Geronimo Stilton

3 in 1

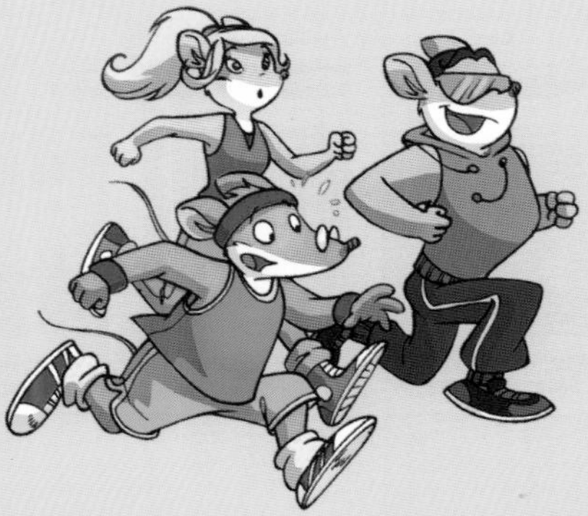

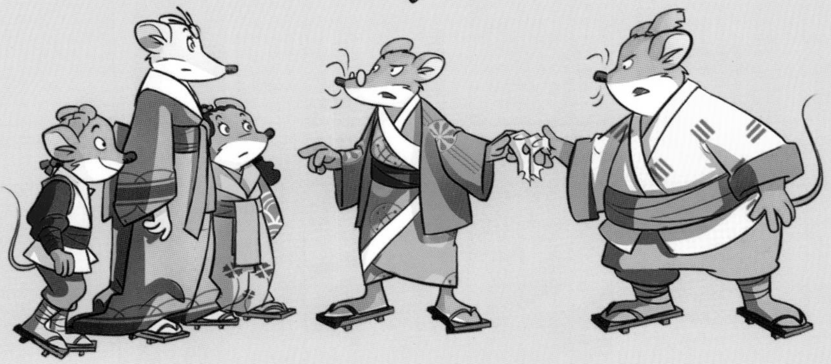

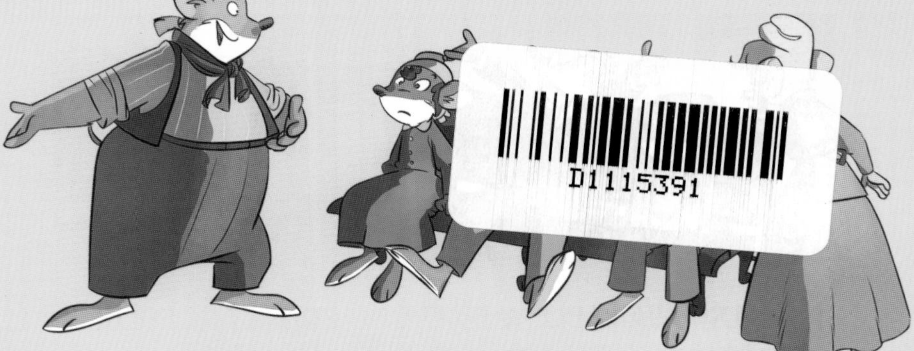

PAPERCUTZ

Geronimo Stilton

GRAPHIC NOVELS AVAILABLE FROM PAPERCUTZ

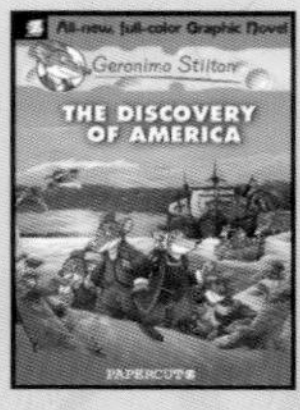
#1 “The Discovery of America”

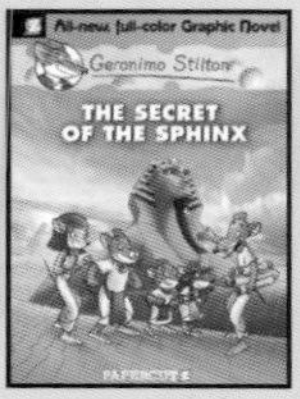
#2 “The Secret of the Sphinx”

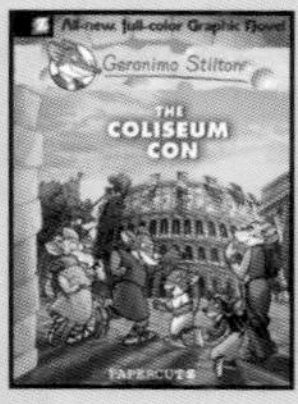
#3 “The Coliseum Con”

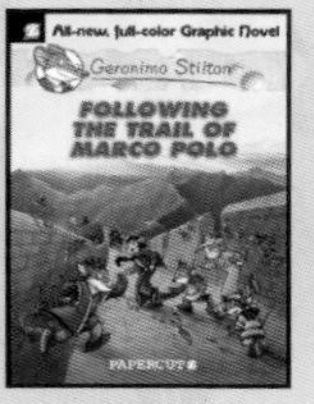
#4 “Following the Trail of Marco Polo”

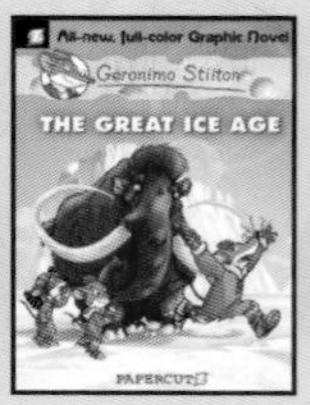
#5 “The Great Ice Age”

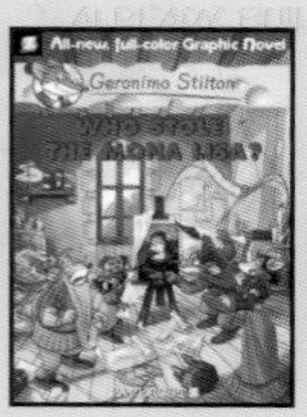
#6 “Who Stole The Mona Lisa?”

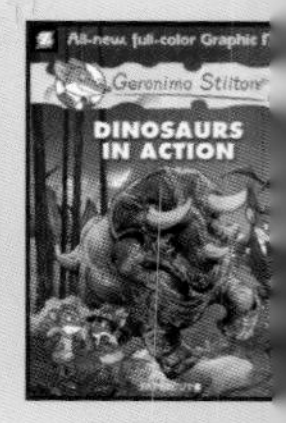
#7 “Dinosaurs in Action”

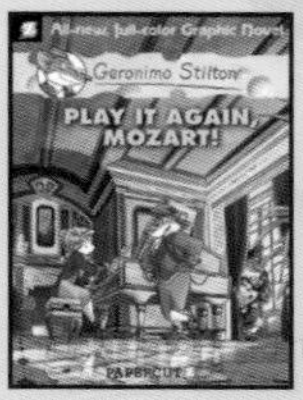
#8 “Play It Again, Mozart!”

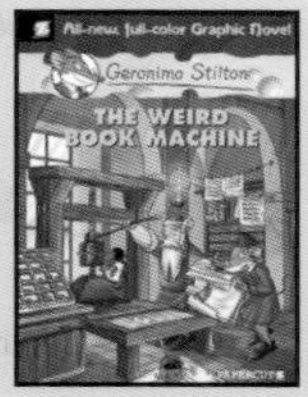
#9 “The Weird Book Machine”

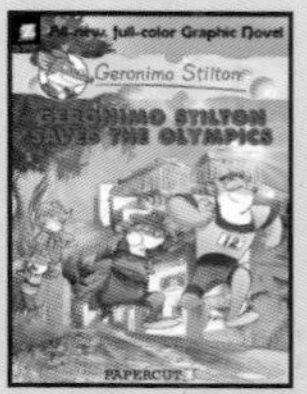
#10 “Geronimo Stilton Saves the Olympics”

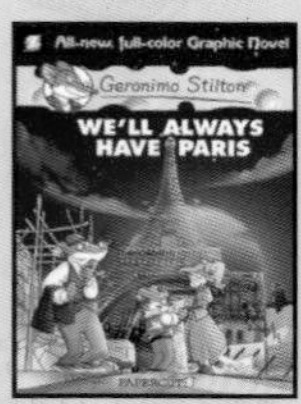
#11 “We’ll Always Have Paris”

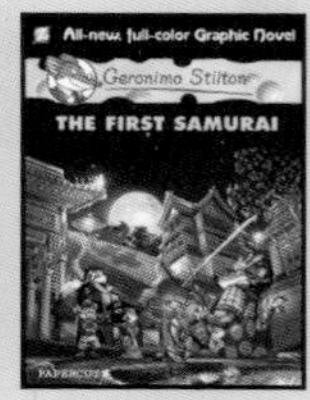
#12 “The First Samurai”

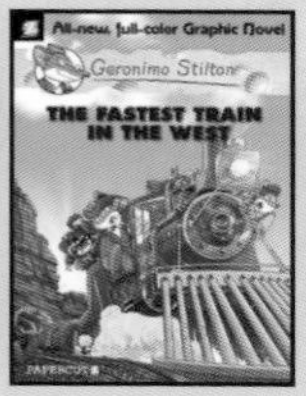
#13 “The Fastest Train in the West”

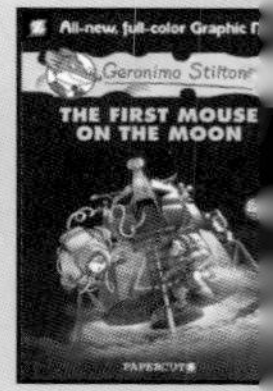
#14 “The First Mo on the Moon”

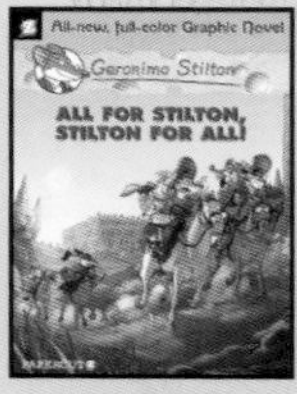
#15 “All for Stilton, Stilton for All!”

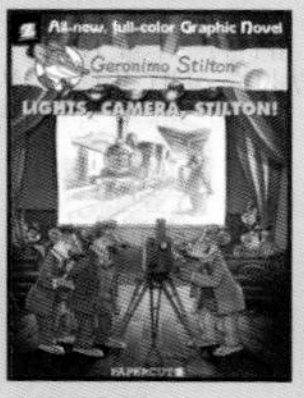
#16 “Lights, Camera, Stilton!”

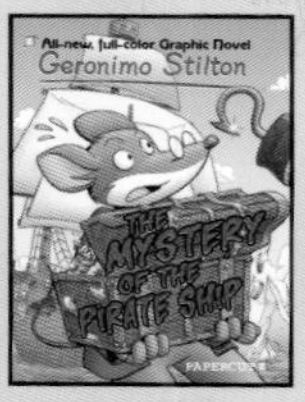
#17 “The Mystery of the Pirate Ship”

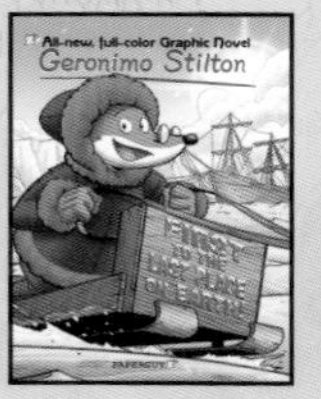
#18 “First to the Last Place on Earth”

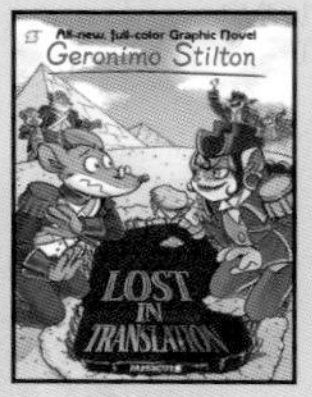
#19 “Lost in Translation”

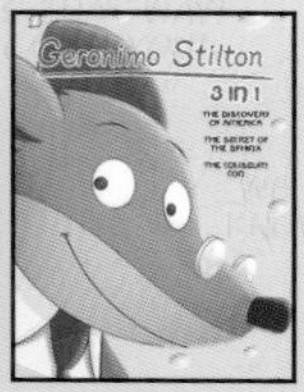
#1 GERONIMO STILTON 3 in 1

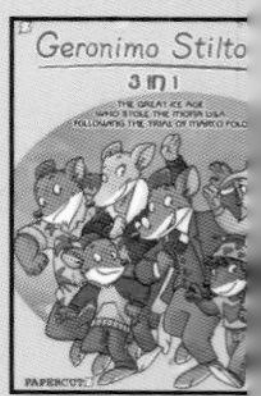
#2 GERONIMO STIL 3 in 1

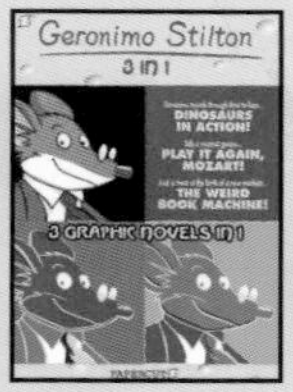
#3 GERONIMO STILTON 3 in 1

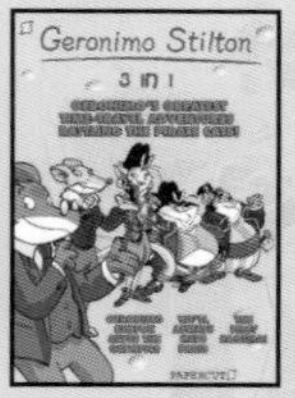
#4 GERONIMO STILTON 3 in 1

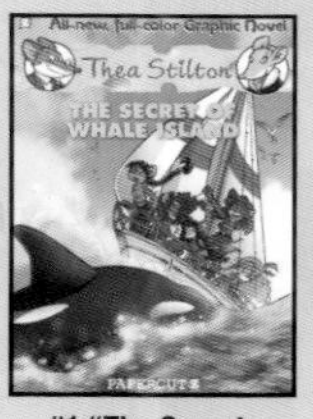
#1 “The Secret of Whale Island”

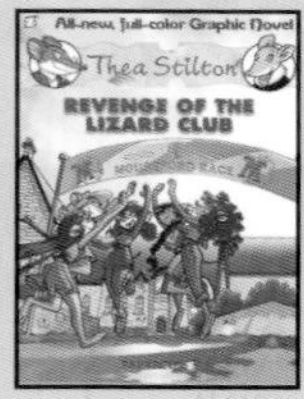
#2 “Revenge of the Lizard Club”

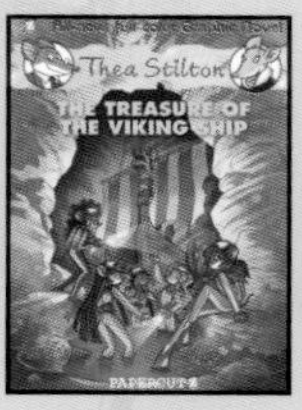
#3 “The Treasure of the Viking Ship”

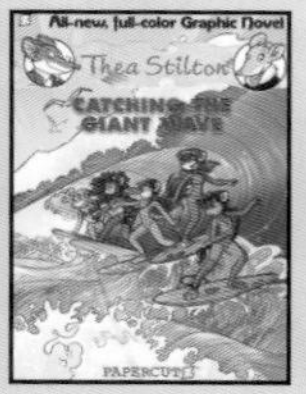
#4 “Catching the Giant Wave”

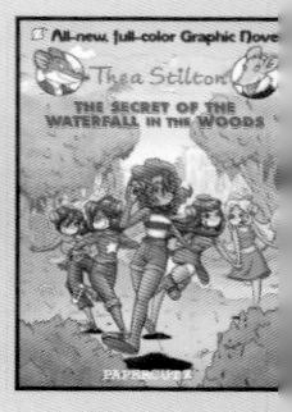
#5 “The Secret of the Waterfall in the Woods”

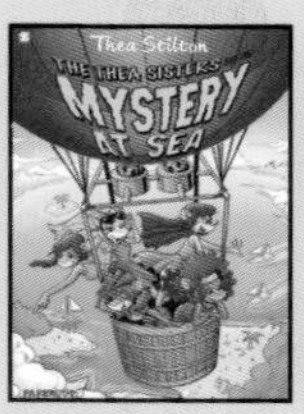
#6 “The Thea Sisters and the Mystery at Sea”

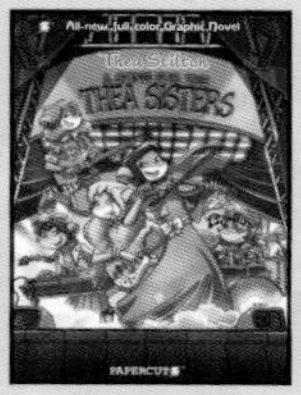
#7 “A Song for the Thea Sisters”

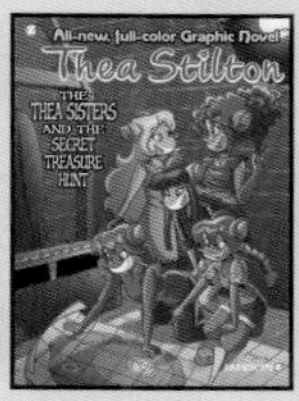
#8 “The Thea Sisters and the Secret Treasure Hunt”

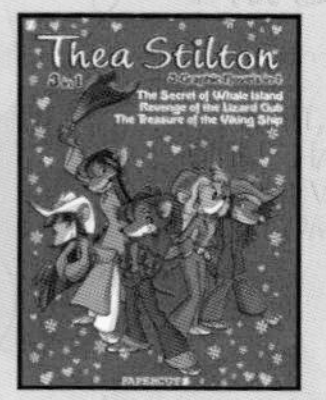
#1 Thea Stilton 3 in 1

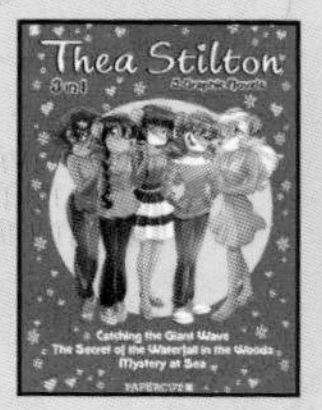
#2 Thea Stilton 3 in 1

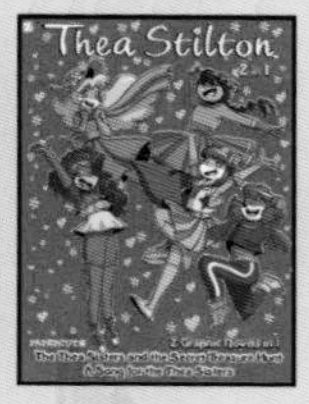
#1 Thea Stilton 2 in 1

...ALSO AVAILABLE WHEREVER E-BOOKS ARE SOLD!

Geronimo Stilton and Thea Stilton Graphic Novels are avaialble for $9.99 each only in hardcover. Geronimo and Thea Stilton 3 in 1s are available for $14.99 each only in paperback. Thea Stilton 2 in 1 is available for $12.99 each only in paperback. Order online at papercutz.com. Or call 1-800-886-1223, Monday through Friday, 9 – 5 EST. MC, Visa, and AmEx accepted. To order by mail, please add $5.00 f postage and handling for first book ordered, $1.00 for each additional book and make check payable to NBM Publishing. Send to: Papercutz, 160 Broadway, Suite 700, East Wing, New York, NY 10038.

See more at papercutz.com

Geronimo Stilton

3 IN 1 #4

By Geronimo Stilton

"Geronimo Stilton Saves the Olympics"

"We'll Always Have Paris"

"The First Samurai"

New York

GERONIMO STILTON 3 IN 1 #4

"Geronimo Stilton Saves the Olympics"
© 2012 Edizioni Piemme © 2022 Mondadori Libri S.p.A.
for PIEMME, Italia
International rights © 2012 Atlantyca S.p.A.
© 2012–for this work in English language by Papercutz
Original Title: *Hai Salvato Le Olimpiadi, Stilton!*
Text by Geronimo Stilton
Editorial Coordination by Patrizia Puricelli
Script by Leonardo Favia
Artistic Coordination by BAO Publishing
Illustrations by Federica Salfo and color by Mirka Andolfo
Original Cover Art and Color by Lorenzo Bolzoni and effeeffestudios

"We'll Always Have Paris"
© 2012 Edizioni Piemme © 2022 Mondadori Libri S.p.A. for
PIEMME, Italia
International rights © 2012 Atlantyca S.p.A.
© 2012–for this work in English language by Papercutz
Original Title: *Il Mistero della Torre Eiffel*
Text by Geronimo Stilton
Editorial Coordination by Patrizia Puricelli
Script by Leonardo Favia
Artistic Coordination by BAO Publishing
Illustrations by Ennio Bufi and Color by Mirka Andolfo
Original Cover Art by Marta Lorini

"The First Samurai"
© 2011 Edizioni Piemme © 2022 Mondadori Libri S.p.A. for PIEMME, Italia
International rights © 2011 Atlantyca S.p.A.
© 2011–for this work in English language by Papercutz
Original title: Il Primo Samurai
Text by Geronimo Stilton
Editorial Coordination by Patrizia Puricelli
Artistic Coordination by BAO Publishing
Script by Leonardo Favia
Story by Michele Foschini
Cover by effeeffestudios
Cover Design by Marta Lorini
Illustrations by Ennio Bufi and Color by Mirka Andolfo

© Atlantyca S.p.A. – via Corso Magenta, 60/62, 20123 Milano, Italia – foreignrights@atlantyca.it
© 2022 for this Work in English language by Papercutz. www.papercutz.com
www.geronimostilton.com
Special thanks to Anita Denti and Alessandra Berello

Translation – Nanette McGuinness
Lettering and Production – Manosaur Martin
Editorial Intern – Lily Lu
Original Associate Editor – Michael Petranek
Managing Editor – Jeff Whitman
Jim Salicrup
Editor-in-Chief

ISBN: 978-1-5458-0859-7
Printed in China
February 2022

Papercutz books may be purchased for business or promotional use.
For information on bulk purchases, please contact Macmillan Corporate and Premium Sales Department at (800) 221-7945 x5442.

Distributed by Macmillan
First Papercutz Printing

GERONIMO STILTON SAVES THE OLYMPICS

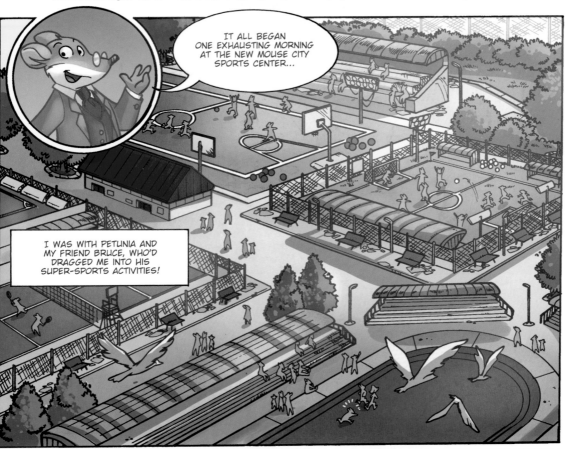

IT ALL BEGAN ONE EXHAUSTING MORNING AT THE NEW MOUSE CITY SPORTS CENTER...

I WAS WITH PETUNIA AND MY FRIEND BRUCE, WHO'D DRAGGED ME INTO HIS SUPER-SPORTS ACTIVITIES!

COME ON, GERONIMO, I WANT YOU TO BE FIT, FIT, FIT!

→PUFF PUFF PUFF!←

CHIN UP, GERONIMO, WE'VE ONLY BEEN RUNNING FOR A FEW MINUTES!

A HEALTHY MIND IN A HEALTHY BODY: THAT'S THE ONLY WAY TO GET THE MOST OUT OF LIFE!

I JUST CAME TO BE WITH MY NEPHEW BENJAMIN. WHAT AM I DOING RUNNING ON A RACE TRACK?

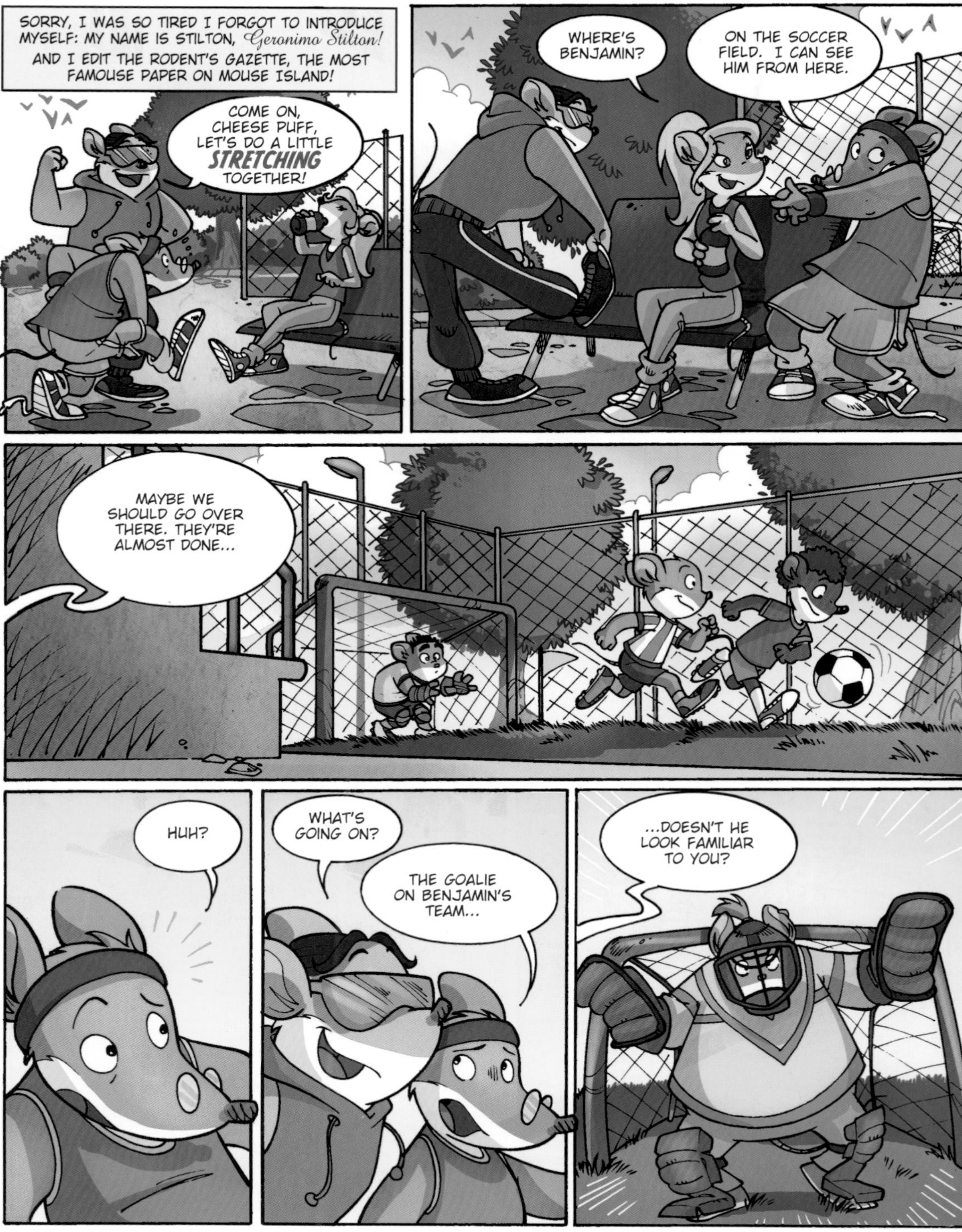
SORRY, I WAS SO TIRED I FORGOT TO INTRODUCE MYSELF: MY NAME IS STILTON, Geronimo Stilton!
AND I EDIT THE RODENT'S GAZETTE, THE MOST FAMOUSE PAPER ON MOUSE ISLAND!
COME ON, CHEESE PUFF, LET'S DO A LITTLE STRETCHING TOGETHER!
WHERE'S BENJAMIN?
ON THE SOCCER FIELD. I CAN SEE HIM FROM HERE.
MAYBE WE SHOULD GO OVER THERE. THEY'RE ALMOST DONE...
HUH?
WHAT'S GOING ON?
THE GOALIE ON BENJAMIN'S TEAM...
...DOESN'T HE LOOK FAMILIAR TO YOU?

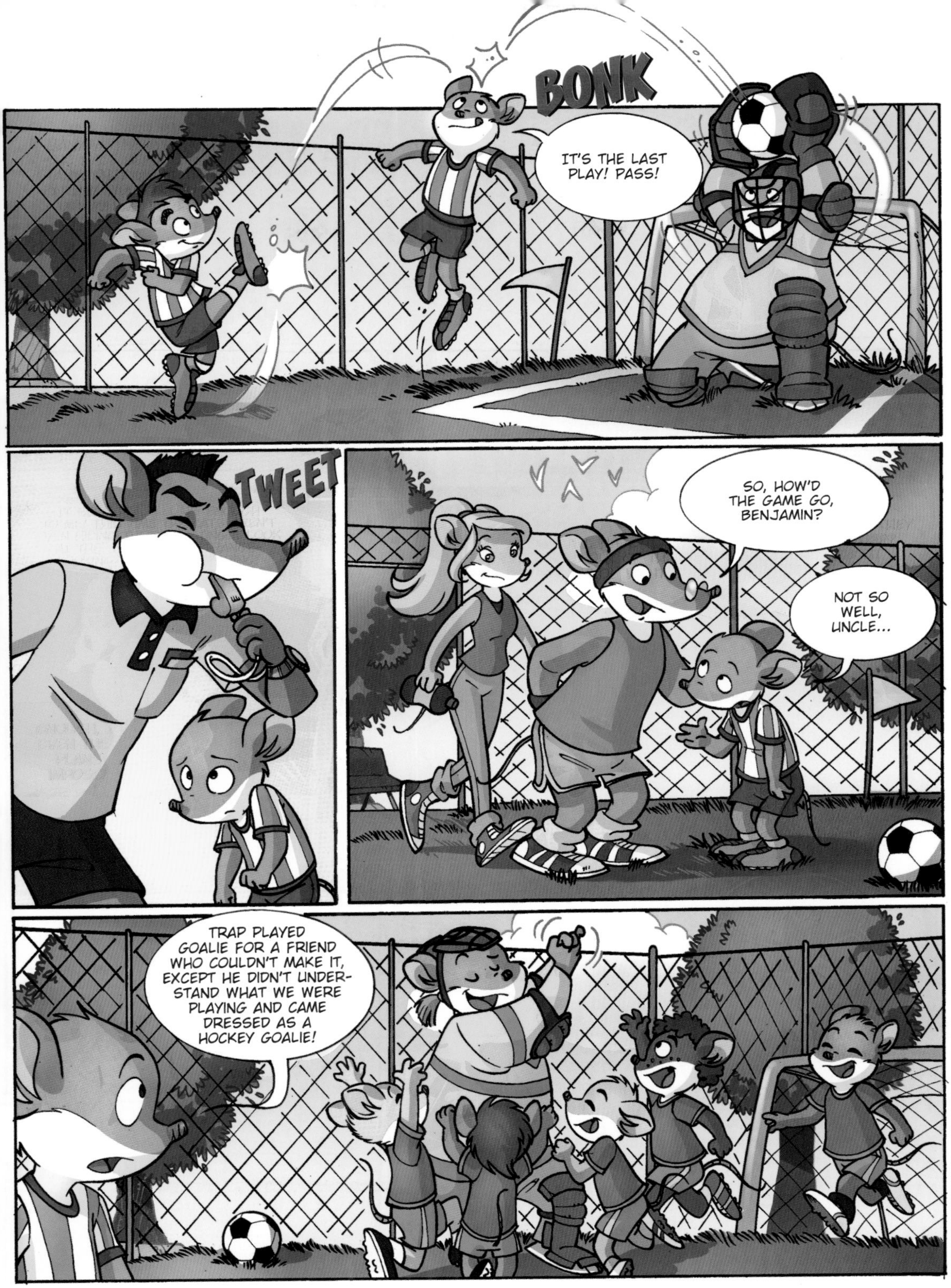
BONK
IT'S THE LAST PLAY! PASS!
TWEET
SO, HOW'D THE GAME GO, BENJAMIN?
NOT SO WELL, UNCLE...
TRAP PLAYED GOALIE FOR A FRIEND WHO COULDN'T MAKE IT, EXCEPT HE DIDN'T UNDER-STAND WHAT WE WERE PLAYING AND CAME DRESSED AS A HOCKEY GOALIE!

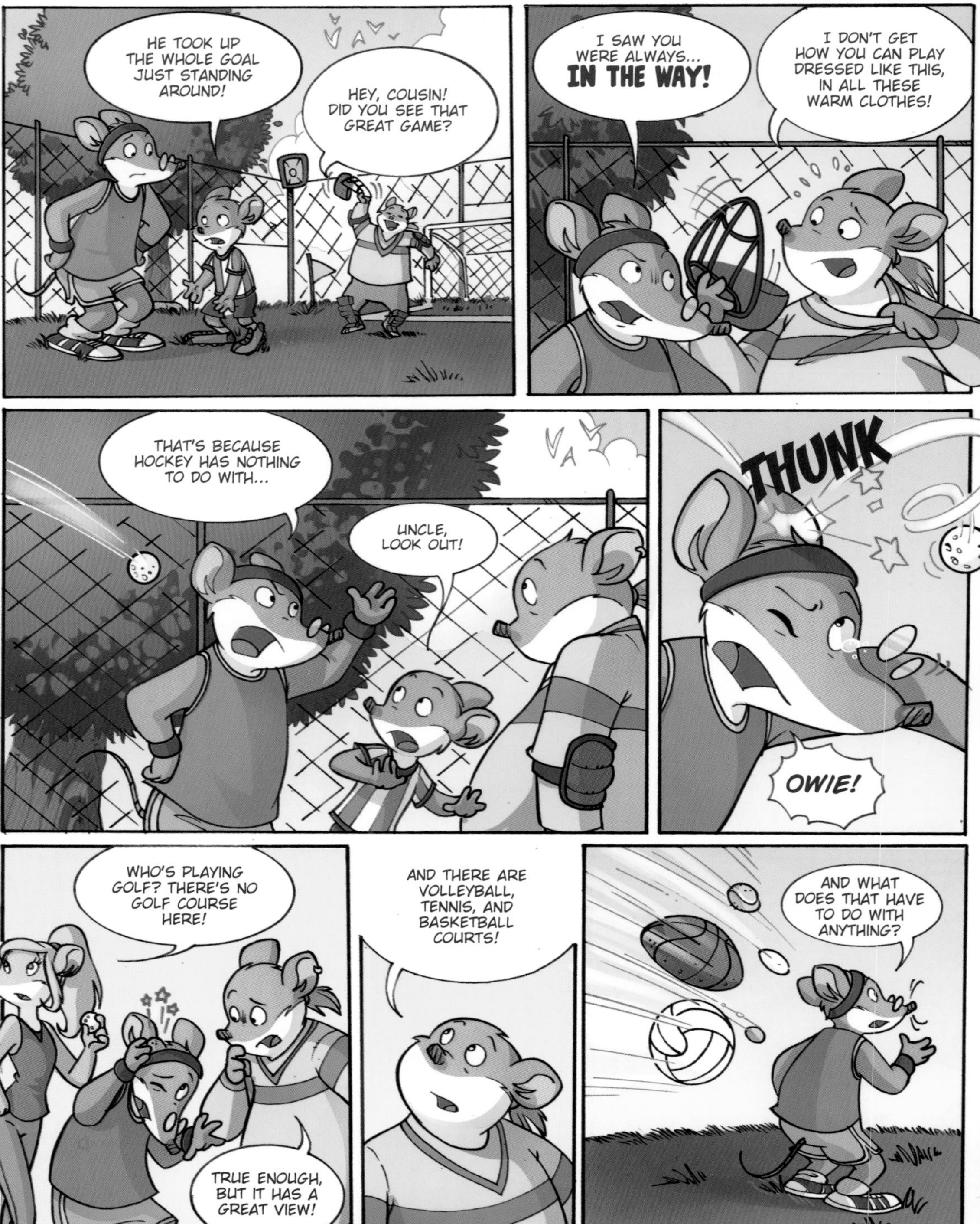
HE TOOK UP THE WHOLE GOAL JUST STANDING AROUND!
HEY, COUSIN! DID YOU SEE THAT GREAT GAME?
I SAW YOU WERE ALWAYS... IN THE WAY!
I DON'T GET HOW YOU CAN PLAY DRESSED LIKE THIS, IN ALL THESE WARM CLOTHES!
THAT'S BECAUSE HOCKEY HAS NOTHING TO DO WITH...
UNCLE, LOOK OUT!
THUNK
OWIE!
WHO'S PLAYING GOLF? THERE'S NO GOLF COURSE HERE!
TRUE ENOUGH, BUT IT HAS A GREAT VIEW!
AND THERE ARE VOLLEYBALL, TENNIS, AND BASKETBALL COURTS!
AND WHAT DOES THAT HAVE TO DO WITH ANYTHING?

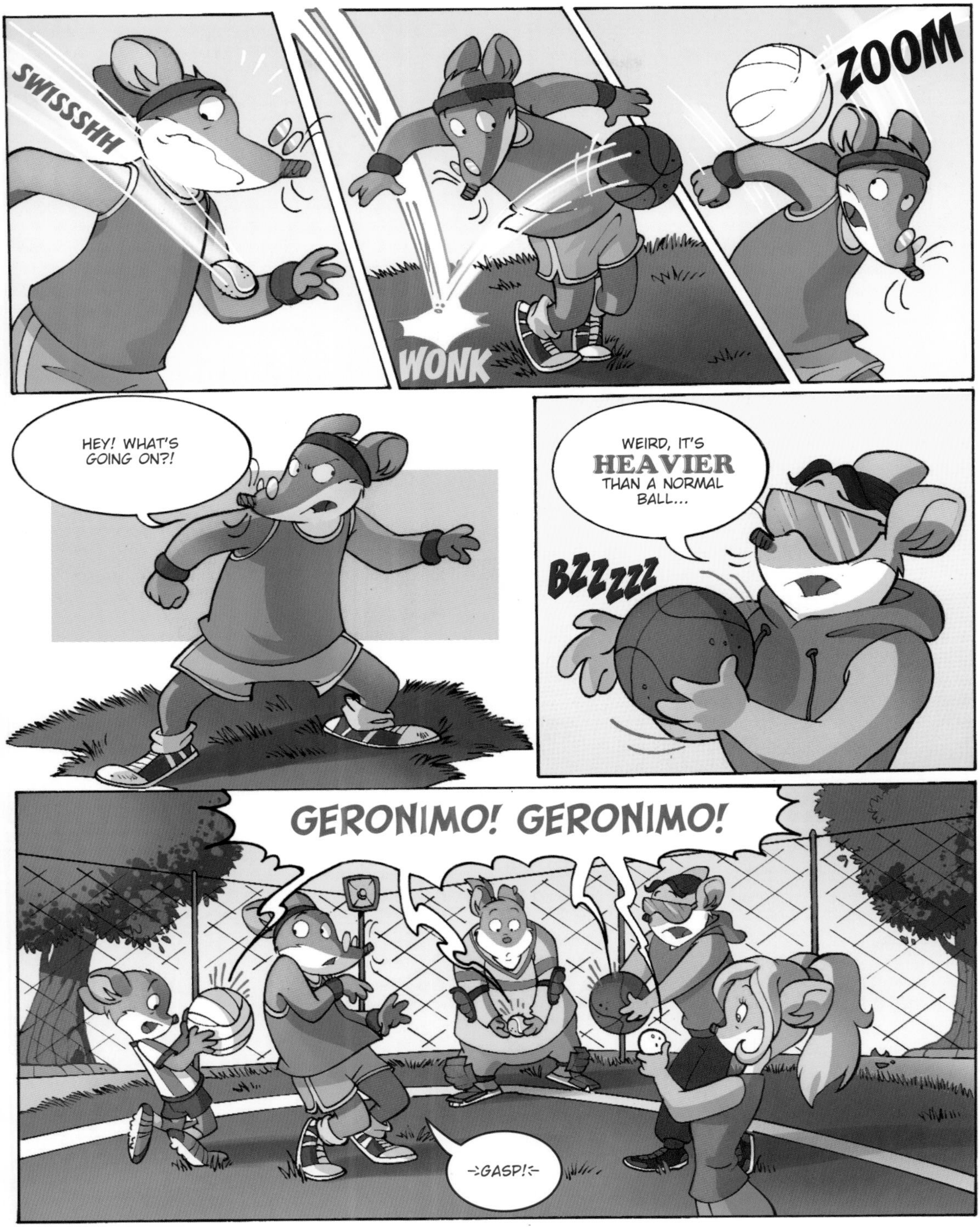
SWISSSHH
WONK
ZOOM
HEY! WHAT'S GOING ON?!
WEIRD, IT'S HEAVIER THAN A NORMAL BALL...
BZZzzz
GERONIMO! GERONIMO!
GASP!

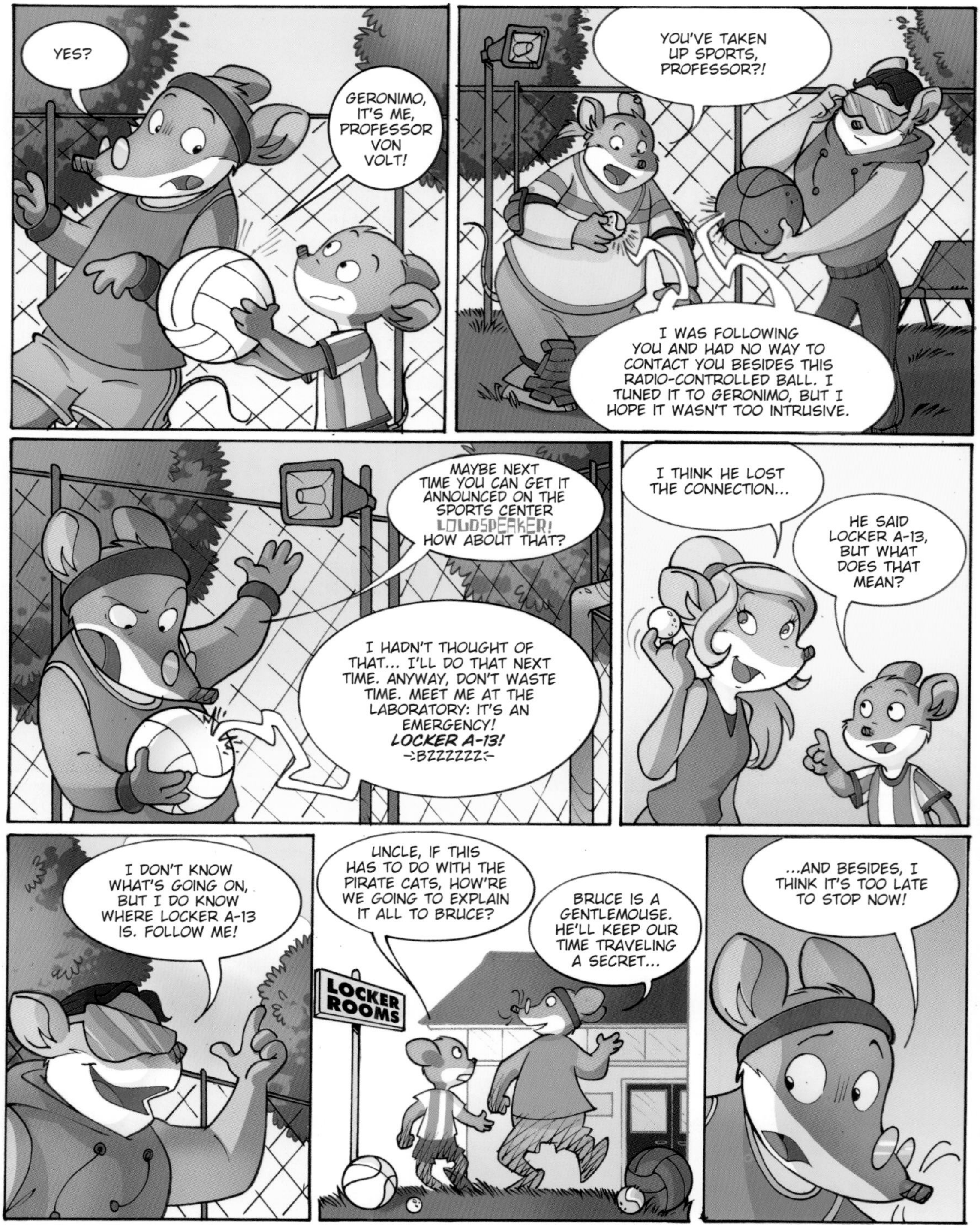
YES?
GERONIMO, IT'S ME, PROFESSOR VON VOLT!
YOU'VE TAKEN UP SPORTS, PROFESSOR?!
I WAS FOLLOWING YOU AND HAD NO WAY TO CONTACT YOU BESIDES THIS RADIO-CONTROLLED BALL. I TUNED IT TO GERONIMO, BUT I HOPE IT WASN'T TOO INTRUSIVE.
MAYBE NEXT TIME YOU CAN GET IT ANNOUNCED ON THE SPORTS CENTER LOUDSPEAKER! HOW ABOUT THAT?
I HADN'T THOUGHT OF THAT... I'LL DO THAT NEXT TIME. ANYWAY, DON'T WASTE TIME. MEET ME AT THE LABORATORY: IT'S AN EMERGENCY! LOCKER A-13! BZZZZZZ
I THINK HE LOST THE CONNECTION...
HE SAID LOCKER A-13, BUT WHAT DOES THAT MEAN?
I DON'T KNOW WHAT'S GOING ON, BUT I DO KNOW WHERE LOCKER A-13 IS. FOLLOW ME!
UNCLE, IF THIS HAS TO DO WITH THE PIRATE CATS, HOW'RE WE GOING TO EXPLAIN IT ALL TO BRUCE?
BRUCE IS A GENTLEMOUSE. HE'LL KEEP OUR TIME TRAVELING A SECRET...
LOCKER ROOMS
...AND BESIDES, I THINK IT'S TOO LATE TO STOP NOW!

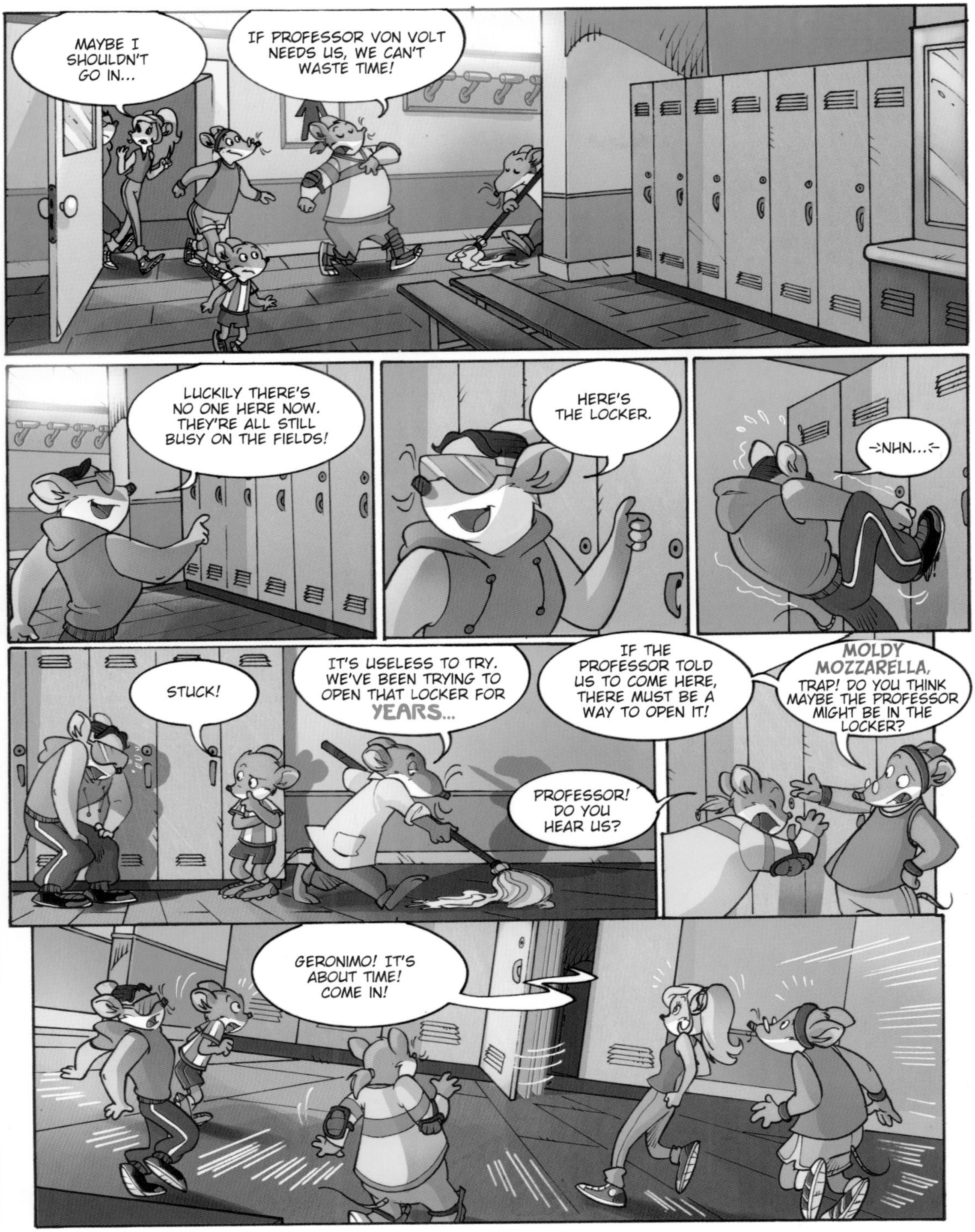
MAYBE I SHOULDN'T GO IN...
IF PROFESSOR VON VOLT NEEDS US, WE CAN'T WASTE TIME!
LUCKILY THERE'S NO ONE HERE NOW. THEY'RE ALL STILL BUSY ON THE FIELDS!
HERE'S THE LOCKER.
NHN...
STUCK!
IT'S USELESS TO TRY. WE'VE BEEN TRYING TO OPEN THAT LOCKER FOR YEARS...
IF THE PROFESSOR TOLD US TO COME HERE, THERE MUST BE A WAY TO OPEN IT!
PROFESSOR! DO YOU HEAR US?
MOLDY MOZZARELLA, TRAP! DO YOU THINK MAYBE THE PROFESSOR MIGHT BE IN THE LOCKER?
GERONIMO! IT'S ABOUT TIME! COME IN!

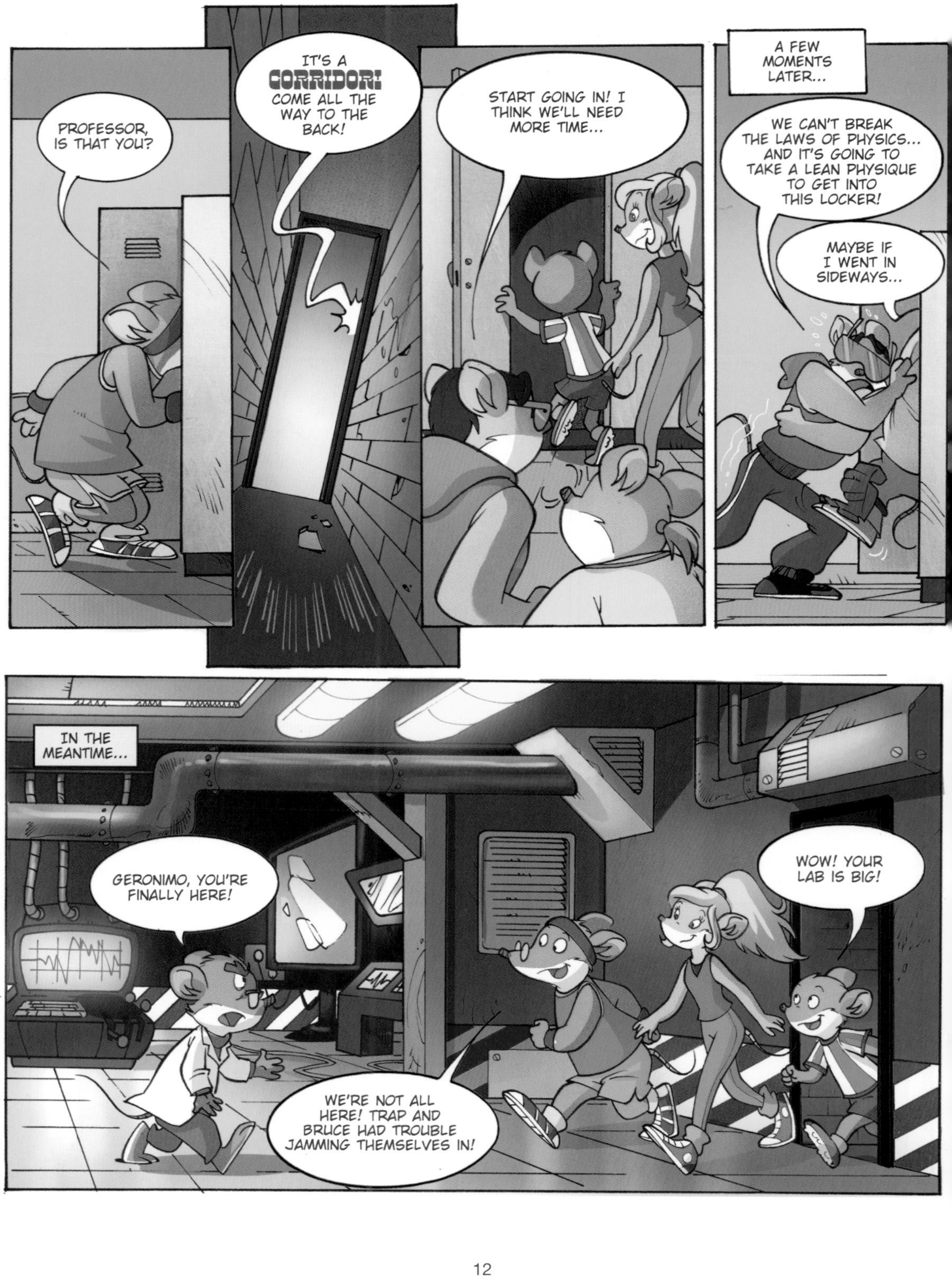
PROFESSOR, IS THAT YOU?
IT'S A CORRIDOR! COME ALL THE WAY TO THE BACK!
START GOING IN! I THINK WE'LL NEED MORE TIME...
A FEW MOMENTS LATER...
WE CAN'T BREAK THE LAWS OF PHYSICS... AND IT'S GOING TO TAKE A LEAN PHYSIQUE TO GET INTO THIS LOCKER!
MAYBE IF I WENT IN SIDEWAYS...
IN THE MEANTIME...
GERONIMO, YOU'RE FINALLY HERE!
WE'RE NOT ALL HERE! TRAP AND BRUCE HAD TROUBLE JAMMING THEMSELVES IN!
WOW! YOUR LAB IS BIG!

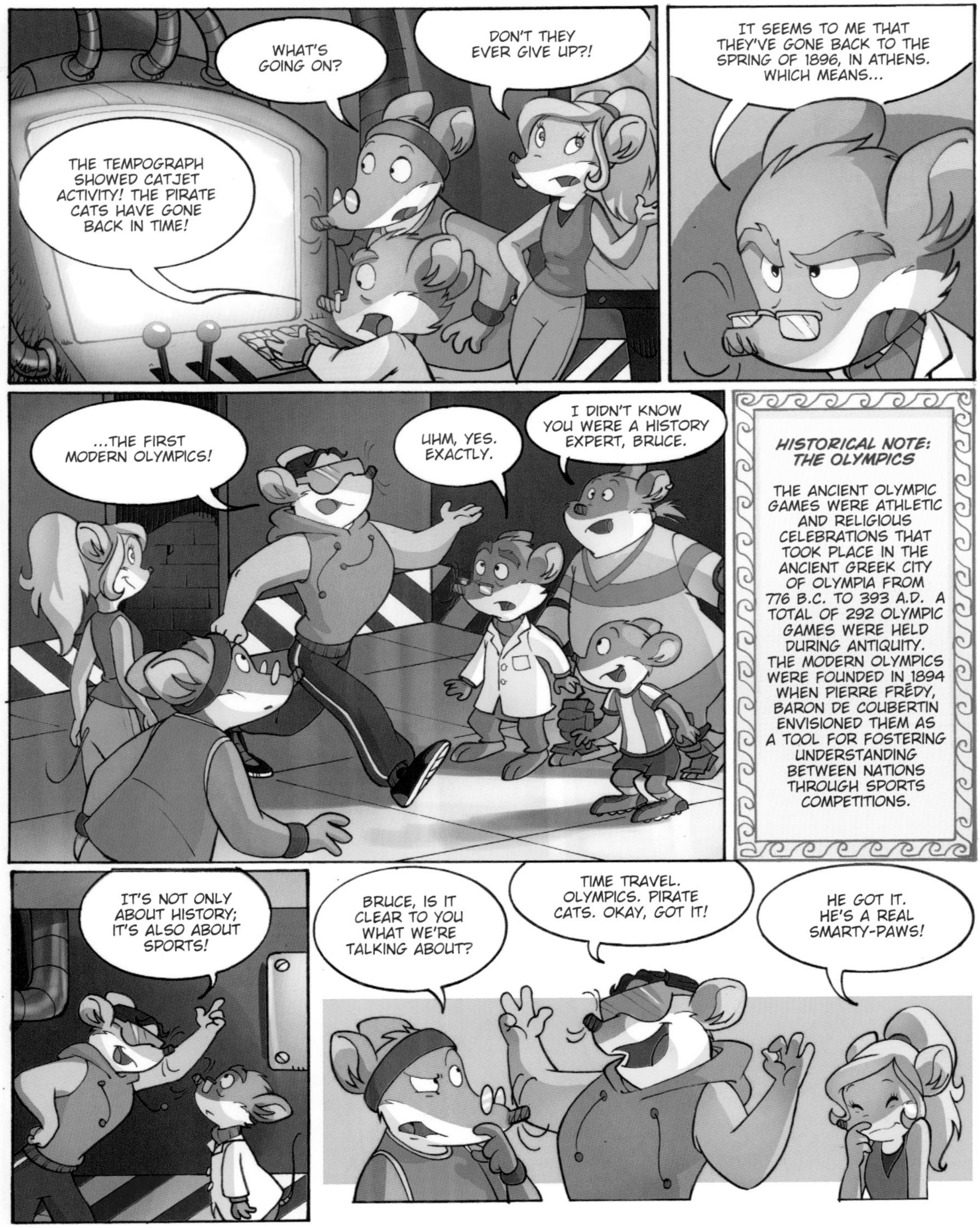
WHAT'S GOING ON?
DON'T THEY EVER GIVE UP?!
THE TEMPOGRAPH SHOWED CATJET ACTIVITY! THE PIRATE CATS HAVE GONE BACK IN TIME!
IT SEEMS TO ME THAT THEY'VE GONE BACK TO THE SPRING OF 1896, IN ATHENS. WHICH MEANS...
...THE FIRST MODERN OLYMPICS!
UHM, YES. EXACTLY.
I DIDN'T KNOW YOU WERE A HISTORY EXPERT, BRUCE.
HISTORICAL NOTE: THE OLYMPICS
THE ANCIENT OLYMPIC GAMES WERE ATHLETIC AND RELIGIOUS CELEBRATIONS THAT TOOK PLACE IN THE ANCIENT GREEK CITY OF OLYMPIA FROM 776 B.C. TO 393 A.D. A TOTAL OF 292 OLYMPIC GAMES WERE HELD DURING ANTIQUITY. THE MODERN OLYMPICS WERE FOUNDED IN 1894 WHEN PIERRE FRÉDY, BARON DE COUBERTIN ENVISIONED THEM AS A TOOL FOR FOSTERING UNDERSTANDING BETWEEN NATIONS THROUGH SPORTS COMPETITIONS.
IT'S NOT ONLY ABOUT HISTORY; IT'S ALSO ABOUT SPORTS!
BRUCE, IS IT CLEAR TO YOU WHAT WE'RE TALKING ABOUT?
TIME TRAVEL. OLYMPICS. PIRATE CATS. OKAY, GOT IT!
HE GOT IT. HE'S A REAL SMARTY-PAWS!

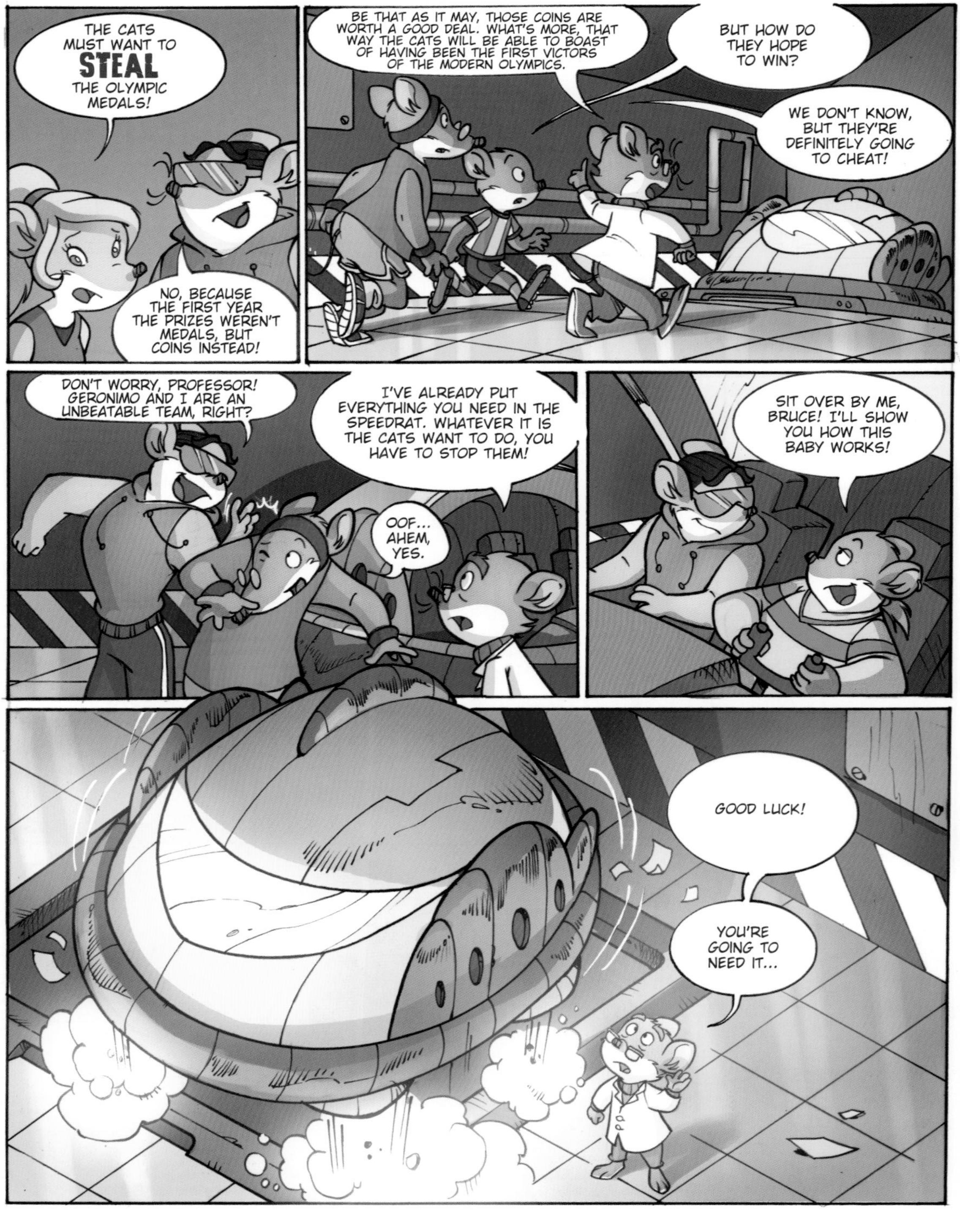
THE CATS MUST WANT TO STEAL THE OLYMPIC MEDALS!
NO, BECAUSE THE FIRST YEAR THE PRIZES WEREN'T MEDALS, BUT COINS INSTEAD!
BE THAT AS IT MAY, THOSE COINS ARE WORTH A GOOD DEAL. WHAT'S MORE, THAT WAY THE CATS WILL BE ABLE TO BOAST OF HAVING BEEN THE FIRST VICTORS OF THE MODERN OLYMPICS.
BUT HOW DO THEY HOPE TO WIN?
WE DON'T KNOW, BUT THEY'RE DEFINITELY GOING TO CHEAT!
DON'T WORRY, PROFESSOR! GERONIMO AND I ARE AN UNBEATABLE TEAM, RIGHT?
I'VE ALREADY PUT EVERYTHING YOU NEED IN THE SPEEDRAT. WHATEVER IT IS THE CATS WANT TO DO, YOU HAVE TO STOP THEM!
OOF... AHEM, YES.
SIT OVER BY ME, BRUCE! I'LL SHOW YOU HOW THIS BABY WORKS!
GOOD LUCK!
YOU'RE GOING TO NEED IT...

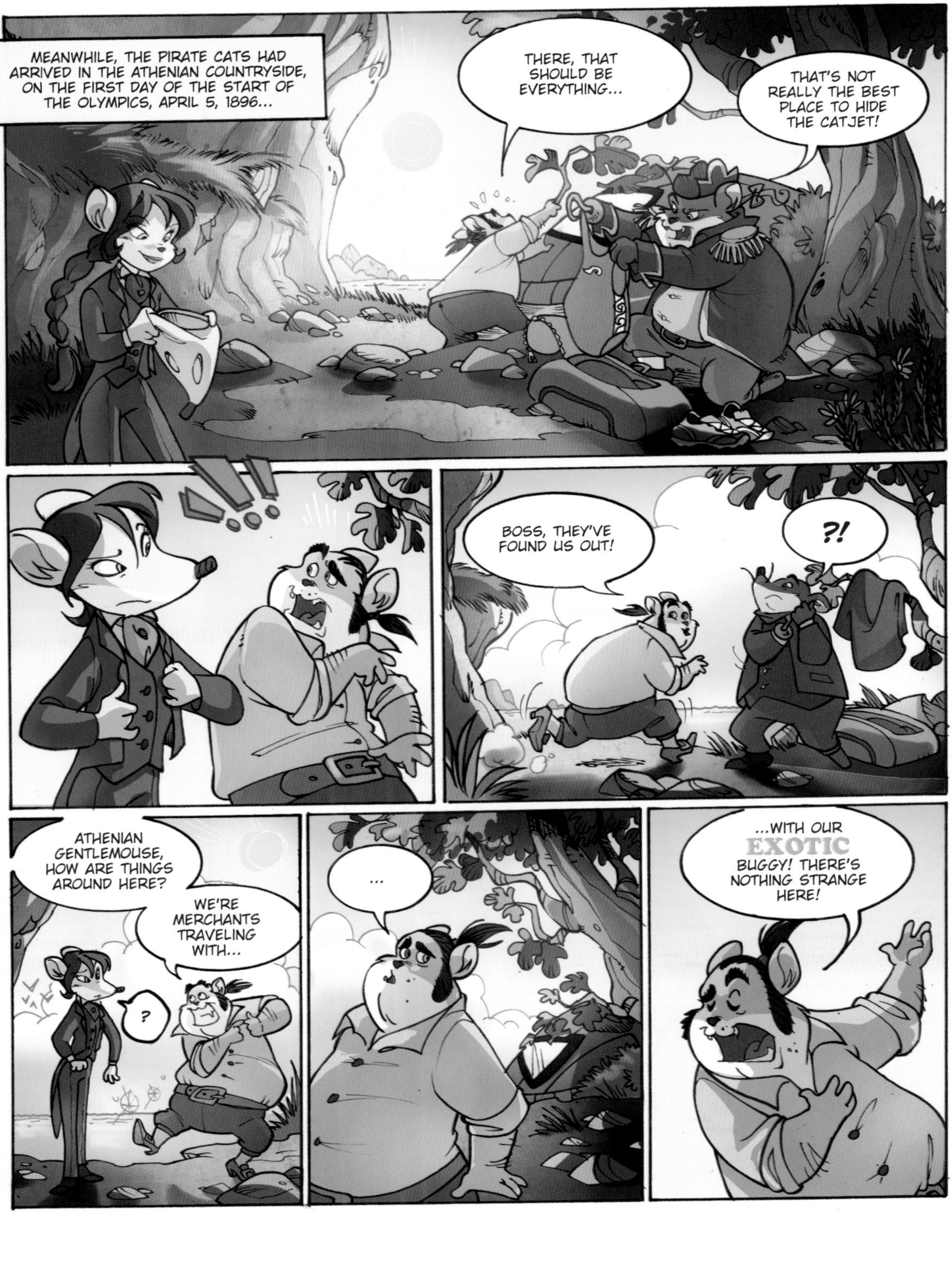
MEANWHILE, THE PIRATE CATS HAD ARRIVED IN THE ATHENIAN COUNTRYSIDE, ON THE FIRST DAY OF THE START OF THE OLYMPICS, APRIL 5, 1896...
THERE, THAT SHOULD BE EVERYTHING...
THAT'S NOT REALLY THE BEST PLACE TO HIDE THE CATJET!
BOSS, THEY'VE FOUND US OUT!
?!
ATHENIAN GENTLEMOUSE, HOW ARE THINGS AROUND HERE?
WE'RE MERCHANTS TRAVELING WITH...
?
...
...WITH OUR EXOTIC BUGGY! THERE'S NOTHING STRANGE HERE!

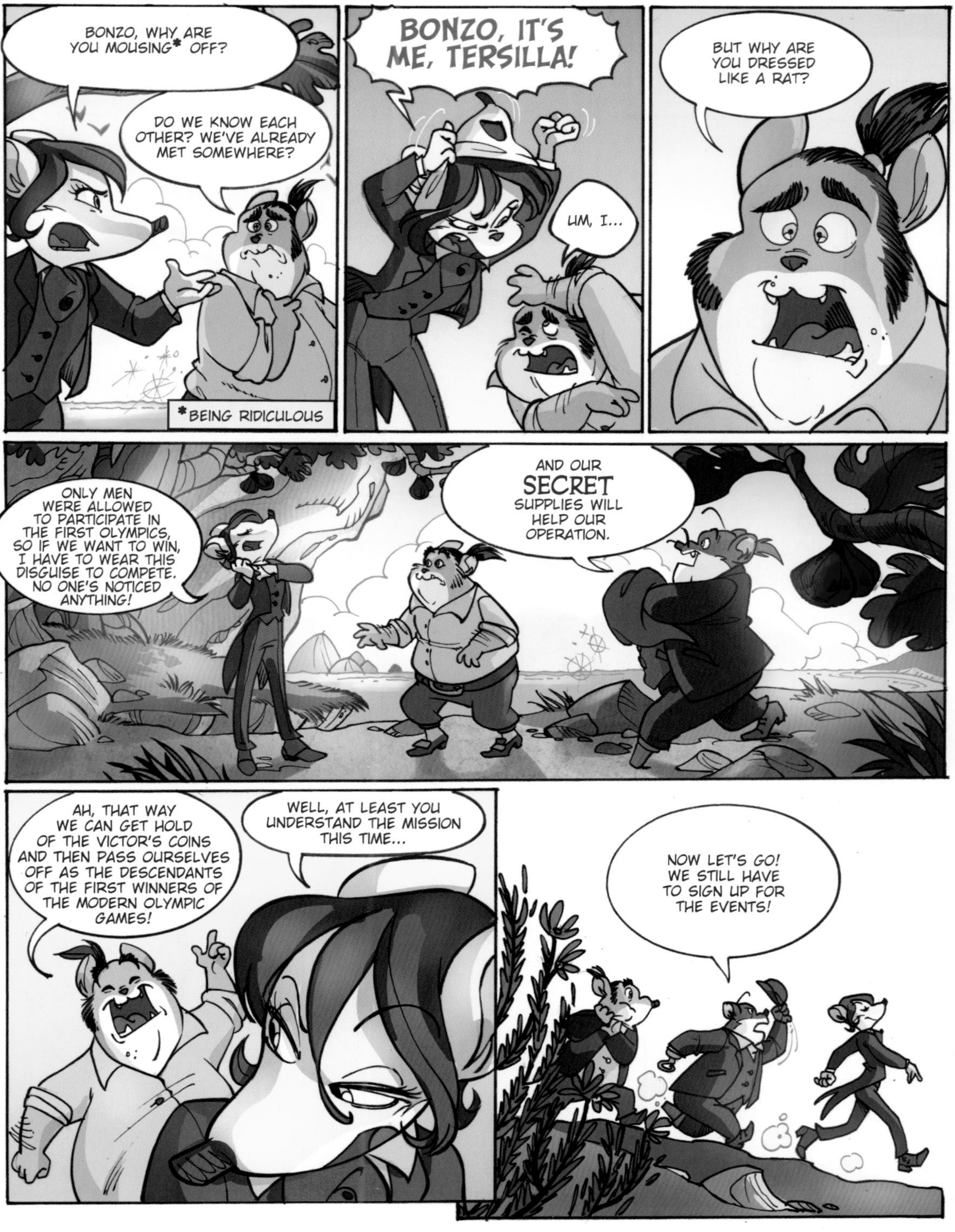
BONZO, WHY ARE YOU MOUSING* OFF?
DO WE KNOW EACH OTHER? WE'VE ALREADY MET SOMEWHERE?
*BEING RIDICULOUS
BONZO, IT'S ME, TERSILLA!
UM, I...
BUT WHY ARE YOU DRESSED LIKE A RAT?
ONLY MEN WERE ALLOWED TO PARTICIPATE IN THE FIRST OLYMPICS, SO IF WE WANT TO WIN, I HAVE TO WEAR THIS DISGUISE TO COMPETE. NO ONE'S NOTICED ANYTHING!
AND OUR SECRET SUPPLIES WILL HELP OUR OPERATION.
AH, THAT WAY WE CAN GET HOLD OF THE VICTOR'S COINS AND THEN PASS OURSELVES OFF AS THE DESCENDANTS OF THE FIRST WINNERS OF THE MODERN OLYMPIC GAMES!
WELL, AT LEAST YOU UNDERSTAND THE MISSION THIS TIME...
NOW LET'S GO! WE STILL HAVE TO SIGN UP FOR THE EVENTS!

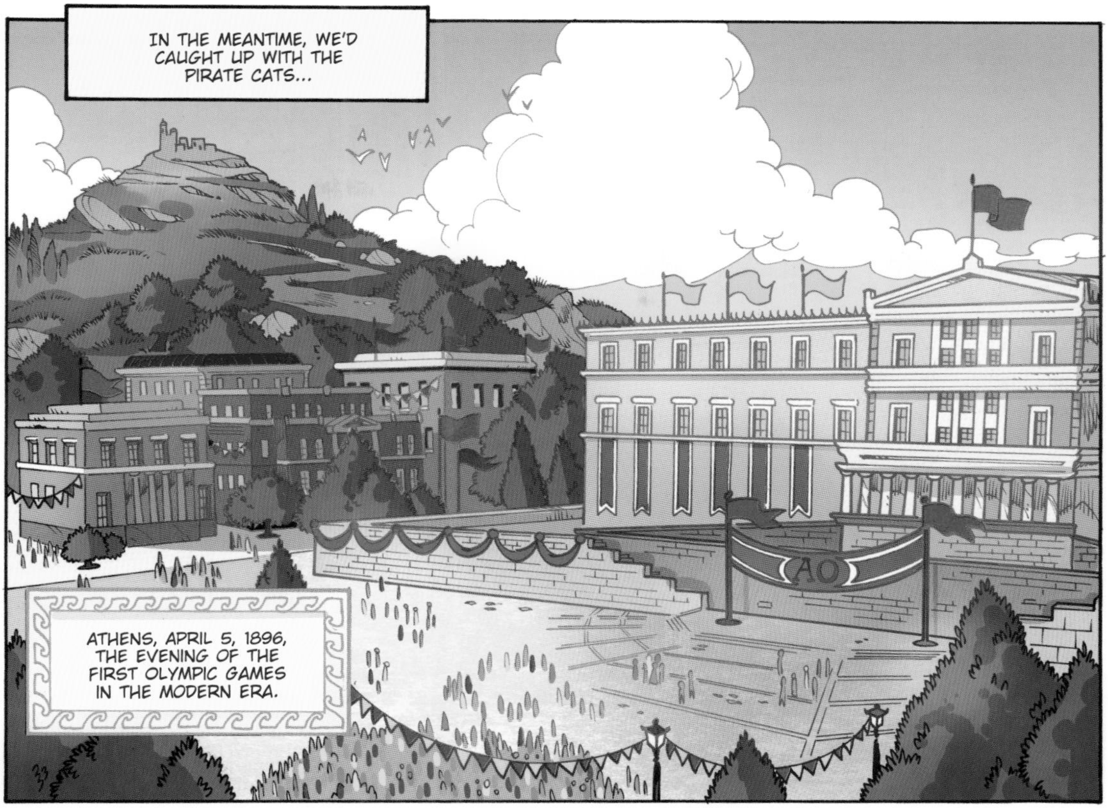
IN THE MEANTIME, WE'D CAUGHT UP WITH THE PIRATE CATS...
ATHENS, APRIL 5, 1896, THE EVENING OF THE FIRST OLYMPIC GAMES IN THE MODERN ERA.

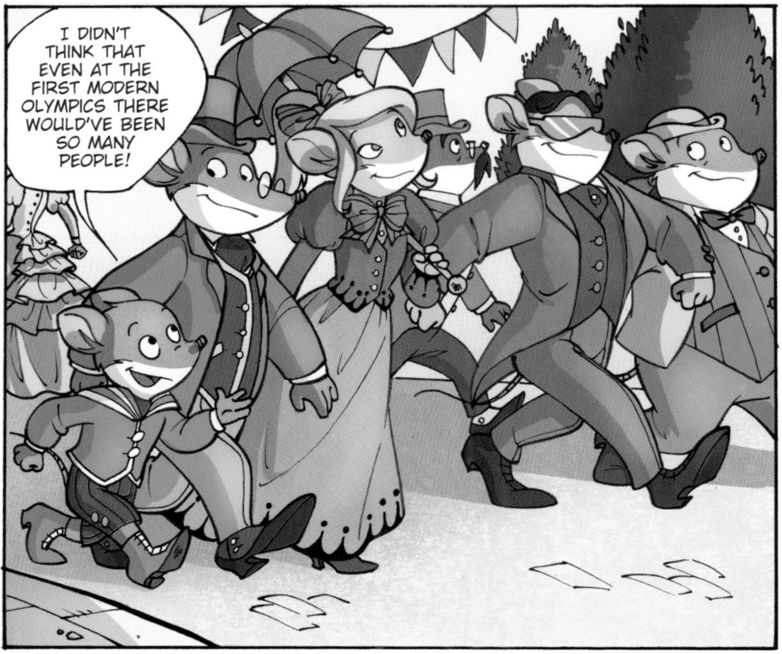
I DIDN'T THINK THAT EVEN AT THE FIRST MODERN OLYMPICS THERE WOULD'VE BEEN SO MANY PEOPLE!

HISTORICAL NOTE: THE MODERN OLYMPICS

THE OLYMPIC GAMES ARE HELD EVERY FOUR YEARS AND ARE A COMPETITION BETWEEN THE BEST ATHLETES IN THE WORLD IN NEARLY ALL THE SPORTS PLAYED ON THE FIVE CONTINENTS. THE NAME OLYMPICS WAS CHOSEN TO COMMEMORATE THE GAMES THAT TOOK PLACE IN ANCIENT GREECE NEAR THE CITY OF OLYMPIA, WHEN THE BEST GREEK ATHLETES COMPETED AGAINST EACH OTHER.

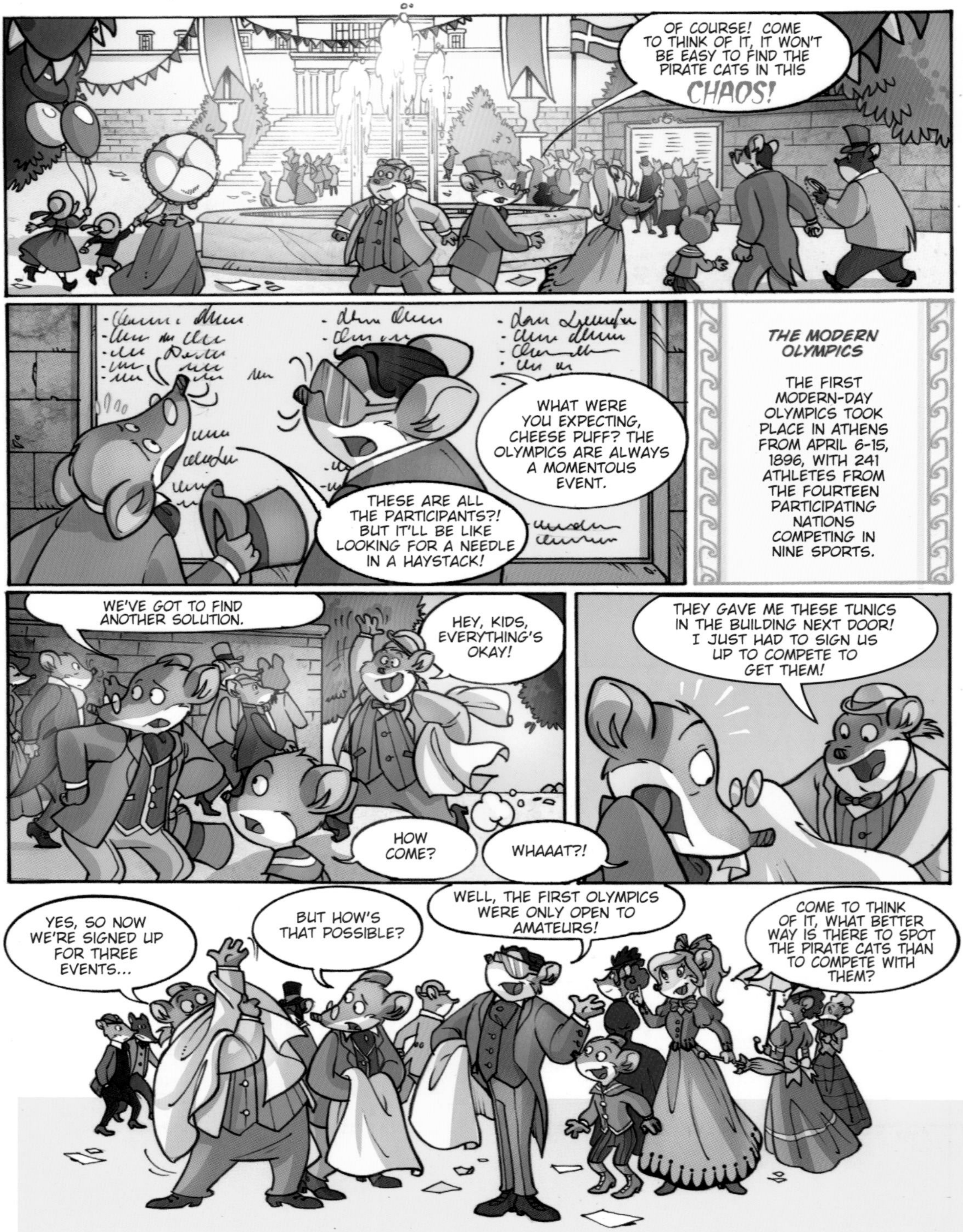
OF COURSE! COME TO THINK OF IT, IT WON'T BE EASY TO FIND THE PIRATE CATS IN THIS CHAOS!
THESE ARE ALL THE PARTICIPANTS?! BUT IT'LL BE LIKE LOOKING FOR A NEEDLE IN A HAYSTACK!
WHAT WERE YOU EXPECTING, CHEESE PUFF? THE OLYMPICS ARE ALWAYS A MOMENTOUS EVENT.
THE MODERN OLYMPICS
THE FIRST MODERN-DAY OLYMPICS TOOK PLACE IN ATHENS FROM APRIL 6-15, 1896, WITH 241 ATHLETES FROM THE FOURTEEN PARTICIPATING NATIONS COMPETING IN NINE SPORTS.
WE'VE GOT TO FIND ANOTHER SOLUTION.
HEY, KIDS, EVERYTHING'S OKAY!
HOW COME?
THEY GAVE ME THESE TUNICS IN THE BUILDING NEXT DOOR! I JUST HAD TO SIGN US UP TO COMPETE TO GET THEM!
WHAAAT?!
YES, SO NOW WE'RE SIGNED UP FOR THREE EVENTS...
BUT HOW'S THAT POSSIBLE?
WELL, THE FIRST OLYMPICS WERE ONLY OPEN TO AMATEURS!
COME TO THINK OF IT, WHAT BETTER WAY IS THERE TO SPOT THE PIRATE CATS THAN TO COMPETE WITH THEM?

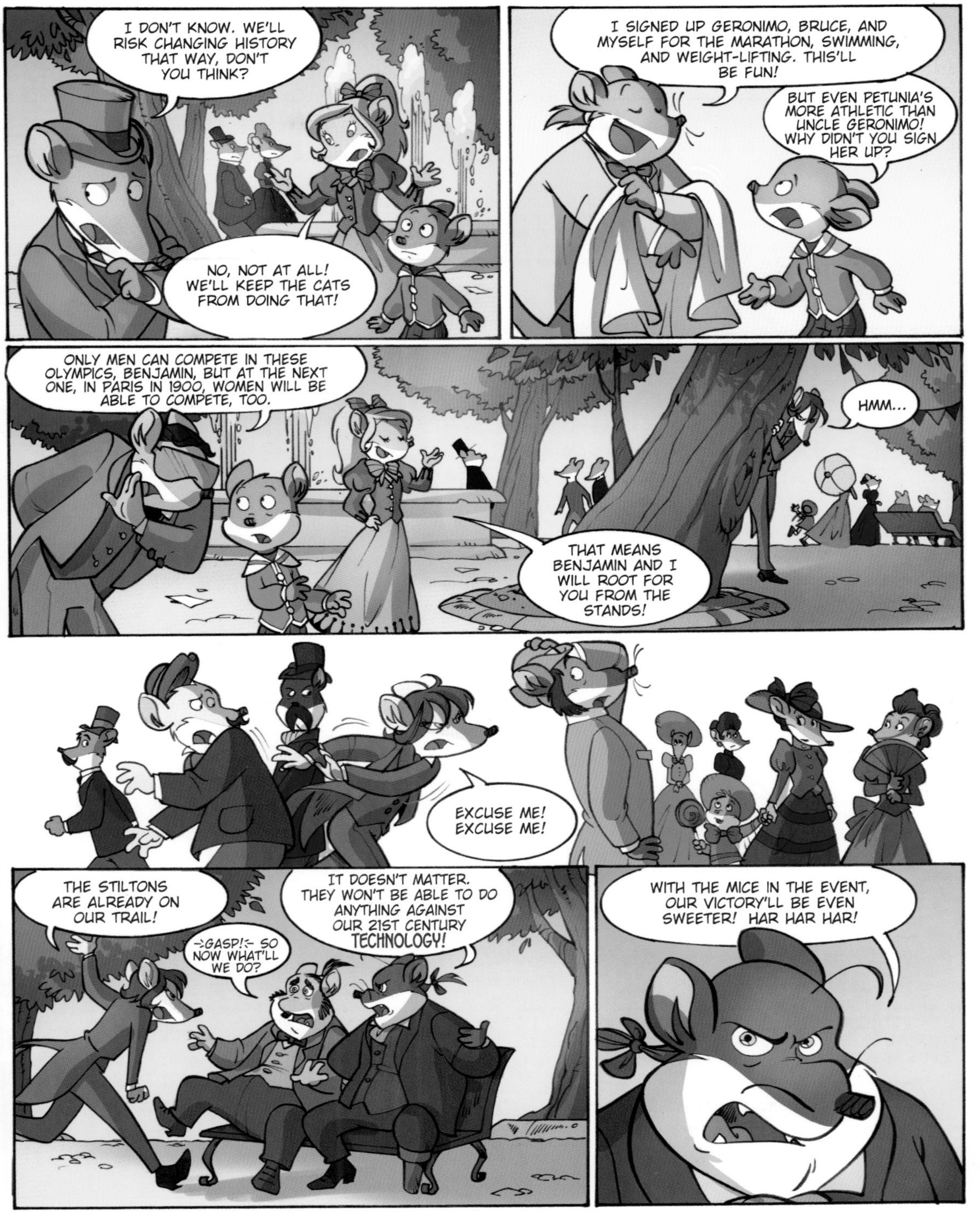
I DON'T KNOW. WE'LL RISK CHANGING HISTORY THAT WAY, DON'T YOU THINK?
NO, NOT AT ALL! WE'LL KEEP THE CATS FROM DOING THAT!
I SIGNED UP GERONIMO, BRUCE, AND MYSELF FOR THE MARATHON, SWIMMING, AND WEIGHT-LIFTING. THIS'LL BE FUN!
BUT EVEN PETUNIA'S MORE ATHLETIC THAN UNCLE GERONIMO! WHY DIDN'T YOU SIGN HER UP?
ONLY MEN CAN COMPETE IN THESE OLYMPICS, BENJAMIN, BUT AT THE NEXT ONE, IN PARIS IN 1900, WOMEN WILL BE ABLE TO COMPETE, TOO.
THAT MEANS BENJAMIN AND I WILL ROOT FOR YOU FROM THE STANDS!
HMM...
EXCUSE ME! EXCUSE ME!
THE STILTONS ARE ALREADY ON OUR TRAIL!
-GASP!- SO NOW WHAT'LL WE DO?
IT DOESN'T MATTER. THEY WON'T BE ABLE TO DO ANYTHING AGAINST OUR 21ST CENTURY TECHNOLOGY!
WITH THE MICE IN THE EVENT, OUR VICTORY'LL BE EVEN SWEETER! HAR HAR HAR!

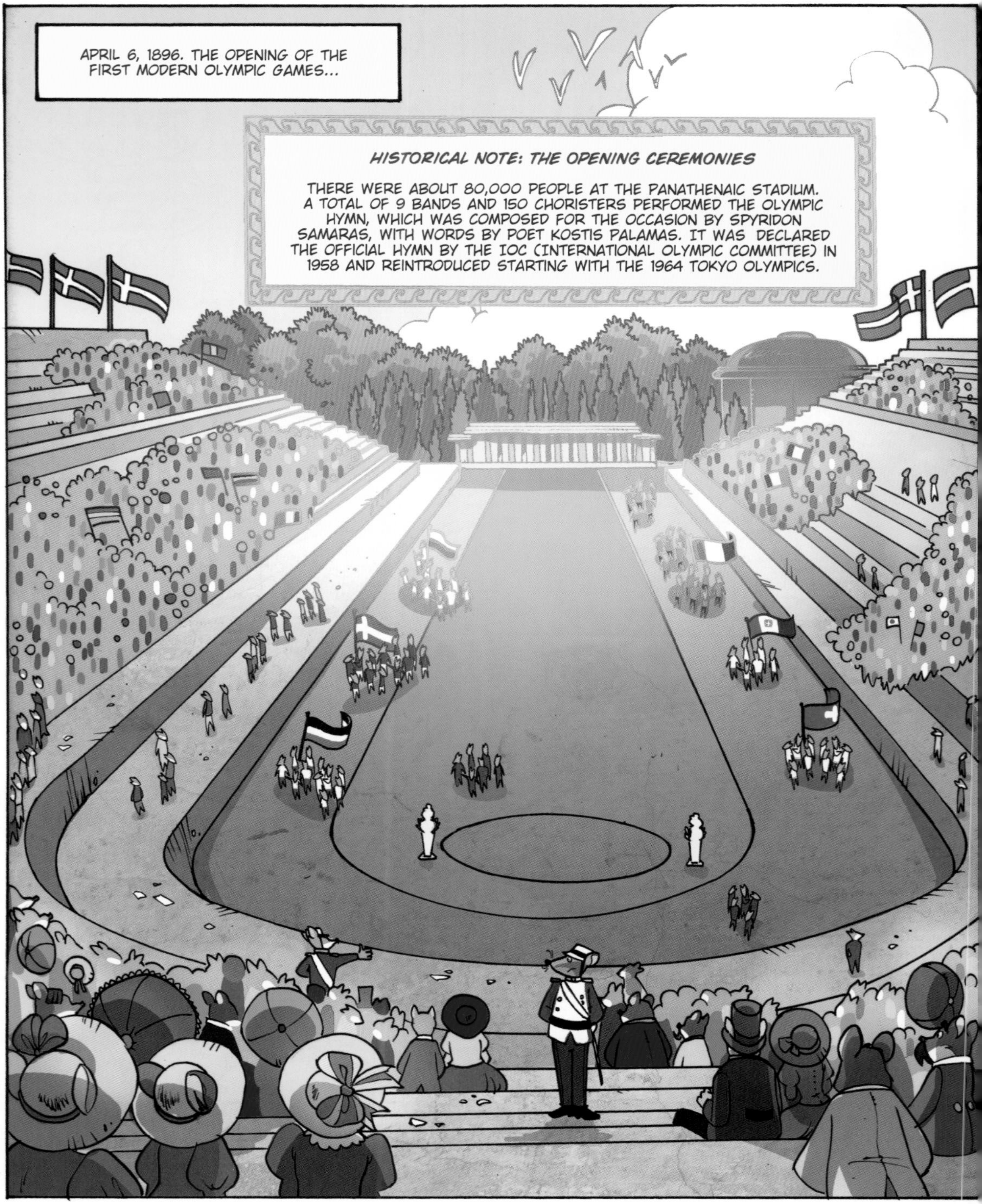
APRIL 6, 1896. THE OPENING OF THE FIRST MODERN OLYMPIC GAMES...
HISTORICAL NOTE: THE OPENING CEREMONIES
THERE WERE ABOUT 80,000 PEOPLE AT THE PANATHENAIC STADIUM. A TOTAL OF 9 BANDS AND 150 CHORISTERS PERFORMED THE OLYMPIC HYMN, WHICH WAS COMPOSED FOR THE OCCASION BY SPYRIDON SAMARAS, WITH WORDS BY POET KOSTIS PALAMAS. IT WAS DECLARED THE OFFICIAL HYMN BY THE IOC (INTERNATIONAL OLYMPIC COMMITTEE) IN 1958 AND REINTRODUCED STARTING WITH THE 1964 TOKYO OLYMPICS.

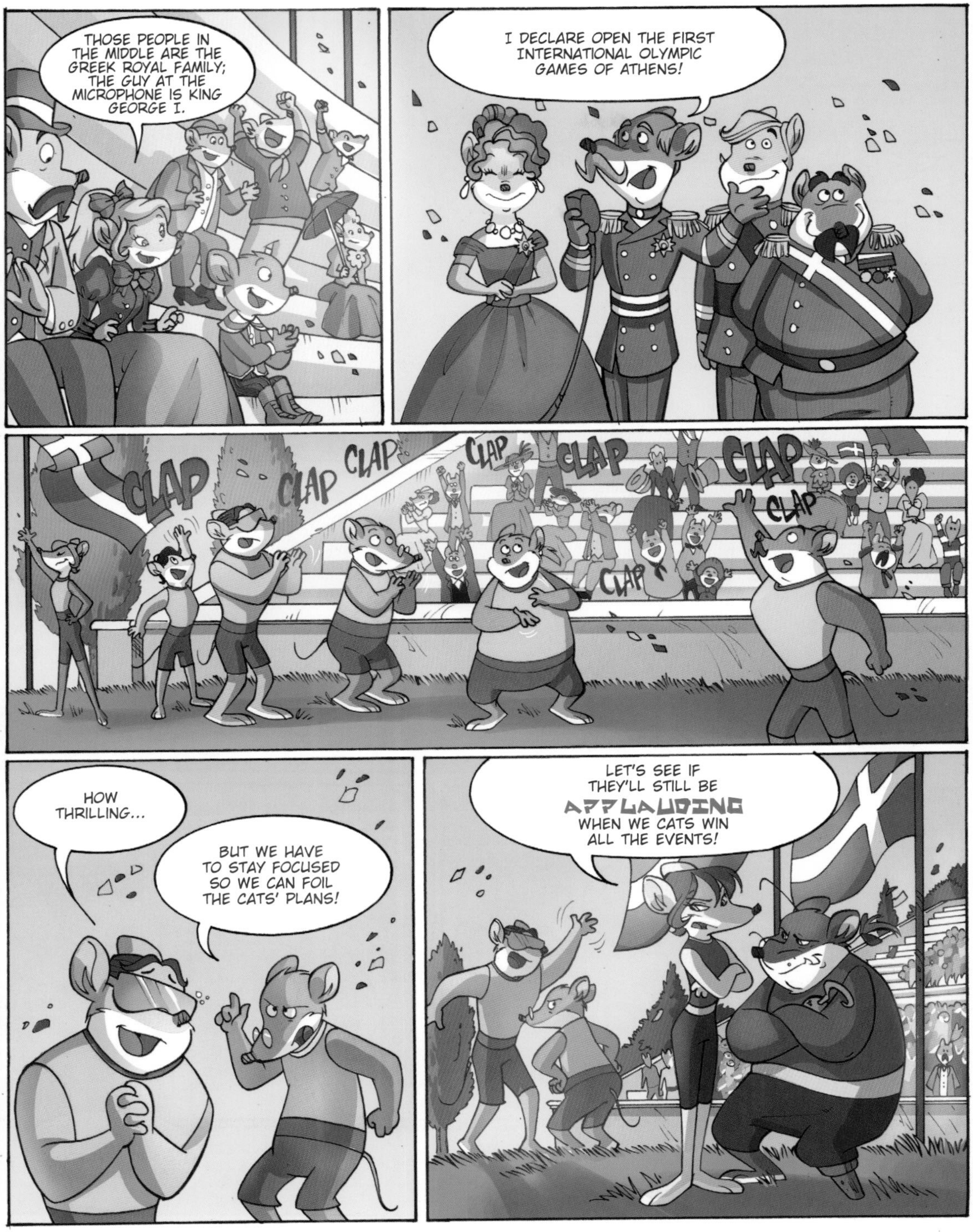
THOSE PEOPLE IN THE MIDDLE ARE THE GREEK ROYAL FAMILY; THE GUY AT THE MICROPHONE IS KING GEORGE I.
I DECLARE OPEN THE FIRST INTERNATIONAL OLYMPIC GAMES OF ATHENS!
CLAP
CLAP
CLAP
CLAP
CLAP
CLAP
CLAP
CLAP
HOW THRILLING...
BUT WE HAVE TO STAY FOCUSED SO WE CAN FOIL THE CATS' PLANS!
LET'S SEE IF THEY'LL STILL BE APPLAUDING WHEN WE CATS WIN ALL THE EVENTS!

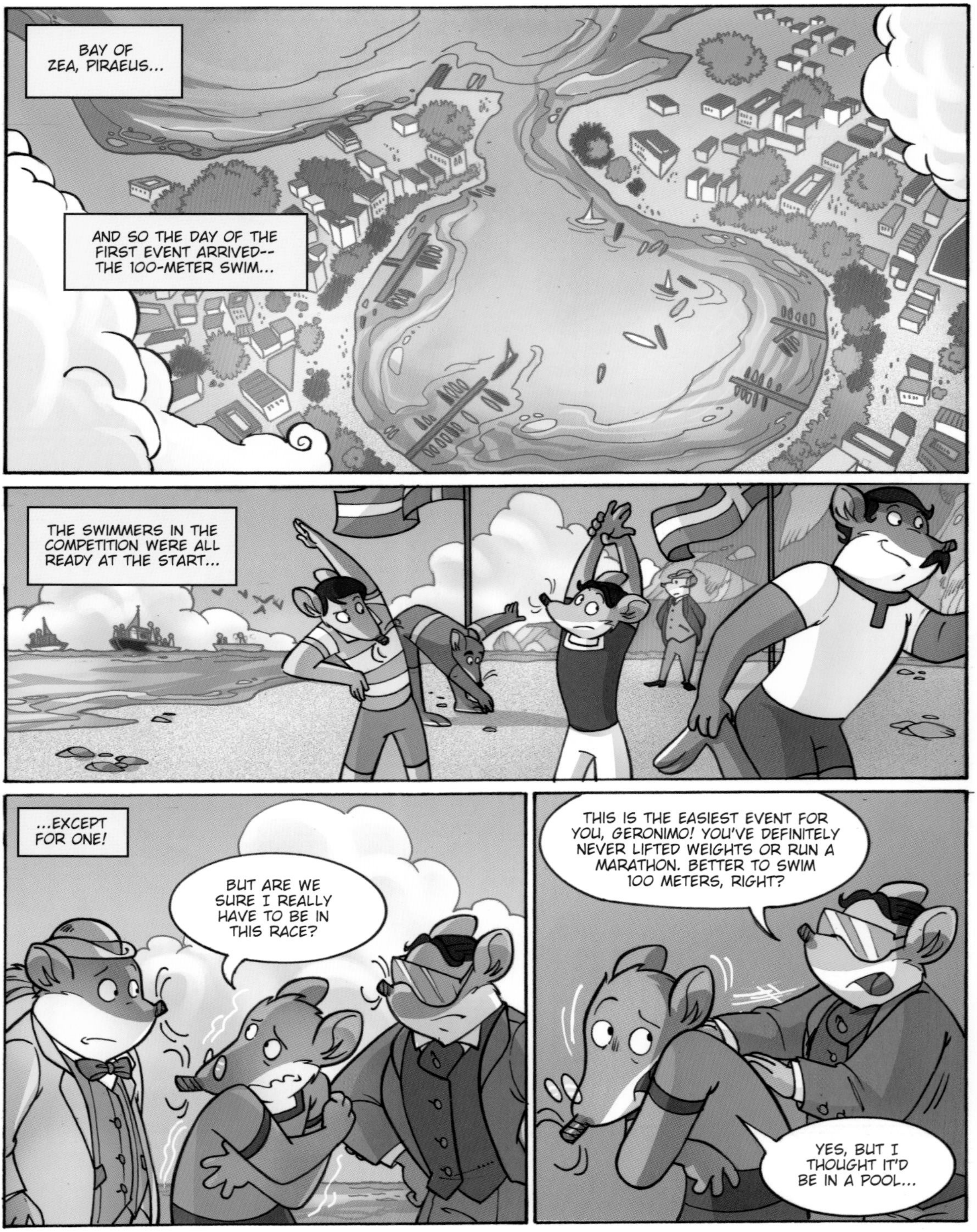
BAY OF ZEA, PIRAEUS...
AND SO THE DAY OF THE FIRST EVENT ARRIVED-- THE 100-METER SWIM...
THE SWIMMERS IN THE COMPETITION WERE ALL READY AT THE START...
...EXCEPT FOR ONE!
BUT ARE WE SURE I REALLY HAVE TO BE IN THIS RACE?
THIS IS THE EASIEST EVENT FOR YOU, GERONIMO! YOU'VE DEFINITELY NEVER LIFTED WEIGHTS OR RUN A MARATHON. BETTER TO SWIM 100 METERS, RIGHT?
YES, BUT I THOUGHT IT'D BE IN A POOL...

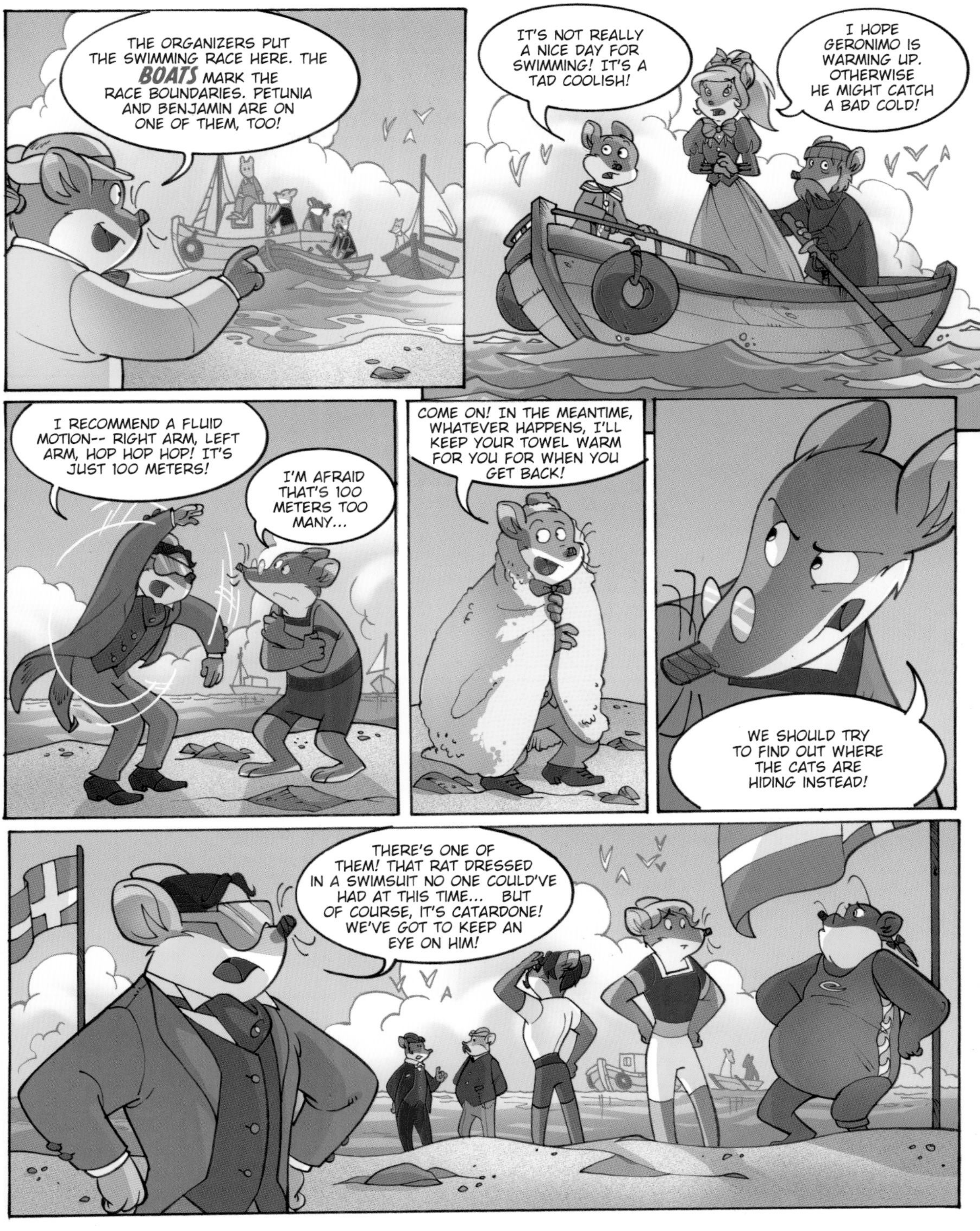
THE ORGANIZERS PUT THE SWIMMING RACE HERE. THE BOATS MARK THE RACE BOUNDARIES. PETUNIA AND BENJAMIN ARE ON ONE OF THEM, TOO!
IT'S NOT REALLY A NICE DAY FOR SWIMMING! IT'S A TAD COOLISH!
I HOPE GERONIMO IS WARMING UP. OTHERWISE HE MIGHT CATCH A BAD COLD!
I RECOMMEND A FLUID MOTION-- RIGHT ARM, LEFT ARM, HOP HOP HOP! IT'S JUST 100 METERS!
I'M AFRAID THAT'S 100 METERS TOO MANY...
COME ON! IN THE MEANTIME, WHATEVER HAPPENS, I'LL KEEP YOUR TOWEL WARM FOR YOU FOR WHEN YOU GET BACK!
WE SHOULD TRY TO FIND OUT WHERE THE CATS ARE HIDING INSTEAD!
THERE'S ONE OF THEM! THAT RAT DRESSED IN A SWIMSUIT NO ONE COULD'VE HAD AT THIS TIME... BUT OF COURSE, IT'S CATARDONE! WE'VE GOT TO KEEP AN EYE ON HIM!

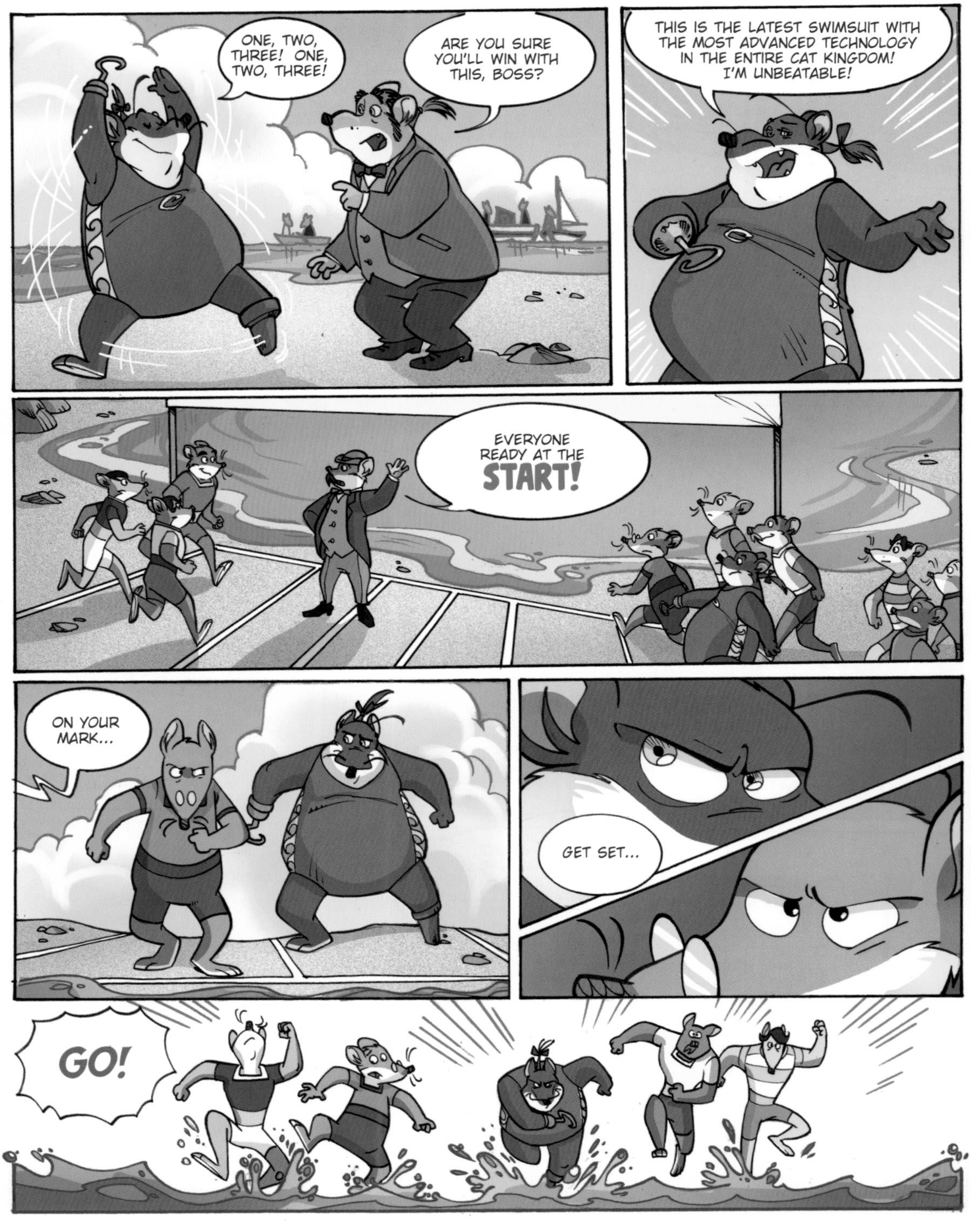
ONE, TWO, THREE! ONE, TWO, THREE!
ARE YOU SURE YOU'LL WIN WITH THIS, BOSS?
THIS IS THE LATEST SWIMSUIT WITH THE MOST ADVANCED TECHNOLOGY IN THE ENTIRE CAT KINGDOM! I'M UNBEATABLE!
EVERYONE READY AT THE START!
ON YOUR MARK...
GET SET...
GO!

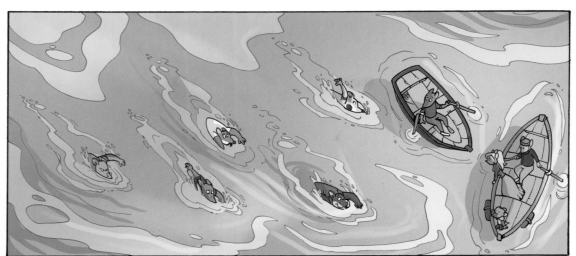

THAT RAT HAS A BIG LEAD!

AND GERONIMO'S NOT DOING WELL...

WE'VE REALLY GOTTEN OFF ON THE WRONG **PAW**... WITH THAT SWIMSUIT, CATARDONE WILL WIN EASILY.

WE'VE ONLY GONE A FEW METERS AND I'M ALREADY THRASHING HIM! THIS SWIMSUIT'S AMAZING!

I'M ALREADY NOT THE BEST MOUSE FOR THIS SPORT AND NOW CATARDONE'S CHEATING! BUT MAYBE...

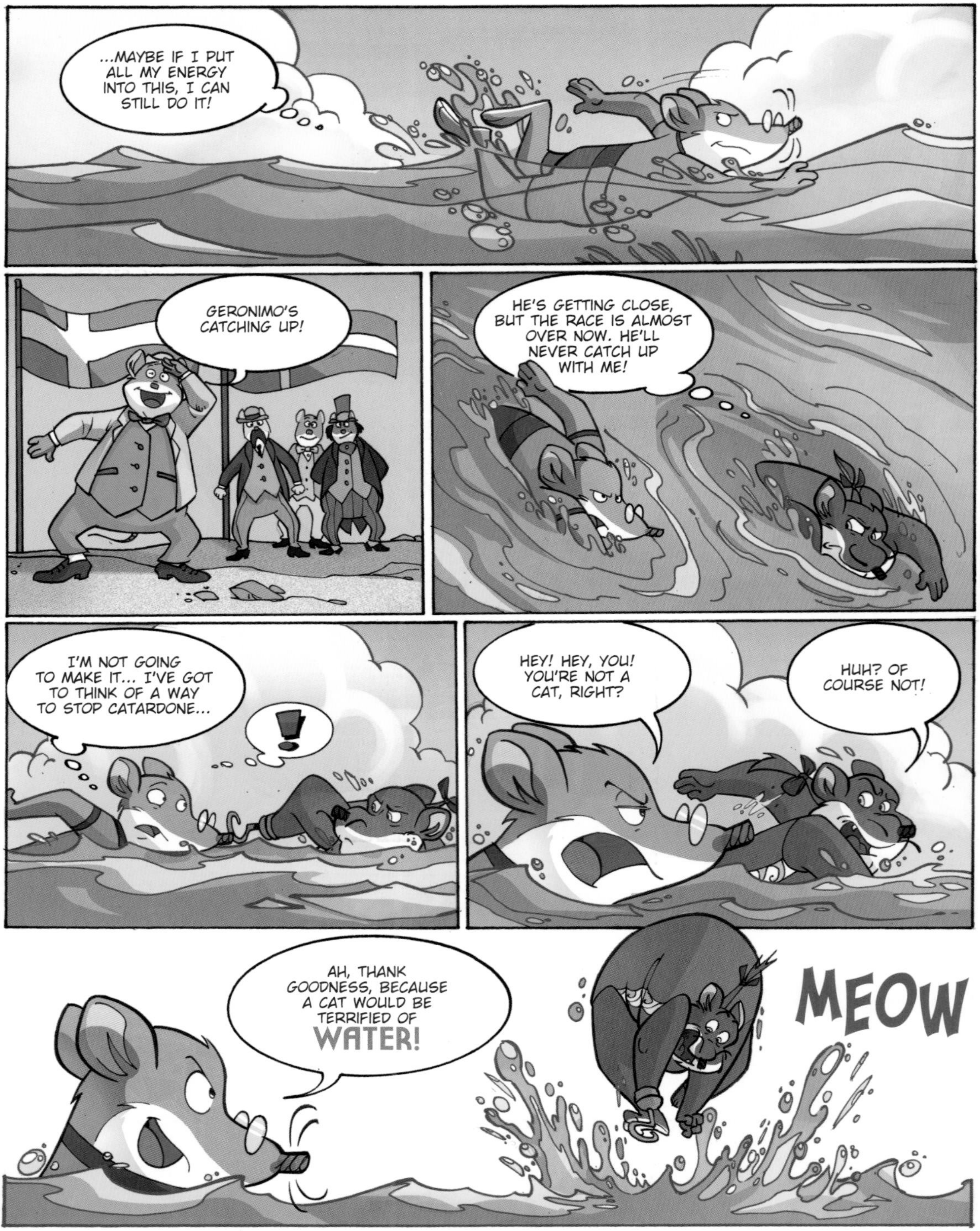
...MAYBE IF I PUT ALL MY ENERGY INTO THIS, I CAN STILL DO IT!
GERONIMO'S CATCHING UP!
HE'S GETTING CLOSE, BUT THE RACE IS ALMOST OVER NOW. HE'LL NEVER CATCH UP WITH ME!
I'M NOT GOING TO MAKE IT... I'VE GOT TO THINK OF A WAY TO STOP CATARDONE...
!
HEY! HEY, YOU! YOU'RE NOT A CAT, RIGHT?
HUH? OF COURSE NOT!
AH, THANK GOODNESS, BECAUSE A CAT WOULD BE TERRIFIED OF WATER!
MEOW

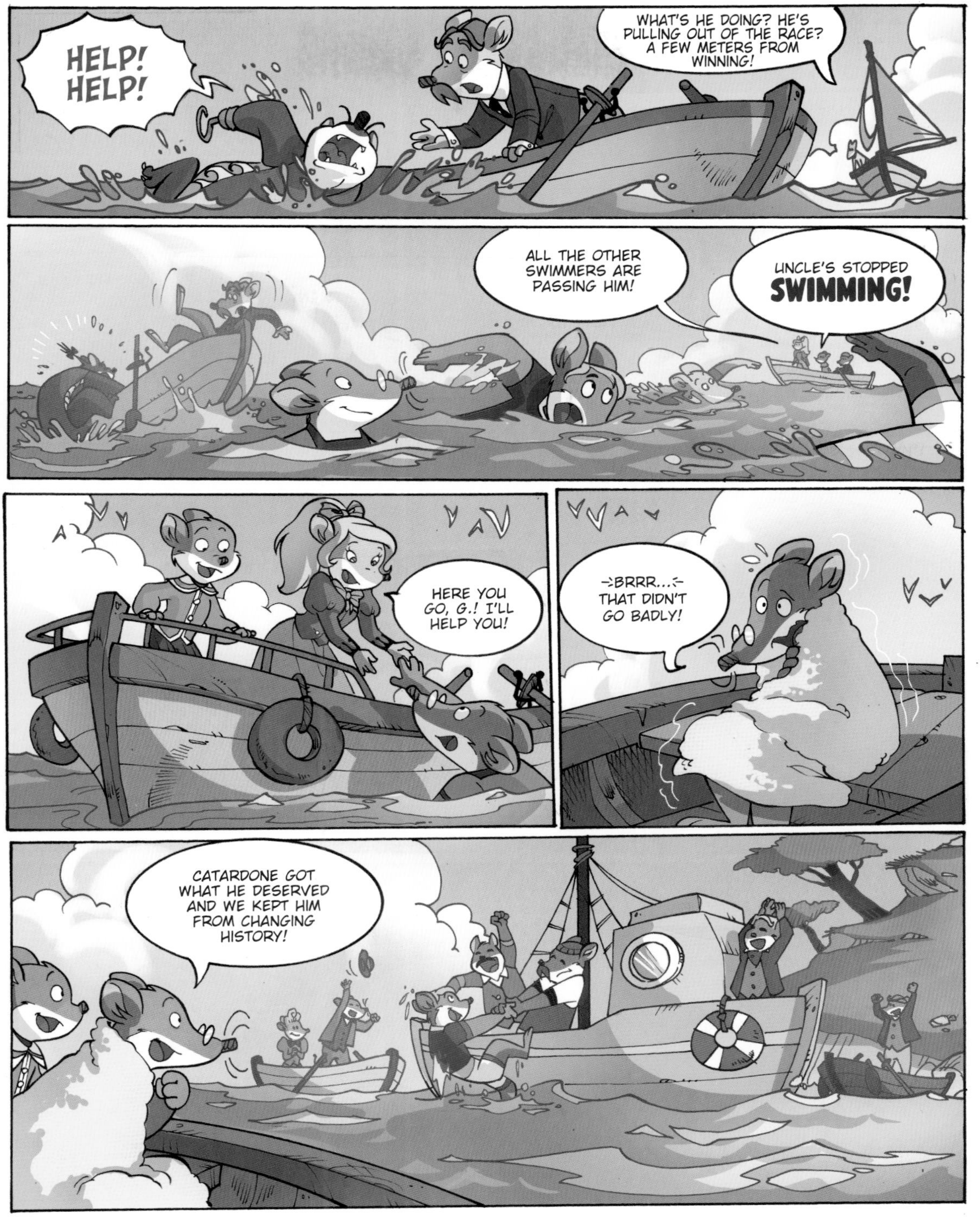
HELP! HELP!
WHAT'S HE DOING? HE'S PULLING OUT OF THE RACE? A FEW METERS FROM WINNING!
ALL THE OTHER SWIMMERS ARE PASSING HIM!
UNCLE'S STOPPED SWIMMING!
HERE YOU GO, G.! I'LL HELP YOU!
BRRR... THAT DIDN'T GO BADLY!
CATARDONE GOT WHAT HE DESERVED AND WE KEPT HIM FROM CHANGING HISTORY!

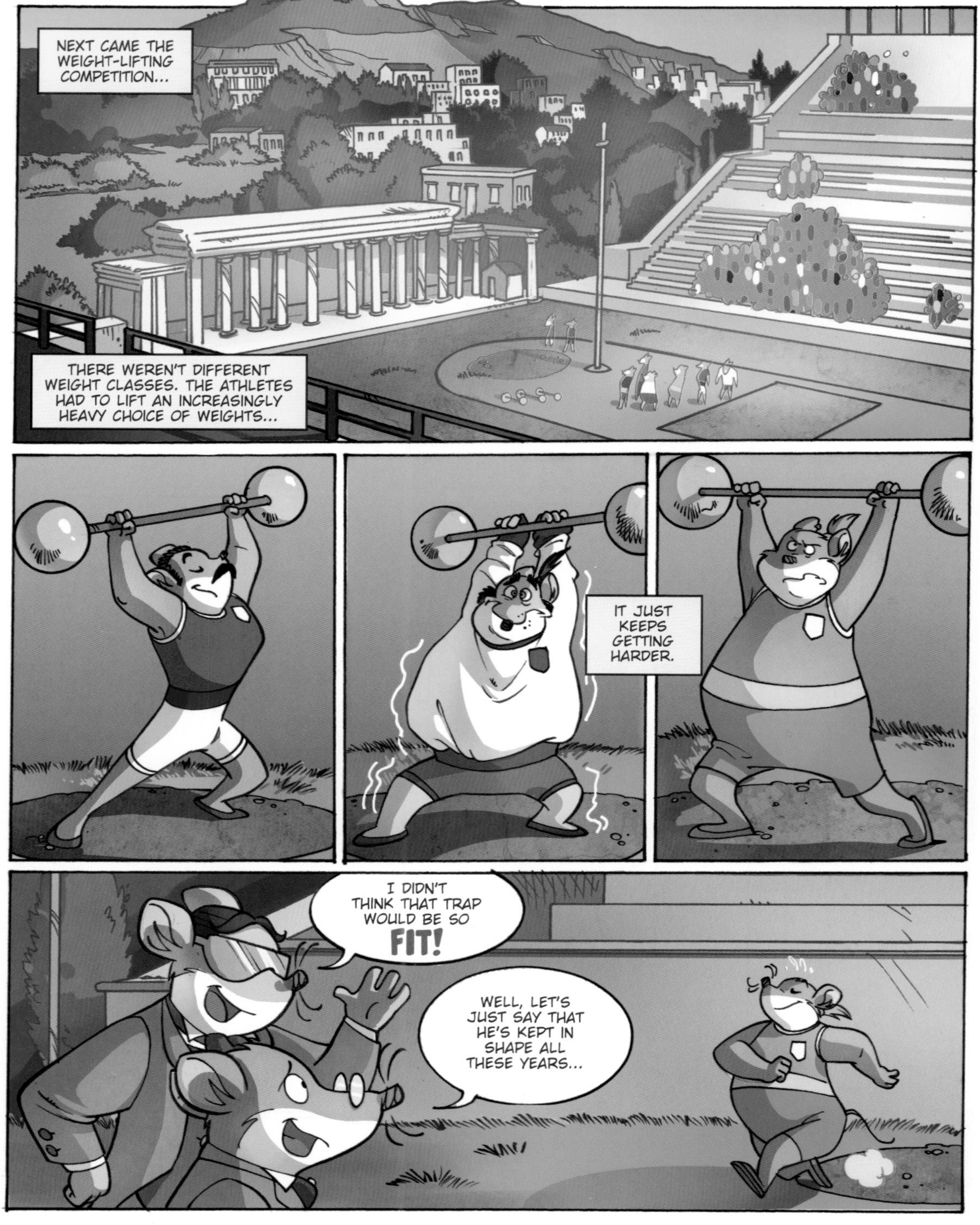

NEXT CAME THE WEIGHT-LIFTING COMPETITION...
THERE WEREN'T DIFFERENT WEIGHT CLASSES. THE ATHLETES HAD TO LIFT AN INCREASINGLY HEAVY CHOICE OF WEIGHTS...
IT JUST KEEPS GETTING HARDER.
I DIDN'T THINK THAT TRAP WOULD BE SO FIT!
WELL, LET'S JUST SAY THAT HE'S KEPT IN SHAPE ALL THESE YEARS...

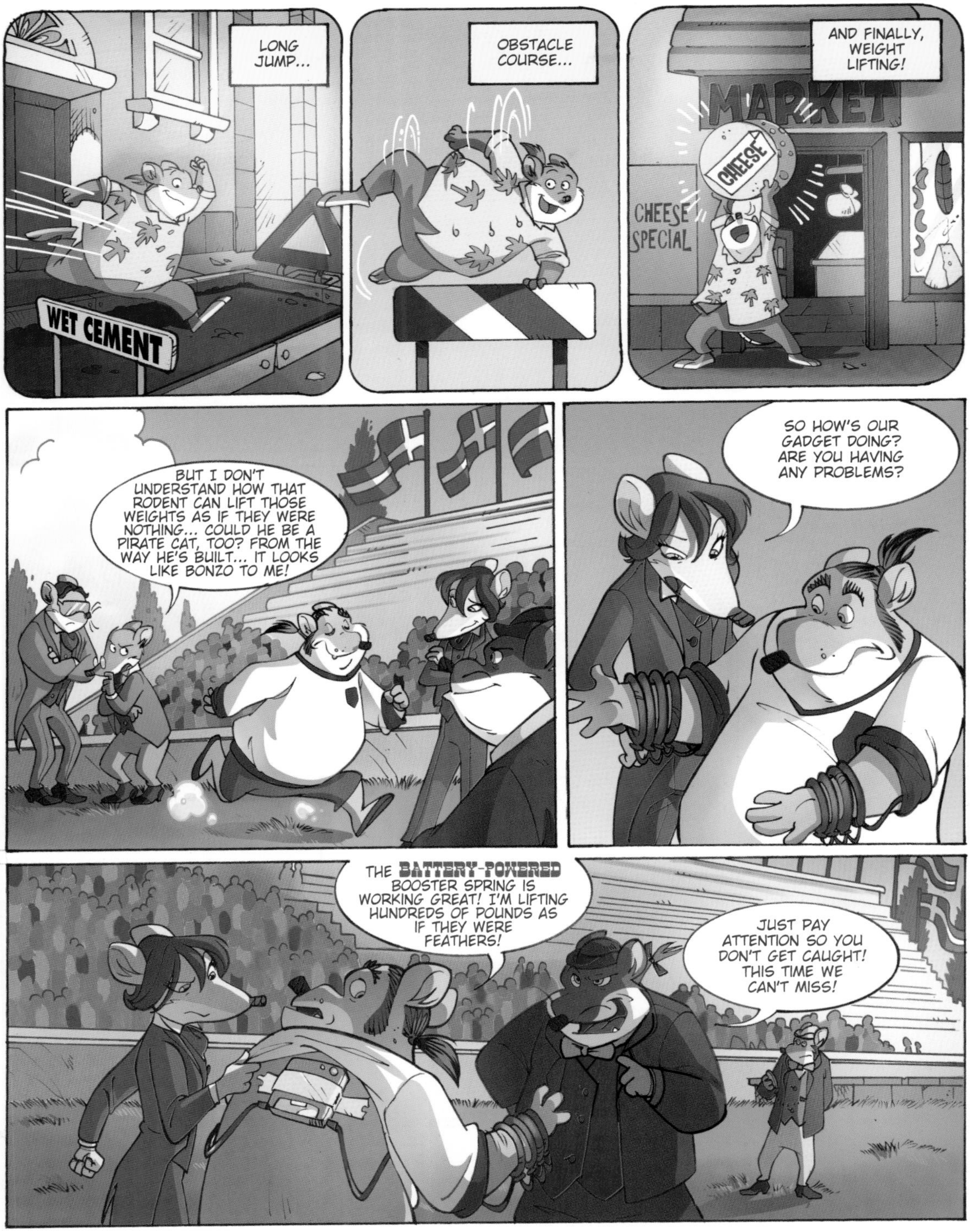
LONG JUMP...
WET CEMENT
OBSTACLE COURSE...
AND FINALLY, WEIGHT LIFTING!
MARKET
CHEESE
CHEESE SPECIAL
BUT I DON'T UNDERSTAND HOW THAT RODENT CAN LIFT THOSE WEIGHTS AS IF THEY WERE NOTHING... COULD HE BE A PIRATE CAT, TOO? FROM THE WAY HE'S BUILT... IT LOOKS LIKE BONZO TO ME!
SO HOW'S OUR GADGET DOING? ARE YOU HAVING ANY PROBLEMS?
THE BATTERY-POWERED BOOSTER SPRING IS WORKING GREAT! I'M LIFTING HUNDREDS OF POUNDS AS IF THEY WERE FEATHERS!
JUST PAY ATTENTION SO YOU DON'T GET CAUGHT! THIS TIME WE CAN'T MISS!

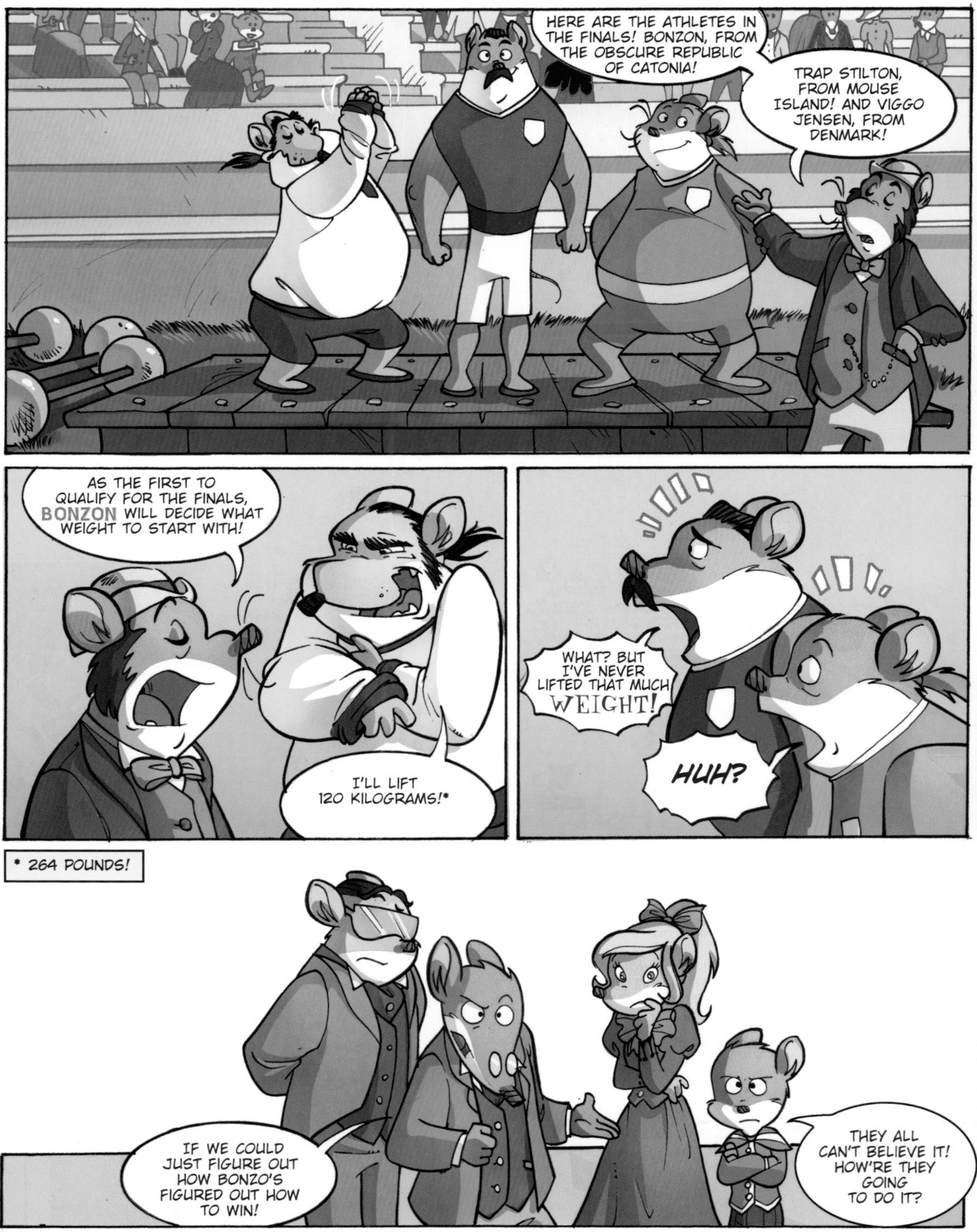
HERE ARE THE ATHLETES IN THE FINALS! BONZON, FROM THE OBSCURE REPUBLIC OF CATONIA!
TRAP STILTON, FROM MOUSE ISLAND! AND VIGGO JENSEN, FROM DENMARK!
AS THE FIRST TO QUALIFY FOR THE FINALS, BONZON WILL DECIDE WHAT WEIGHT TO START WITH!
I'LL LIFT 120 KILOGRAMS!*
WHAT? BUT I'VE NEVER LIFTED THAT MUCH WEIGHT!
HUH?
* 264 POUNDS!
IF WE COULD JUST FIGURE OUT HOW BONZO'S FIGURED OUT HOW TO WIN!
THEY ALL CAN'T BELIEVE IT! HOW'RE THEY GOING TO DO IT?

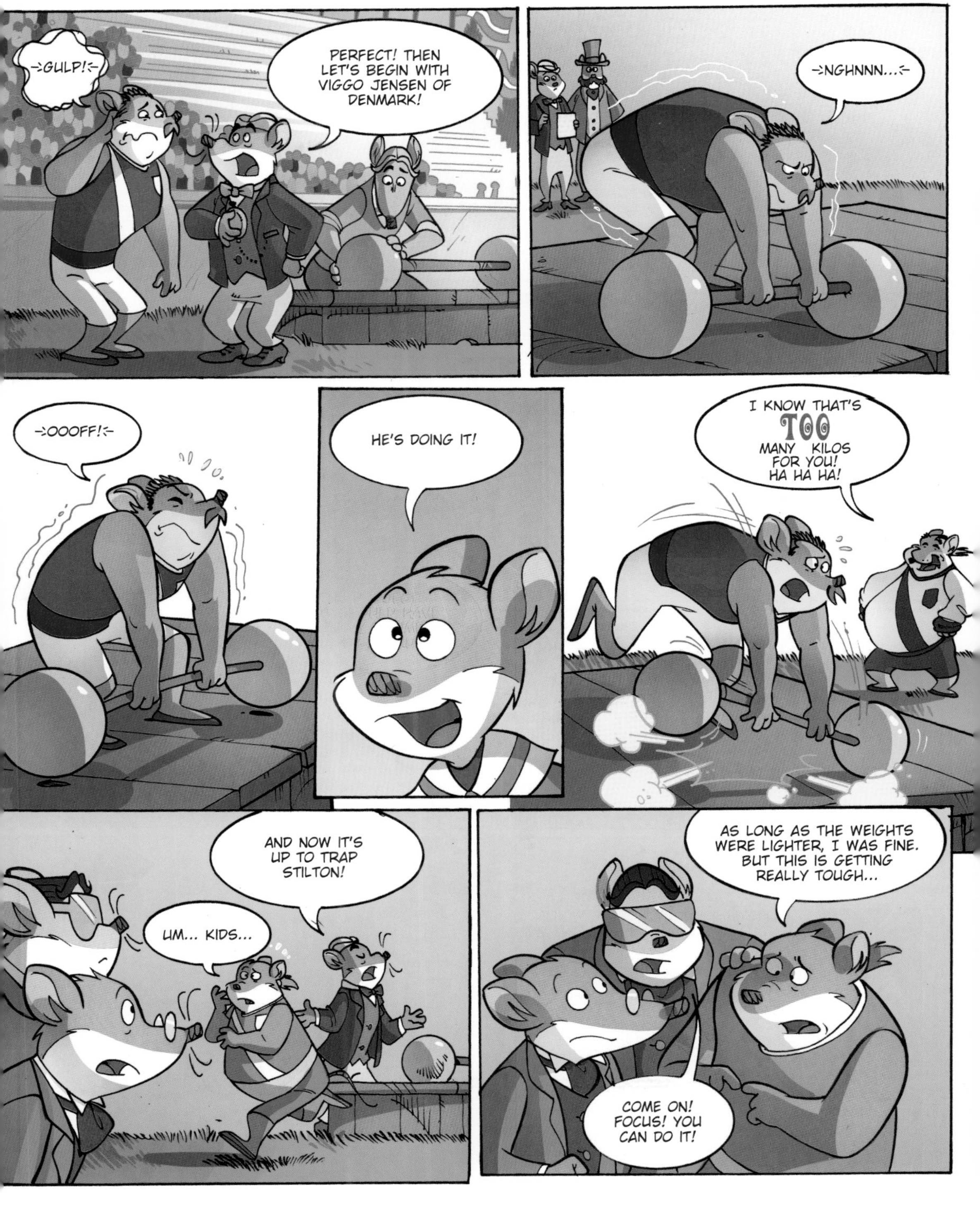

-GULP!-
PERFECT! THEN LET'S BEGIN WITH VIGGO JENSEN OF DENMARK!
-NGHNNN...-
-OOOFF!-
HE'S DOING IT!
I KNOW THAT'S TOO MANY KILOS FOR YOU! HA HA HA!
AND NOW IT'S UP TO TRAP STILTON!
UM... KIDS...
AS LONG AS THE WEIGHTS WERE LIGHTER, I WAS FINE. BUT THIS IS GETTING REALLY TOUGH...
COME ON! FOCUS! YOU CAN DO IT!

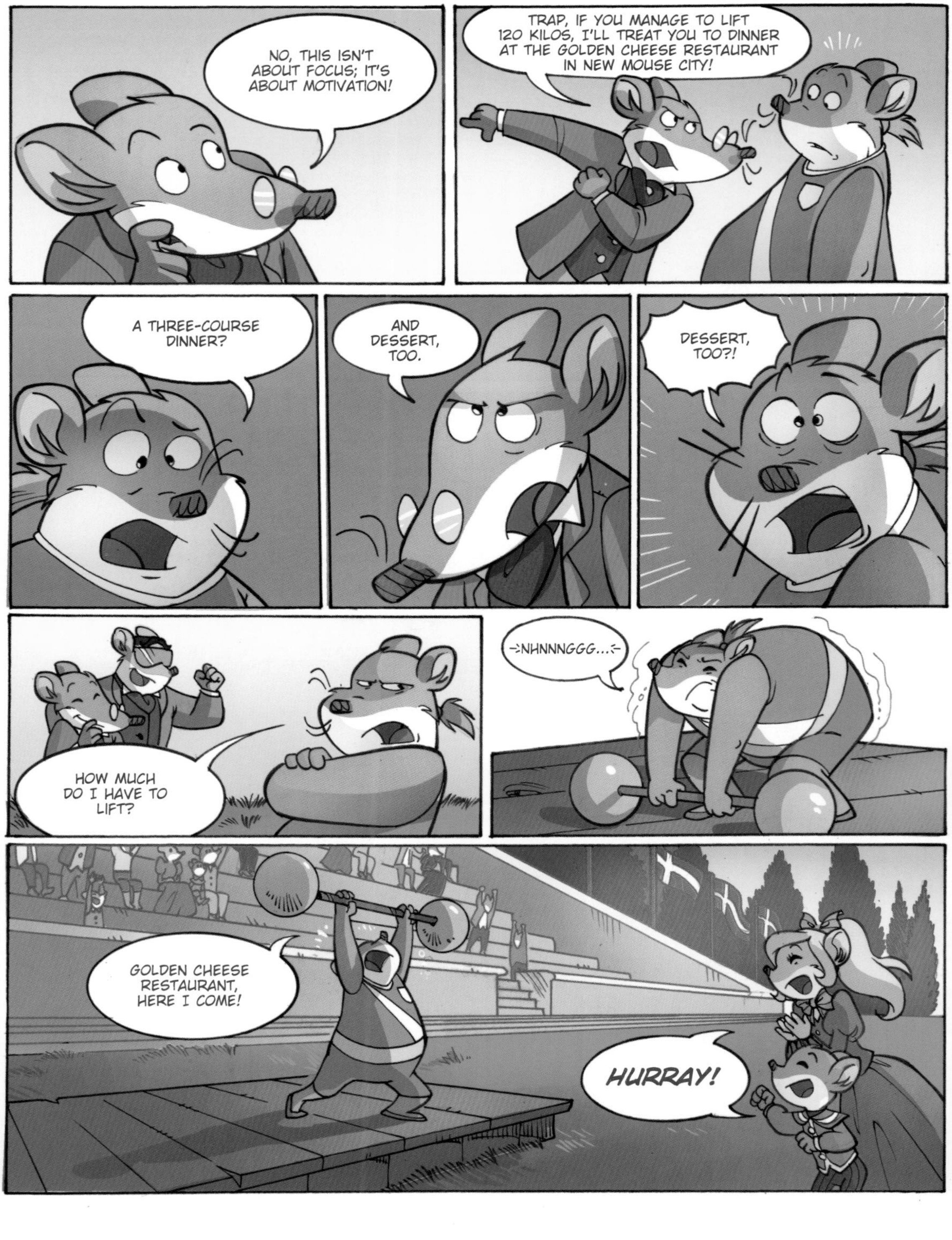
NO, THIS ISN'T ABOUT FOCUS; IT'S ABOUT MOTIVATION!
TRAP, IF YOU MANAGE TO LIFT 120 KILOS, I'LL TREAT YOU TO DINNER AT THE GOLDEN CHEESE RESTAURANT IN NEW MOUSE CITY!
A THREE-COURSE DINNER?
AND DESSERT, TOO.
DESSERT, TOO?!
HOW MUCH DO I HAVE TO LIFT?
NHNNNGGG...
GOLDEN CHEESE RESTAURANT, HERE I COME!
HURRAY!

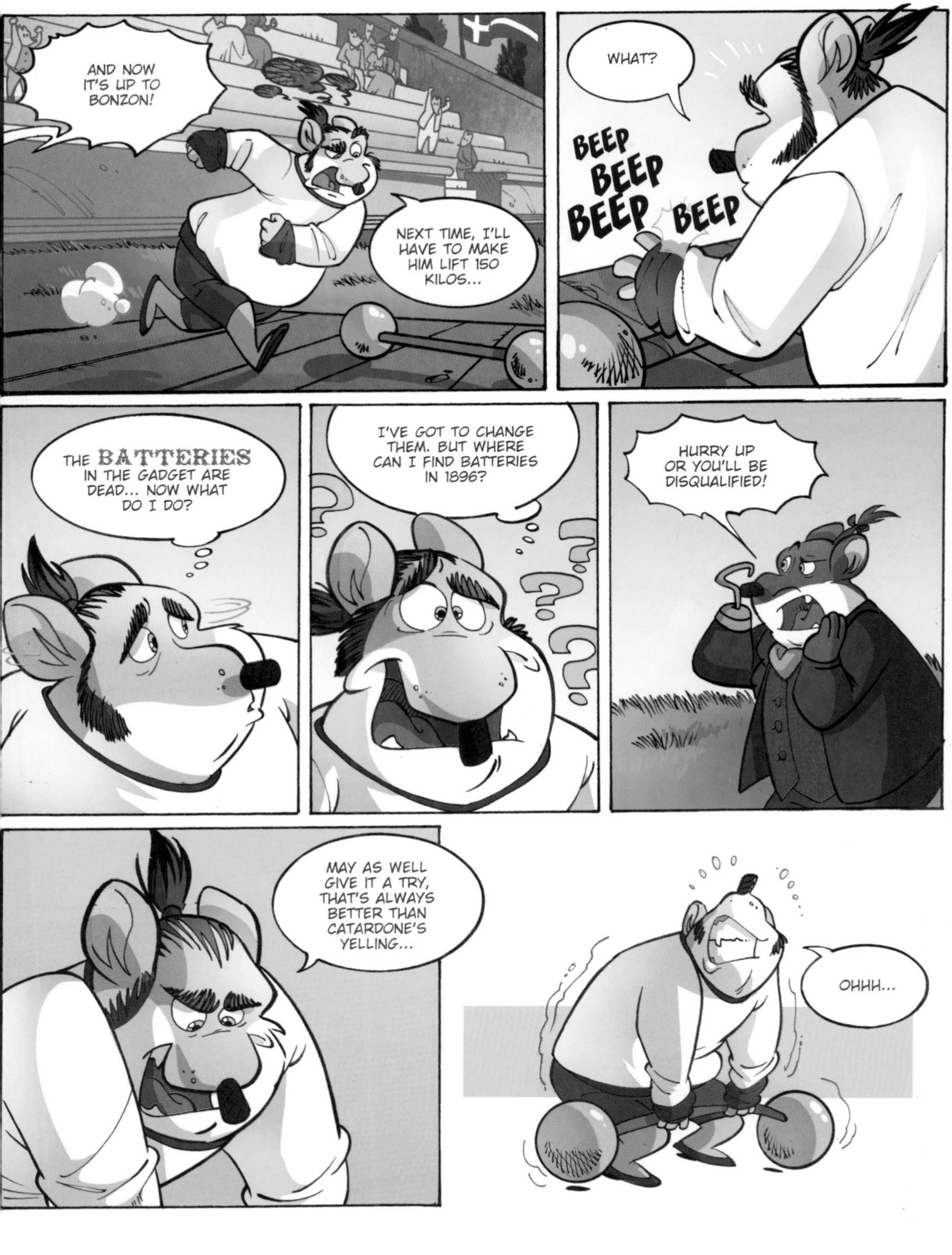
AND NOW IT'S UP TO BONZON!
NEXT TIME, I'LL HAVE TO MAKE HIM LIFT 150 KILOS...
WHAT?
BEEP BEEP BEEP BEEP
THE BATTERIES IN THE GADGET ARE DEAD... NOW WHAT DO I DO?
I'VE GOT TO CHANGE THEM. BUT WHERE CAN I FIND BATTERIES IN 1896?
HURRY UP OR YOU'LL BE DISQUALIFIED!
MAY AS WELL GIVE IT A TRY, THAT'S ALWAYS BETTER THAN CATARDONE'S YELLING...
OHHH...

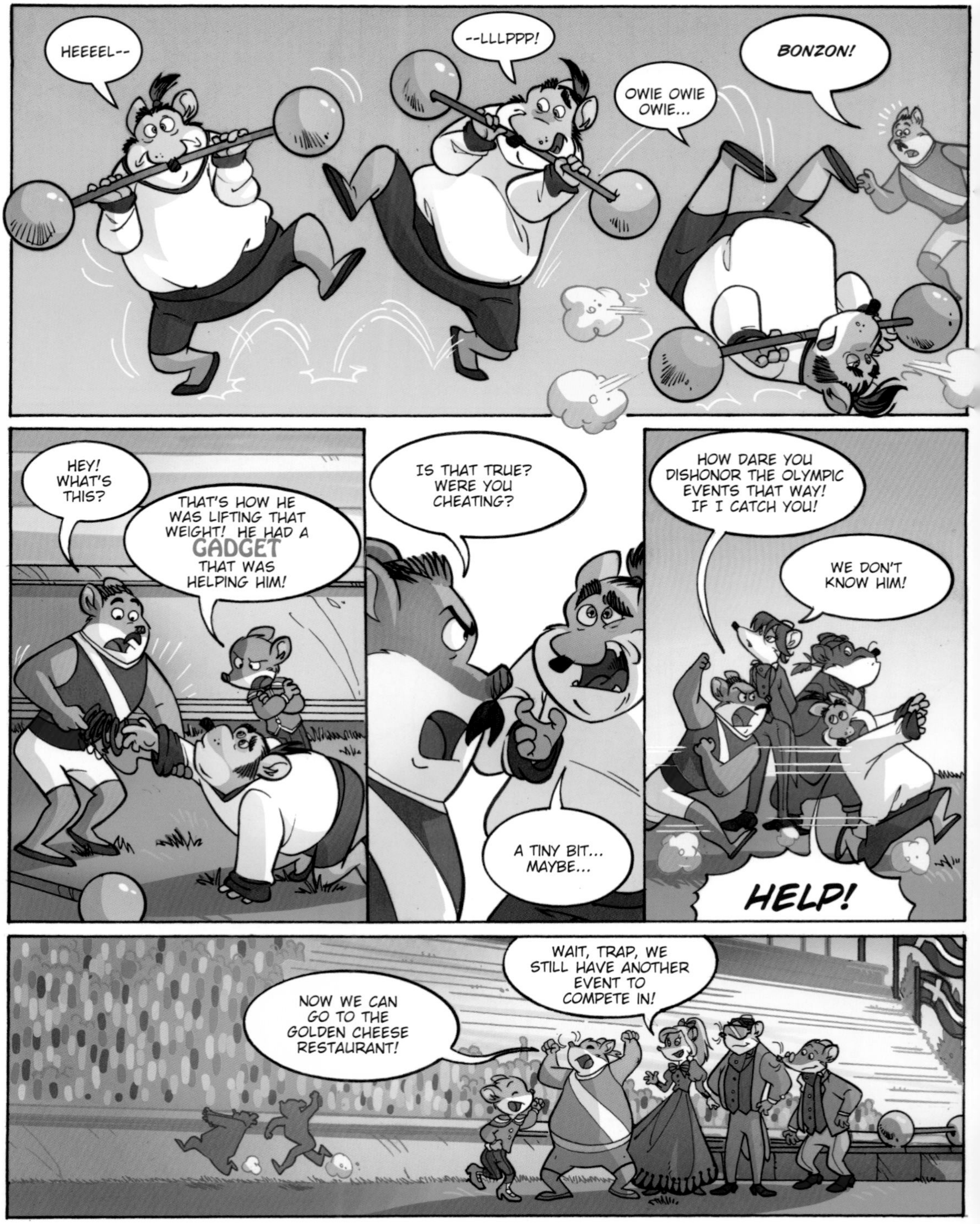
HEEEEL--
--LLLPPP!
OWIE OWIE OWIE...
BONZON!
HEY! WHAT'S THIS?
THAT'S HOW HE WAS LIFTING THAT WEIGHT! HE HAD A GADGET THAT WAS HELPING HIM!
IS THAT TRUE? WERE YOU CHEATING?
A TINY BIT... MAYBE...
HOW DARE YOU DISHONOR THE OLYMPIC EVENTS THAT WAY! IF I CATCH YOU!
WE DON'T KNOW HIM!
HELP!
NOW WE CAN GO TO THE GOLDEN CHEESE RESTAURANT!
WAIT, TRAP, WE STILL HAVE ANOTHER EVENT TO COMPETE IN!

THE DAY OFF BETWEEN EVENTS...

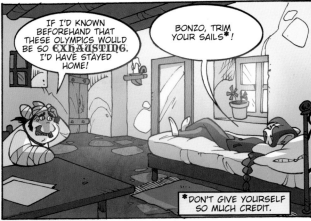

IF I'D KNOWN BEFOREHAND THAT THESE OLYMPICS WOULD BE SO **EXHAUSTING**, I'D HAVE STAYED HOME!

BONZO, TRIM YOUR SAILS*!

*DON'T GIVE YOURSELF SO MUCH CREDIT.

YOU COULDN'T EVEN MANAGE TO WIN BY CHEATING!

HERE ARE THE SHOES... I KEPT THEM IN THE CATJET, IT SEEMED LIKE THE SAFEST PLACE TO ME.

HMM...

BUT I DON'T UNDERSTAND HOW YOU THINK YOU'RE GOING TO WIN THE MARATHON WITH THOSE. THEY'RE JUST SHOES!

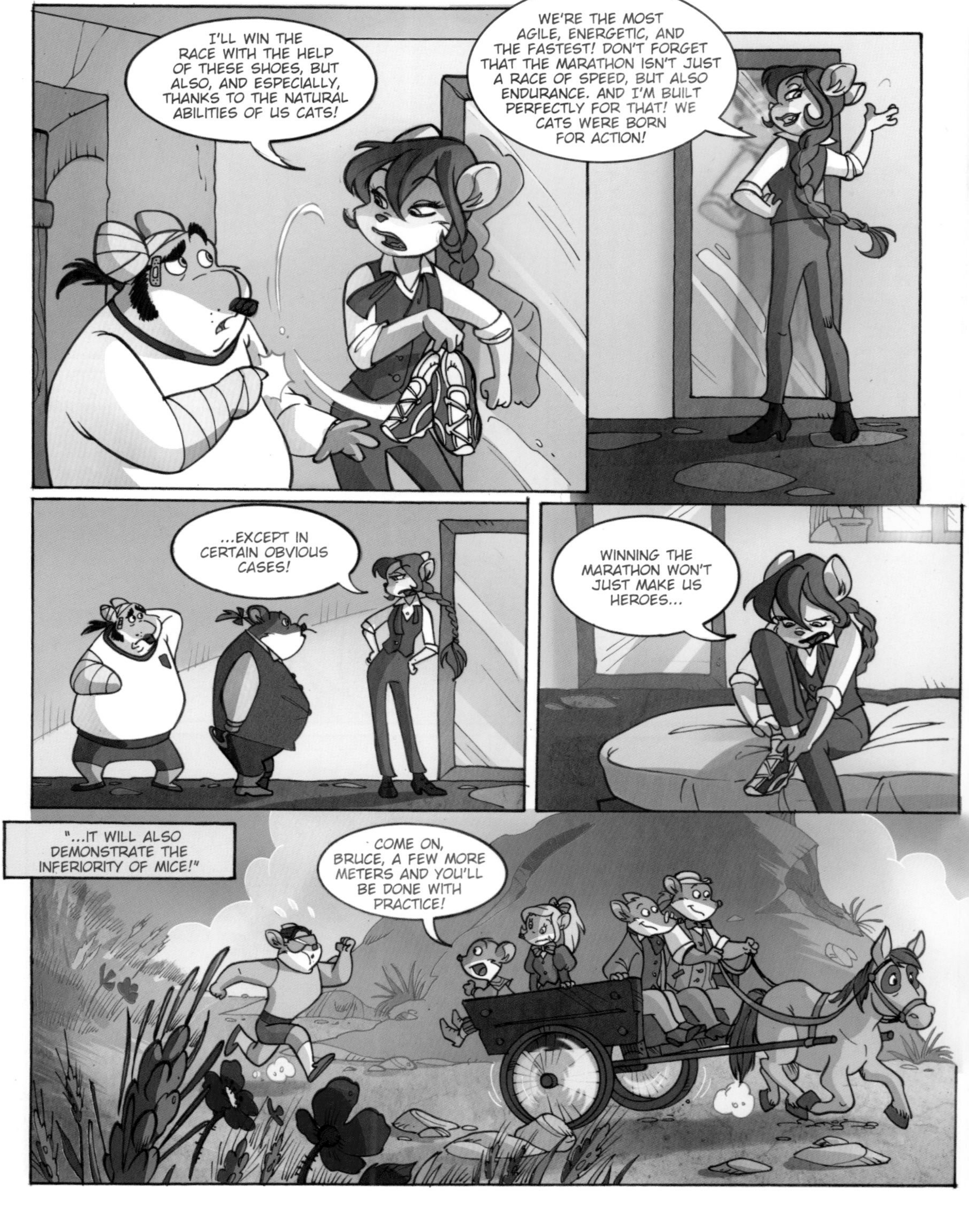
I'LL WIN THE RACE WITH THE HELP OF THESE SHOES, BUT ALSO, AND ESPECIALLY, THANKS TO THE NATURAL ABILITIES OF US CATS!
WE'RE THE MOST AGILE, ENERGETIC, AND THE FASTEST! DON'T FORGET THAT THE MARATHON ISN'T JUST A RACE OF SPEED, BUT ALSO ENDURANCE. AND I'M BUILT PERFECTLY FOR THAT! WE CATS WERE BORN FOR ACTION!
...EXCEPT IN CERTAIN OBVIOUS CASES!
WINNING THE MARATHON WON'T JUST MAKE US HEROES...
"...IT WILL ALSO DEMONSTRATE THE INFERIORITY OF MICE!"
COME ON, BRUCE, A FEW MORE METERS AND YOU'LL BE DONE WITH PRACTICE!

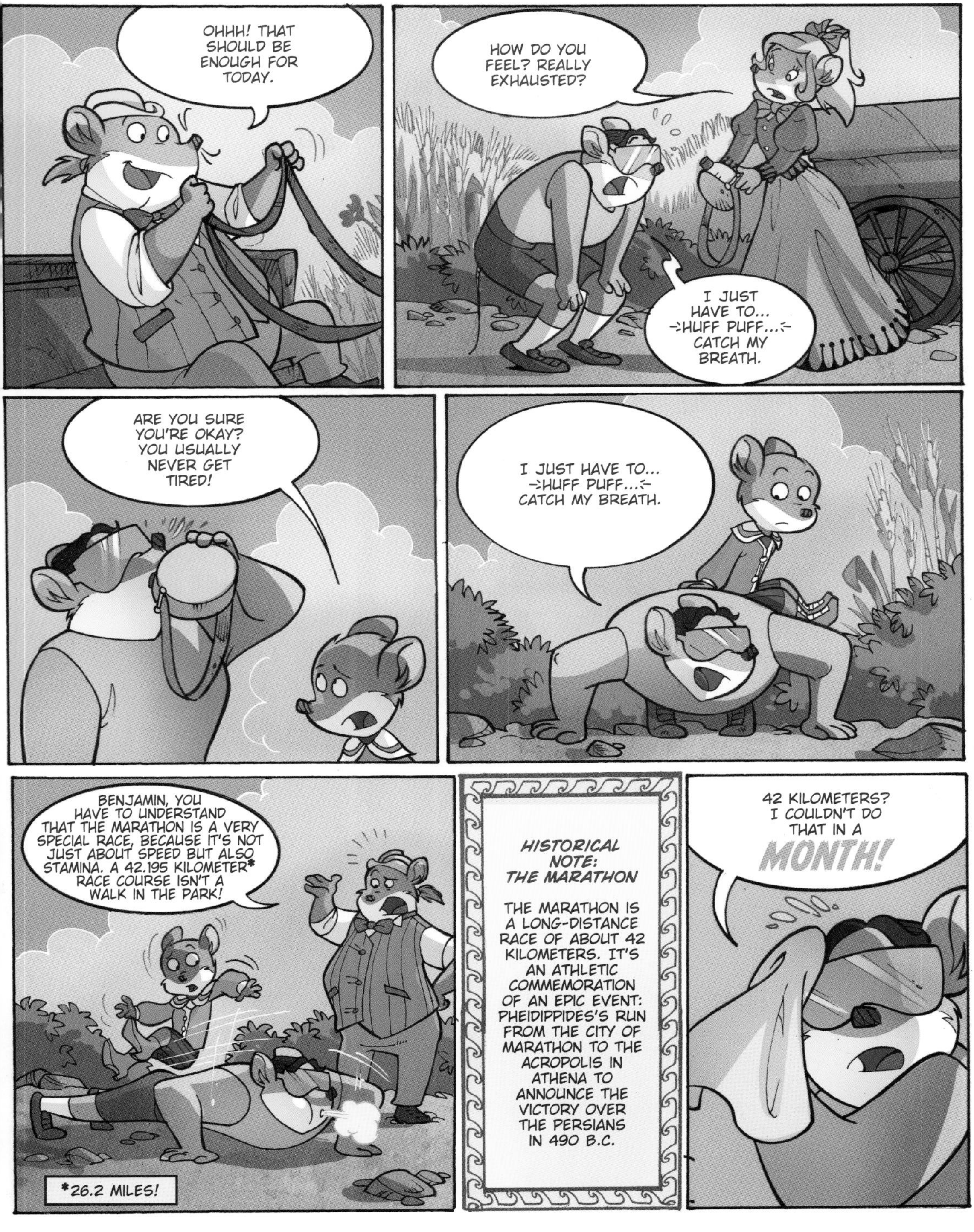
OHHH! THAT SHOULD BE ENOUGH FOR TODAY.
HOW DO YOU FEEL? REALLY EXHAUSTED?
I JUST HAVE TO... HUFF PUFF... CATCH MY BREATH.
ARE YOU SURE YOU'RE OKAY? YOU USUALLY NEVER GET TIRED!
I JUST HAVE TO... HUFF PUFF... CATCH MY BREATH.
BENJAMIN, YOU HAVE TO UNDERSTAND THAT THE MARATHON IS A VERY SPECIAL RACE, BECAUSE IT'S NOT JUST ABOUT SPEED BUT ALSO STAMINA. A 42.195 KILOMETER* RACE COURSE ISN'T A WALK IN THE PARK!
*26.2 MILES!
HISTORICAL NOTE: THE MARATHON
THE MARATHON IS A LONG-DISTANCE RACE OF ABOUT 42 KILOMETERS. IT'S AN ATHLETIC COMMEMORATION OF AN EPIC EVENT: PHEIDIPPIDES'S RUN FROM THE CITY OF MARATHON TO THE ACROPOLIS IN ATHENA TO ANNOUNCE THE VICTORY OVER THE PERSIANS IN 490 B.C.
42 KILOMETERS? I COULDN'T DO THAT IN A MONTH!

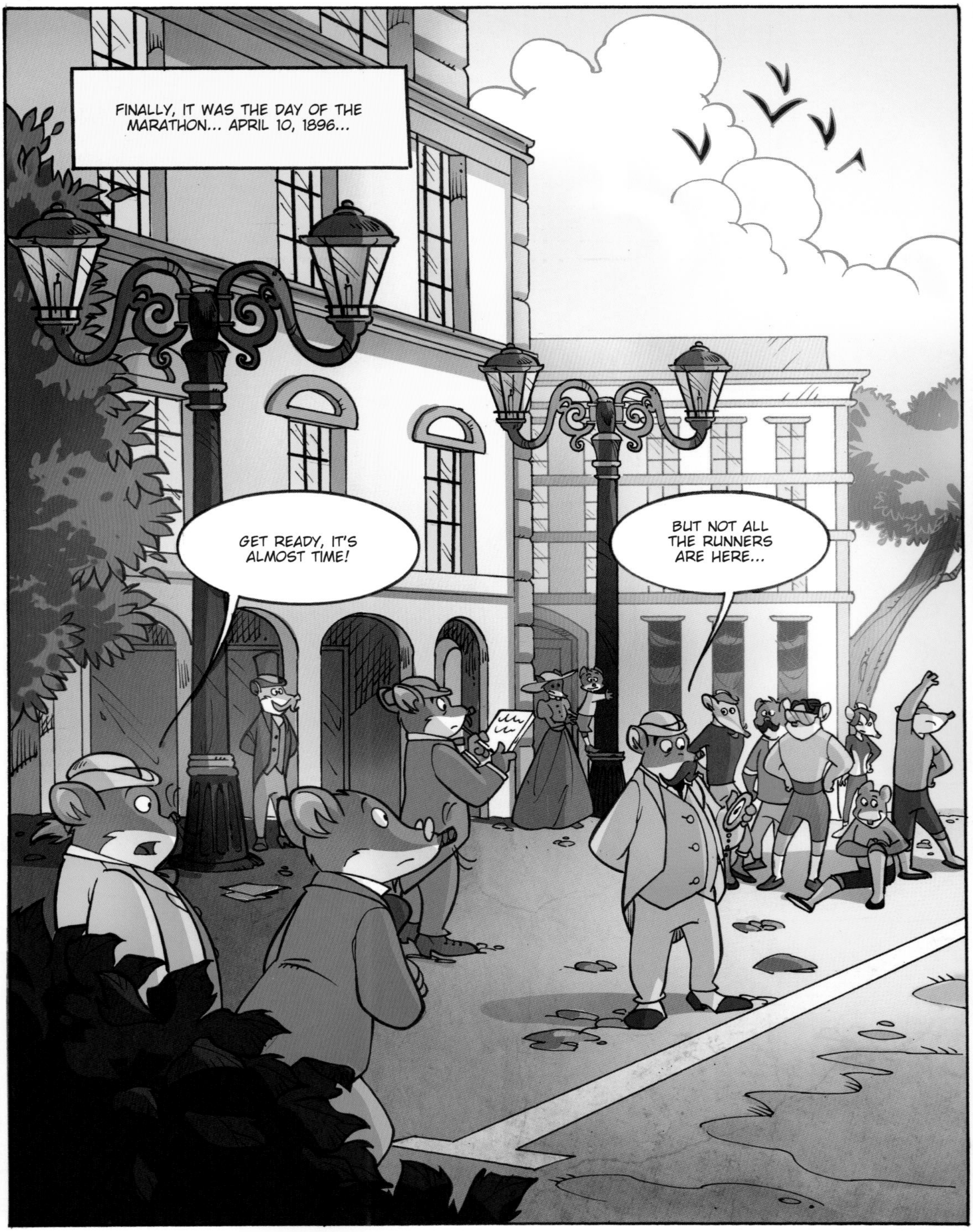
FINALLY, IT WAS THE DAY OF THE MARATHON... APRIL 10, 1896...
GET READY, IT'S ALMOST TIME!
BUT NOT ALL THE RUNNERS ARE HERE...

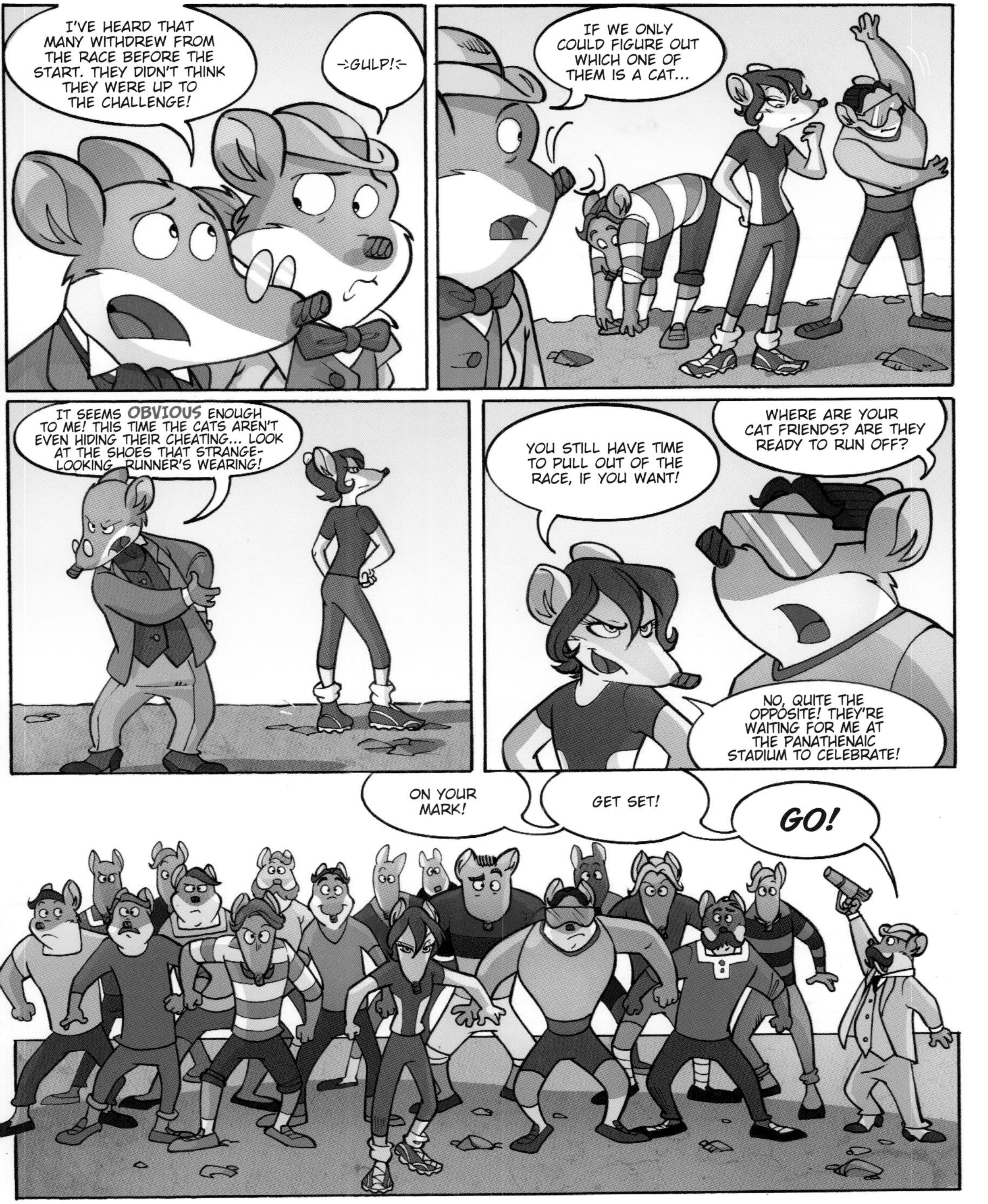
I'VE HEARD THAT MANY WITHDREW FROM THE RACE BEFORE THE START. THEY DIDN'T THINK THEY WERE UP TO THE CHALLENGE!
GULP!
IF WE ONLY COULD FIGURE OUT WHICH ONE OF THEM IS A CAT...
IT SEEMS OBVIOUS ENOUGH TO ME! THIS TIME THE CATS AREN'T EVEN HIDING THEIR CHEATING... LOOK AT THE SHOES THAT STRANGE-LOOKING RUNNER'S WEARING!
YOU STILL HAVE TIME TO PULL OUT OF THE RACE, IF YOU WANT!
WHERE ARE YOUR CAT FRIENDS? ARE THEY READY TO RUN OFF?
NO, QUITE THE OPPOSITE! THEY'RE WAITING FOR ME AT THE PANATHENAIC STADIUM TO CELEBRATE!
ON YOUR MARK!
GET SET!
GO!

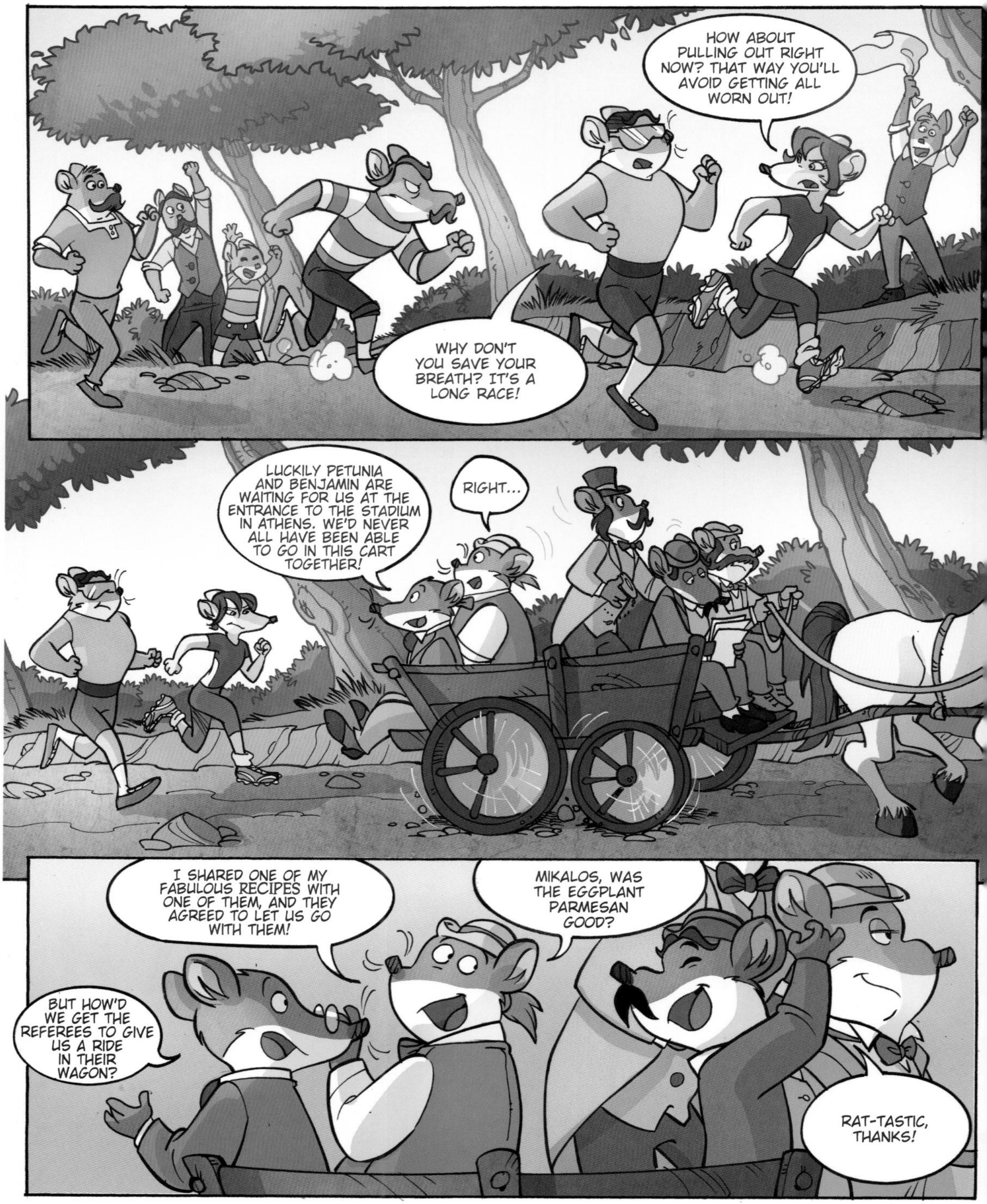
HOW ABOUT PULLING OUT RIGHT NOW? THAT WAY YOU'LL AVOID GETTING ALL WORN OUT!
WHY DON'T YOU SAVE YOUR BREATH? IT'S A LONG RACE!
LUCKILY PETUNIA AND BENJAMIN ARE WAITING FOR US AT THE ENTRANCE TO THE STADIUM IN ATHENS. WE'D NEVER ALL HAVE BEEN ABLE TO GO IN THIS CART TOGETHER!
RIGHT...
BUT HOW'D WE GET THE REFEREES TO GIVE US A RIDE IN THEIR WAGON?
I SHARED ONE OF MY FABULOUS RECIPES WITH ONE OF THEM, AND THEY AGREED TO LET US GO WITH THEM!
MIKALOS, WAS THE EGGPLANT PARMESAN GOOD?
RAT-TASTIC, THANKS!

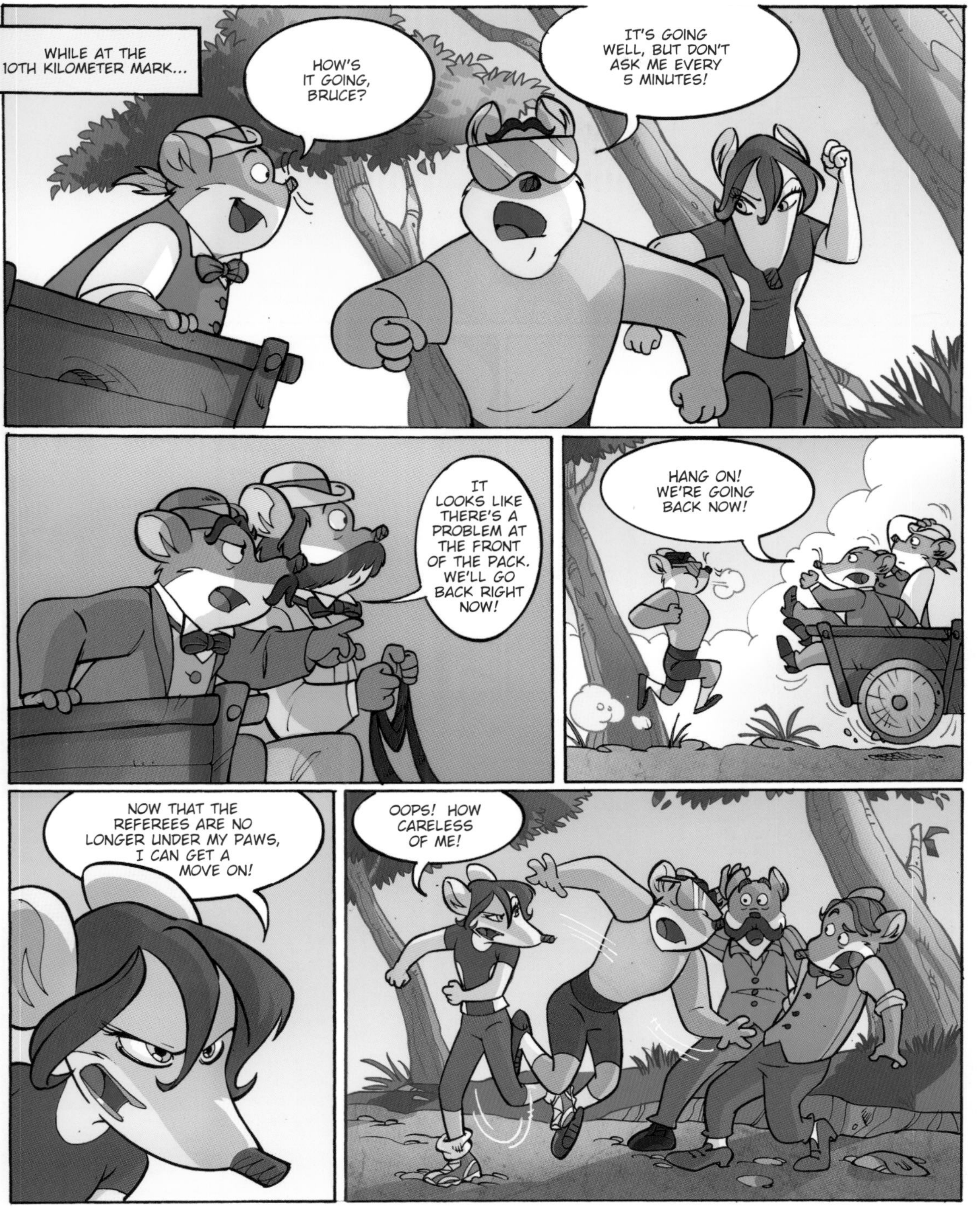
WHILE AT THE 10TH KILOMETER MARK...
HOW'S IT GOING, BRUCE?
IT'S GOING WELL, BUT DON'T ASK ME EVERY 5 MINUTES!
IT LOOKS LIKE THERE'S A PROBLEM AT THE FRONT OF THE PACK. WE'LL GO BACK RIGHT NOW!
HANG ON! WE'RE GOING BACK NOW!
NOW THAT THE REFEREES ARE NO LONGER UNDER MY PAWS, I CAN GET A MOVE ON!
OOPS! HOW CARELESS OF ME!

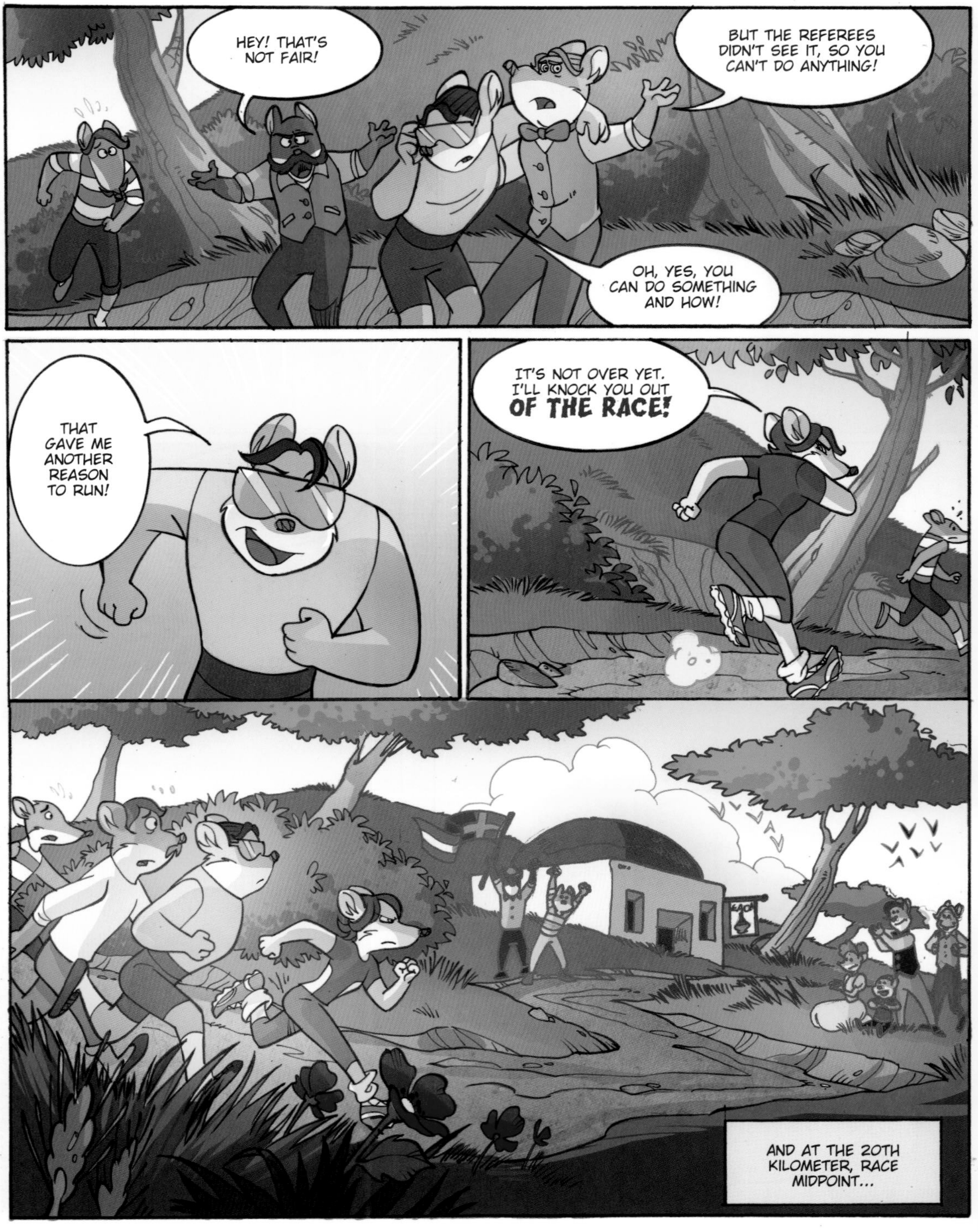

HEY! THAT'S NOT FAIR!
BUT THE REFEREES DIDN'T SEE IT, SO YOU CAN'T DO ANYTHING!
OH, YES, YOU CAN DO SOMETHING AND HOW!
THAT GAVE ME ANOTHER REASON TO RUN!
IT'S NOT OVER YET. I'LL KNOCK YOU OUT OF THE RACE!
AND AT THE 20TH KILOMETER, RACE MIDPOINT...

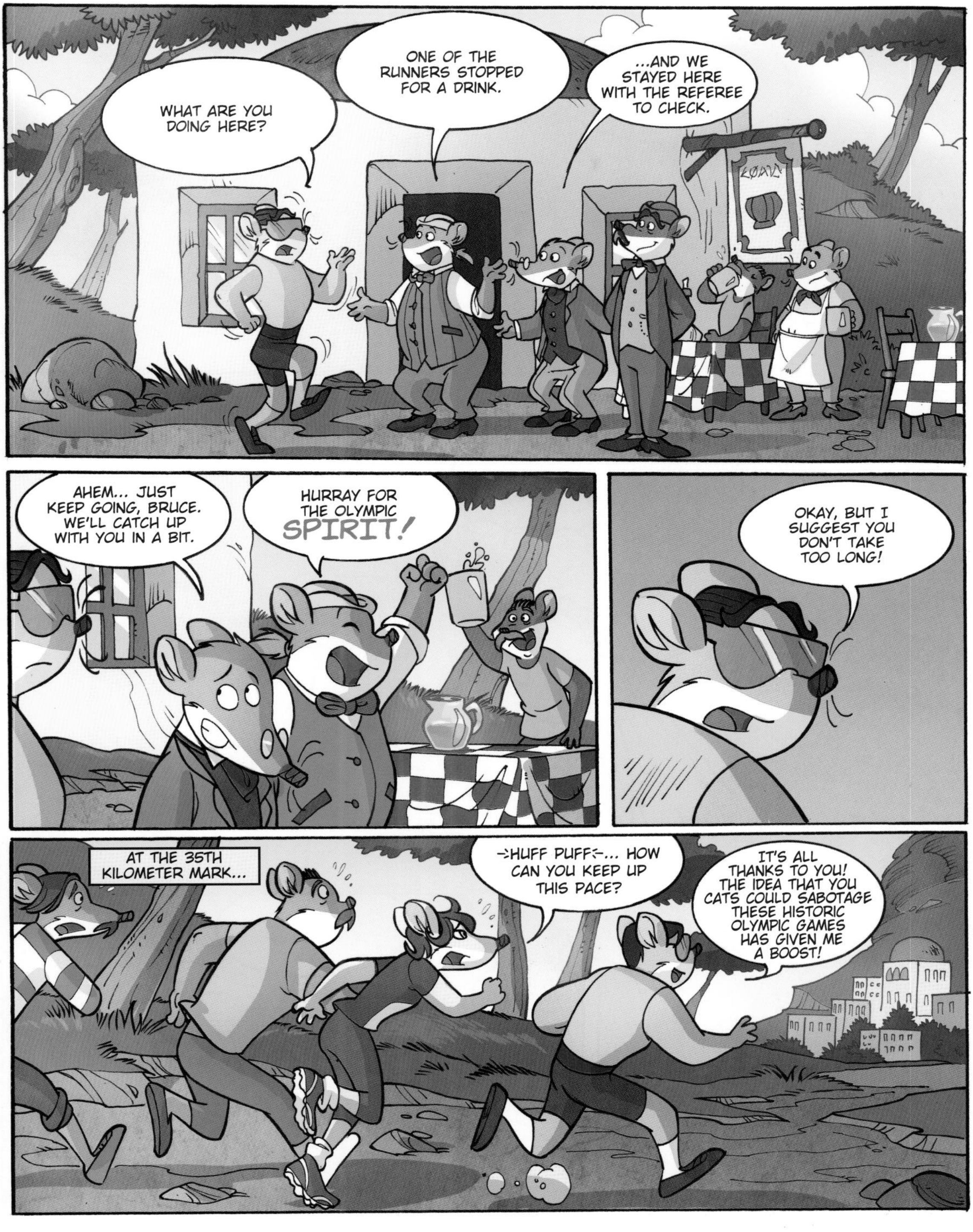
WHAT ARE YOU DOING HERE?
ONE OF THE RUNNERS STOPPED FOR A DRINK.
...AND WE STAYED HERE WITH THE REFEREE TO CHECK.
AHEM... JUST KEEP GOING, BRUCE. WE'LL CATCH UP WITH YOU IN A BIT.
HURRAY FOR THE OLYMPIC SPIRIT!
OKAY, BUT I SUGGEST YOU DON'T TAKE TOO LONG!
AT THE 35TH KILOMETER MARK...
-HUFF PUFF-... HOW CAN YOU KEEP UP THIS PACE?
IT'S ALL THANKS TO YOU! THE IDEA THAT YOU CATS COULD SABOTAGE THESE HISTORIC OLYMPIC GAMES HAS GIVEN ME A BOOST!

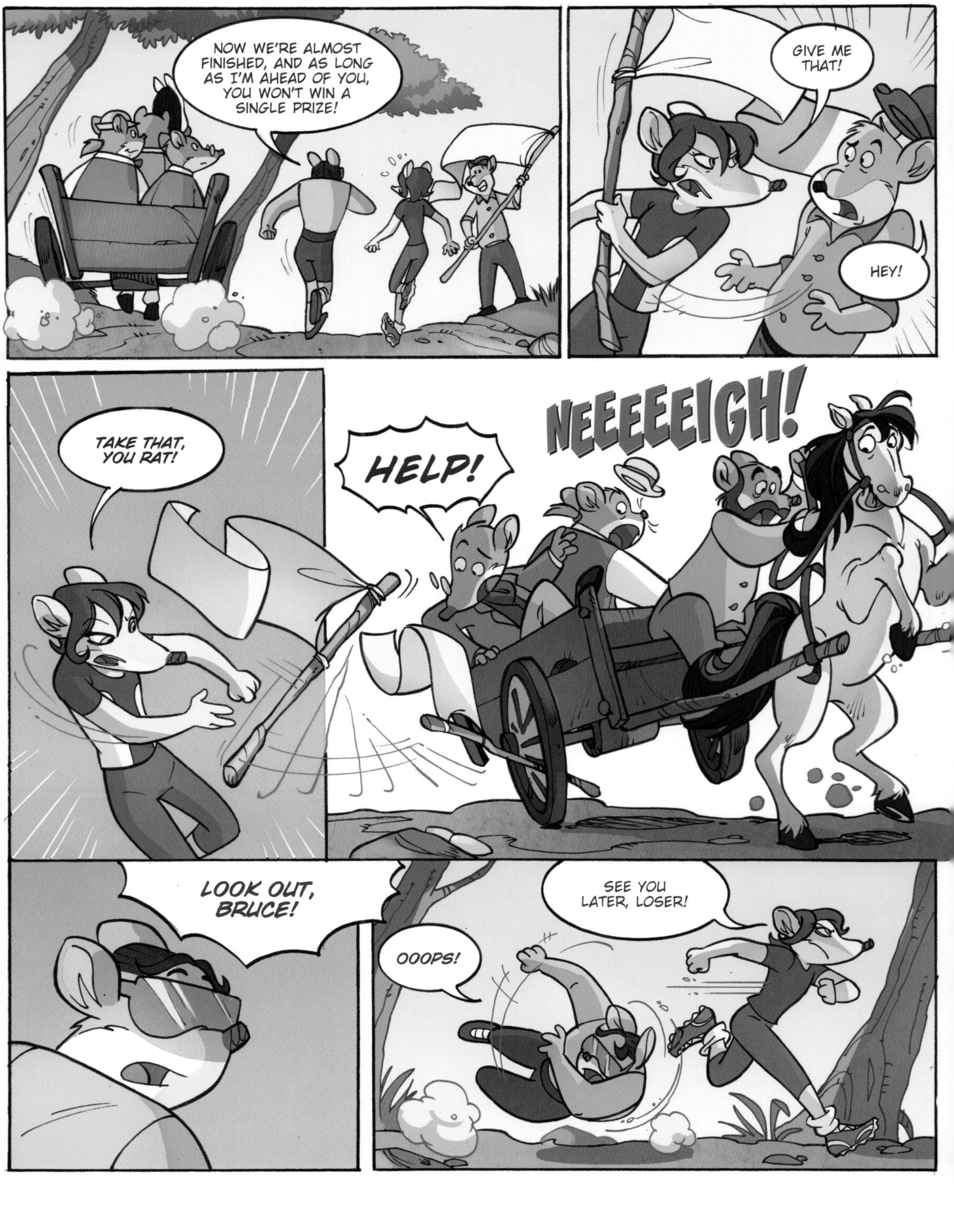
NOW WE'RE ALMOST FINISHED, AND AS LONG AS I'M AHEAD OF YOU, YOU WON'T WIN A SINGLE PRIZE!
GIVE ME THAT!
HEY!
TAKE THAT, YOU RAT!
HELP!
NEEEEEEIGH!
LOOK OUT, BRUCE!
SEE YOU LATER, LOSER!
OOOPS!

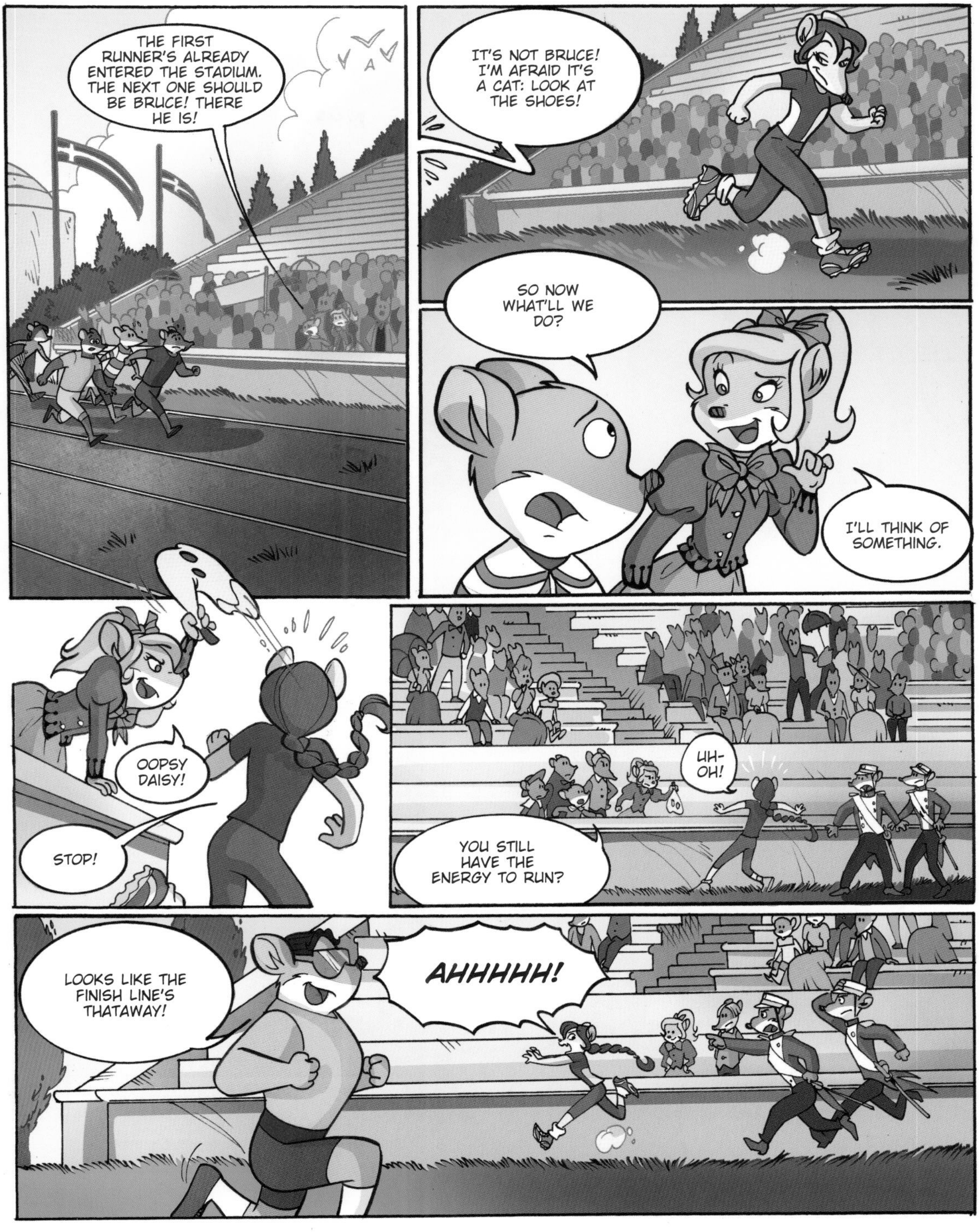
THE FIRST RUNNER'S ALREADY ENTERED THE STADIUM. THE NEXT ONE SHOULD BE BRUCE! THERE HE IS!
IT'S NOT BRUCE! I'M AFRAID IT'S A CAT: LOOK AT THE SHOES!
SO NOW WHAT'LL WE DO?
I'LL THINK OF SOMETHING.
OOPSY DAISY!
STOP!
UH-OH!
YOU STILL HAVE THE ENERGY TO RUN?
LOOKS LIKE THE FINISH LINE'S THATAWAY!
AHHHHH!

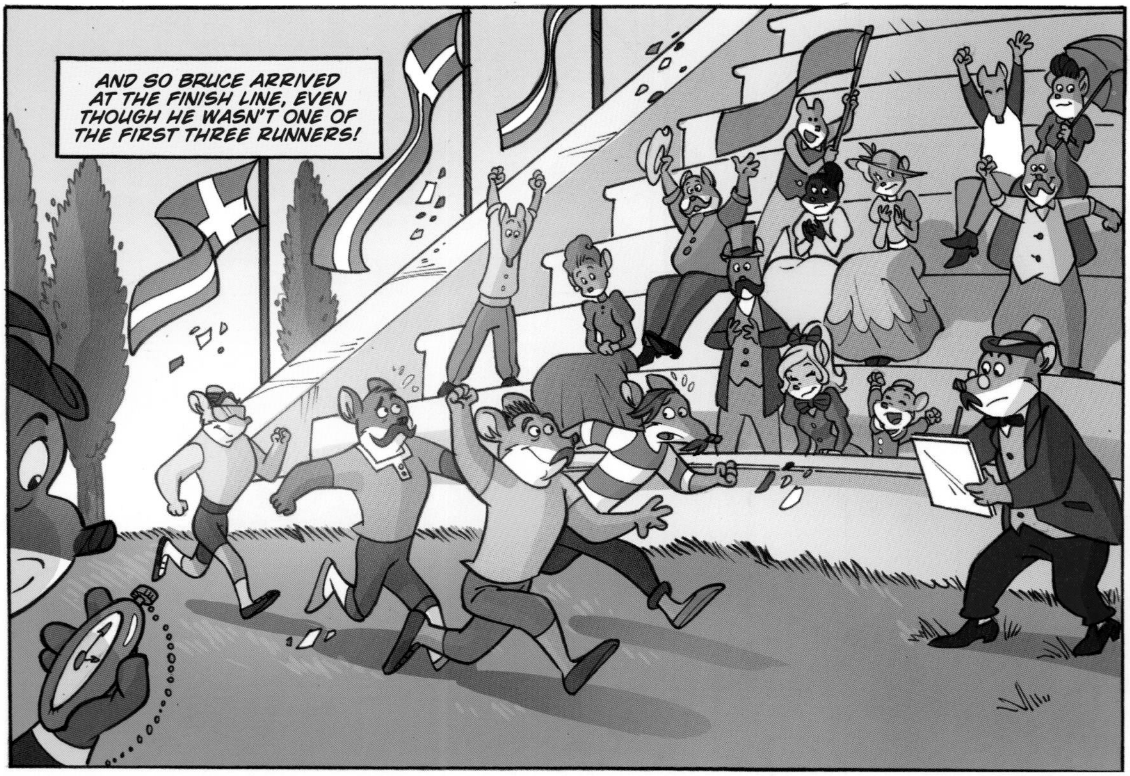
AND SO BRUCE ARRIVED AT THE FINISH LINE, EVEN THOUGH HE WASN'T ONE OF THE FIRST THREE RUNNERS!

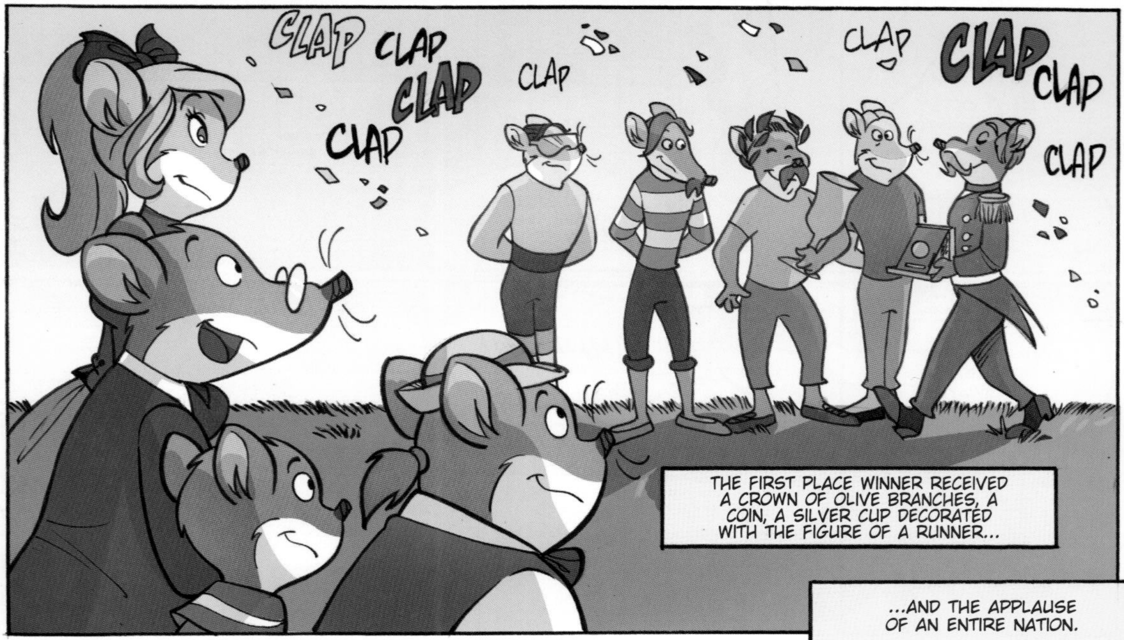
CLAP
CLAP
CLAP
CLAP
CLAP
CLAP
CLAP
CLAP
CLAP
THE FIRST PLACE WINNER RECEIVED A CROWN OF OLIVE BRANCHES, A COIN, A SILVER CUP DECORATED WITH THE FIGURE OF A RUNNER...
...AND THE APPLAUSE OF AN ENTIRE NATION.

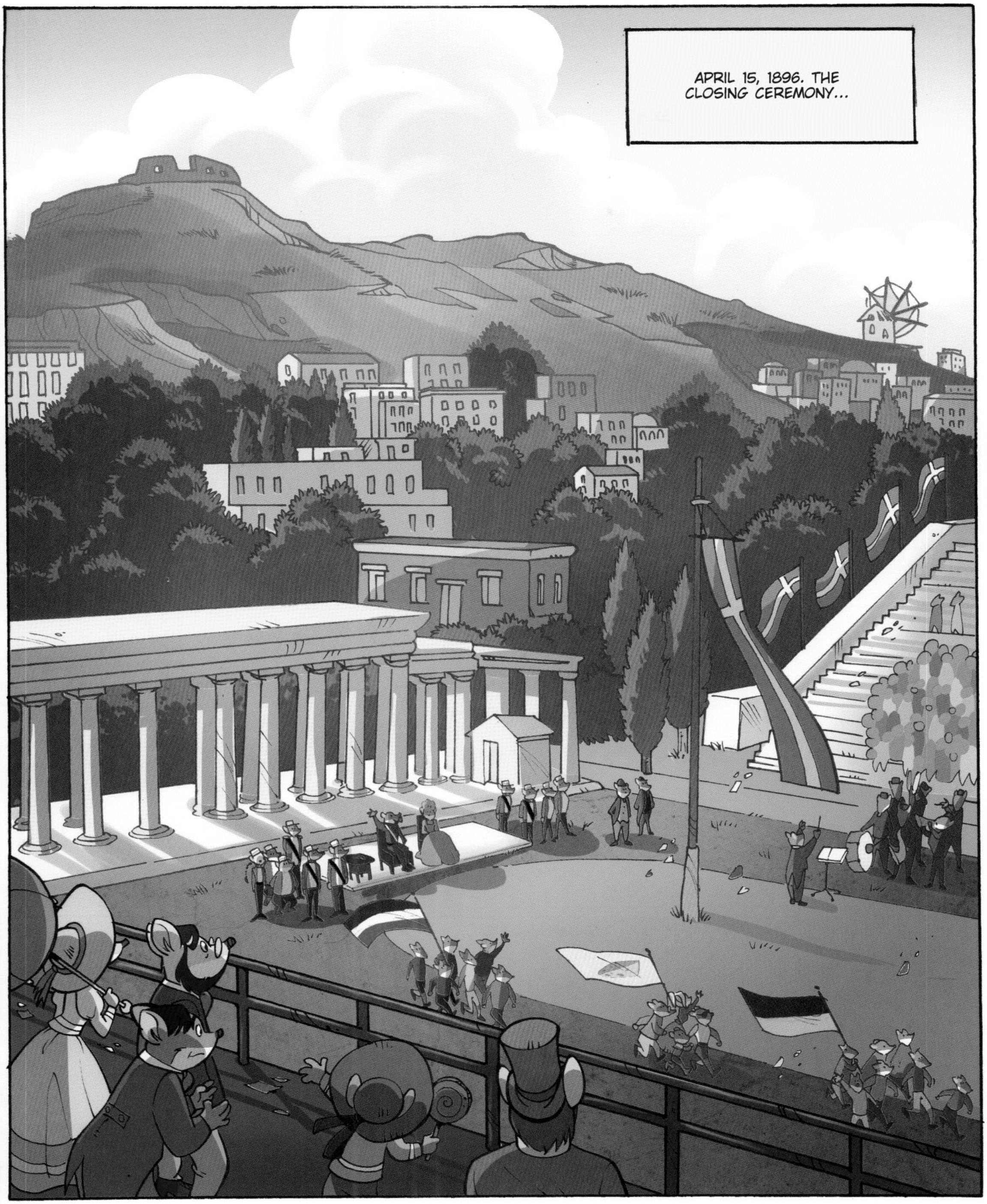
APRIL 15, 1896. THE CLOSING CEREMONY...

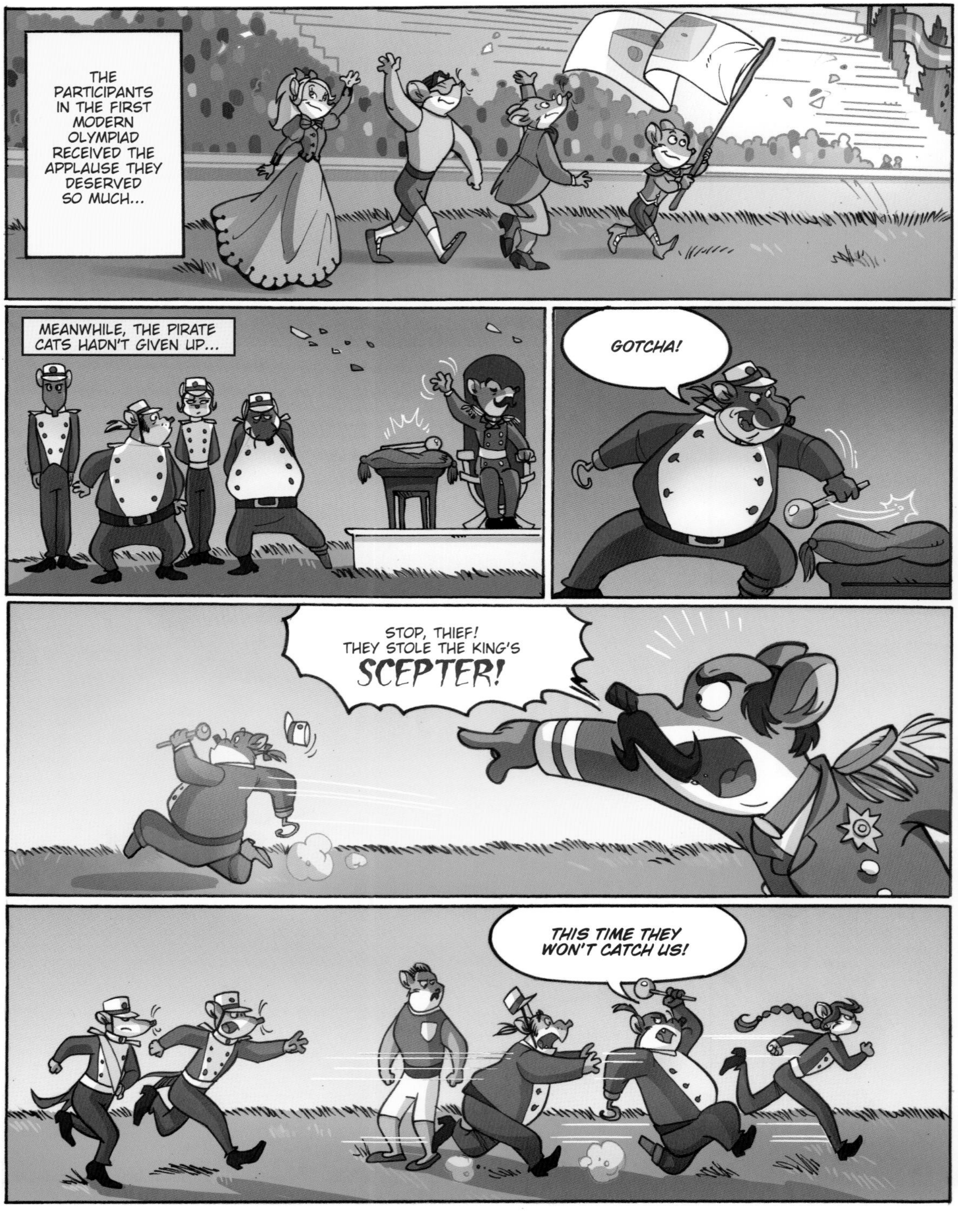
THE PARTICIPANTS IN THE FIRST MODERN OLYMPIAD RECEIVED THE APPLAUSE THEY DESERVED SO MUCH...
MEANWHILE, THE PIRATE CATS HADN'T GIVEN UP...
GOTCHA!
STOP, THIEF! THEY STOLE THE KING'S SCEPTER!
THIS TIME THEY WON'T CATCH US!

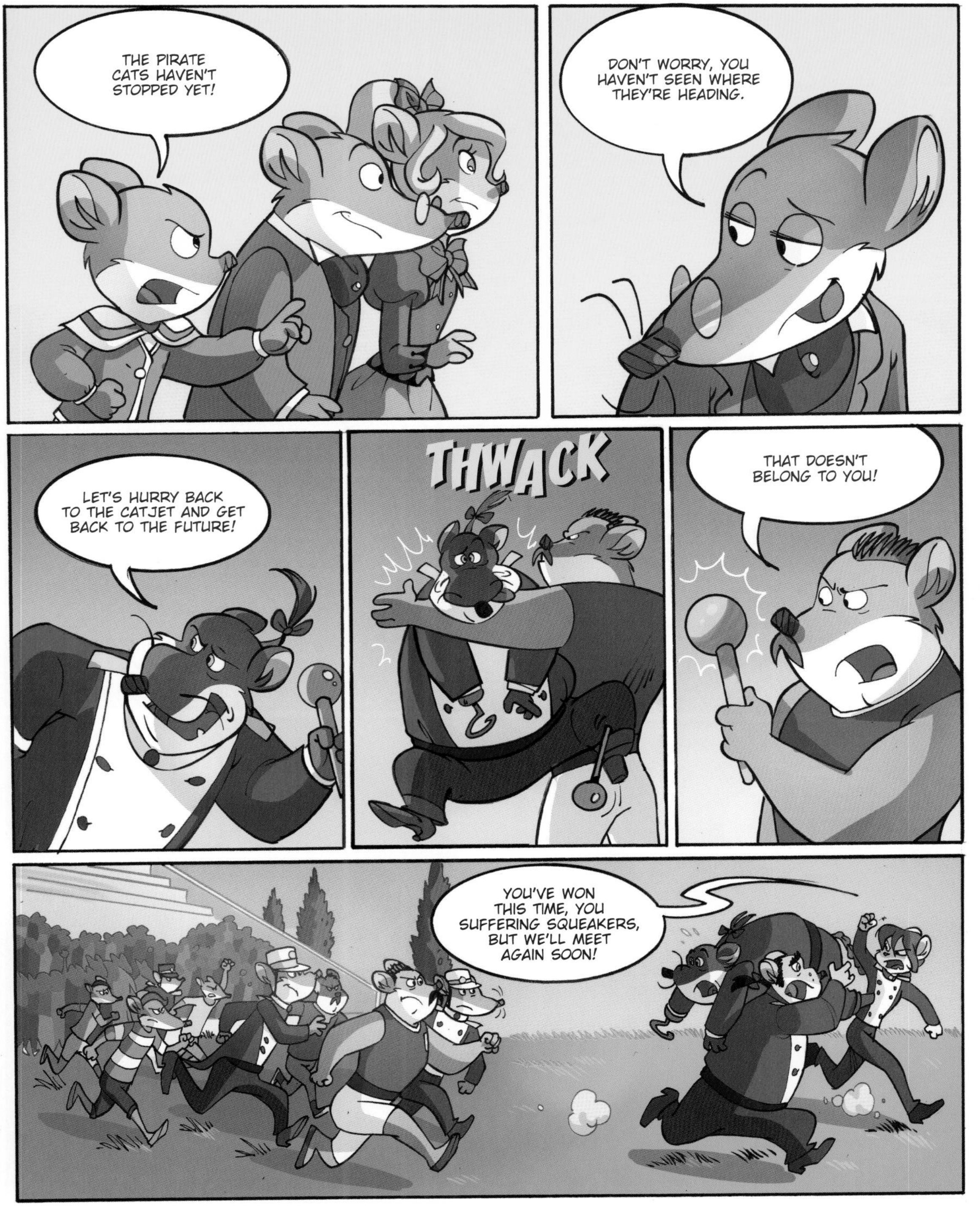
THE PIRATE CATS HAVEN'T STOPPED YET!
DON'T WORRY, YOU HAVEN'T SEEN WHERE THEY'RE HEADING.
LET'S HURRY BACK TO THE CATJET AND GET BACK TO THE FUTURE!
THWACK
THAT DOESN'T BELONG TO YOU!
YOU'VE WON THIS TIME, YOU SUFFERING SQUEAKERS, BUT WE'LL MEET AGAIN SOON!

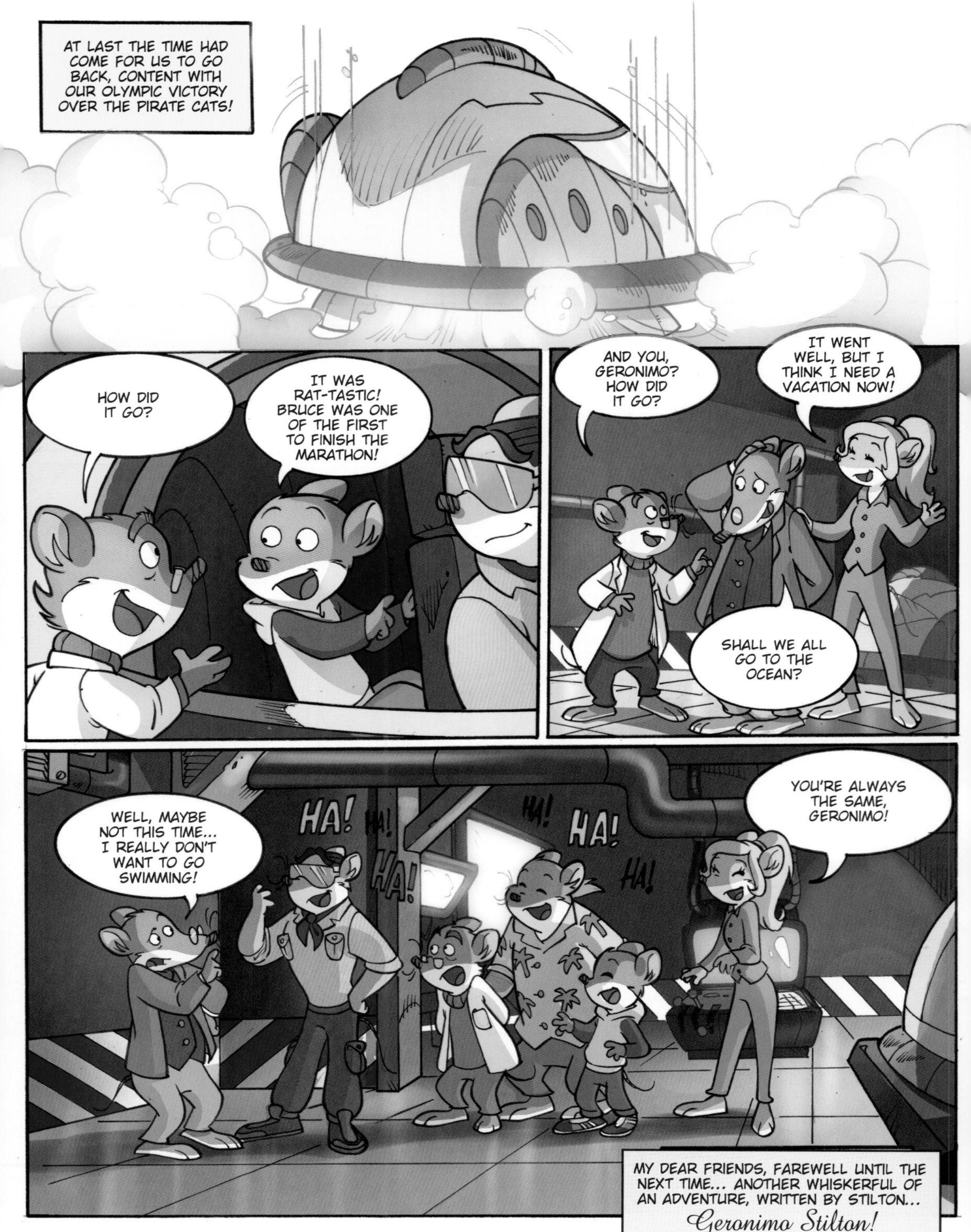
AT LAST THE TIME HAD COME FOR US TO GO BACK, CONTENT WITH OUR OLYMPIC VICTORY OVER THE PIRATE CATS!
HOW DID IT GO?
IT WAS RAT-TASTIC! BRUCE WAS ONE OF THE FIRST TO FINISH THE MARATHON!
AND YOU, GERONIMO? HOW DID IT GO?
IT WENT WELL, BUT I THINK I NEED A VACATION NOW!
SHALL WE ALL GO TO THE OCEAN?
WELL, MAYBE NOT THIS TIME... I REALLY DON'T WANT TO GO SWIMMING!
HA! HA! HA! HA! HA! HA!
YOU'RE ALWAYS THE SAME, GERONIMO!
MY DEAR FRIENDS, FAREWELL UNTIL THE NEXT TIME... ANOTHER WHISKERFUL OF AN ADVENTURE, WRITTEN BY STILTON...
Geronimo Stilton!

WE'LL ALWAYS HAVE PARIS

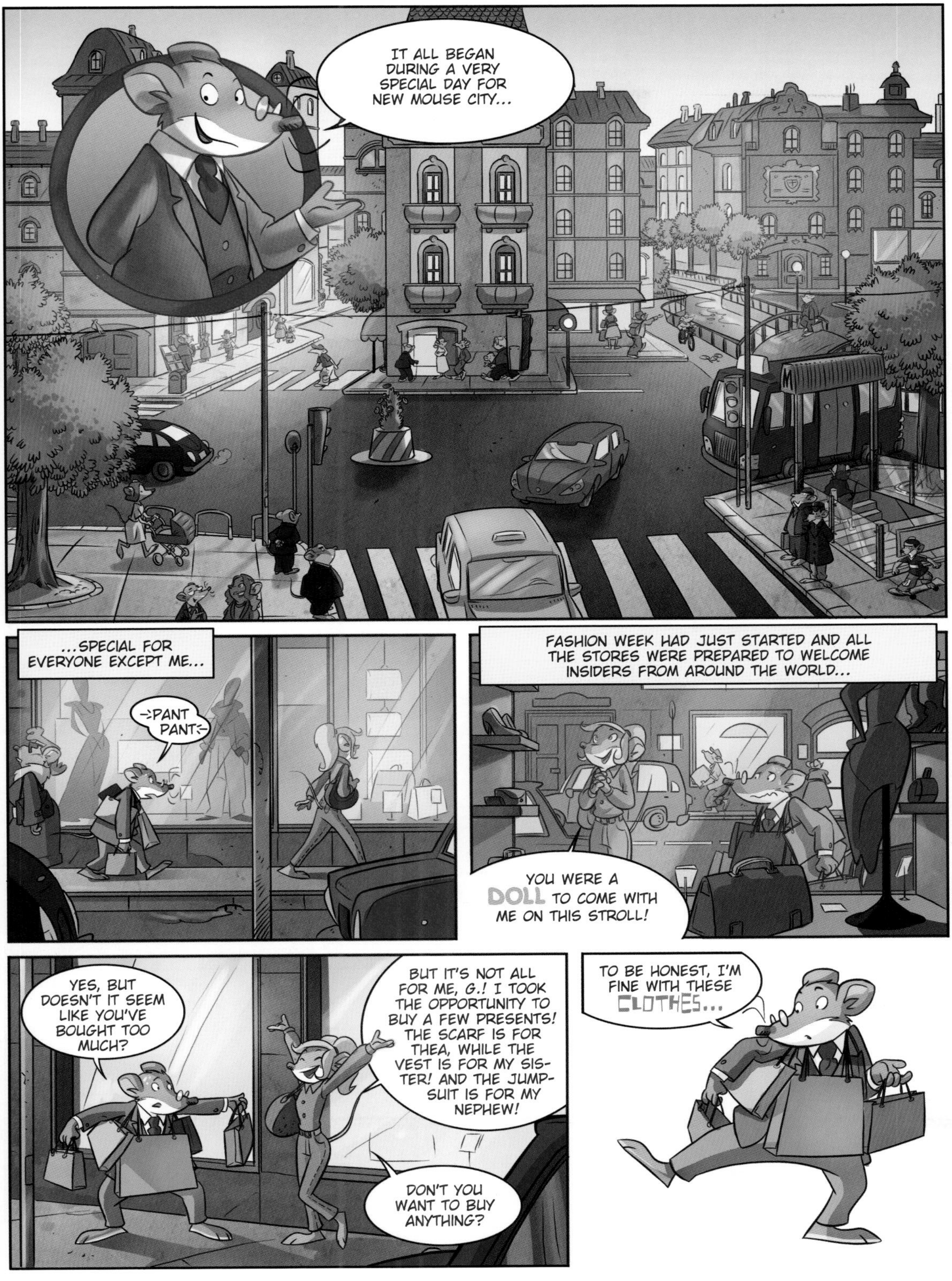
IT ALL BEGAN DURING A VERY SPECIAL DAY FOR NEW MOUSE CITY...
...SPECIAL FOR EVERYONE EXCEPT ME...
PANT PANT
FASHION WEEK HAD JUST STARTED AND ALL THE STORES WERE PREPARED TO WELCOME INSIDERS FROM AROUND THE WORLD...
YOU WERE A DOLL TO COME WITH ME ON THIS STROLL!
YES, BUT DOESN'T IT SEEM LIKE YOU'VE BOUGHT TOO MUCH?
BUT IT'S NOT ALL FOR ME, G.! I TOOK THE OPPORTUNITY TO BUY A FEW PRESENTS! THE SCARF IS FOR THEA, WHILE THE VEST IS FOR MY SISTER! AND THE JUMPSUIT IS FOR MY NEPHEW!
DON'T YOU WANT TO BUY ANYTHING?
TO BE HONEST, I'M FINE WITH THESE CLOTHES...

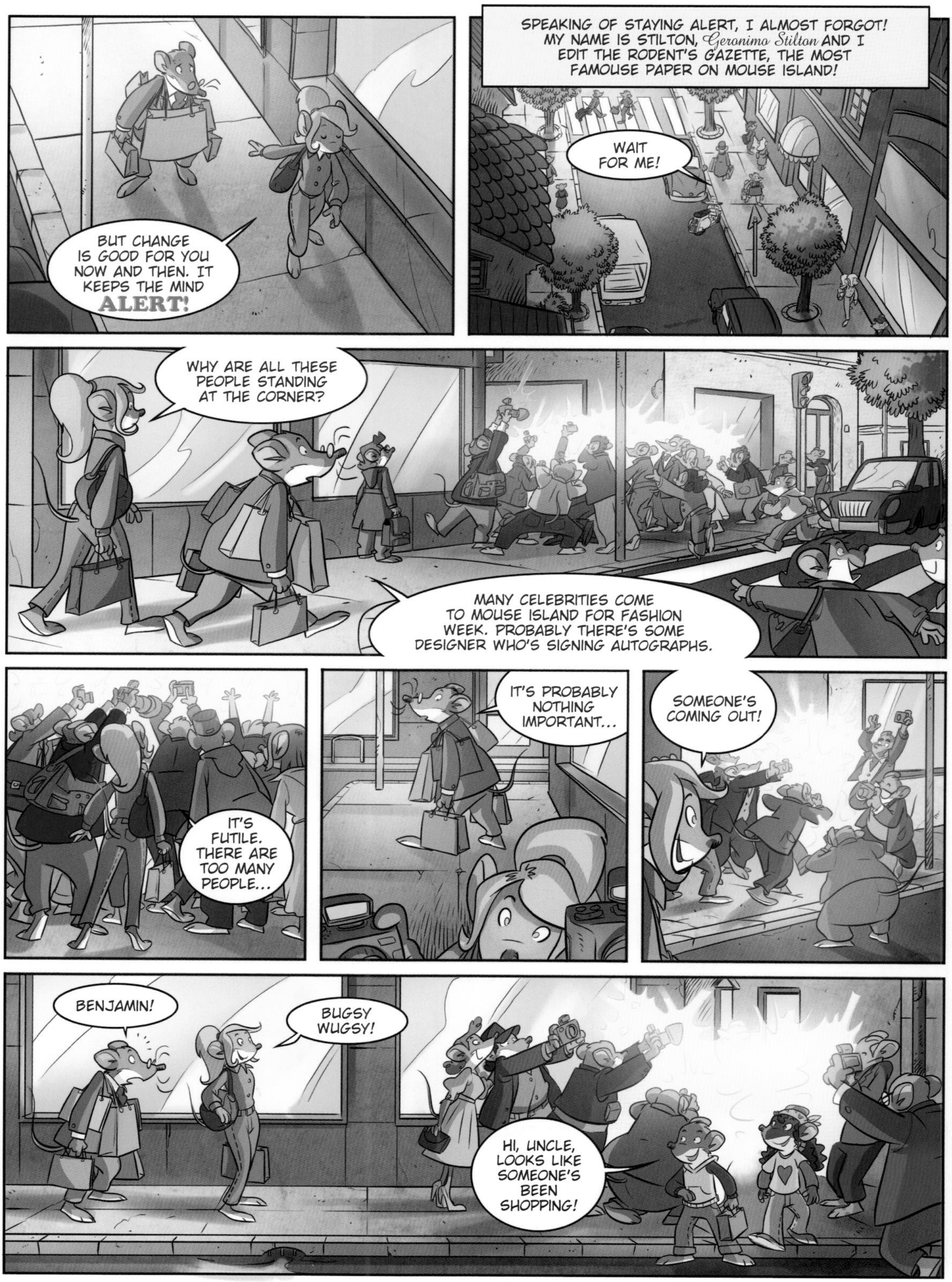

BUT CHANGE IS GOOD FOR YOU NOW AND THEN. IT KEEPS THE MIND ALERT!
SPEAKING OF STAYING ALERT, I ALMOST FORGOT! MY NAME IS STILTON, Geronimo Stilton AND I EDIT THE RODENT'S GAZETTE, THE MOST FAMOUSE PAPER ON MOUSE ISLAND!
WAIT FOR ME!
WHY ARE ALL THESE PEOPLE STANDING AT THE CORNER?
MANY CELEBRITIES COME TO MOUSE ISLAND FOR FASHION WEEK. PROBABLY THERE'S SOME DESIGNER WHO'S SIGNING AUTOGRAPHS.
IT'S FUTILE. THERE ARE TOO MANY PEOPLE...
IT'S PROBABLY NOTHING IMPORTANT...
SOMEONE'S COMING OUT!
BENJAMIN!
BUGSY WUGSY!
HI, UNCLE, LOOKS LIKE SOMEONE'S BEEN SHOPPING!

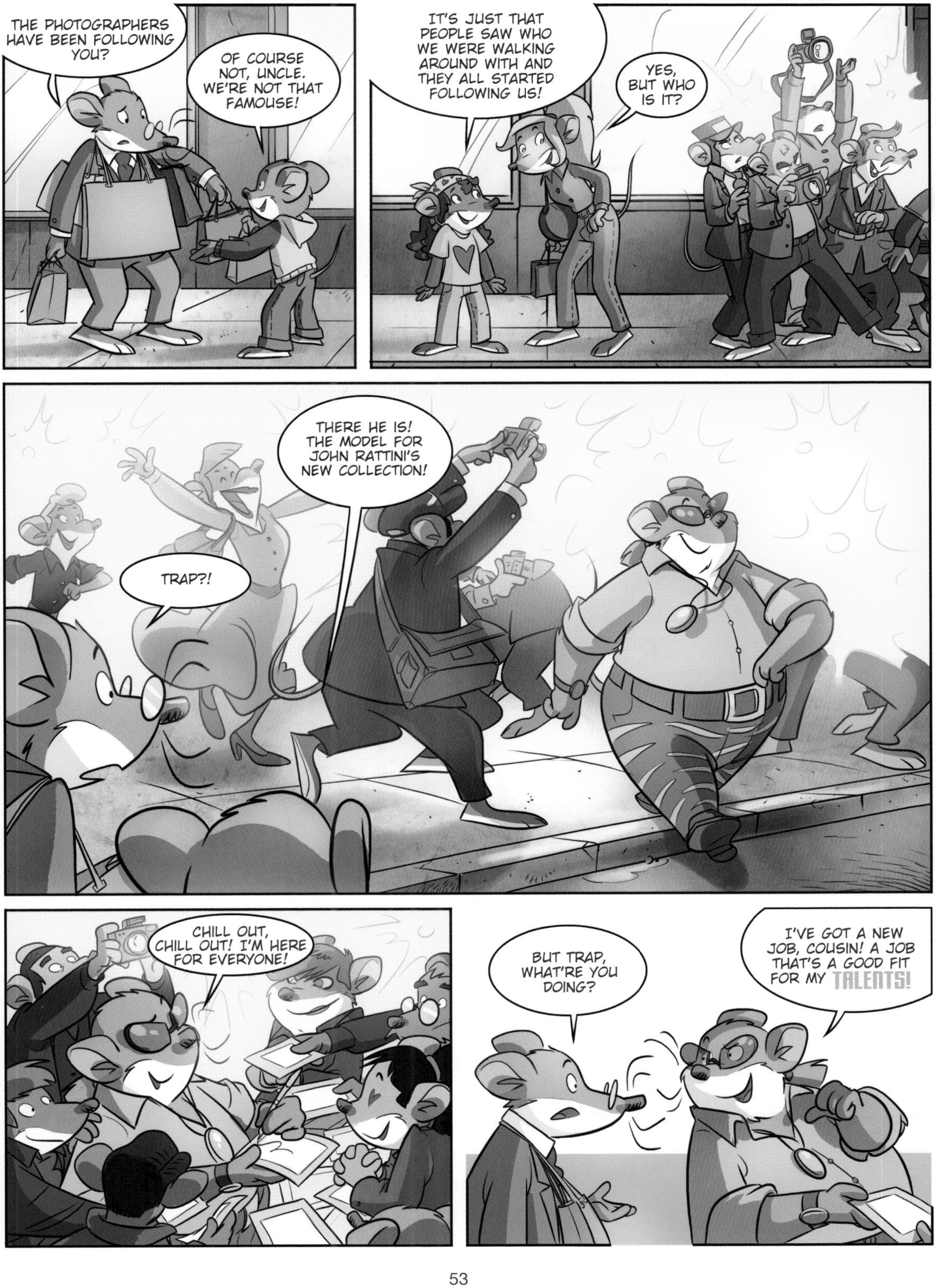
THE PHOTOGRAPHERS HAVE BEEN FOLLOWING YOU?
OF COURSE NOT, UNCLE. WE'RE NOT THAT FAMOUSE!
IT'S JUST THAT PEOPLE SAW WHO WE WERE WALKING AROUND WITH AND THEY ALL STARTED FOLLOWING US!
YES, BUT WHO IS IT?
THERE HE IS! THE MODEL FOR JOHN RATTINI'S NEW COLLECTION!
TRAP?!
CHILL OUT, CHILL OUT! I'M HERE FOR EVERYONE!
BUT TRAP, WHAT'RE YOU DOING?
I'VE GOT A NEW JOB, COUSIN! A JOB THAT'S A GOOD FIT FOR MY TALENTS!

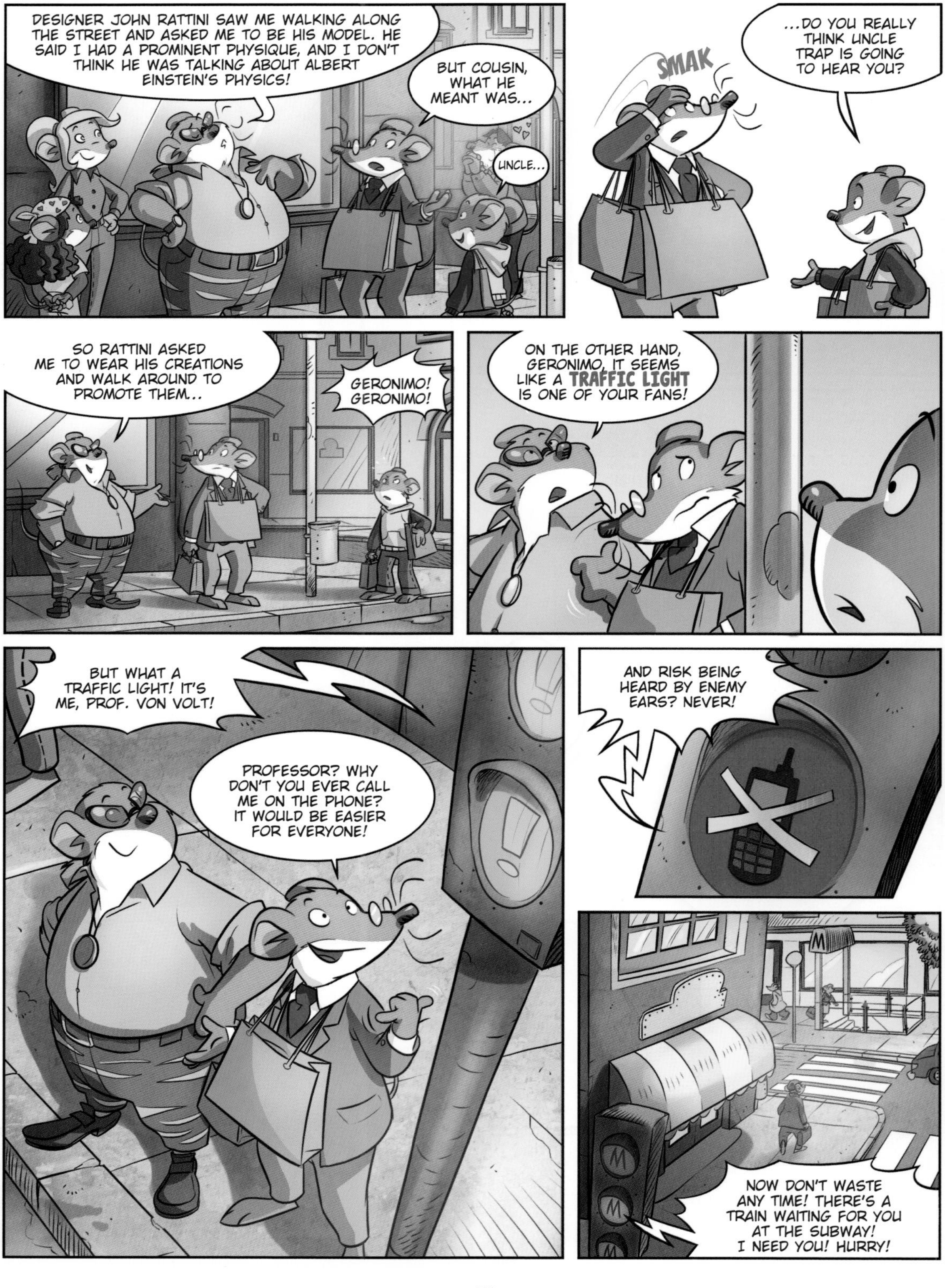

DESIGNER JOHN RATTINI SAW ME WALKING ALONG THE STREET AND ASKED ME TO BE HIS MODEL. HE SAID I HAD A PROMINENT PHYSIQUE, AND I DON'T THINK HE WAS TALKING ABOUT ALBERT EINSTEIN'S PHYSICS!
BUT COUSIN, WHAT HE MEANT WAS...
UNCLE...
SMAK
...DO YOU REALLY THINK UNCLE TRAP IS GOING TO HEAR YOU?
SO RATTINI ASKED ME TO WEAR HIS CREATIONS AND WALK AROUND TO PROMOTE THEM...
GERONIMO! GERONIMO!
ON THE OTHER HAND, GERONIMO, IT SEEMS LIKE A TRAFFIC LIGHT IS ONE OF YOUR FANS!
BUT WHAT A TRAFFIC LIGHT! IT'S ME, PROF. VON VOLT!
PROFESSOR? WHY DON'T YOU EVER CALL ME ON THE PHONE? IT WOULD BE EASIER FOR EVERYONE!
AND RISK BEING HEARD BY ENEMY EARS? NEVER!
NOW DON'T WASTE ANY TIME! THERE'S A TRAIN WAITING FOR YOU AT THE SUBWAY! I NEED YOU! HURRY!

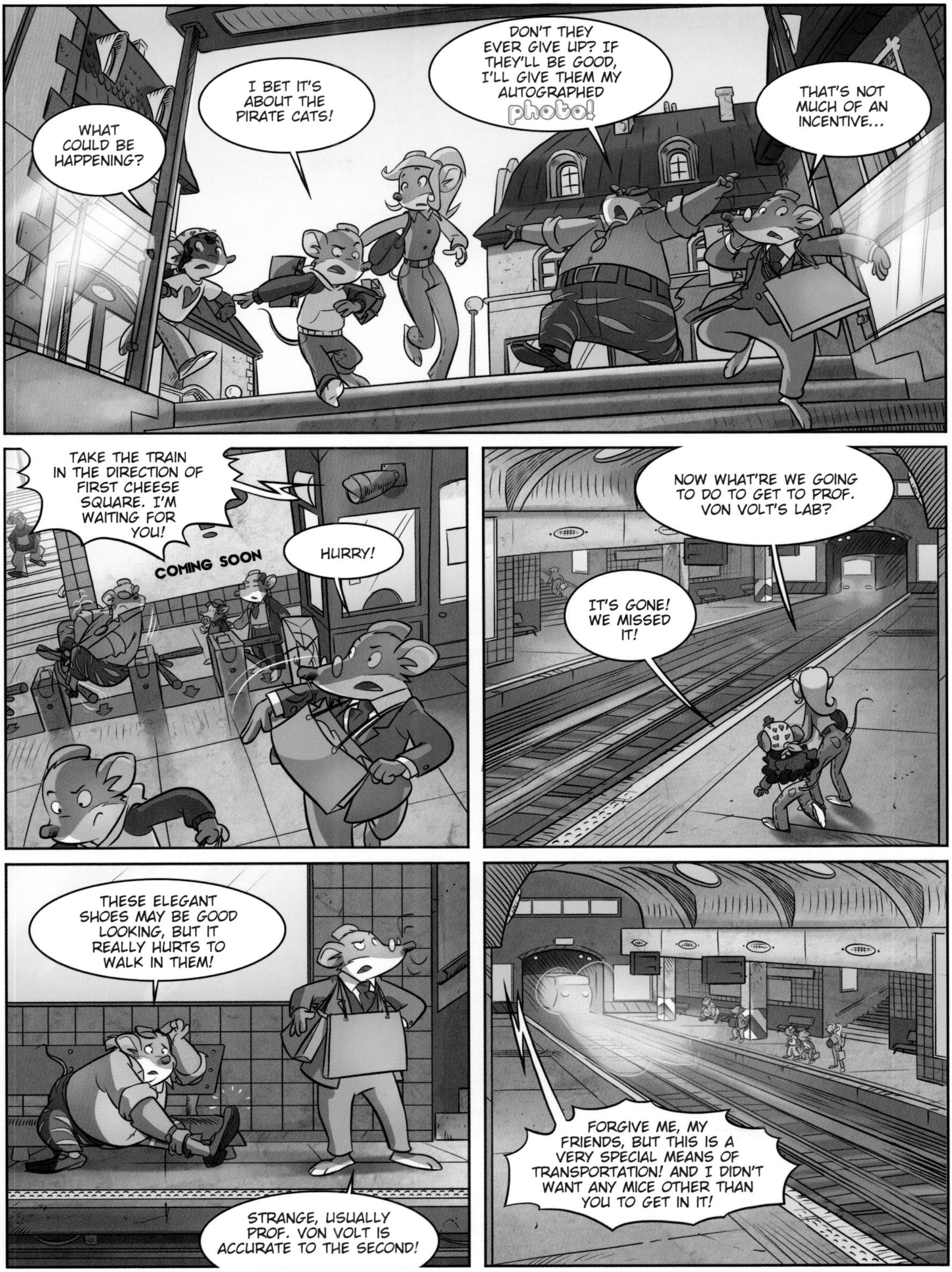

WHAT COULD BE HAPPENING?
I BET IT'S ABOUT THE PIRATE CATS!
DON'T THEY EVER GIVE UP? IF THEY'LL BE GOOD, I'LL GIVE THEM MY AUTOGRAPHED photo!
THAT'S NOT MUCH OF AN INCENTIVE...
TAKE THE TRAIN IN THE DIRECTION OF FIRST CHEESE SQUARE. I'M WAITING FOR YOU!
COMING SOON
HURRY!
NOW WHAT'RE WE GOING TO DO TO GET TO PROF. VON VOLT'S LAB?
IT'S GONE! WE MISSED IT!
THESE ELEGANT SHOES MAY BE GOOD LOOKING, BUT IT REALLY HURTS TO WALK IN THEM!
STRANGE, USUALLY PROF. VON VOLT IS ACCURATE TO THE SECOND!
FORGIVE ME, MY FRIENDS, BUT THIS IS A VERY SPECIAL MEANS OF TRANSPORTATION! AND I DIDN'T WANT ANY MICE OTHER THAN YOU TO GET IN IT!

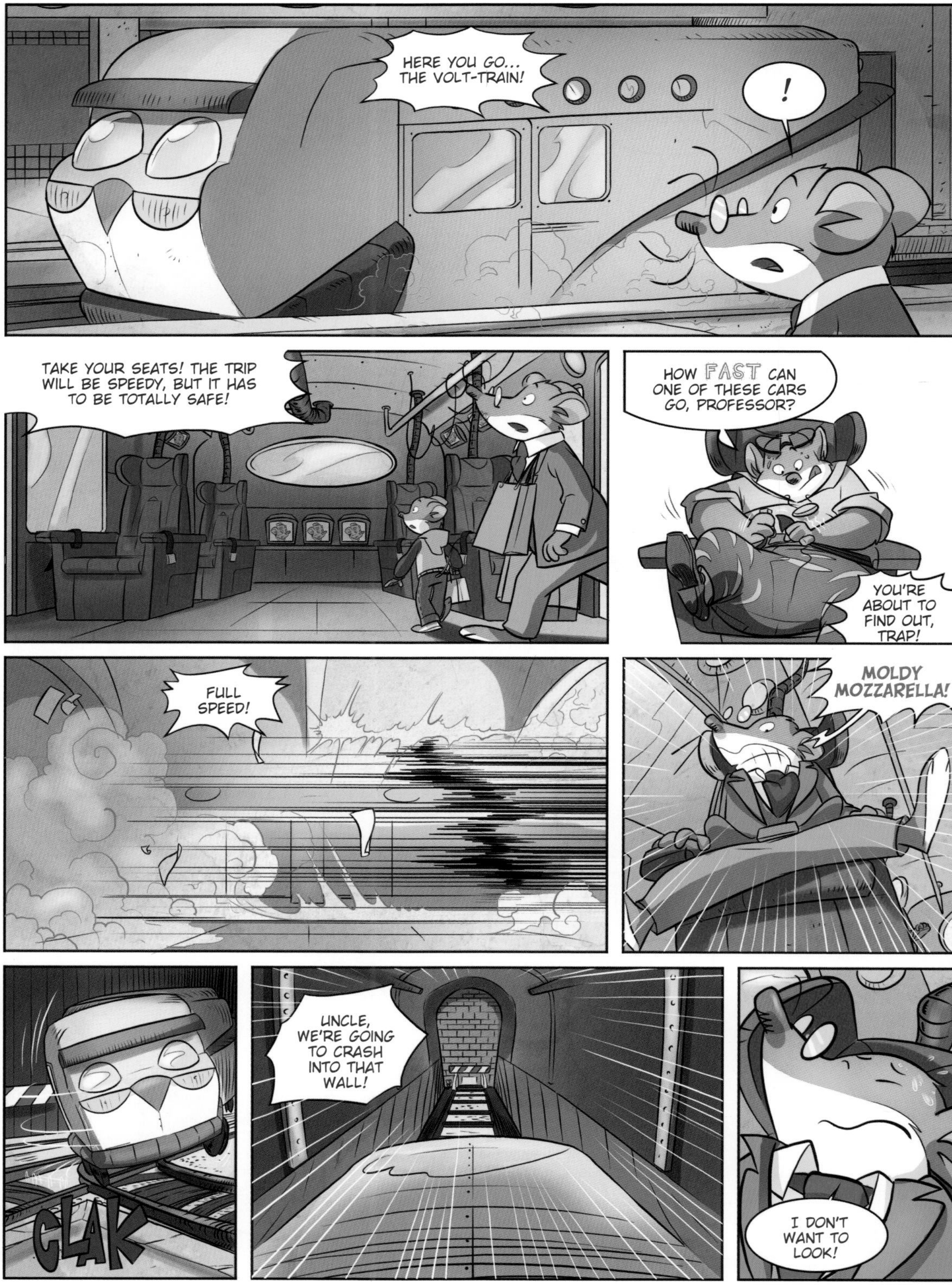
HERE YOU GO... THE VOLT-TRAIN!
!
TAKE YOUR SEATS! THE TRIP WILL BE SPEEDY, BUT IT HAS TO BE TOTALLY SAFE!
HOW FAST CAN ONE OF THESE CARS GO, PROFESSOR?
YOU'RE ABOUT TO FIND OUT, TRAP!
FULL SPEED!
MOLDY MOZZARELLA!
CLAK
UNCLE, WE'RE GOING TO CRASH INTO THAT WALL!
I DON'T WANT TO LOOK!

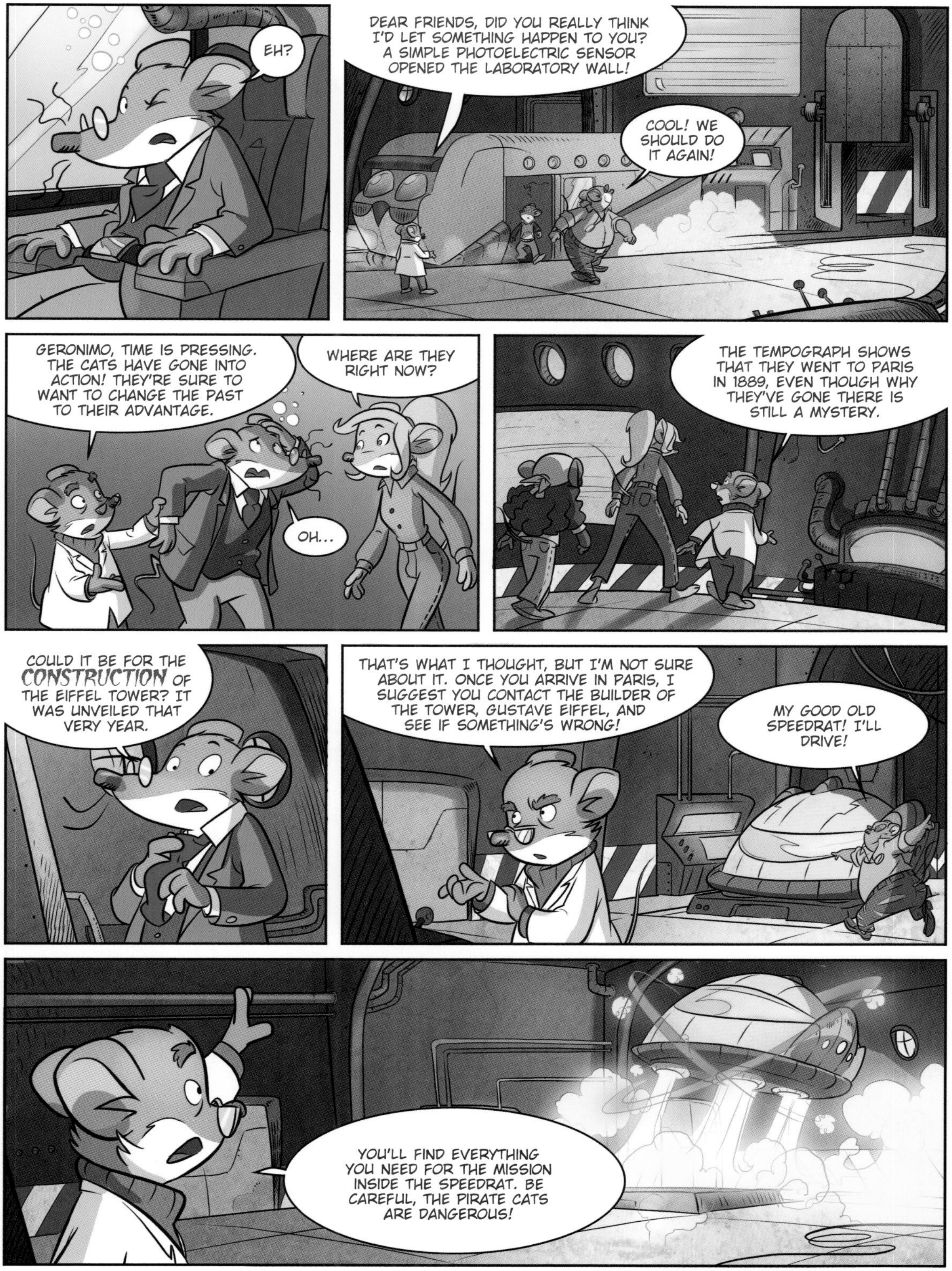
EH?
DEAR FRIENDS, DID YOU REALLY THINK I'D LET SOMETHING HAPPEN TO YOU? A SIMPLE PHOTOELECTRIC SENSOR OPENED THE LABORATORY WALL!
COOL! WE SHOULD DO IT AGAIN!
GERONIMO, TIME IS PRESSING. THE CATS HAVE GONE INTO ACTION! THEY'RE SURE TO WANT TO CHANGE THE PAST TO THEIR ADVANTAGE.
WHERE ARE THEY RIGHT NOW?
OH...
THE TEMPOGRAPH SHOWS THAT THEY WENT TO PARIS IN 1889, EVEN THOUGH WHY THEY'VE GONE THERE IS STILL A MYSTERY.
COULD IT BE FOR THE CONSTRUCTION OF THE EIFFEL TOWER? IT WAS UNVEILED THAT VERY YEAR.
THAT'S WHAT I THOUGHT, BUT I'M NOT SURE ABOUT IT. ONCE YOU ARRIVE IN PARIS, I SUGGEST YOU CONTACT THE BUILDER OF THE TOWER, GUSTAVE EIFFEL, AND SEE IF SOMETHING'S WRONG!
MY GOOD OLD SPEEDRAT! I'LL DRIVE!
YOU'LL FIND EVERYTHING YOU NEED FOR THE MISSION INSIDE THE SPEEDRAT. BE CAREFUL, THE PIRATE CATS ARE DANGEROUS!

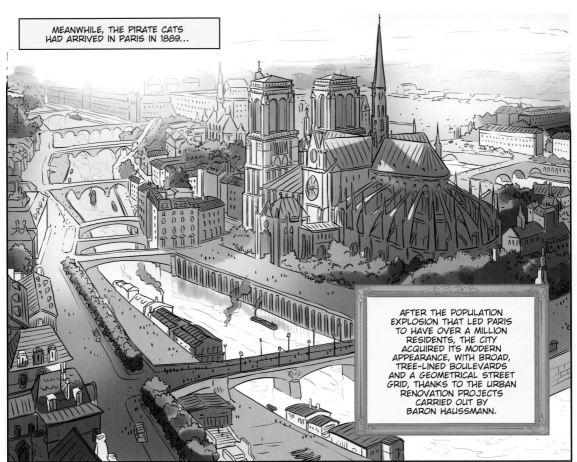

MEANWHILE, THE PIRATE CATS HAD ARRIVED IN PARIS IN 1889...

AFTER THE POPULATION EXPLOSION THAT LED PARIS TO HAVE OVER A MILLION RESIDENTS, THE CITY ACQUIRED ITS MODERN APPEARANCE, WITH BROAD, TREE-LINED BOULEVARDS AND A GEOMETRICAL STREET GRID, THANKS TO THE URBAN RENOVATION PROJECTS CARRIED OUT BY BARON HAUSSMANN.

I CAN'T STAND THESE MASKS. THEY PINCH!

MEOW DOWN*, DADDY DEAR! IF WE TRAVELED AROUND AMONG THESE LOUSY RATS WITHOUT A DISGUISE, OUR PLANS WOULD GO RIGHT UP IN SMOKE!

*CALM DOWN!

58

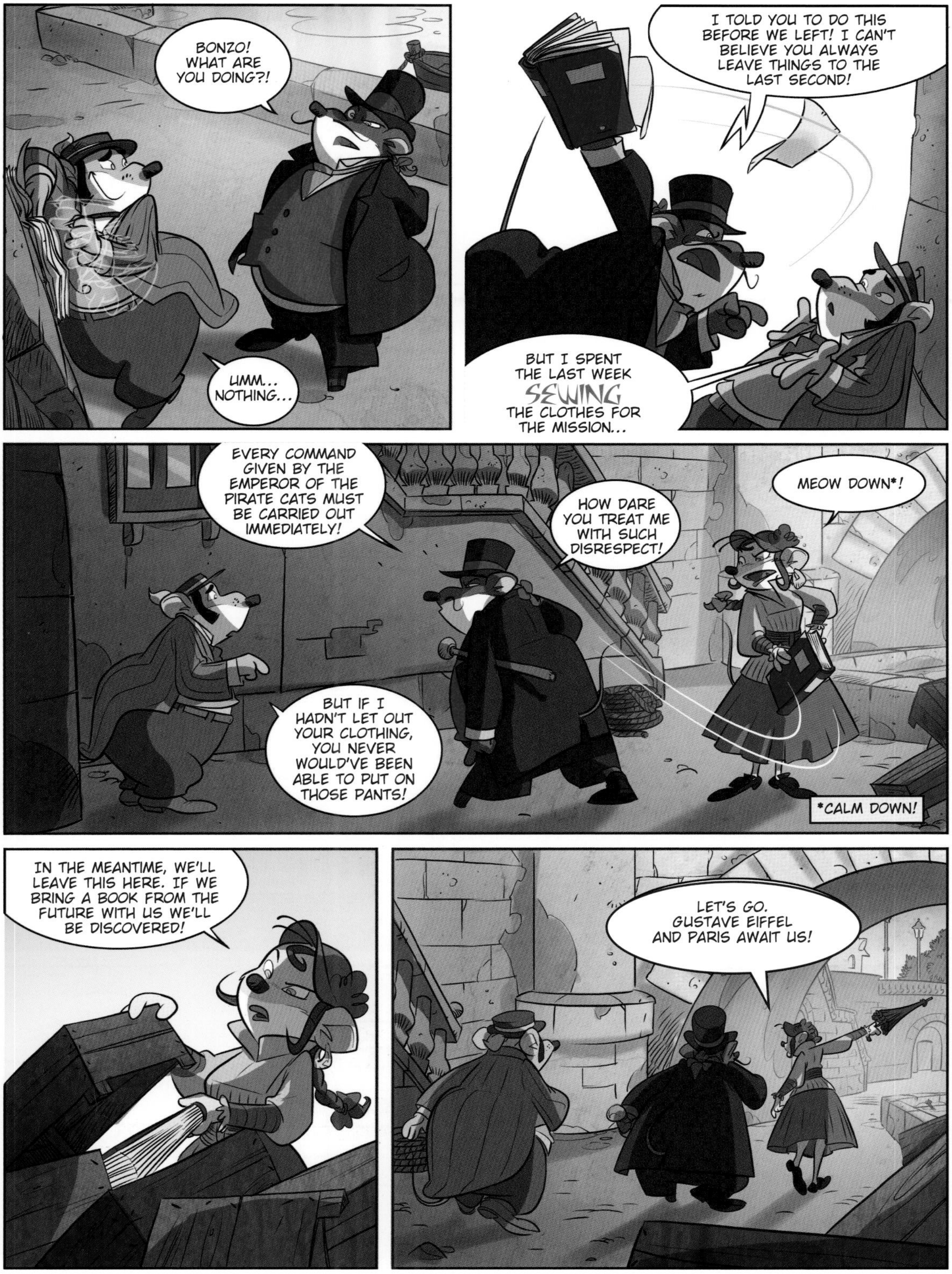
BONZO! WHAT ARE YOU DOING?!
UMM... NOTHING...
I TOLD YOU TO DO THIS BEFORE WE LEFT! I CAN'T BELIEVE YOU ALWAYS LEAVE THINGS TO THE LAST SECOND!
BUT I SPENT THE LAST WEEK SEWING THE CLOTHES FOR THE MISSION...
EVERY COMMAND GIVEN BY THE EMPEROR OF THE PIRATE CATS MUST BE CARRIED OUT IMMEDIATELY!
BUT IF I HADN'T LET OUT YOUR CLOTHING, YOU NEVER WOULD'VE BEEN ABLE TO PUT ON THOSE PANTS!
HOW DARE YOU TREAT ME WITH SUCH DISRESPECT!
MEOW DOWN*!
*CALM DOWN!
IN THE MEANTIME, WE'LL LEAVE THIS HERE. IF WE BRING A BOOK FROM THE FUTURE WITH US WE'LL BE DISCOVERED!
LET'S GO. GUSTAVE EIFFEL AND PARIS AWAIT US!

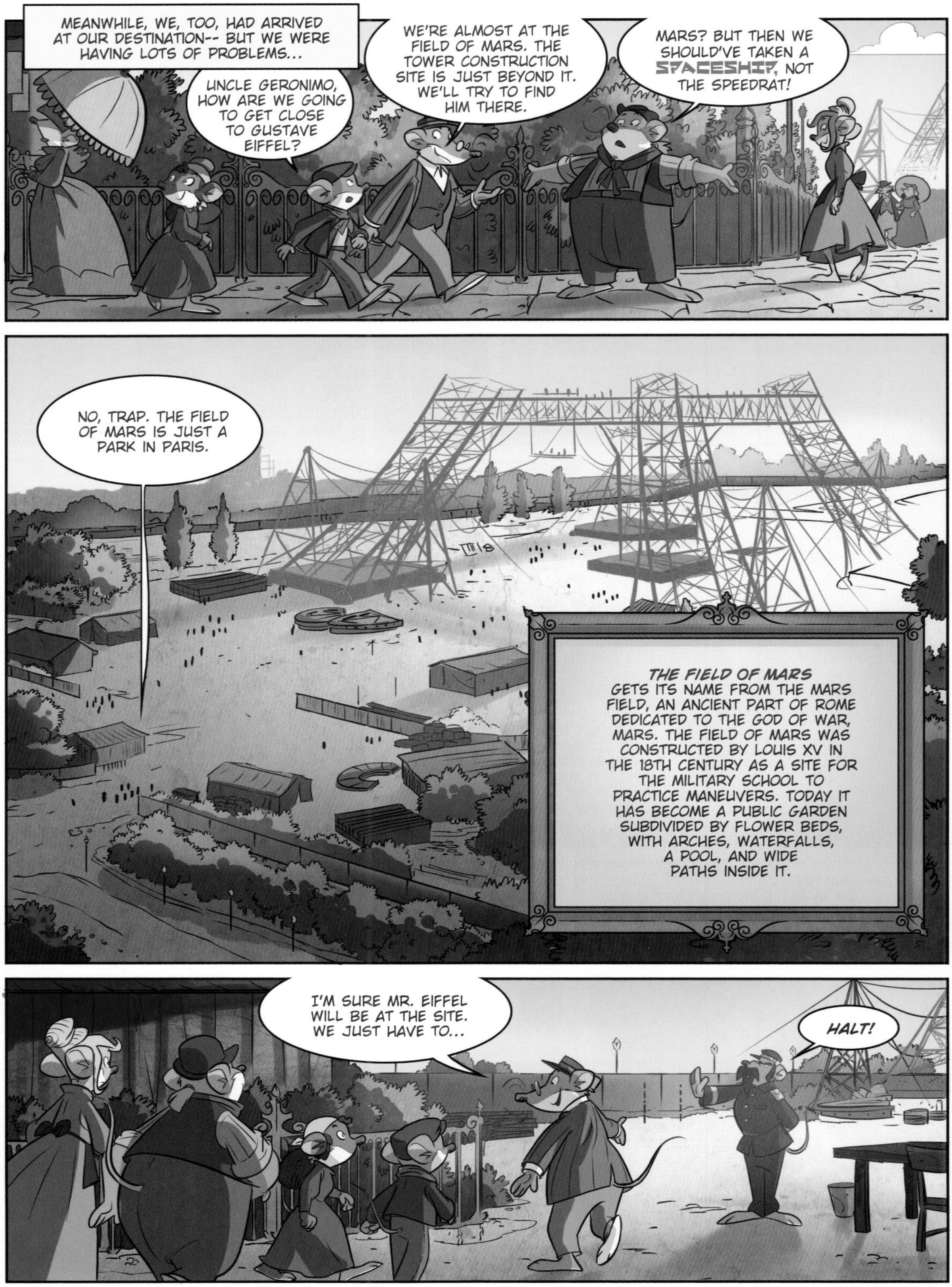
MEANWHILE, WE, TOO, HAD ARRIVED AT OUR DESTINATION-- BUT WE WERE HAVING LOTS OF PROBLEMS...
UNCLE GERONIMO, HOW ARE WE GOING TO GET CLOSE TO GUSTAVE EIFFEL?
WE'RE ALMOST AT THE FIELD OF MARS. THE TOWER CONSTRUCTION SITE IS JUST BEYOND IT. WE'LL TRY TO FIND HIM THERE.
MARS? BUT THEN WE SHOULD'VE TAKEN A SPACESHIP, NOT THE SPEEDRAT!
NO, TRAP. THE FIELD OF MARS IS JUST A PARK IN PARIS.
THE FIELD OF MARS
GETS ITS NAME FROM THE MARS FIELD, AN ANCIENT PART OF ROME DEDICATED TO THE GOD OF WAR, MARS. THE FIELD OF MARS WAS CONSTRUCTED BY LOUIS XV IN THE 18TH CENTURY AS A SITE FOR THE MILITARY SCHOOL TO PRACTICE MANEUVERS. TODAY IT HAS BECOME A PUBLIC GARDEN SUBDIVIDED BY FLOWER BEDS, WITH ARCHES, WATERFALLS, A POOL, AND WIDE PATHS INSIDE IT.
I'M SURE MR. EIFFEL WILL BE AT THE SITE. WE JUST HAVE TO...
HALT!

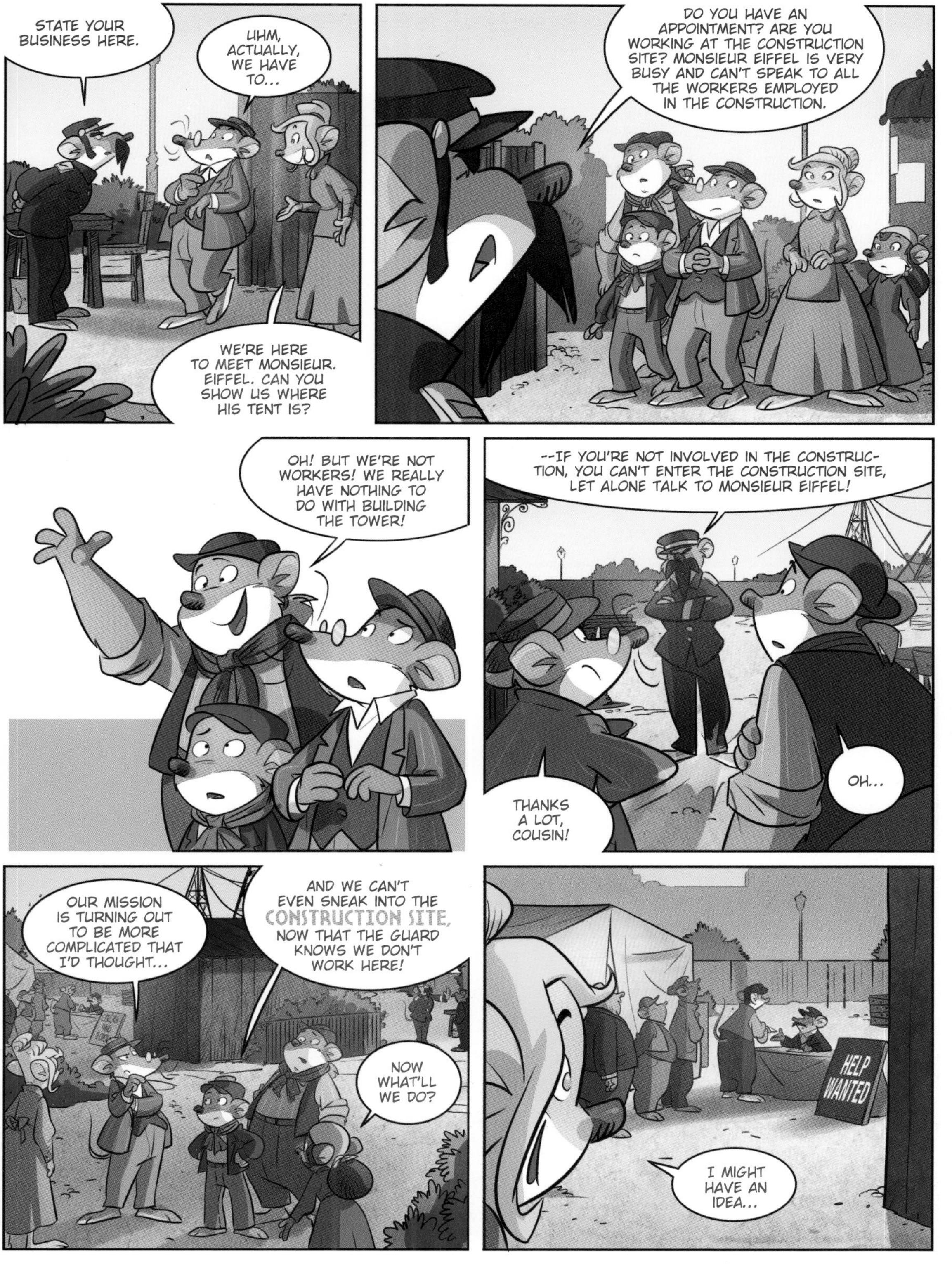
STATE YOUR BUSINESS HERE.
UHM, ACTUALLY, WE HAVE TO...
WE'RE HERE TO MEET MONSIEUR. EIFFEL. CAN YOU SHOW US WHERE HIS TENT IS?
DO YOU HAVE AN APPOINTMENT? ARE YOU WORKING AT THE CONSTRUCTION SITE? MONSIEUR EIFFEL IS VERY BUSY AND CAN'T SPEAK TO ALL THE WORKERS EMPLOYED IN THE CONSTRUCTION.
OH! BUT WE'RE NOT WORKERS! WE REALLY HAVE NOTHING TO DO WITH BUILDING THE TOWER!
--IF YOU'RE NOT INVOLVED IN THE CONSTRUCTION, YOU CAN'T ENTER THE CONSTRUCTION SITE, LET ALONE TALK TO MONSIEUR EIFFEL!
THANKS A LOT, COUSIN!
OH...
OUR MISSION IS TURNING OUT TO BE MORE COMPLICATED THAT I'D THOUGHT...
AND WE CAN'T EVEN SNEAK INTO THE CONSTRUCTION SITE, NOW THAT THE GUARD KNOWS WE DON'T WORK HERE!
NOW WHAT'LL WE DO?
HELP WANTED
I MIGHT HAVE AN IDEA...

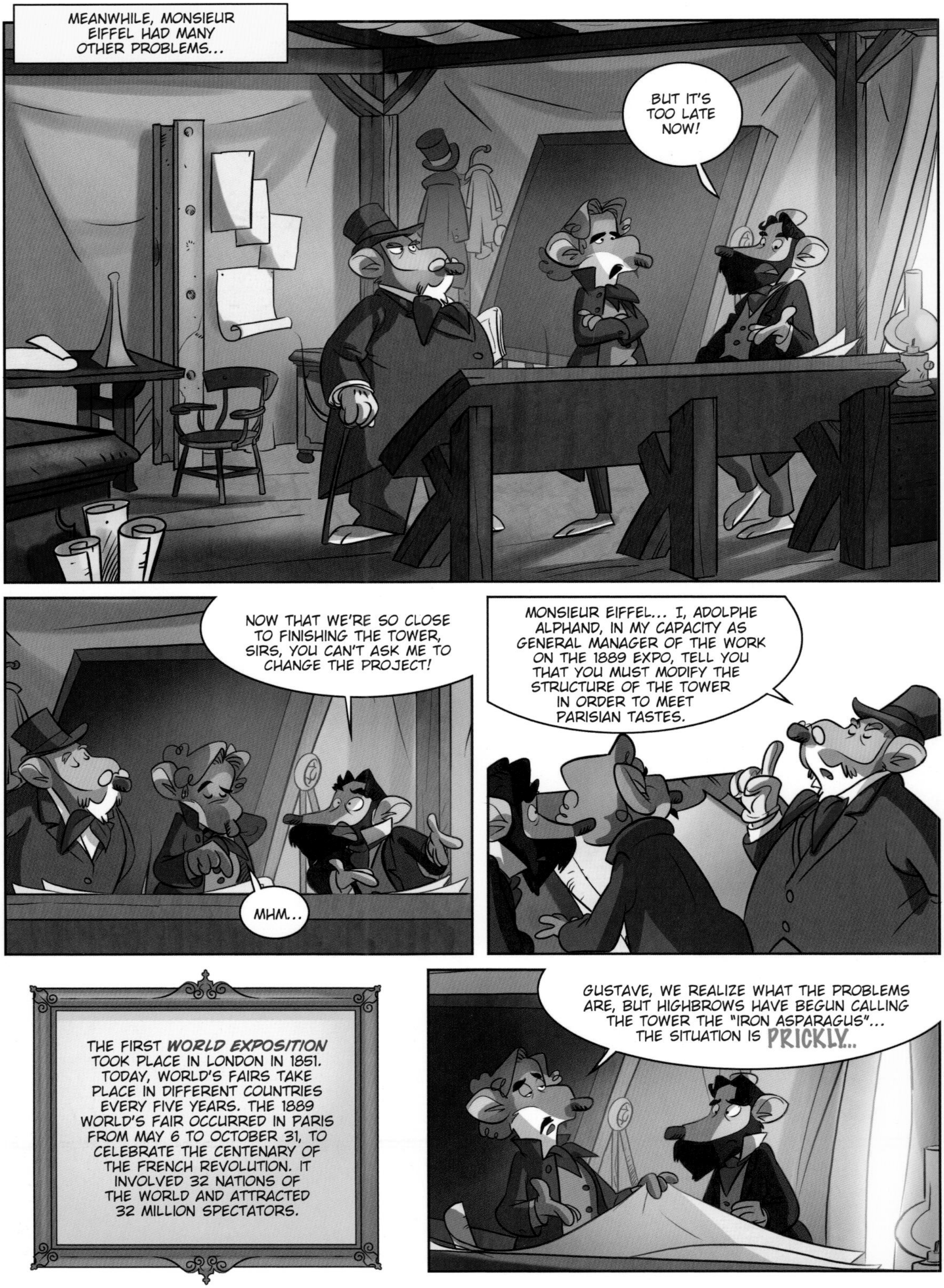
MEANWHILE, MONSIEUR EIFFEL HAD MANY OTHER PROBLEMS...
BUT IT'S TOO LATE NOW!
NOW THAT WE'RE SO CLOSE TO FINISHING THE TOWER, SIRS, YOU CAN'T ASK ME TO CHANGE THE PROJECT!
MHM...
MONSIEUR EIFFEL... I, ADOLPHE ALPHAND, IN MY CAPACITY AS GENERAL MANAGER OF THE WORK ON THE 1889 EXPO, TELL YOU THAT YOU MUST MODIFY THE STRUCTURE OF THE TOWER IN ORDER TO MEET PARISIAN TASTES.
THE FIRST WORLD EXPOSITION TOOK PLACE IN LONDON IN 1851. TODAY, WORLD'S FAIRS TAKE PLACE IN DIFFERENT COUNTRIES EVERY FIVE YEARS. THE 1889 WORLD'S FAIR OCCURRED IN PARIS FROM MAY 6 TO OCTOBER 31, TO CELEBRATE THE CENTENARY OF THE FRENCH REVOLUTION. IT INVOLVED 32 NATIONS OF THE WORLD AND ATTRACTED 32 MILLION SPECTATORS.
GUSTAVE, WE REALIZE WHAT THE PROBLEMS ARE, BUT HIGHBROWS HAVE BEGUN CALLING THE TOWER THE "IRON ASPARAGUS"... THE SITUATION IS PRICKLY...

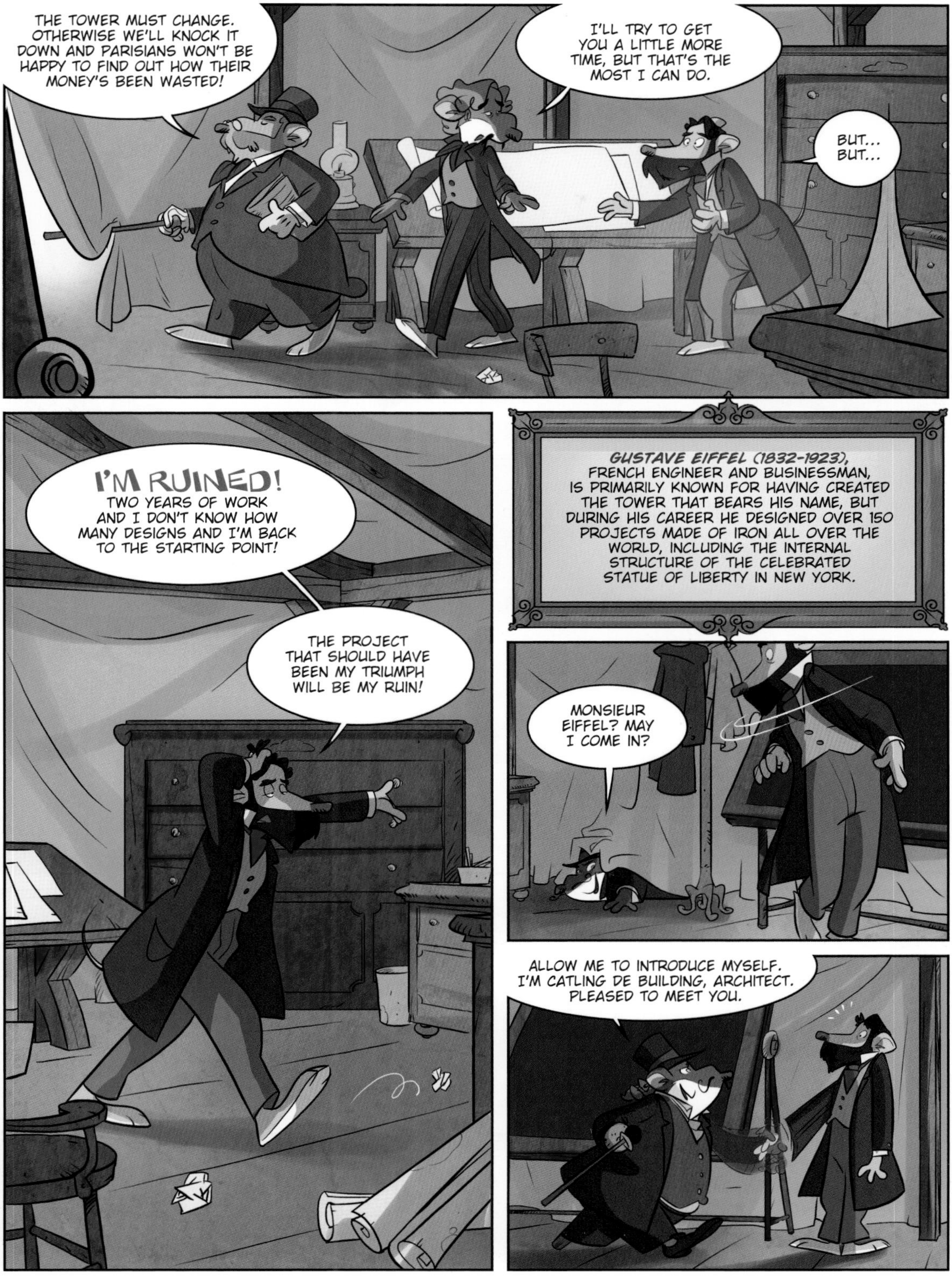
THE TOWER MUST CHANGE. OTHERWISE WE'LL KNOCK IT DOWN AND PARISIANS WON'T BE HAPPY TO FIND OUT HOW THEIR MONEY'S BEEN WASTED!
I'LL TRY TO GET YOU A LITTLE MORE TIME, BUT THAT'S THE MOST I CAN DO.
BUT... BUT...
I'M RUINED! TWO YEARS OF WORK AND I DON'T KNOW HOW MANY DESIGNS AND I'M BACK TO THE STARTING POINT!
THE PROJECT THAT SHOULD HAVE BEEN MY TRIUMPH WILL BE MY RUIN!
GUSTAVE EIFFEL (1832-1923), FRENCH ENGINEER AND BUSINESSMAN, IS PRIMARILY KNOWN FOR HAVING CREATED THE TOWER THAT BEARS HIS NAME, BUT DURING HIS CAREER HE DESIGNED OVER 150 PROJECTS MADE OF IRON ALL OVER THE WORLD, INCLUDING THE INTERNAL STRUCTURE OF THE CELEBRATED STATUE OF LIBERTY IN NEW YORK.
MONSIEUR EIFFEL? MAY I COME IN?
ALLOW ME TO INTRODUCE MYSELF. I'M CATLING DE BUILDING, ARCHITECT. PLEASED TO MEET YOU.

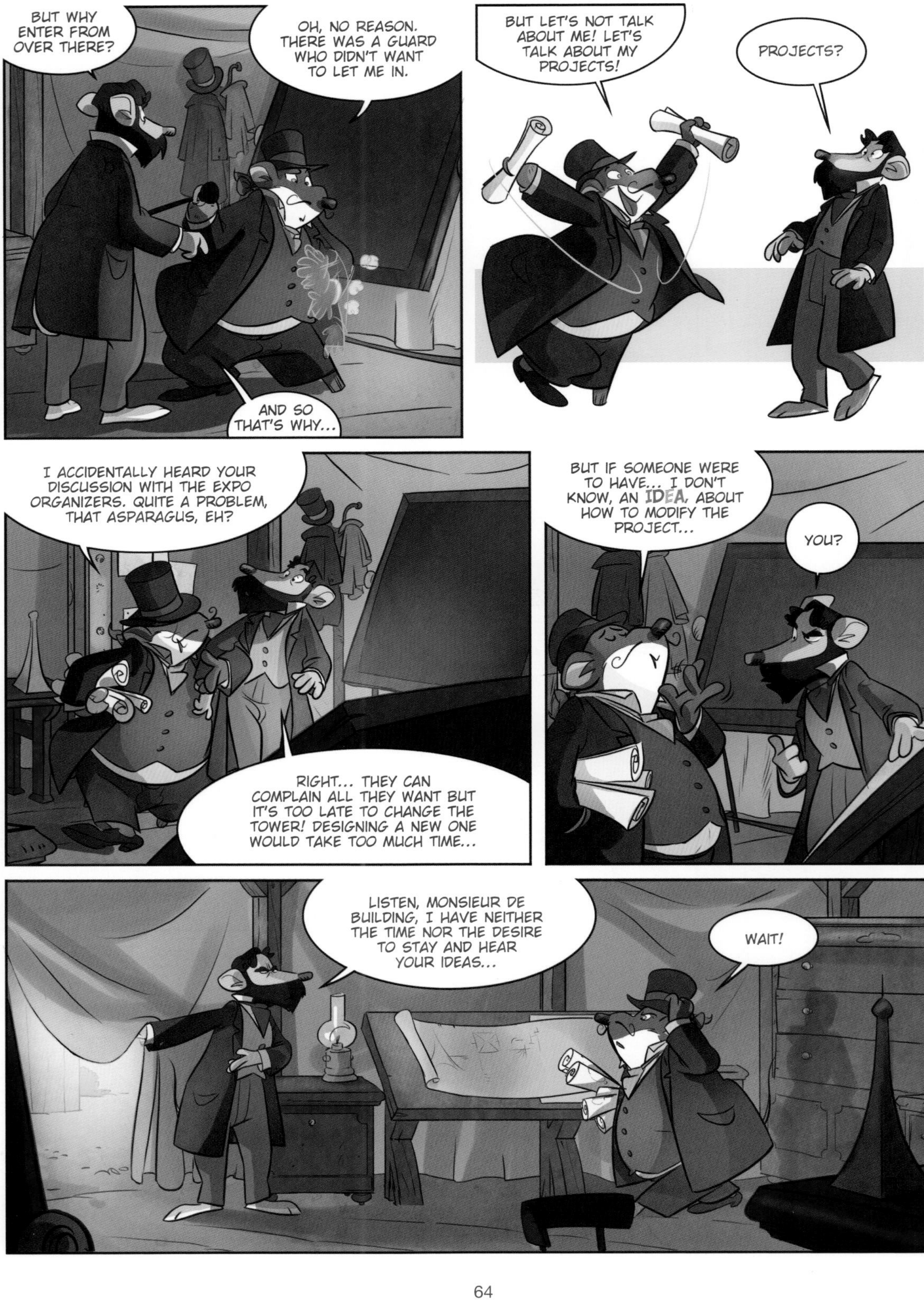
BUT WHY ENTER FROM OVER THERE?
OH, NO REASON. THERE WAS A GUARD WHO DIDN'T WANT TO LET ME IN.
AND SO THAT'S WHY...
BUT LET'S NOT TALK ABOUT ME! LET'S TALK ABOUT MY PROJECTS!
PROJECTS?
I ACCIDENTALLY HEARD YOUR DISCUSSION WITH THE EXPO ORGANIZERS. QUITE A PROBLEM, THAT ASPARAGUS, EH?
RIGHT... THEY CAN COMPLAIN ALL THEY WANT BUT IT'S TOO LATE TO CHANGE THE TOWER! DESIGNING A NEW ONE WOULD TAKE TOO MUCH TIME...
BUT IF SOMEONE WERE TO HAVE... I DON'T KNOW, AN IDEA, ABOUT HOW TO MODIFY THE PROJECT...
YOU?
LISTEN, MONSIEUR DE BUILDING, I HAVE NEITHER THE TIME NOR THE DESIRE TO STAY AND HEAR YOUR IDEAS...
WAIT!

JUST TAKE A LOOK HERE. YOU'LL SEE SOMETHING THAT'LL AMAZE YOU!

BUT... BUT...

BUT YOU...

BUT YOU'RE A *GENIUS!*

OF COURSE, THE WAY YOU'VE DESIGNED IT IS TERRIFIC, BUT THE IDEAS IT'S BASED ON ARE VISIONARY!

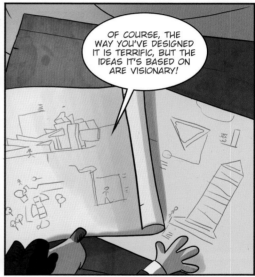

I DON'T KNOW, HOWEVER, HOW YOUR IDEAS CAN BE APPLIED TO MY TOWER. WE STILL NEED THE RIGHT PROJECT...

I JUST HAD ONE THAT MIGHT BE EXACTLY WHAT WE NEED... BUT WHERE IS IT?

HERE IT IS: "THE GHERKIN."

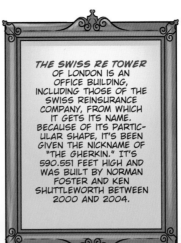

THE SWISS RE TOWER OF LONDON IS AN OFFICE BUILDING, INCLUDING THOSE OF THE SWISS REINSURANCE COMPANY, FROM WHICH IT GETS ITS NAME. BECAUSE OF ITS PARTIC- ULAR SHAPE, IT'S BEEN GIVEN THE NICKNAME OF "THE GHERKIN." IT'S 590.551 FEET HIGH AND WAS BUILT BY NORMAN FOSTER AND KEN SHUTTLEWORTH BETWEEN 2000 AND 2004.

IT'S A BOLD PROJECT, BUT I DON'T SEE HOW IT COULD BE USEFUL TO OUR CURRENT SITUATION. WE CAN'T KNOCK DOWN SOMETHING WE'VE ALREADY BUILT!

NATURALLY! BUT I KNOW YOU ALSO BUILT THE INTERNAL FRAME OF THE AMERICAN STATUE OF LIBERTY. OUR PROJECT WOULD BE SIMILAR.

IT WOULD BE ENOUGH TO USE "YOUR" TOWER AS THE SHELL FOR "MY" TOWER! THAT WAY YOUR WORK WOULDN'T BE WASTED!

LIKE THIS?

EXACTLY!

OF COURSE, MAKING SOME MODIFICATIONS HERE AND THERE...

I THINK IT WOULD BE AN UNPARALLELED **SIGHT!**

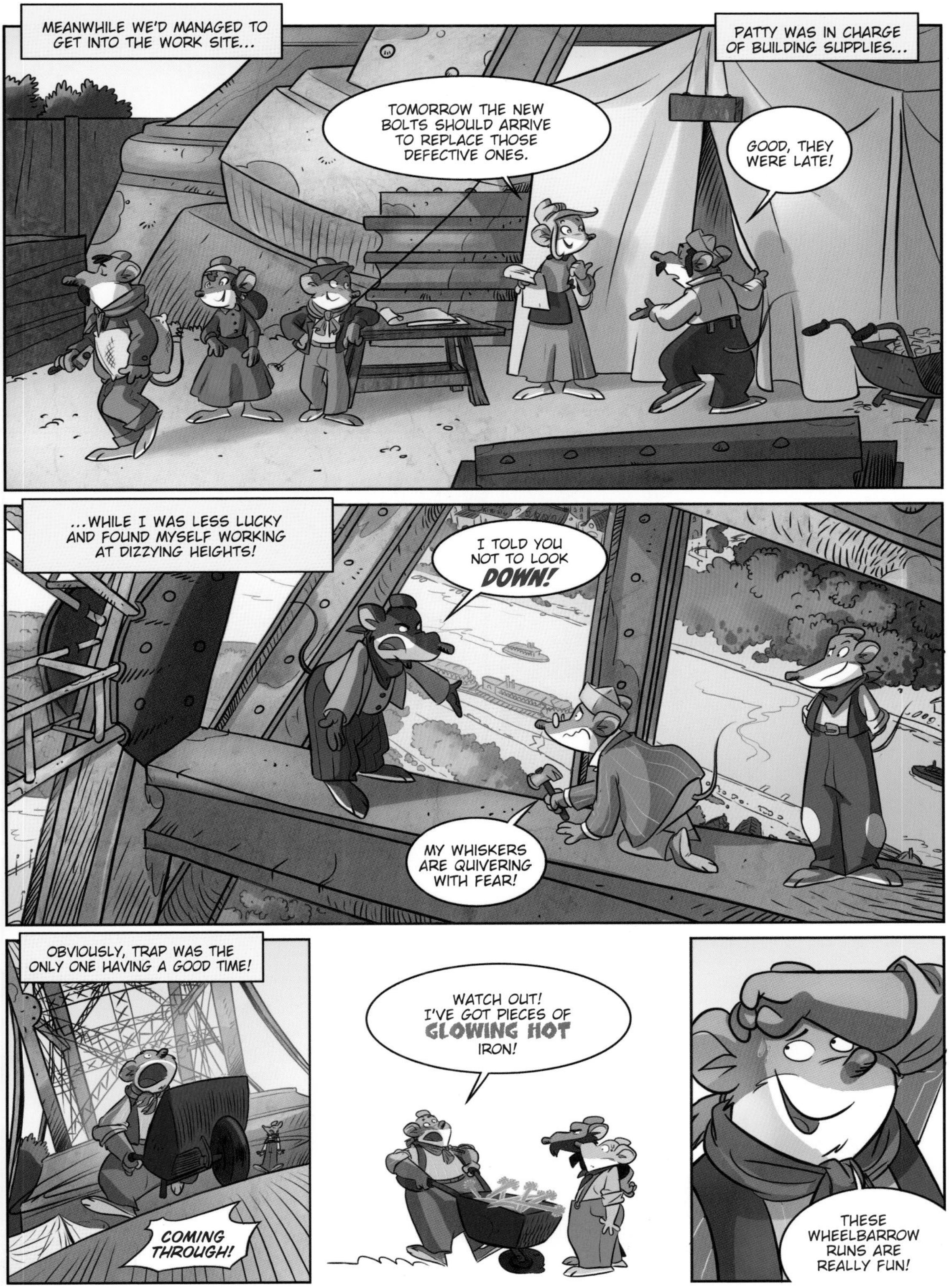
MEANWHILE WE'D MANAGED TO GET INTO THE WORK SITE...
TOMORROW THE NEW BOLTS SHOULD ARRIVE TO REPLACE THOSE DEFECTIVE ONES.
PATTY WAS IN CHARGE OF BUILDING SUPPLIES...
GOOD, THEY WERE LATE!
...WHILE I WAS LESS LUCKY AND FOUND MYSELF WORKING AT DIZZYING HEIGHTS!
I TOLD YOU NOT TO LOOK DOWN!
MY WHISKERS ARE QUIVERING WITH FEAR!
OBVIOUSLY, TRAP WAS THE ONLY ONE HAVING A GOOD TIME!
COMING THROUGH!
WATCH OUT! I'VE GOT PIECES OF GLOWING HOT IRON!
THESE WHEELBARROW RUNS ARE REALLY FUN!

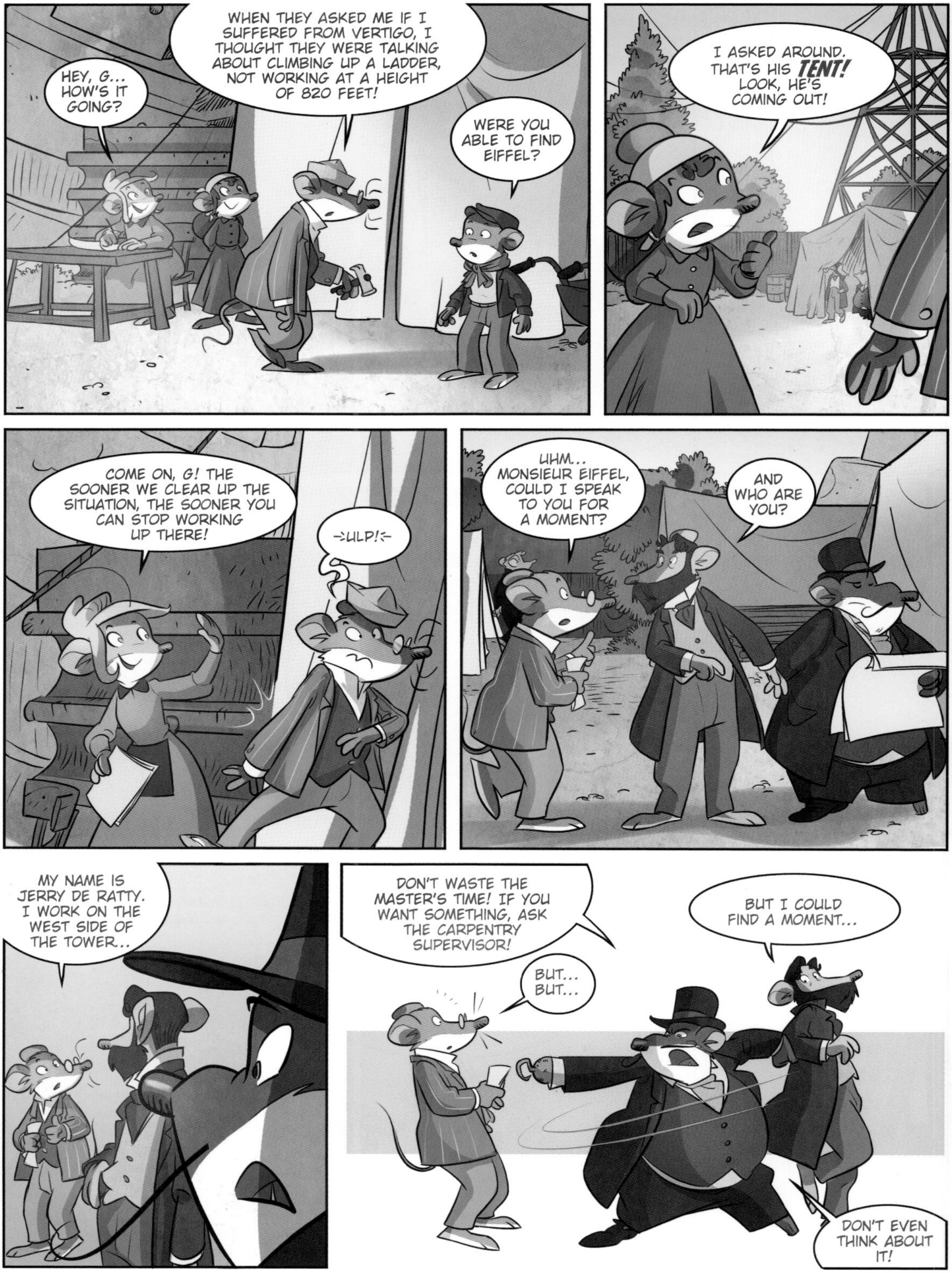
HEY, G... HOW'S IT GOING?
WHEN THEY ASKED ME IF I SUFFERED FROM VERTIGO, I THOUGHT THEY WERE TALKING ABOUT CLIMBING UP A LADDER, NOT WORKING AT A HEIGHT OF 820 FEET!
WERE YOU ABLE TO FIND EIFFEL?
I ASKED AROUND. THAT'S HIS TENT! LOOK, HE'S COMING OUT!
COME ON, G! THE SOONER WE CLEAR UP THE SITUATION, THE SOONER YOU CAN STOP WORKING UP THERE!
ULP!
UHM... MONSIEUR EIFFEL, COULD I SPEAK TO YOU FOR A MOMENT?
AND WHO ARE YOU?
MY NAME IS JERRY DE RATTY. I WORK ON THE WEST SIDE OF THE TOWER...
DON'T WASTE THE MASTER'S TIME! IF YOU WANT SOMETHING, ASK THE CARPENTRY SUPERVISOR!
BUT... BUT...
BUT I COULD FIND A MOMENT...
DON'T EVEN THINK ABOUT IT!

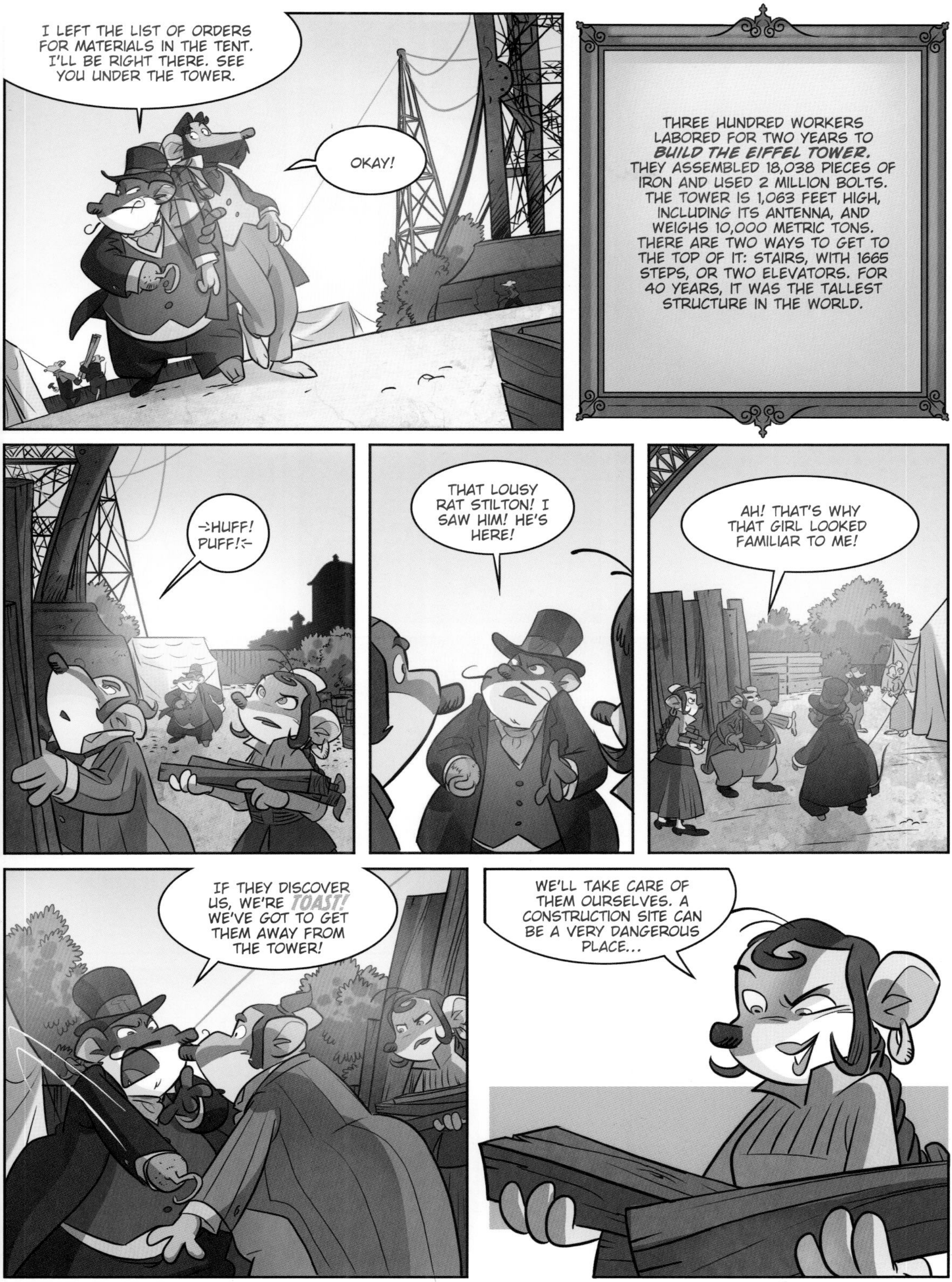
I LEFT THE LIST OF ORDERS FOR MATERIALS IN THE TENT. I'LL BE RIGHT THERE. SEE YOU UNDER THE TOWER.
OKAY!
THREE HUNDRED WORKERS LABORED FOR TWO YEARS TO BUILD THE EIFFEL TOWER. THEY ASSEMBLED 18,038 PIECES OF IRON AND USED 2 MILLION BOLTS. THE TOWER IS 1,063 FEET HIGH, INCLUDING ITS ANTENNA, AND WEIGHS 10,000 METRIC TONS. THERE ARE TWO WAYS TO GET TO THE TOP OF IT: STAIRS, WITH 1665 STEPS, OR TWO ELEVATORS. FOR 40 YEARS, IT WAS THE TALLEST STRUCTURE IN THE WORLD.
HUFF! PUFF!
THAT LOUSY RAT STILTON! I SAW HIM! HE'S HERE!
AH! THAT'S WHY THAT GIRL LOOKED FAMILIAR TO ME!
IF THEY DISCOVER US, WE'RE TOAST! WE'VE GOT TO GET THEM AWAY FROM THE TOWER!
WE'LL TAKE CARE OF THEM OURSELVES. A CONSTRUCTION SITE CAN BE A VERY DANGEROUS PLACE...

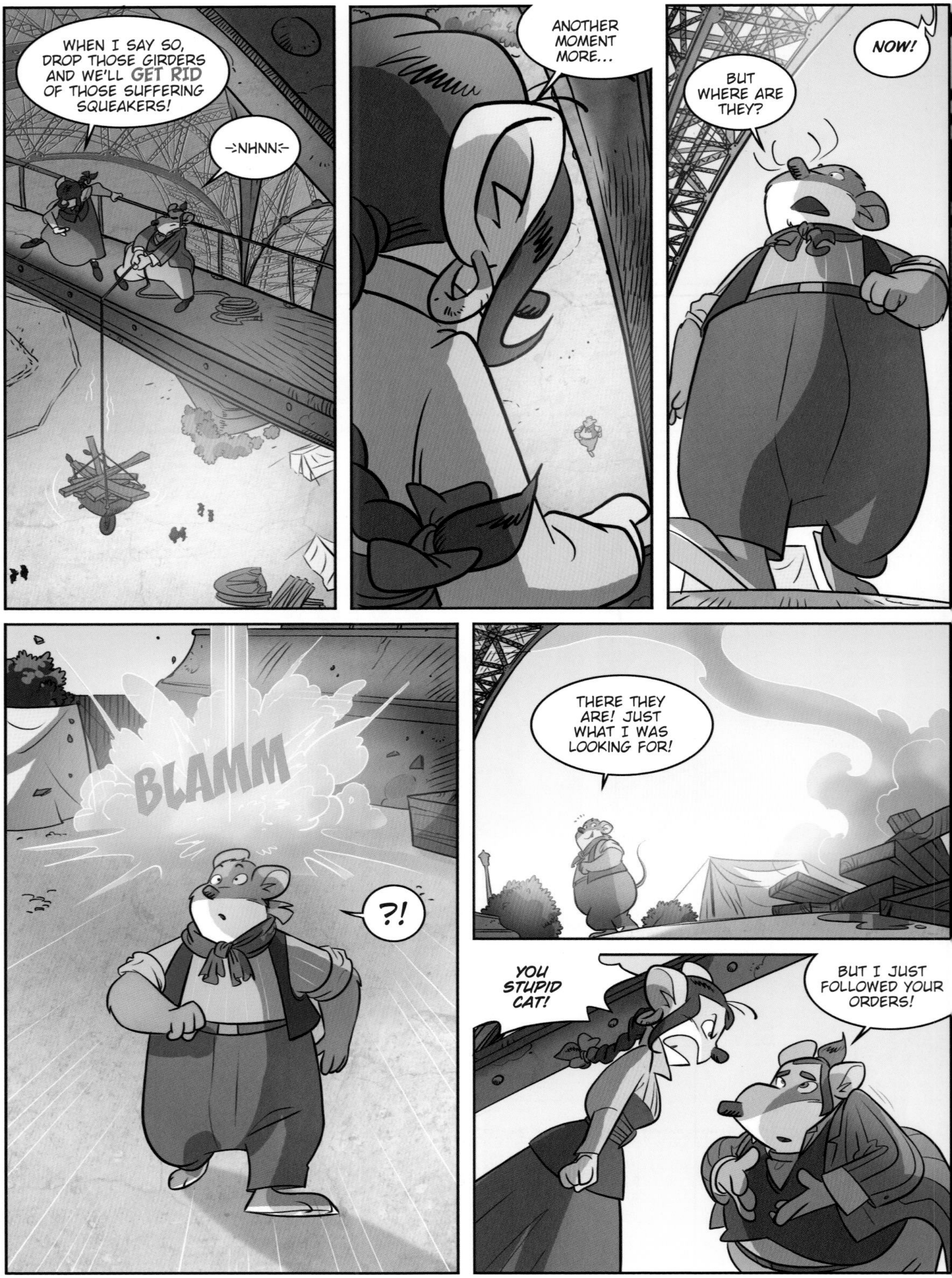
WHEN I SAY SO, DROP THOSE GIRDERS AND WE'LL GET RID OF THOSE SUFFERING SQUEAKERS!
-NHNN-
ANOTHER MOMENT MORE...
NOW!
BUT WHERE ARE THEY?
BLAMM
?!
THERE THEY ARE! JUST WHAT I WAS LOOKING FOR!
YOU STUPID CAT!
BUT I JUST FOLLOWED YOUR ORDERS!

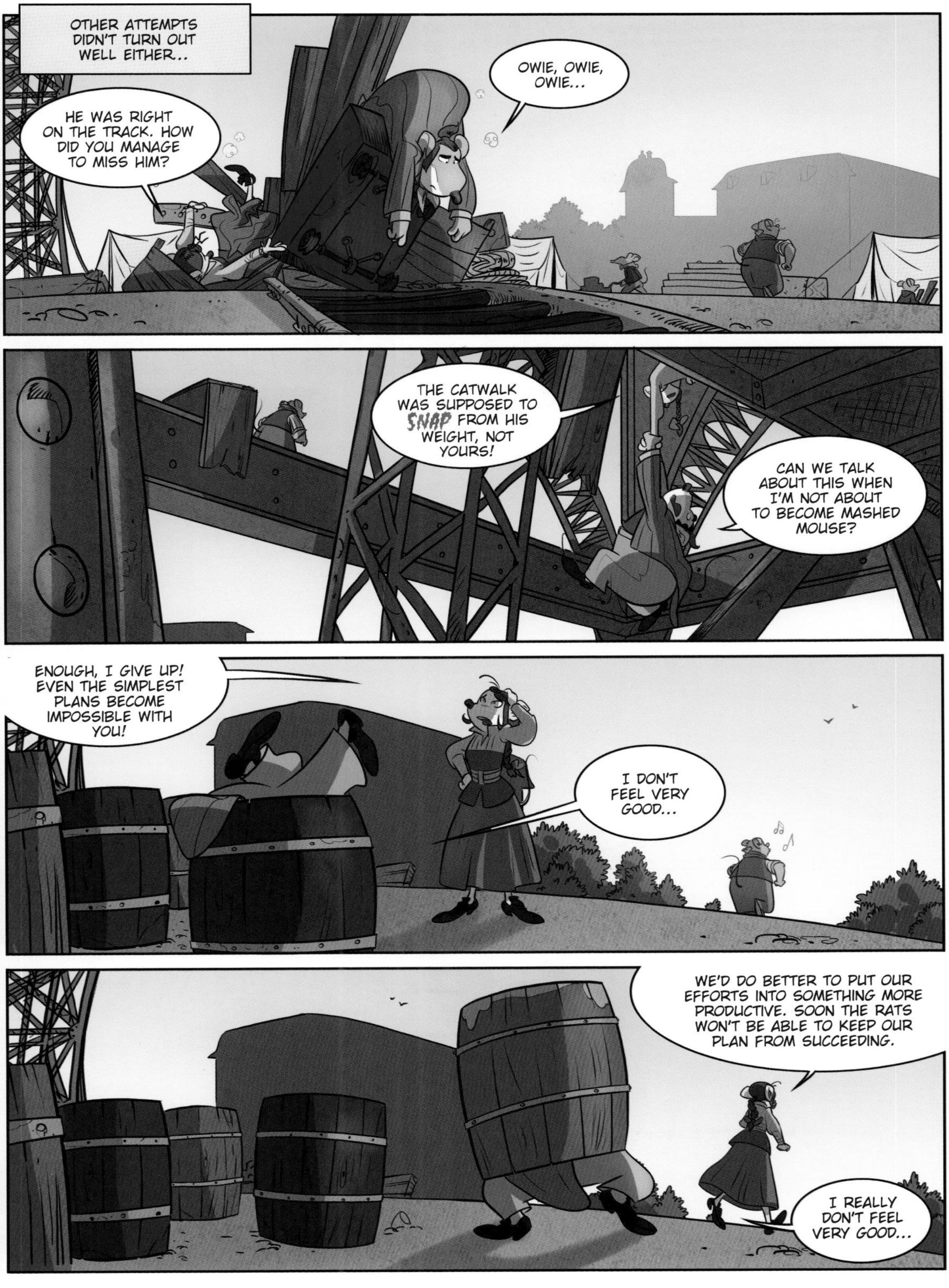

OTHER ATTEMPTS DIDN'T TURN OUT WELL EITHER...
HE WAS RIGHT ON THE TRACK. HOW DID YOU MANAGE TO MISS HIM?
OWIE, OWIE, OWIE...
THE CATWALK WAS SUPPOSED TO SNAP FROM HIS WEIGHT, NOT YOURS!
CAN WE TALK ABOUT THIS WHEN I'M NOT ABOUT TO BECOME MASHED MOUSE?
ENOUGH, I GIVE UP! EVEN THE SIMPLEST PLANS BECOME IMPOSSIBLE WITH YOU!
I DON'T FEEL VERY GOOD...
WE'D DO BETTER TO PUT OUR EFFORTS INTO SOMETHING MORE PRODUCTIVE. SOON THE RATS WON'T BE ABLE TO KEEP OUR PLAN FROM SUCCEEDING.
I REALLY DON'T FEEL VERY GOOD...

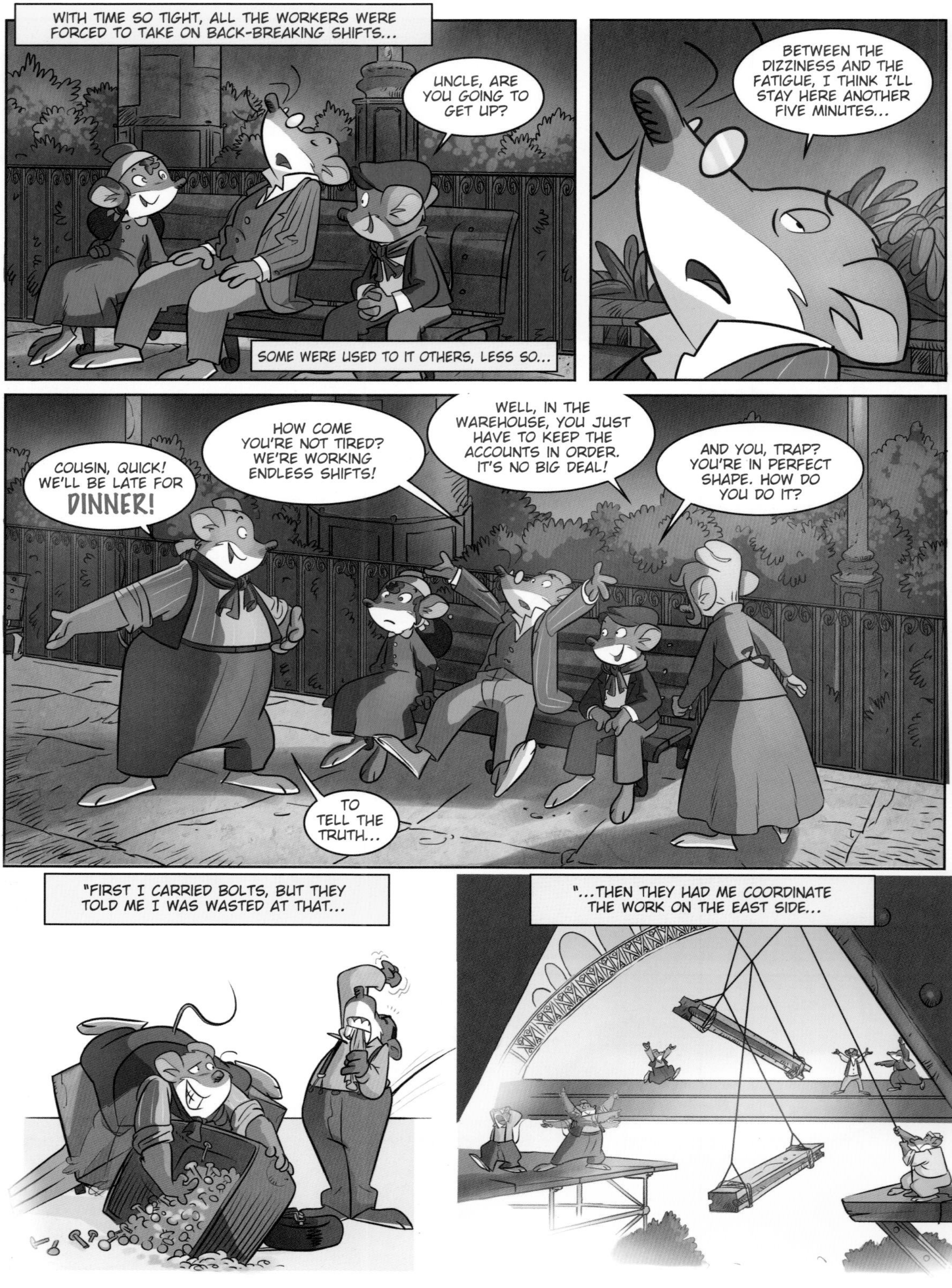
WITH TIME SO TIGHT, ALL THE WORKERS WERE FORCED TO TAKE ON BACK-BREAKING SHIFTS...
UNCLE, ARE YOU GOING TO GET UP?
SOME WERE USED TO IT OTHERS, LESS SO...
BETWEEN THE DIZZINESS AND THE FATIGUE, I THINK I'LL STAY HERE ANOTHER FIVE MINUTES...
COUSIN, QUICK! WE'LL BE LATE FOR DINNER!
HOW COME YOU'RE NOT TIRED? WE'RE WORKING ENDLESS SHIFTS!
WELL, IN THE WAREHOUSE, YOU JUST HAVE TO KEEP THE ACCOUNTS IN ORDER. IT'S NO BIG DEAL!
AND YOU, TRAP? YOU'RE IN PERFECT SHAPE. HOW DO YOU DO IT?
TO TELL THE TRUTH...
"FIRST I CARRIED BOLTS, BUT THEY TOLD ME I WAS WASTED AT THAT...
"...THEN THEY HAD ME COORDINATE THE WORK ON THE EAST SIDE...

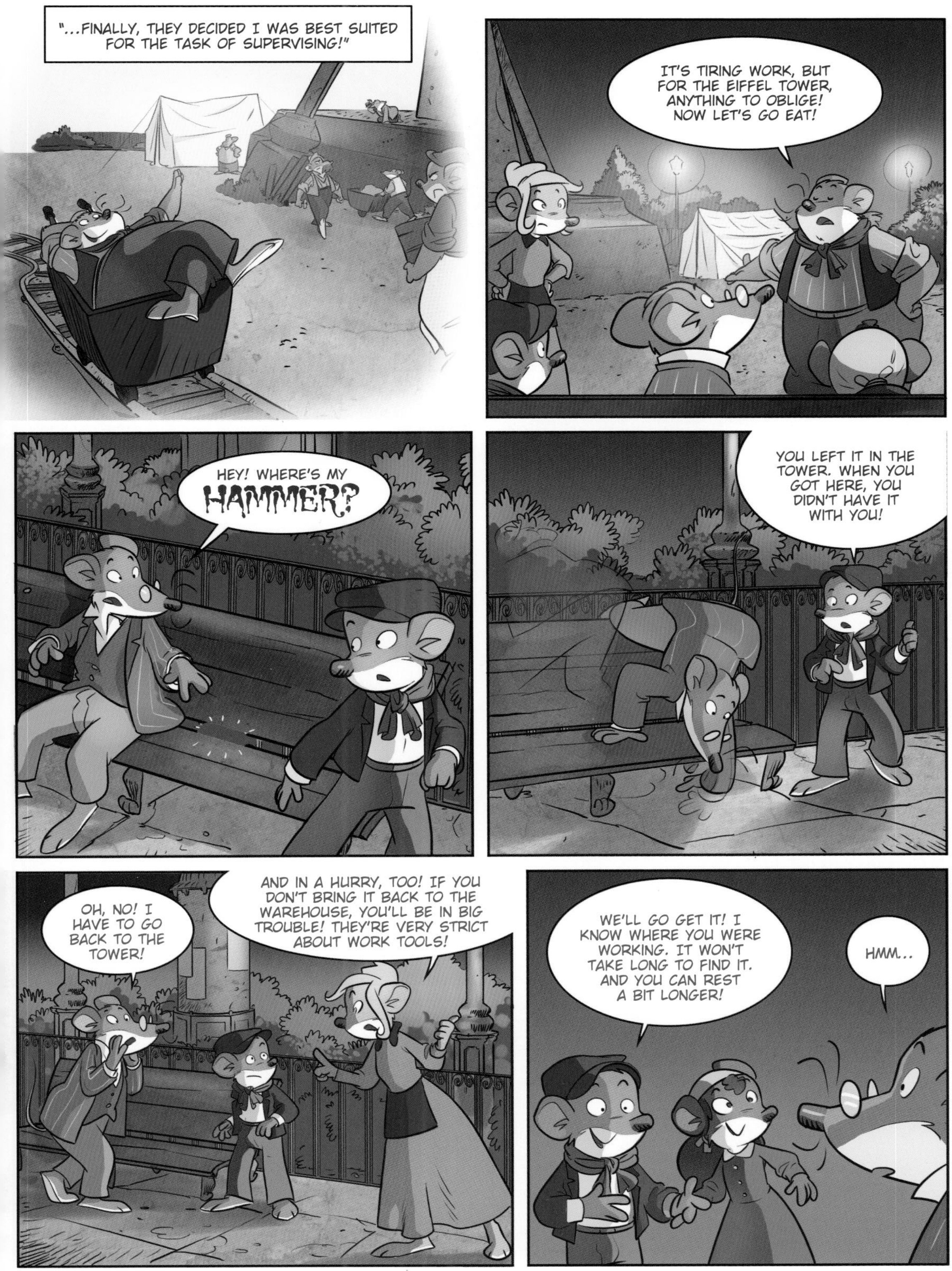

"...FINALLY, THEY DECIDED I WAS BEST SUITED FOR THE TASK OF SUPERVISING!"
IT'S TIRING WORK, BUT FOR THE EIFFEL TOWER, ANYTHING TO OBLIGE! NOW LET'S GO EAT!
HEY! WHERE'S MY HAMMER?
YOU LEFT IT IN THE TOWER. WHEN YOU GOT HERE, YOU DIDN'T HAVE IT WITH YOU!
OH, NO! I HAVE TO GO BACK TO THE TOWER!
AND IN A HURRY, TOO! IF YOU DON'T BRING IT BACK TO THE WAREHOUSE, YOU'LL BE IN BIG TROUBLE! THEY'RE VERY STRICT ABOUT WORK TOOLS!
WE'LL GO GET IT! I KNOW WHERE YOU WERE WORKING. IT WON'T TAKE LONG TO FIND IT. AND YOU CAN REST A BIT LONGER!
HMM...

WE'LL BE CAREFUL, I PROMISE!

THE AREA IS **WELL-LIT.** PLUS YOU WERE WORKING IN A SAFE AREA TODAY!

OKAY...

IT'LL JUST TAKE US A MOMENT. WE'LL BE RIGHT BACK.

BE CAREFUL!

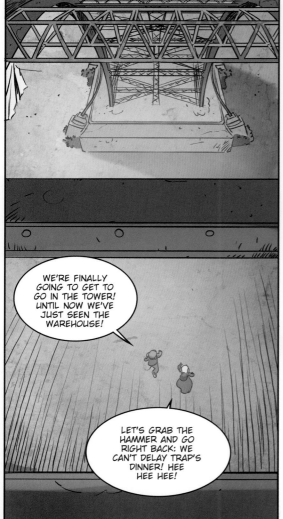

WE'RE FINALLY GOING TO GET TO GO IN THE TOWER! UNTIL NOW WE'VE JUST SEEN THE WAREHOUSE!

LET'S GRAB THE HAMMER AND GO RIGHT BACK: WE CAN'T DELAY TRAP'S DINNER! HEE HEE HEE!

HUH?

THERE'S SOMEONE THERE...

THAT'S STRANGE. THEY SHOULD ALL BE AT DINNER NOW...

MAYBE ONE OF THEM ALSO FORGOT SOMETHING...

THAT MAY BE, BUT ALL THAT MOVEMENT IS SUSPICIOUS. WE'D BETTER CHECK!

HURRY OR WE'LL LOSE THEM!

THEY'RE GOING UP.

LUCKILY THE LOWER PART OF THE TOWER IS FINISHED NOW, SO IT'S SAFE!

COME ON, WE'RE ALMOST THERE!

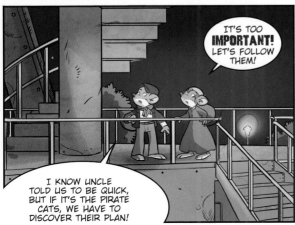

IT'S TOO **IMPORTANT!** LET'S FOLLOW THEM!

I KNOW UNCLE TOLD US TO BE QUICK, BUT IF IT'S THE PIRATE CATS, WE HAVE TO DISCOVER THEIR PLAN!

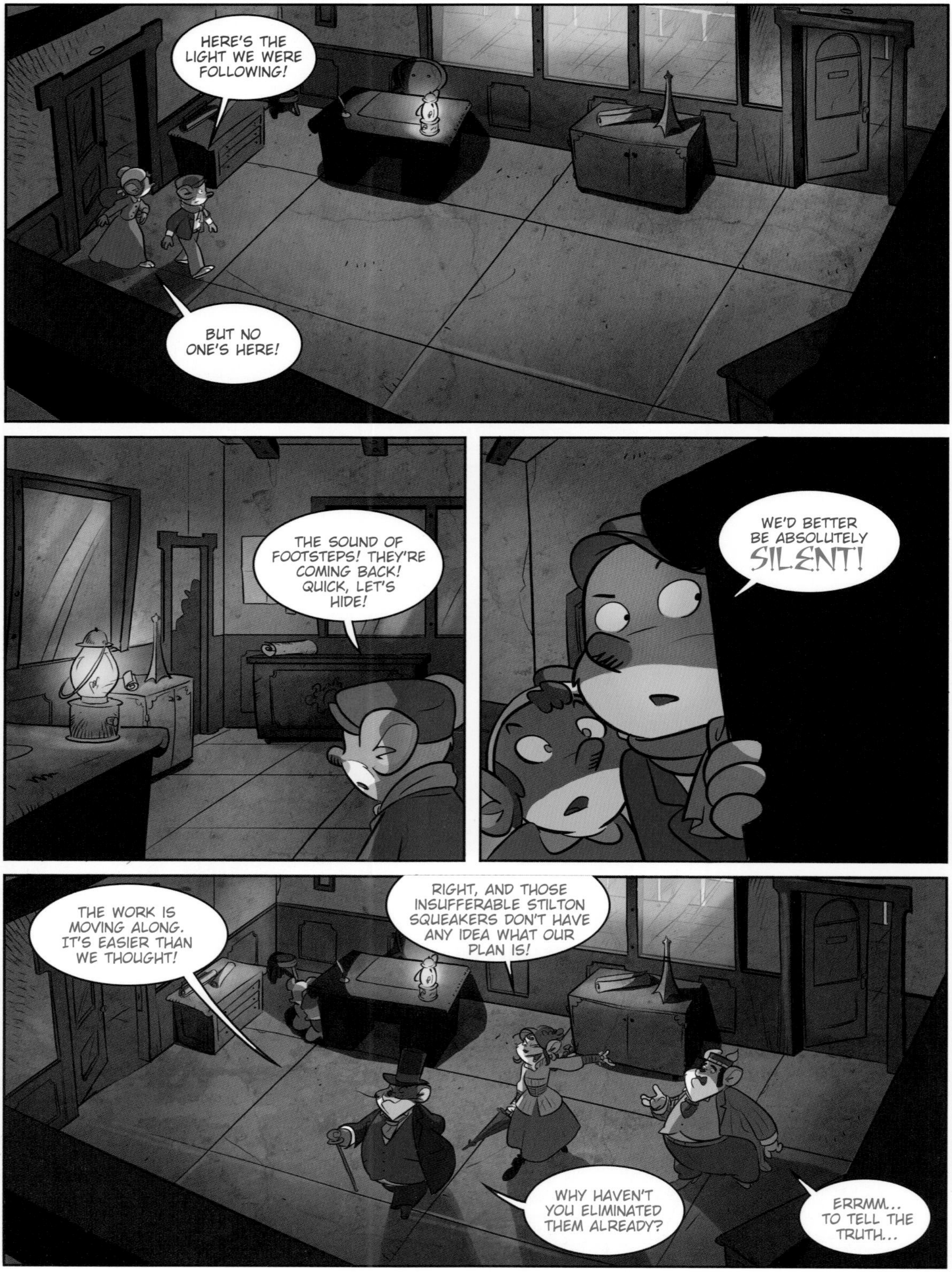
HERE'S THE LIGHT WE WERE FOLLOWING!
BUT NO ONE'S HERE!
THE SOUND OF FOOTSTEPS! THEY'RE COMING BACK! QUICK, LET'S HIDE!
WE'D BETTER BE ABSOLUTELY SILENT!
THE WORK IS MOVING ALONG. IT'S EASIER THAN WE THOUGHT!
RIGHT, AND THOSE INSUFFERABLE STILTON SQUEAKERS DON'T HAVE ANY IDEA WHAT OUR PLAN IS!
WHY HAVEN'T YOU ELIMINATED THEM ALREADY?
ERRMM... TO TELL THE TRUTH...

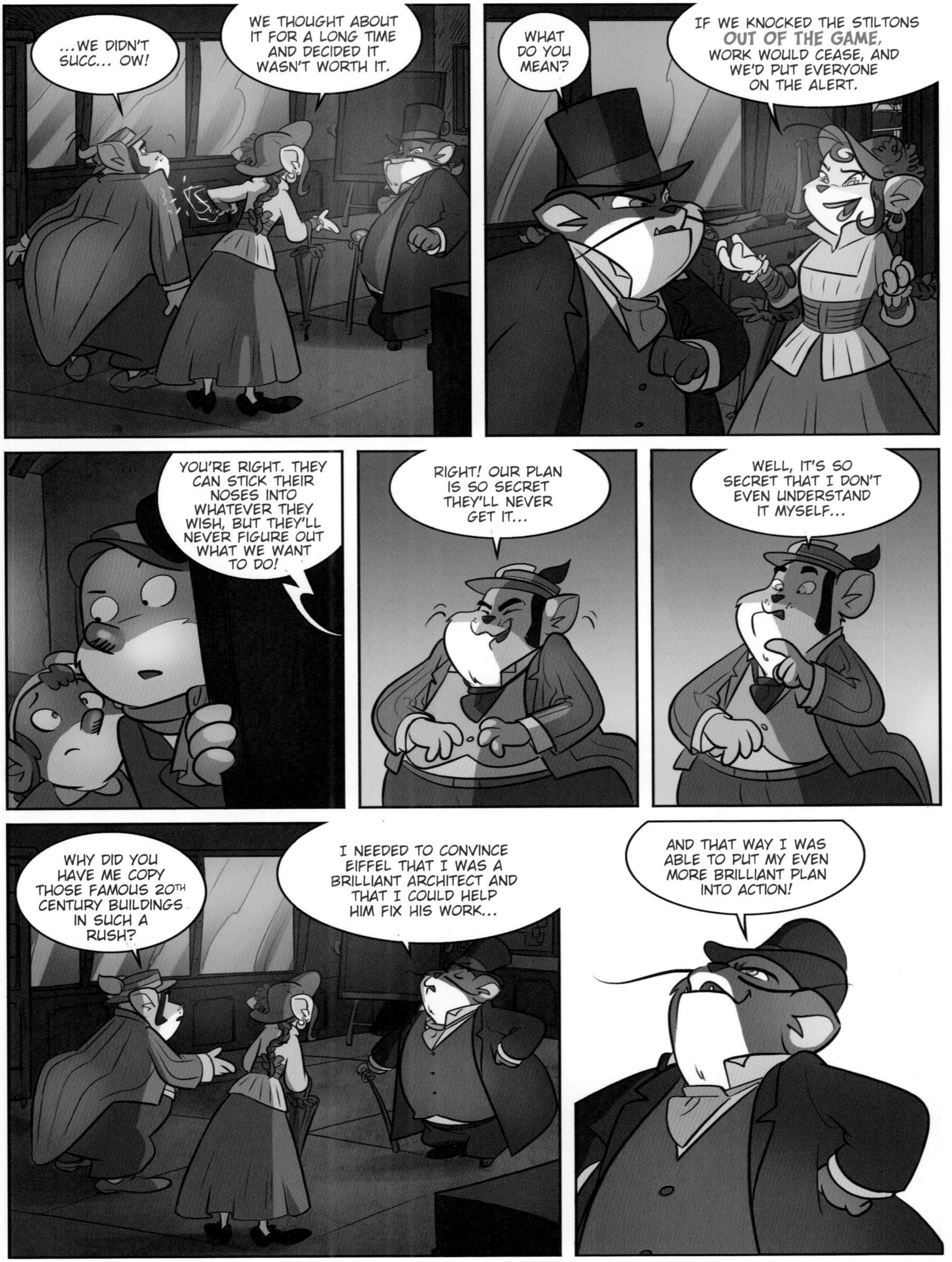
...WE DIDN'T SUCC... OW!
WE THOUGHT ABOUT IT FOR A LONG TIME AND DECIDED IT WASN'T WORTH IT.
WHAT DO YOU MEAN?
IF WE KNOCKED THE STILTONS OUT OF THE GAME, WORK WOULD CEASE, AND WE'D PUT EVERYONE ON THE ALERT.
YOU'RE RIGHT. THEY CAN STICK THEIR NOSES INTO WHATEVER THEY WISH, BUT THEY'LL NEVER FIGURE OUT WHAT WE WANT TO DO!
RIGHT! OUR PLAN IS SO SECRET THEY'LL NEVER GET IT...
WELL, IT'S SO SECRET THAT I DON'T EVEN UNDERSTAND IT MYSELF...
WHY DID YOU HAVE ME COPY THOSE FAMOUS 20TH CENTURY BUILDINGS IN SUCH A RUSH?
I NEEDED TO CONVINCE EIFFEL THAT I WAS A BRILLIANT ARCHITECT AND THAT I COULD HELP HIM FIX HIS WORK...
AND THAT WAY I WAS ABLE TO PUT MY EVEN MORE BRILLIANT PLAN INTO ACTION!

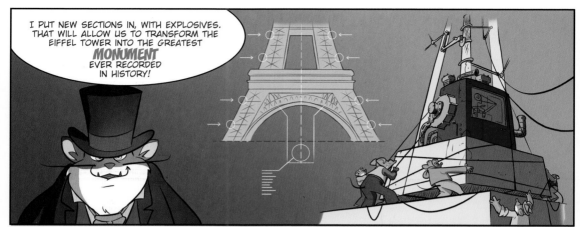

I PUT NEW SECTIONS IN, WITH EXPLOSIVES. THAT WILL ALLOW US TO TRANSFORM THE EIFFEL TOWER INTO THE GREATEST **MONUMENT** EVER RECORDED IN HISTORY!

THE GARGANTUAN TOWER OF CATARDONE III OF CATATONIA, THE GREAT EMPEROR OF THE CATS!

?!

UMM... GARGANTUAN?

THAT MEANS "GIGANTIC," "ENORMOUS."

OH, WELL, THEN IT WILL BE PRETTY FAITHFUL TO THE ORIGINAL, HA, HA, HA!

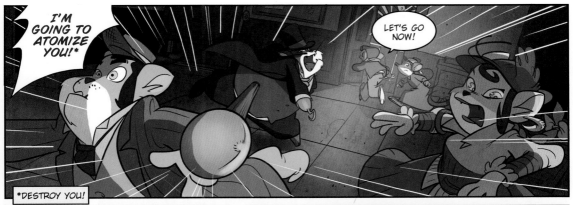

I'M GOING TO ATOMIZE YOU!*

LET'S GO NOW!

*DESTROY YOU!

LET'S HIGHTAIL IT! WE HAVE TO WARN UNCLE GERONIMO RIGHT AWAY!

WHERE HAVE YOU BEEN? WE'VE BEEN WORRIED!

UNCLE! UNCLE! THE CATS!

WHAT HAPPENED?

WE DISCOVERED THAT CATARDONE IS WORKING ON THE CONSTRUCTION OF THE TOWER. AND HE WANTS TO CREATE A STATUE IN HIS IMAGE AND LIKENESS!

AND HOW IS CATARDONE GOING TO LOOK LIKE A TOWER?

HE SAID HE'D PUT EXPLOSIVES IN THE TOWER, TO BLOW UP THE PIECES NEEDED TO TRANSFORM THE TOWER!

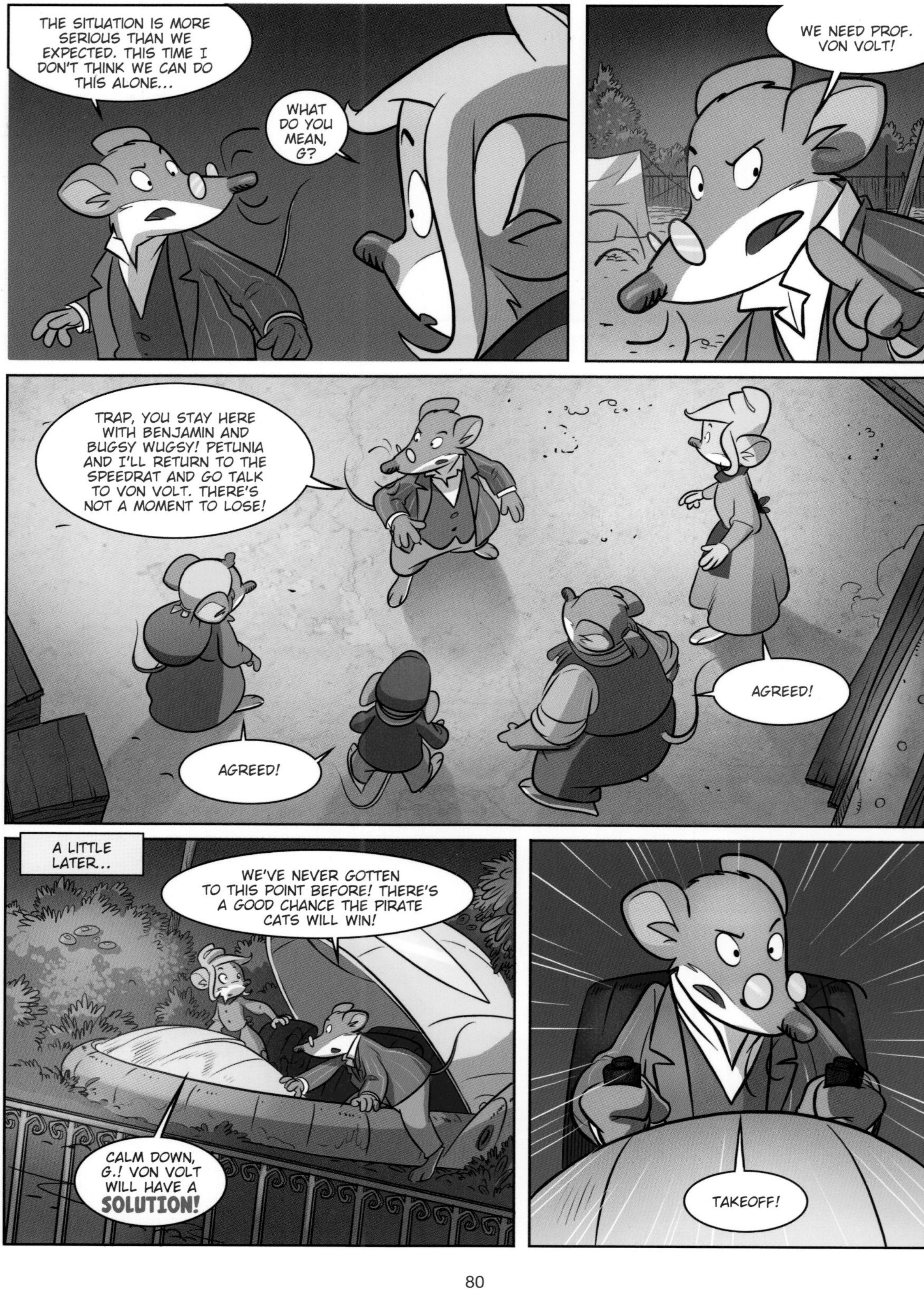

THE SITUATION IS MORE SERIOUS THAN WE EXPECTED. THIS TIME I DON'T THINK WE CAN DO THIS ALONE...
WHAT DO YOU MEAN, G?
WE NEED PROF. VON VOLT!
TRAP, YOU STAY HERE WITH BENJAMIN AND BUGSY WUGSY! PETUNIA AND I'LL RETURN TO THE SPEEDRAT AND GO TALK TO VON VOLT. THERE'S NOT A MOMENT TO LOSE!
AGREED!
AGREED!
A LITTLE LATER...
WE'VE NEVER GOTTEN TO THIS POINT BEFORE! THERE'S A GOOD CHANCE THE PIRATE CATS WILL WIN!
CALM DOWN, G.! VON VOLT WILL HAVE A SOLUTION!
TAKEOFF!

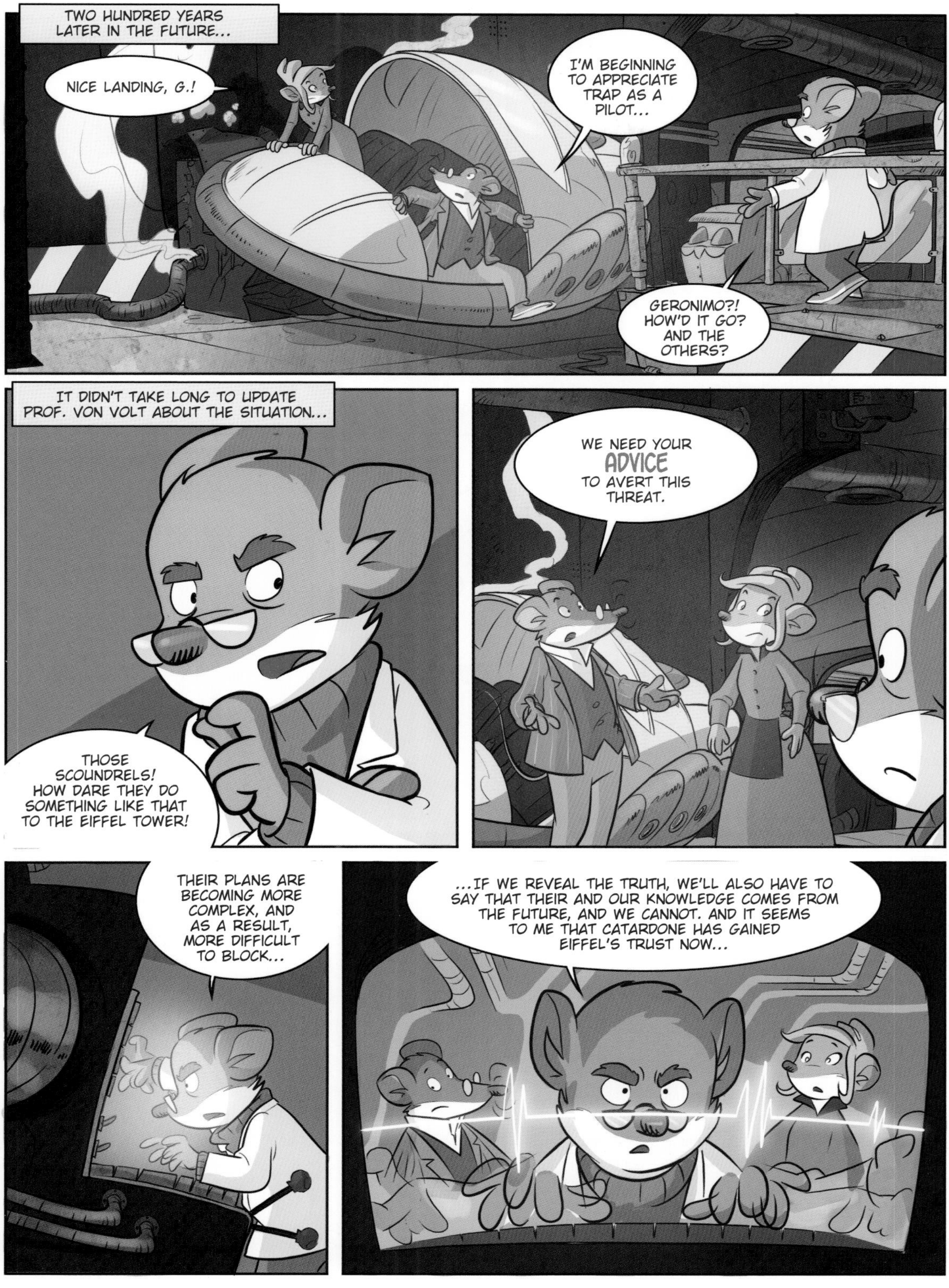
TWO HUNDRED YEARS LATER IN THE FUTURE...
NICE LANDING, G.!
I'M BEGINNING TO APPRECIATE TRAP AS A PILOT...
GERONIMO?! HOW'D IT GO? AND THE OTHERS?
IT DIDN'T TAKE LONG TO UPDATE PROF. VON VOLT ABOUT THE SITUATION...
THOSE SCOUNDRELS! HOW DARE THEY DO SOMETHING LIKE THAT TO THE EIFFEL TOWER!
WE NEED YOUR ADVICE TO AVERT THIS THREAT.
THEIR PLANS ARE BECOMING MORE COMPLEX, AND AS A RESULT, MORE DIFFICULT TO BLOCK...
...IF WE REVEAL THE TRUTH, WE'LL ALSO HAVE TO SAY THAT THEIR AND OUR KNOWLEDGE COMES FROM THE FUTURE, AND WE CANNOT. AND IT SEEMS TO ME THAT CATARDONE HAS GAINED EIFFEL'S TRUST NOW...

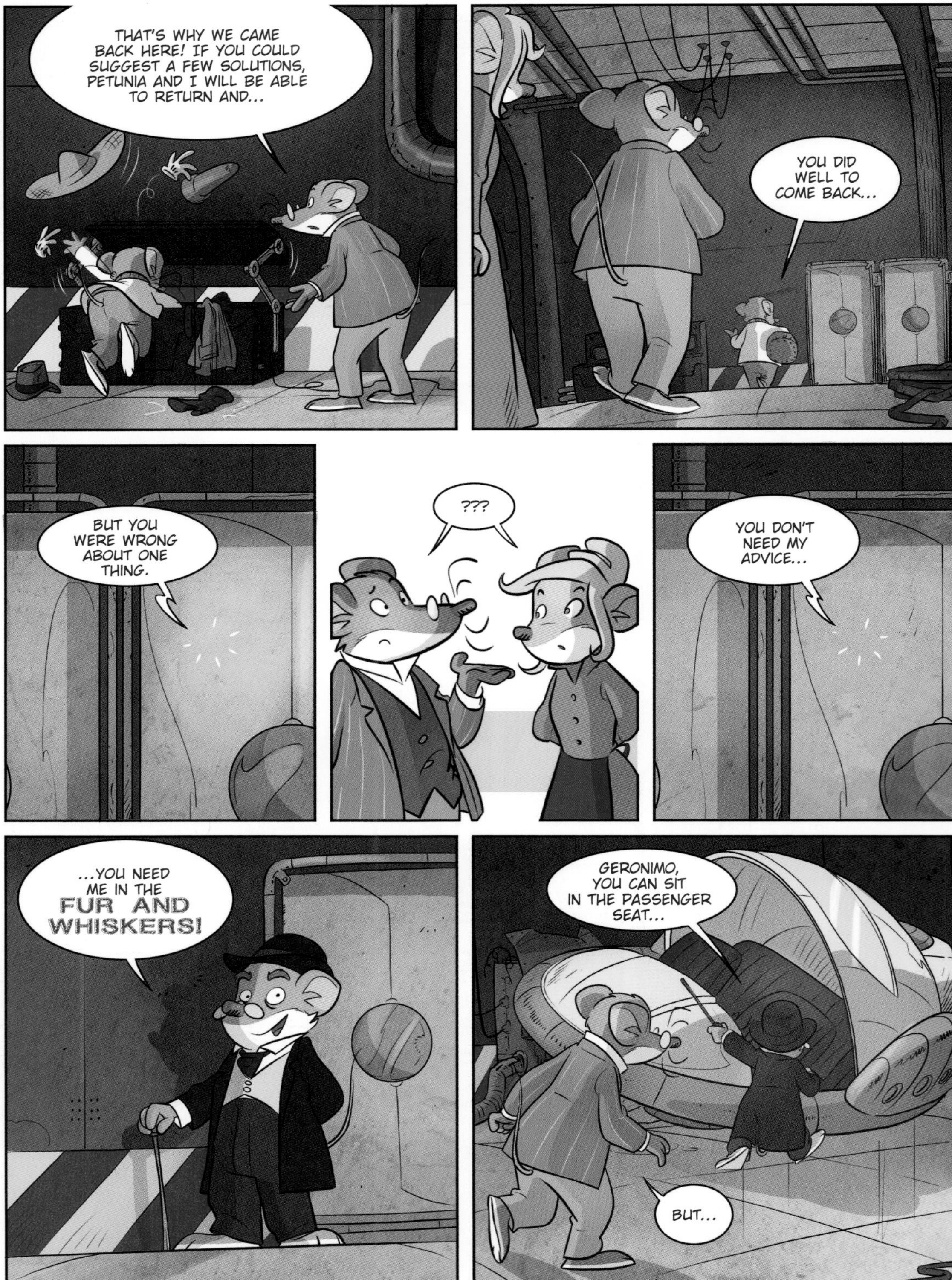
THAT'S WHY WE CAME BACK HERE! IF YOU COULD SUGGEST A FEW SOLUTIONS, PETUNIA AND I WILL BE ABLE TO RETURN AND...
YOU DID WELL TO COME BACK...
BUT YOU WERE WRONG ABOUT ONE THING.
???
YOU DON'T NEED MY ADVICE...
...YOU NEED ME IN THE FUR AND WHISKERS!
GERONIMO, YOU CAN SIT IN THE PASSENGER SEAT...
BUT...

YOU'LL SEE HOW THE SPEEDRAT **TAKES OFF** WHEN I FLY IT!

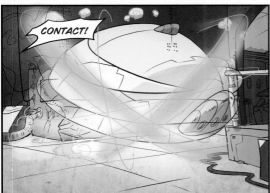

CONTACT!

MOLDY MOZZARELLA! I'VE NEVER TRAVELED SO QUICKLY AND WITHOUT THE SLIGHTEST BUMP! BUT WHERE ARE WE?

THIS PLACE LOOKS FAMILIAR TO ME...

WE'RE IN THE TOWER WAREHOUSE. IT'S THE NEAREST POINT WHERE WE COULD LAND WITHOUT ATTRACTING ATTENTION.

PROFESSOR, YOU'RE A **GENIUS!**

NOW, NOW, I HAVEN'T DONE ANYTHING SPECIAL...

...THE BEST IS YET TO COME.

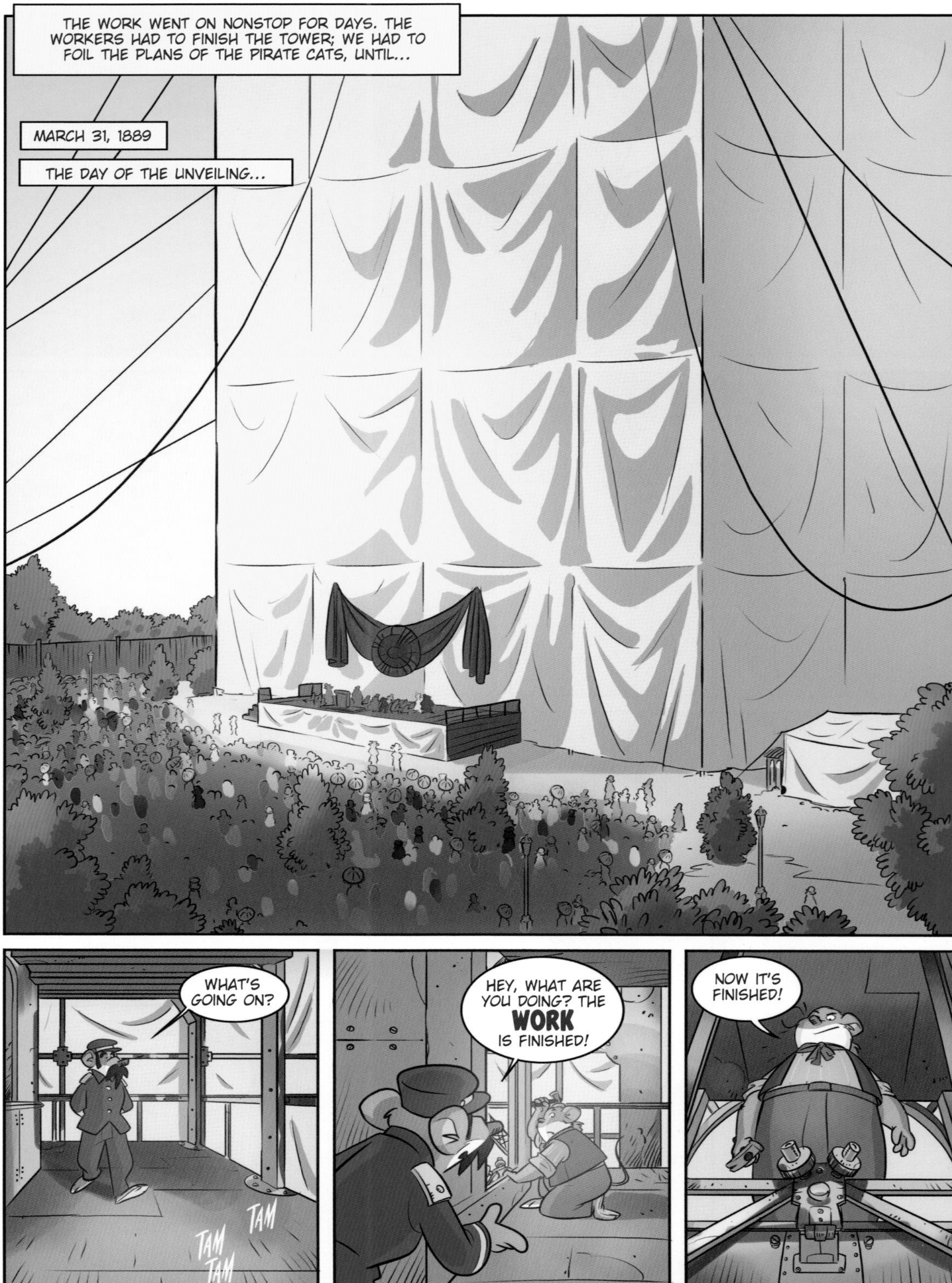
THE WORK WENT ON NONSTOP FOR DAYS. THE WORKERS HAD TO FINISH THE TOWER; WE HAD TO FOIL THE PLANS OF THE PIRATE CATS, UNTIL...
MARCH 31, 1889
THE DAY OF THE UNVEILING...
WHAT'S GOING ON?
TAM
TAM TAM
HEY, WHAT ARE YOU DOING? THE WORK IS FINISHED!
NOW IT'S FINISHED!

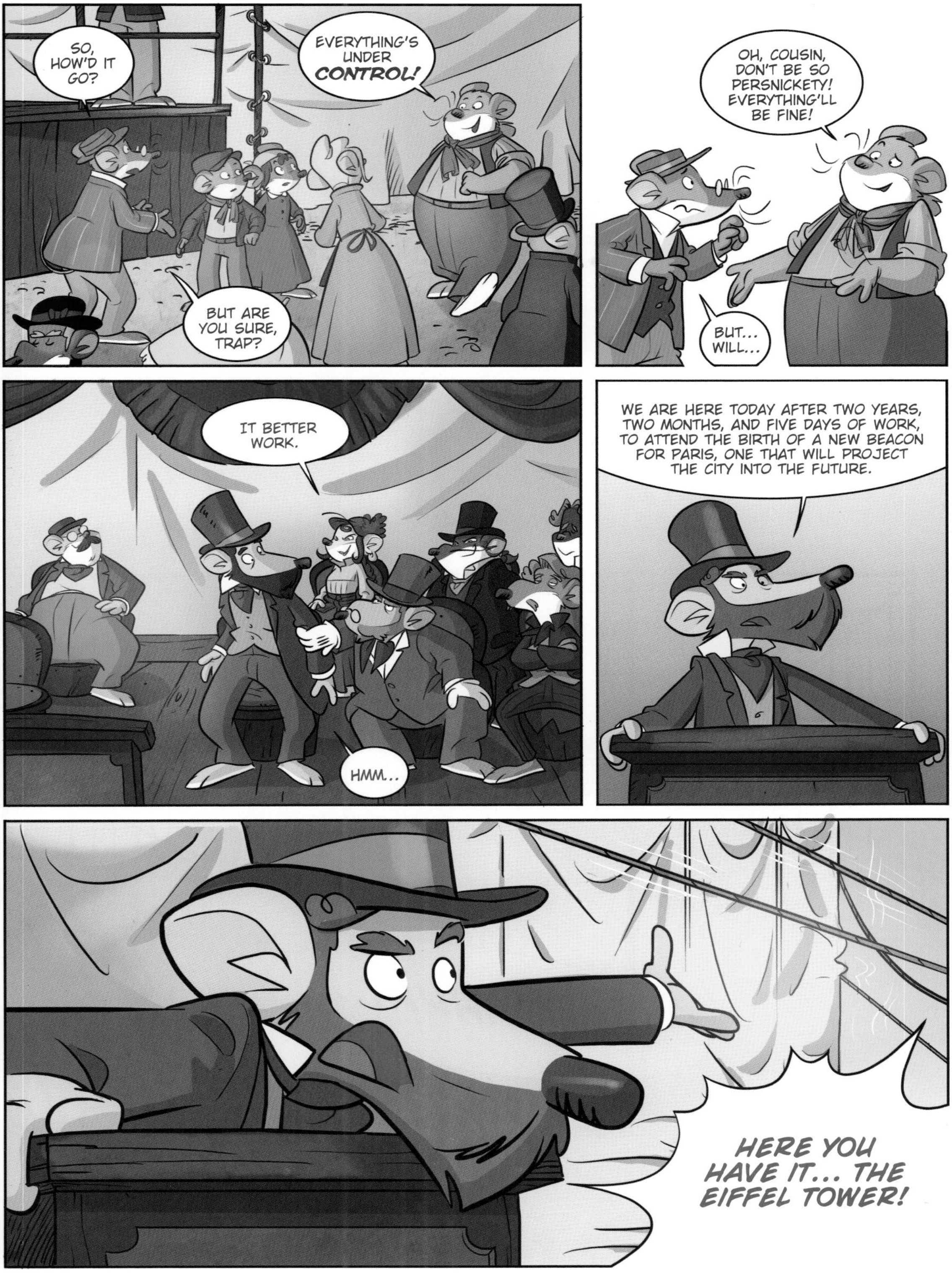
SO, HOW'D IT GO?
EVERYTHING'S UNDER CONTROL!
BUT ARE YOU SURE, TRAP?
OH, COUSIN, DON'T BE SO PERSNICKETY! EVERYTHING'LL BE FINE!
BUT... WILL...
IT BETTER WORK.
HMM...
WE ARE HERE TODAY AFTER TWO YEARS, TWO MONTHS, AND FIVE DAYS OF WORK, TO ATTEND THE BIRTH OF A NEW BEACON FOR PARIS, ONE THAT WILL PROJECT THE CITY INTO THE FUTURE.
HERE YOU HAVE IT... THE EIFFEL TOWER!

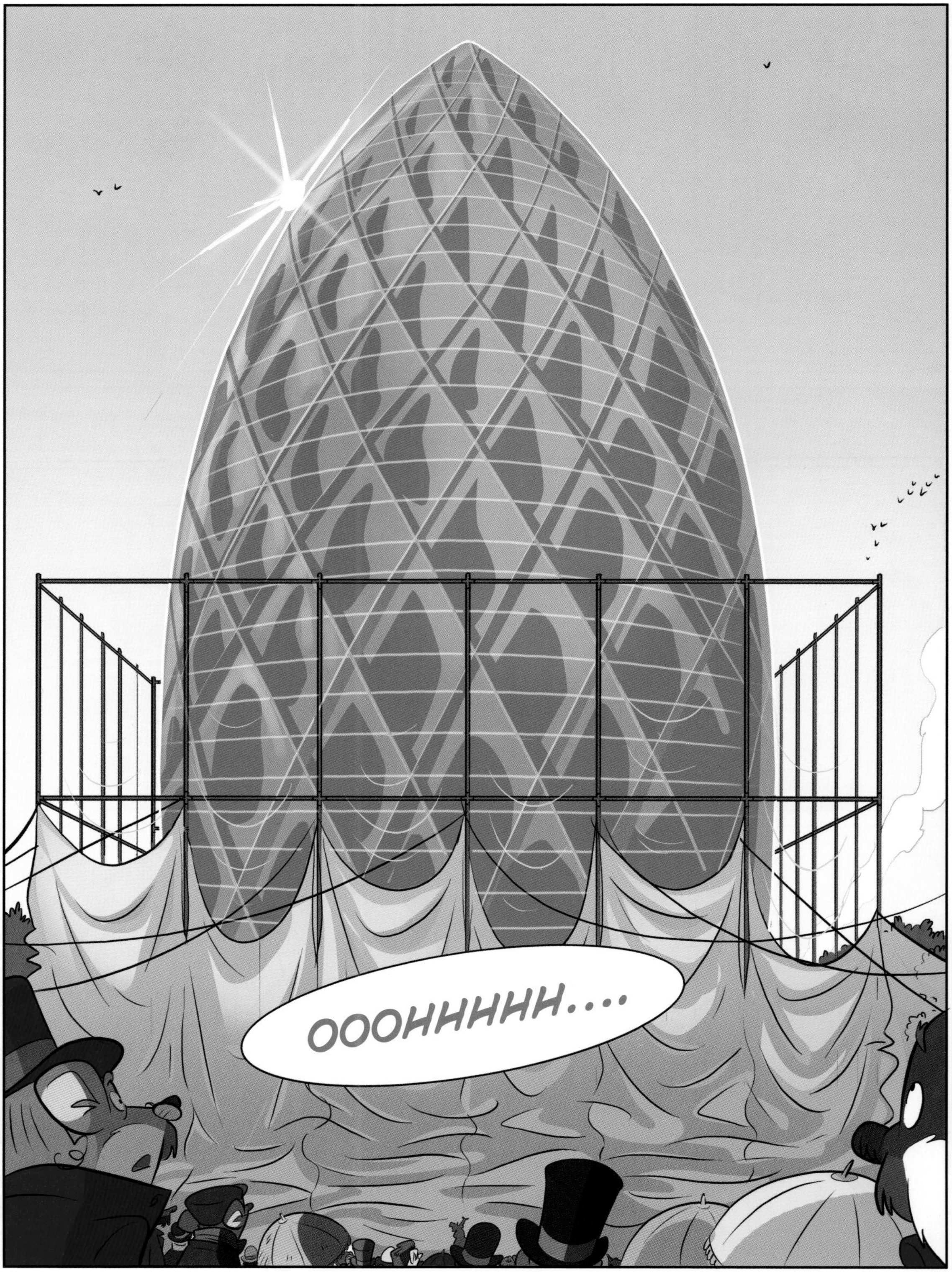
OOOHHHHH....

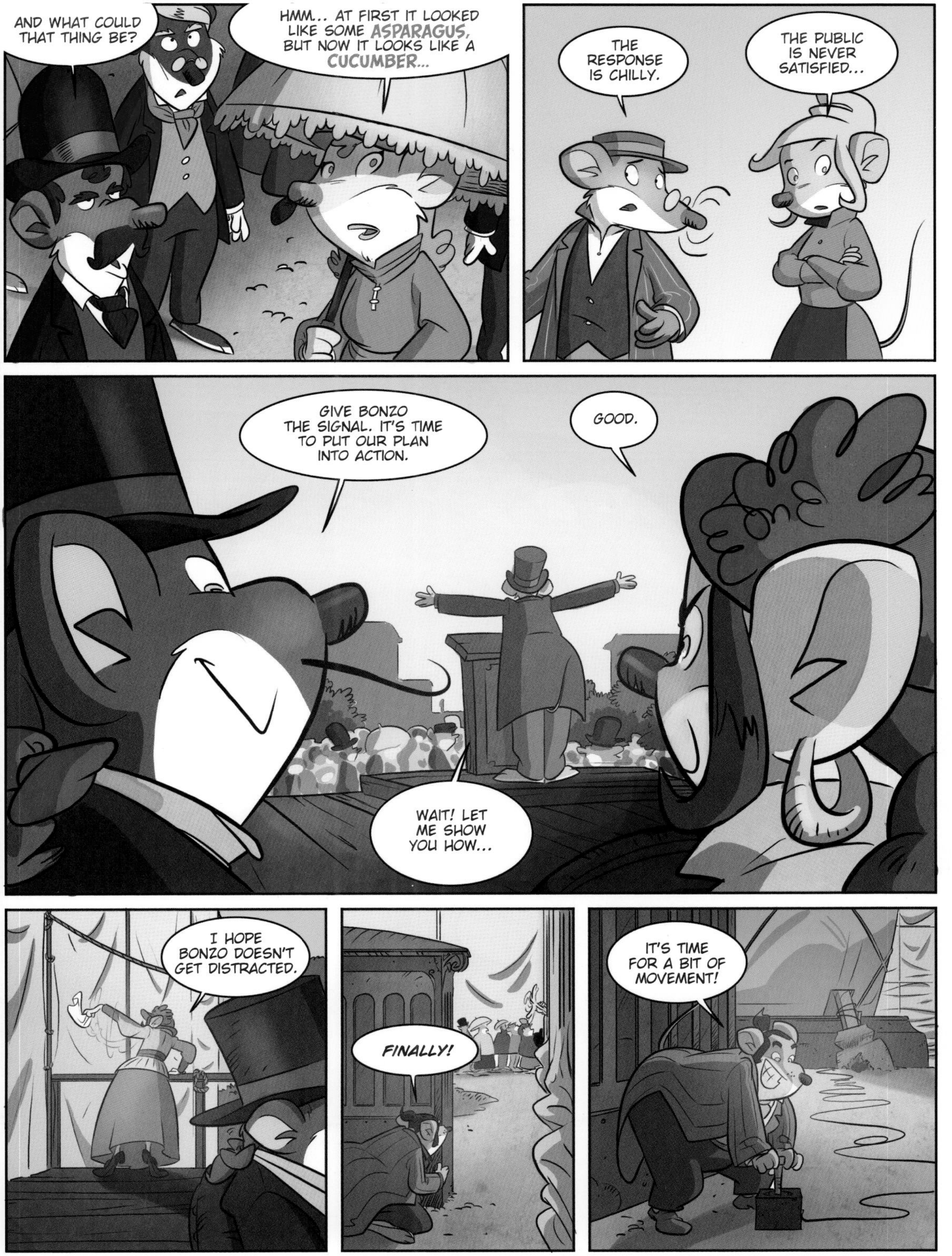
AND WHAT COULD THAT THING BE?
HMM... AT FIRST IT LOOKED LIKE SOME ASPARAGUS, BUT NOW IT LOOKS LIKE A CUCUMBER...
THE RESPONSE IS CHILLY.
THE PUBLIC IS NEVER SATISFIED...
GIVE BONZO THE SIGNAL. IT'S TIME TO PUT OUR PLAN INTO ACTION.
GOOD.
WAIT! LET ME SHOW YOU HOW...
I HOPE BONZO DOESN'T GET DISTRACTED.
FINALLY!
IT'S TIME FOR A BIT OF MOVEMENT!

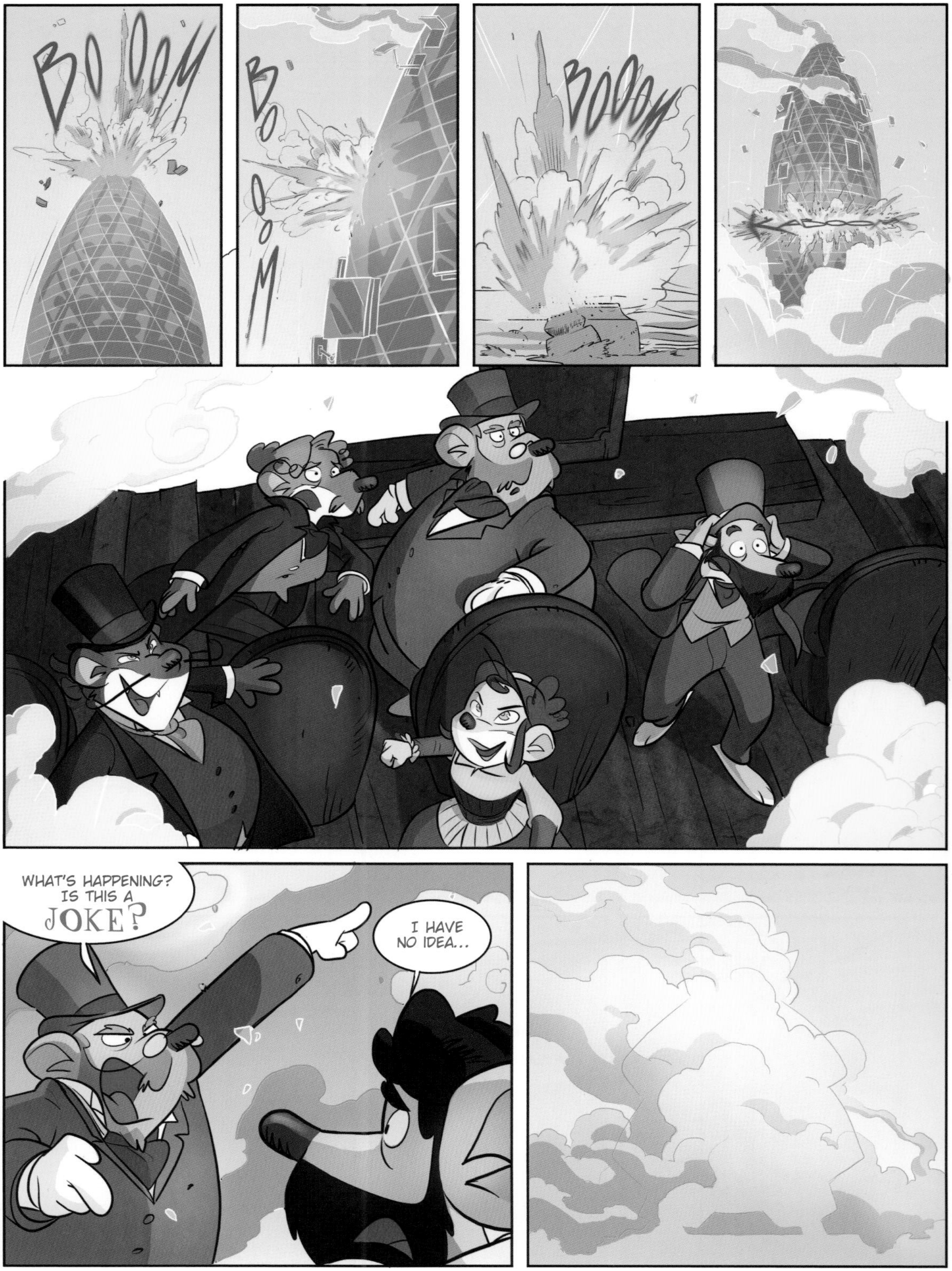
BOOOOM
BOOOOM
BOOOOM
WHAT'S HAPPENING? IS THIS A JOKE?
I HAVE NO IDEA...

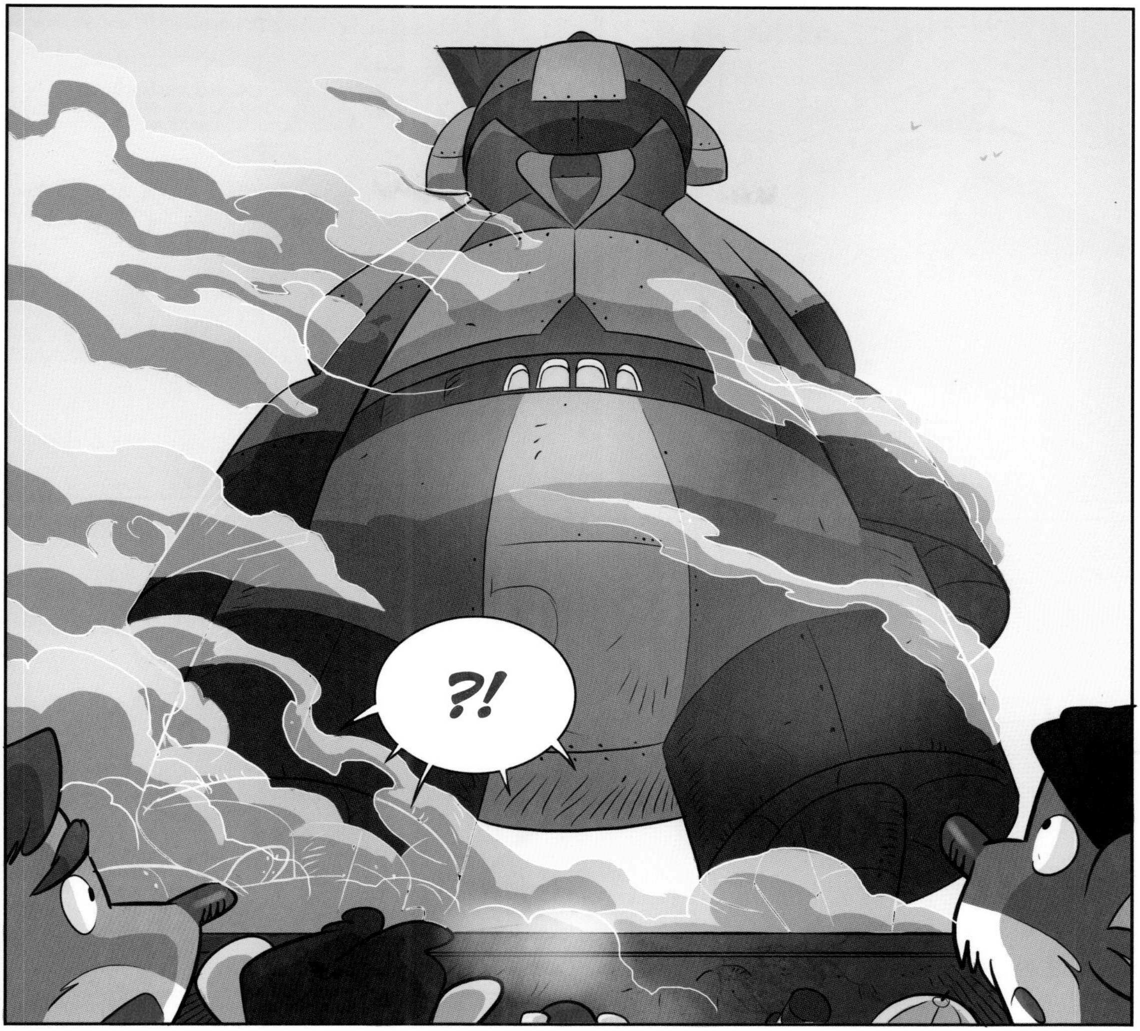
?!

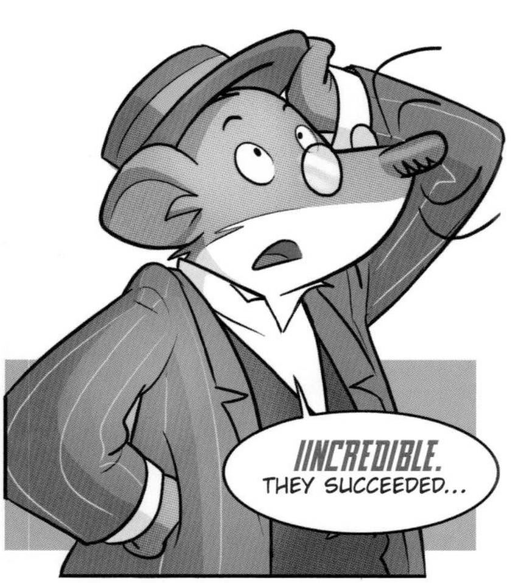
INCREDIBLE.
THEY SUCCEEDED...

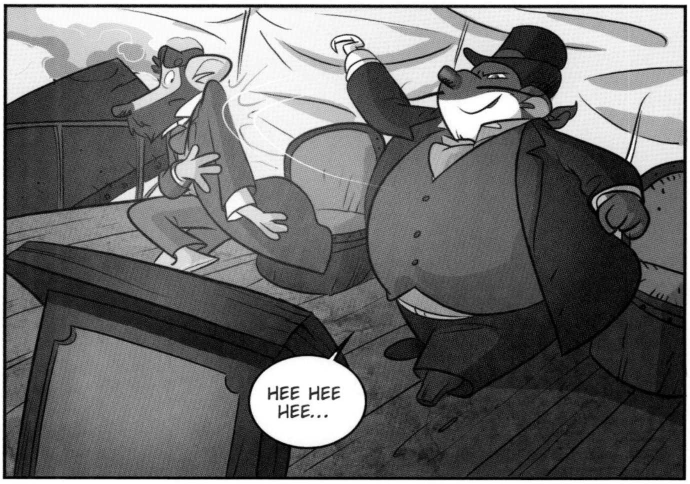
HEE HEE HEE...

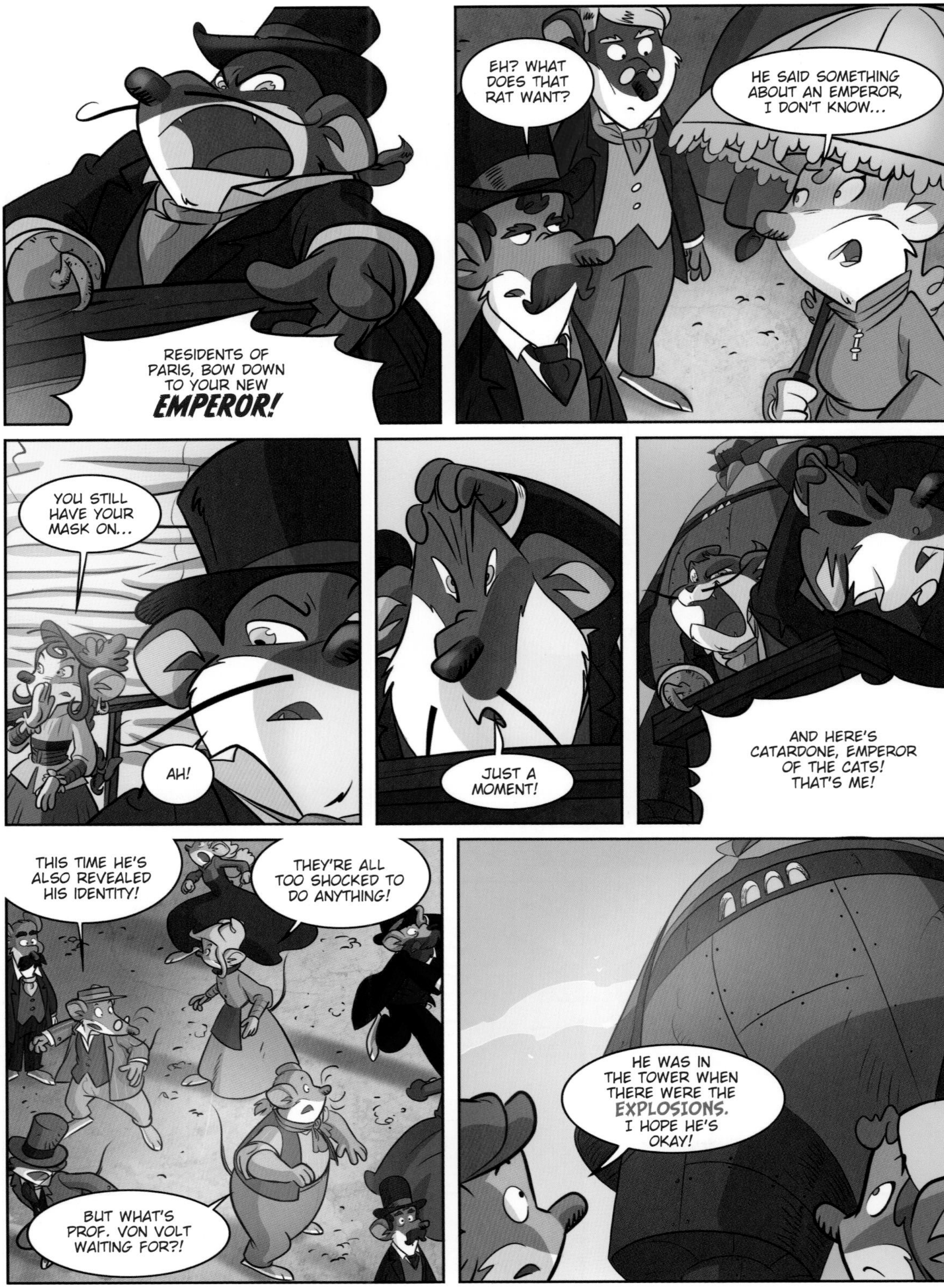
RESIDENTS OF PARIS, BOW DOWN TO YOUR NEW EMPEROR!
EH? WHAT DOES THAT RAT WANT?
HE SAID SOMETHING ABOUT AN EMPEROR, I DON'T KNOW...
YOU STILL HAVE YOUR MASK ON...
AH!
JUST A MOMENT!
AND HERE'S CATARDONE, EMPEROR OF THE CATS! THAT'S ME!
THIS TIME HE'S ALSO REVEALED HIS IDENTITY!
THEY'RE ALL TOO SHOCKED TO DO ANYTHING!
BUT WHAT'S PROF. VON VOLT WAITING FOR?!
HE WAS IN THE TOWER WHEN THERE WERE THE EXPLOSIONS. I HOPE HE'S OKAY!

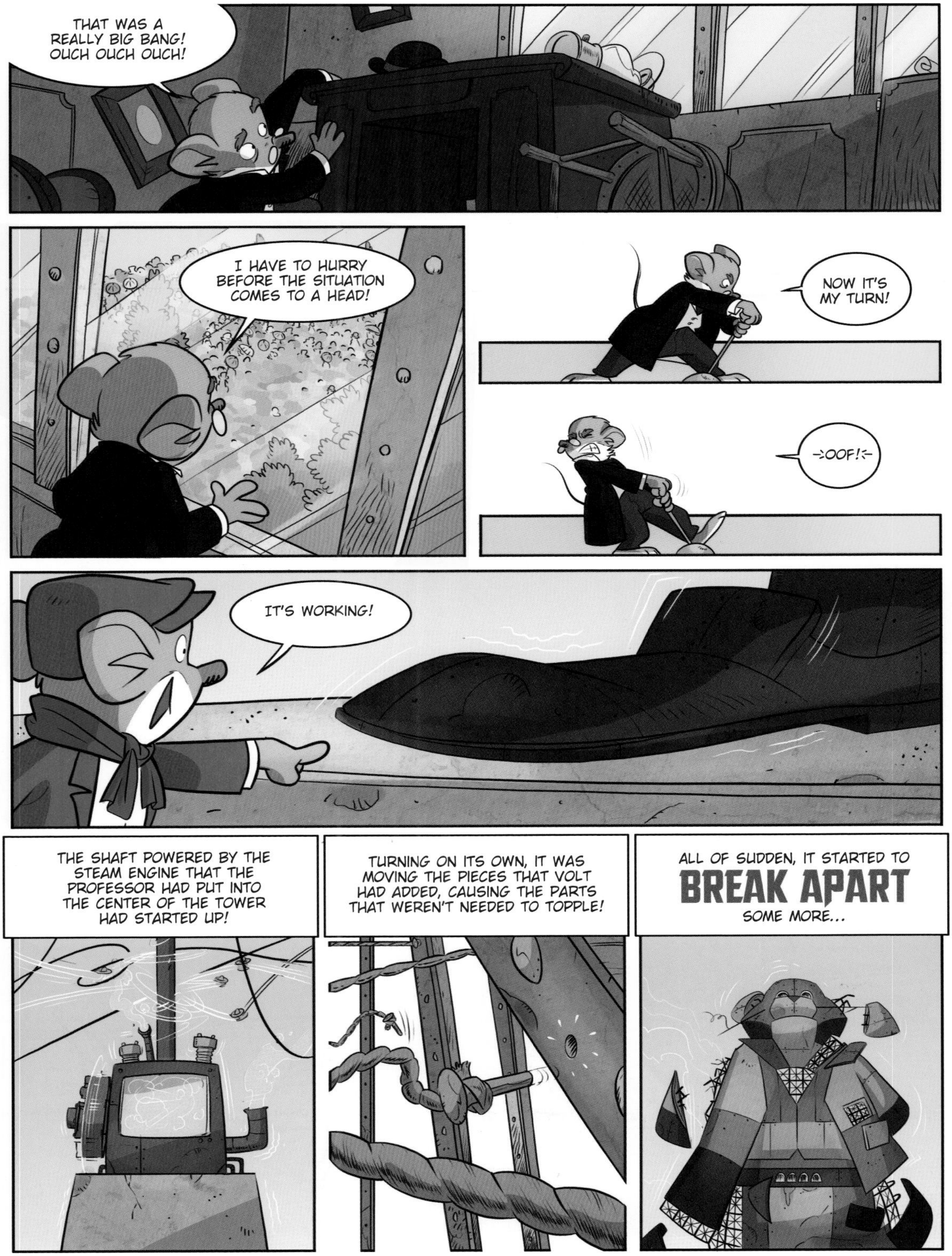
THAT WAS A REALLY BIG BANG! OUCH OUCH OUCH!
I HAVE TO HURRY BEFORE THE SITUATION COMES TO A HEAD!
NOW IT'S MY TURN!
OOF!
IT'S WORKING!
THE SHAFT POWERED BY THE STEAM ENGINE THAT THE PROFESSOR HAD PUT INTO THE CENTER OF THE TOWER HAD STARTED UP!
TURNING ON ITS OWN, IT WAS MOVING THE PIECES THAT VOLT HAD ADDED, CAUSING THE PARTS THAT WEREN'T NEEDED TO TOPPLE!
ALL OF SUDDEN, IT STARTED TO
BREAK APART
SOME MORE...

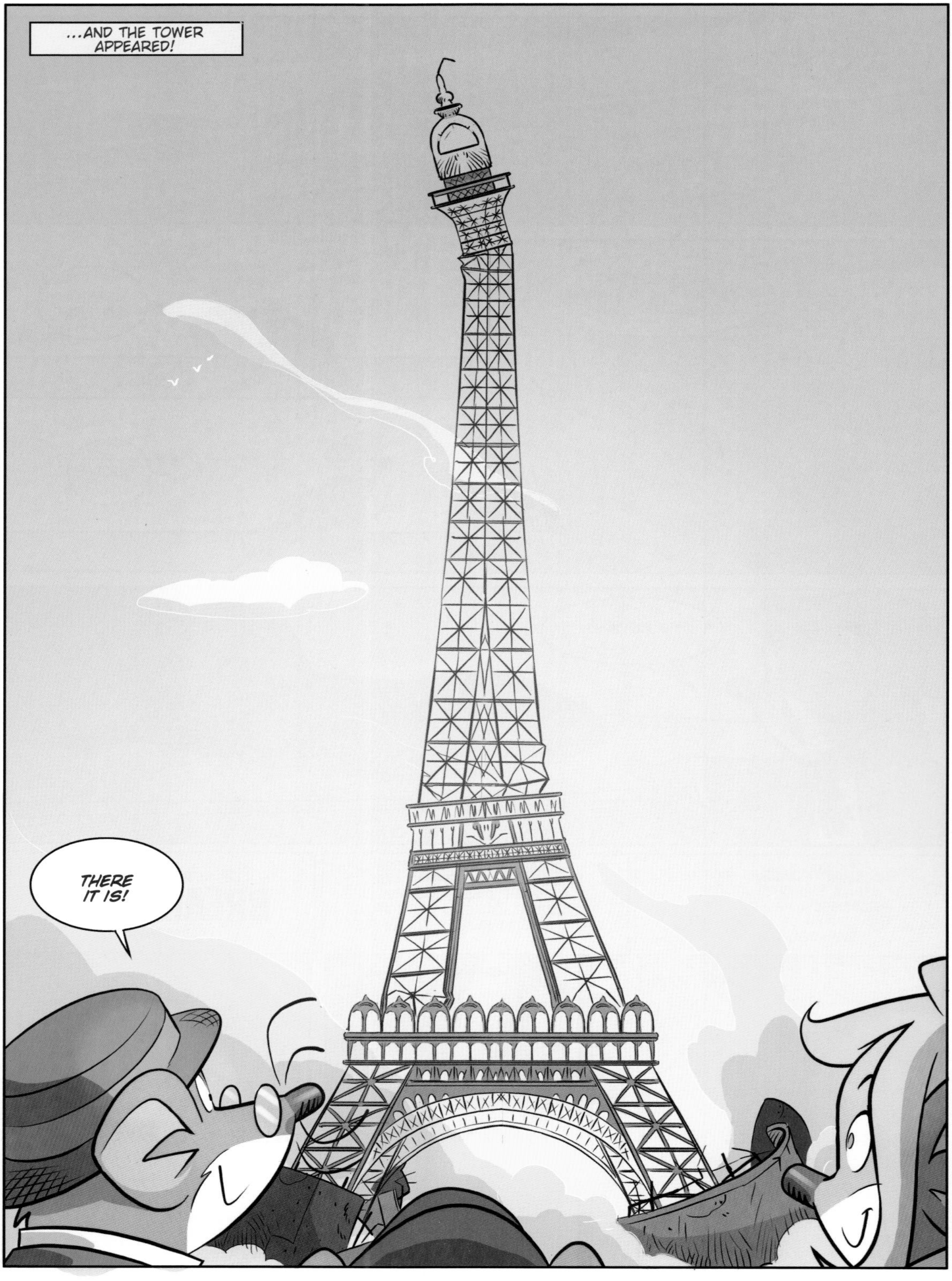
...AND THE TOWER APPEARED!
THERE IT IS!

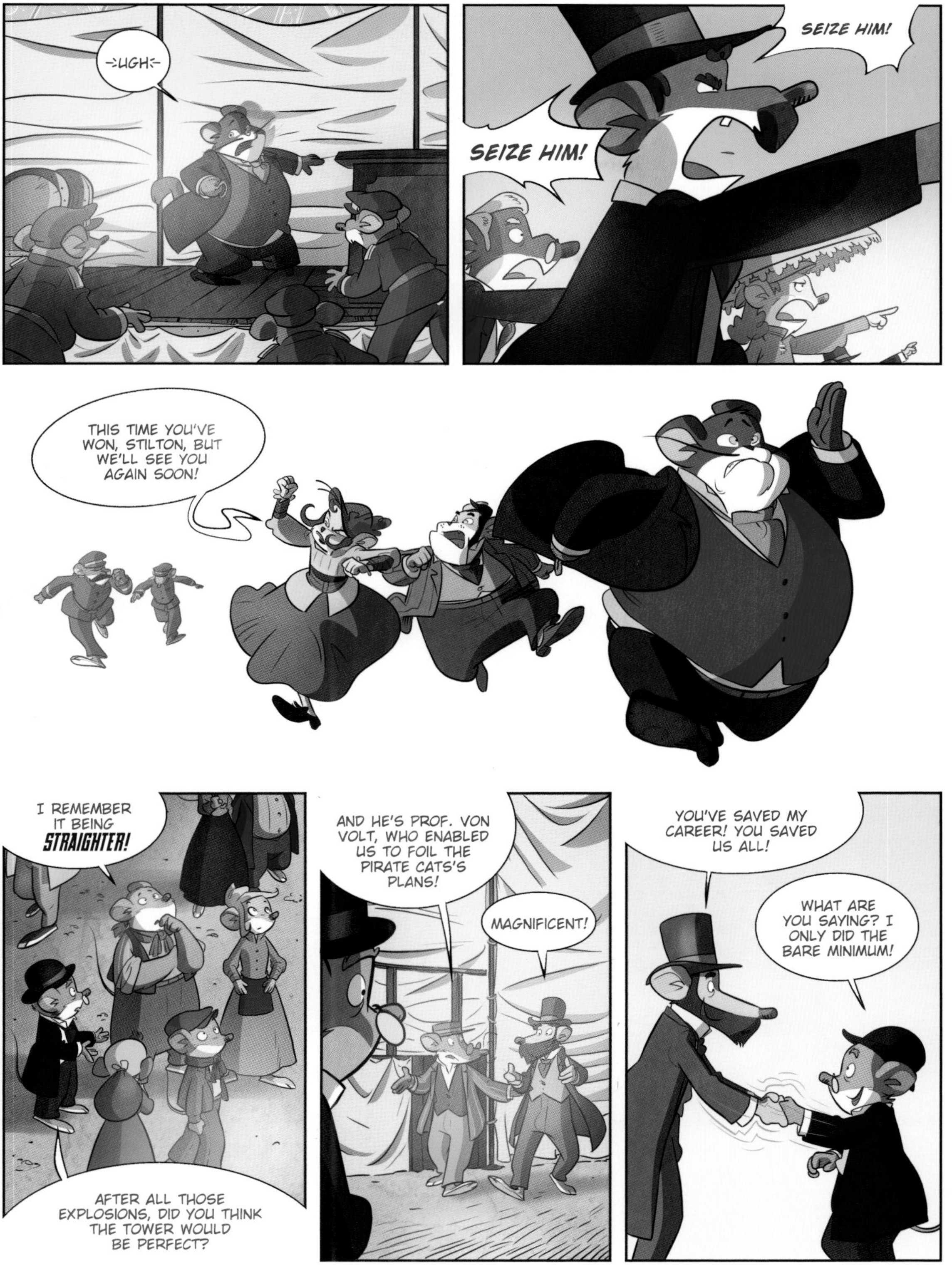

UGH
SEIZE HIM!
SEIZE HIM!
THIS TIME YOU'VE WON, STILTON, BUT WE'LL SEE YOU AGAIN SOON!
I REMEMBER IT BEING STRAIGHTER!
AFTER ALL THOSE EXPLOSIONS, DID YOU THINK THE TOWER WOULD BE PERFECT?
AND HE'S PROF. VON VOLT, WHO ENABLED US TO FOIL THE PIRATE CATS'S PLANS!
MAGNIFICENT!
YOU'VE SAVED MY CAREER! YOU SAVED US ALL!
WHAT ARE YOU SAYING? I ONLY DID THE BARE MINIMUM!

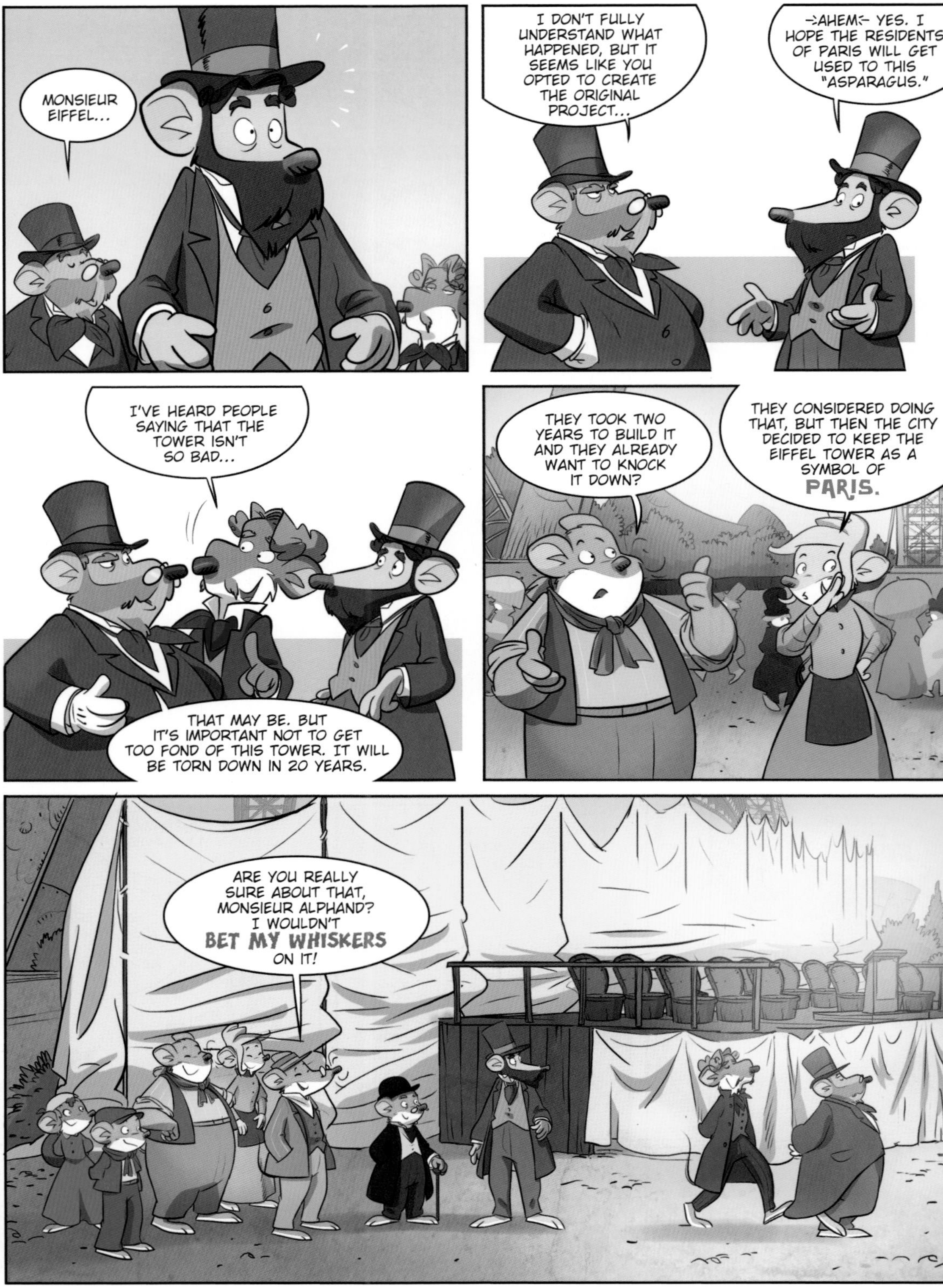
MONSIEUR EIFFEL...
I DON'T FULLY UNDERSTAND WHAT HAPPENED, BUT IT SEEMS LIKE YOU OPTED TO CREATE THE ORIGINAL PROJECT...
AHEM YES. I HOPE THE RESIDENTS OF PARIS WILL GET USED TO THIS "ASPARAGUS."
I'VE HEARD PEOPLE SAYING THAT THE TOWER ISN'T SO BAD...
THAT MAY BE. BUT IT'S IMPORTANT NOT TO GET TOO FOND OF THIS TOWER. IT WILL BE TORN DOWN IN 20 YEARS.
THEY TOOK TWO YEARS TO BUILD IT AND THEY ALREADY WANT TO KNOCK IT DOWN?
THEY CONSIDERED DOING THAT, BUT THEN THE CITY DECIDED TO KEEP THE EIFFEL TOWER AS A SYMBOL OF PARIS.
ARE YOU REALLY SURE ABOUT THAT, MONSIEUR ALPHAND? I WOULDN'T BET MY WHISKERS ON IT!

I'M LEAVING IN A FEW DAYS TO BUILD A BRIDGE. WOULD YOU LIKE TO COME WITH ME?

OH, I APPRECIATE THE OFFER, BUT I'M MORE OF A LABORATORY GUY, OR RATHER A LAB RAT!

IF YOU NEED HELP, I'M HERE!

NO, TODAY'S CRASHES ARE ENOUGH FOR THE REST OF MY CAREER, THANKS!

ALL THAT REMAINED FOR US WAS TO RETURN HOME...

HA HA HA!

HA HA HA!

HA HA HA!

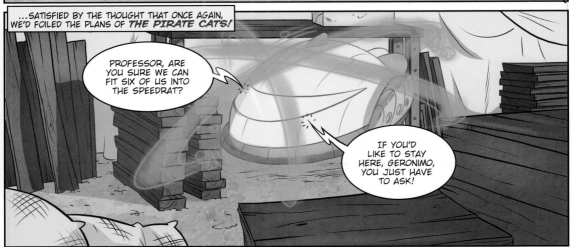

...SATISFIED BY THE THOUGHT THAT ONCE AGAIN, WE'D FOILED THE PLANS OF *THE PIRATE CATS!*

PROFESSOR, ARE YOU SURE WE CAN FIT SIX OF US INTO THE SPEEDRAT?

IF YOU'D LIKE TO STAY HERE, GERONIMO, YOU JUST HAVE TO ASK!

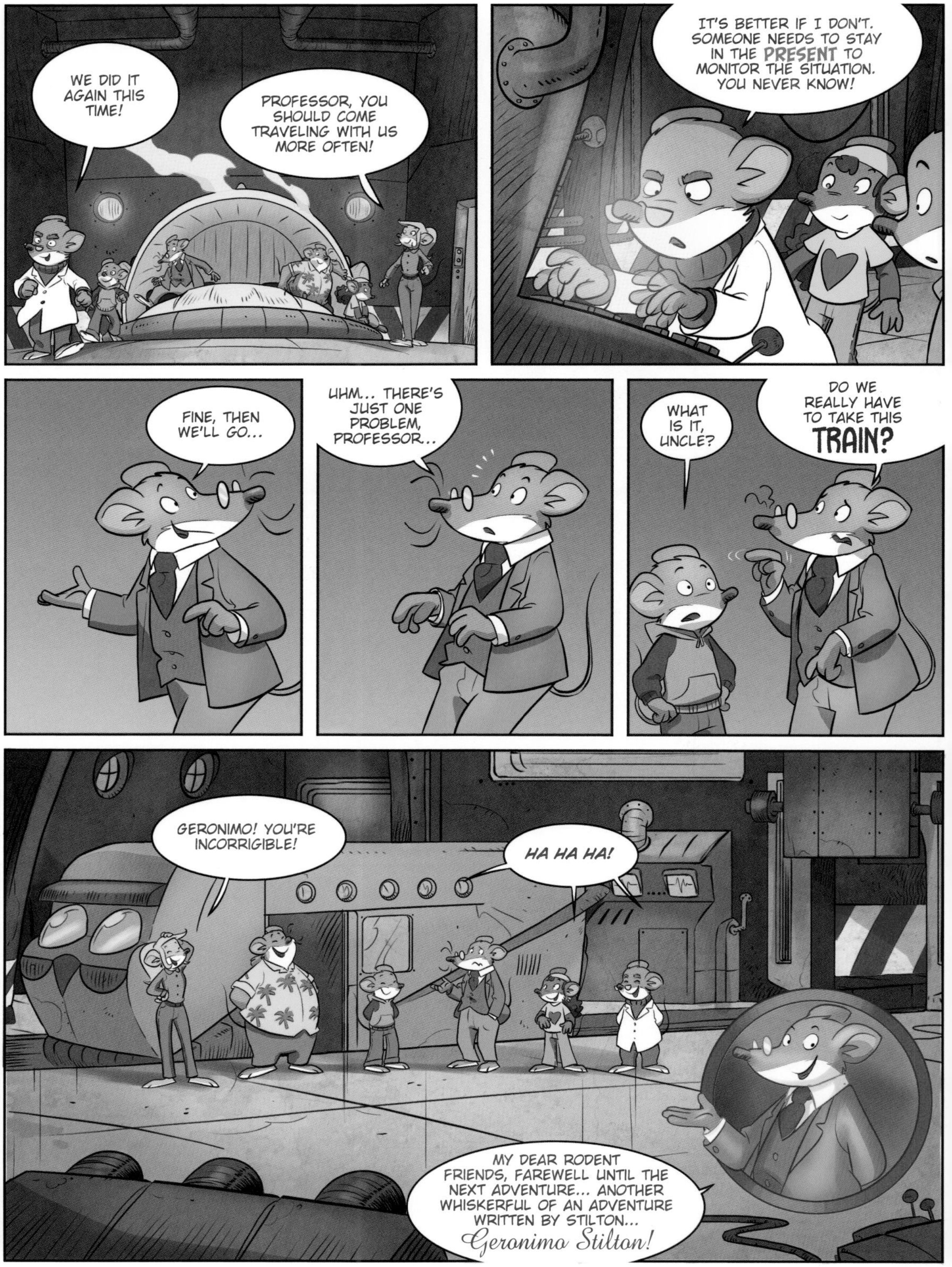
WE DID IT AGAIN THIS TIME!
PROFESSOR, YOU SHOULD COME TRAVELING WITH US MORE OFTEN!
IT'S BETTER IF I DON'T. SOMEONE NEEDS TO STAY IN THE PRESENT TO MONITOR THE SITUATION. YOU NEVER KNOW!
FINE, THEN WE'LL GO...
UHM... THERE'S JUST ONE PROBLEM, PROFESSOR...
WHAT IS IT, UNCLE?
DO WE REALLY HAVE TO TAKE THIS TRAIN?
GERONIMO! YOU'RE INCORRIGIBLE!
HA HA HA!
MY DEAR RODENT FRIENDS, FAREWELL UNTIL THE NEXT ADVENTURE... ANOTHER WHISKERFUL OF AN ADVENTURE WRITTEN BY STILTON...
Geronimo Stilton!

THE LAST SAMURAI

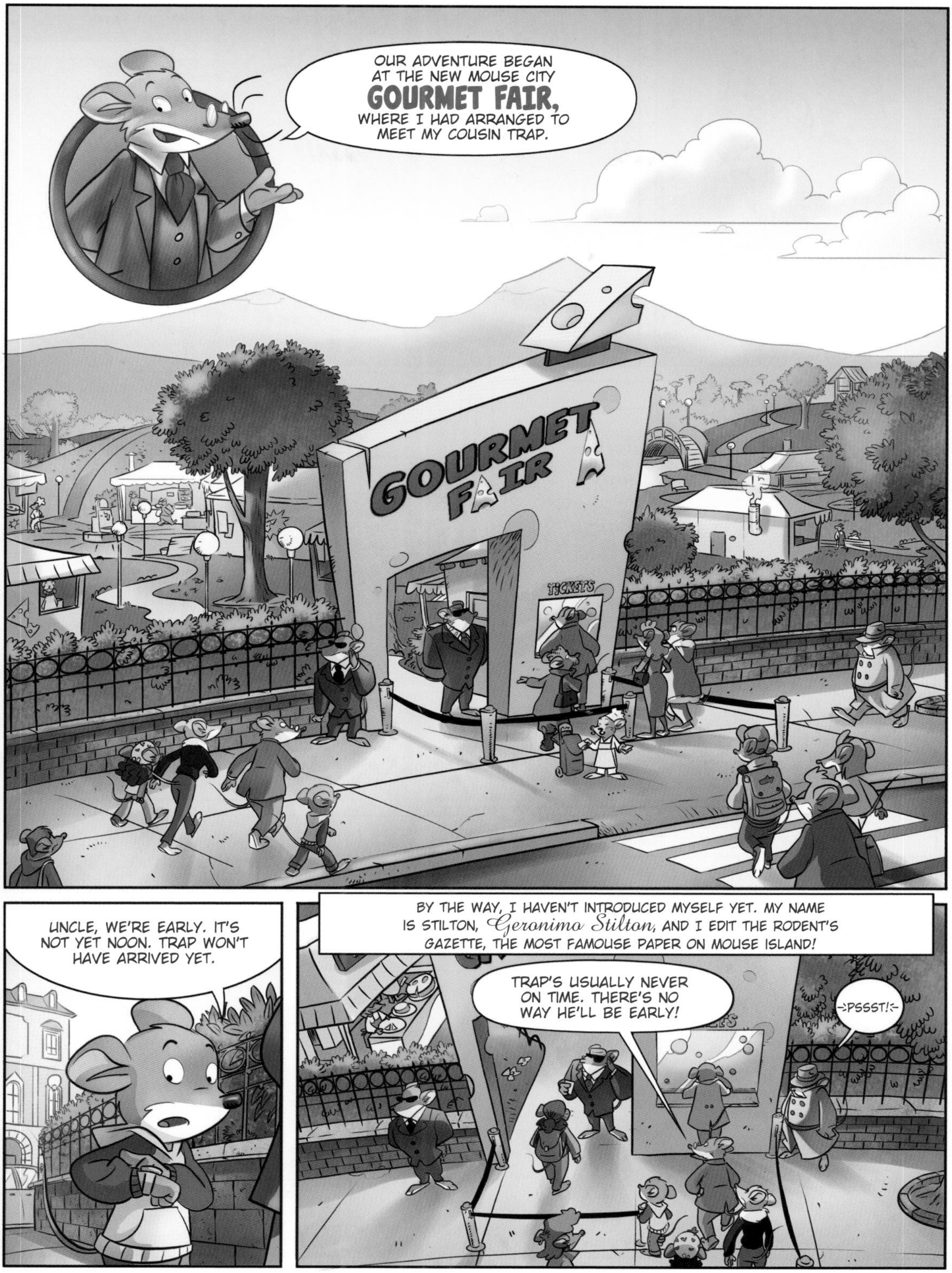
OUR ADVENTURE BEGAN AT THE NEW MOUSE CITY GOURMET FAIR, WHERE I HAD ARRANGED TO MEET MY COUSIN TRAP.
GOURMET FAIR
TICKETS
UNCLE, WE'RE EARLY. IT'S NOT YET NOON. TRAP WON'T HAVE ARRIVED YET.
BY THE WAY, I HAVEN'T INTRODUCED MYSELF YET. MY NAME IS STILTON, *Geronimo Stilton*, AND I EDIT THE RODENT'S GAZETTE, THE MOST FAMOUSE PAPER ON MOUSE ISLAND!
TRAP'S USUALLY NEVER ON TIME. THERE'S NO WAY HE'LL BE EARLY!
PSSST!

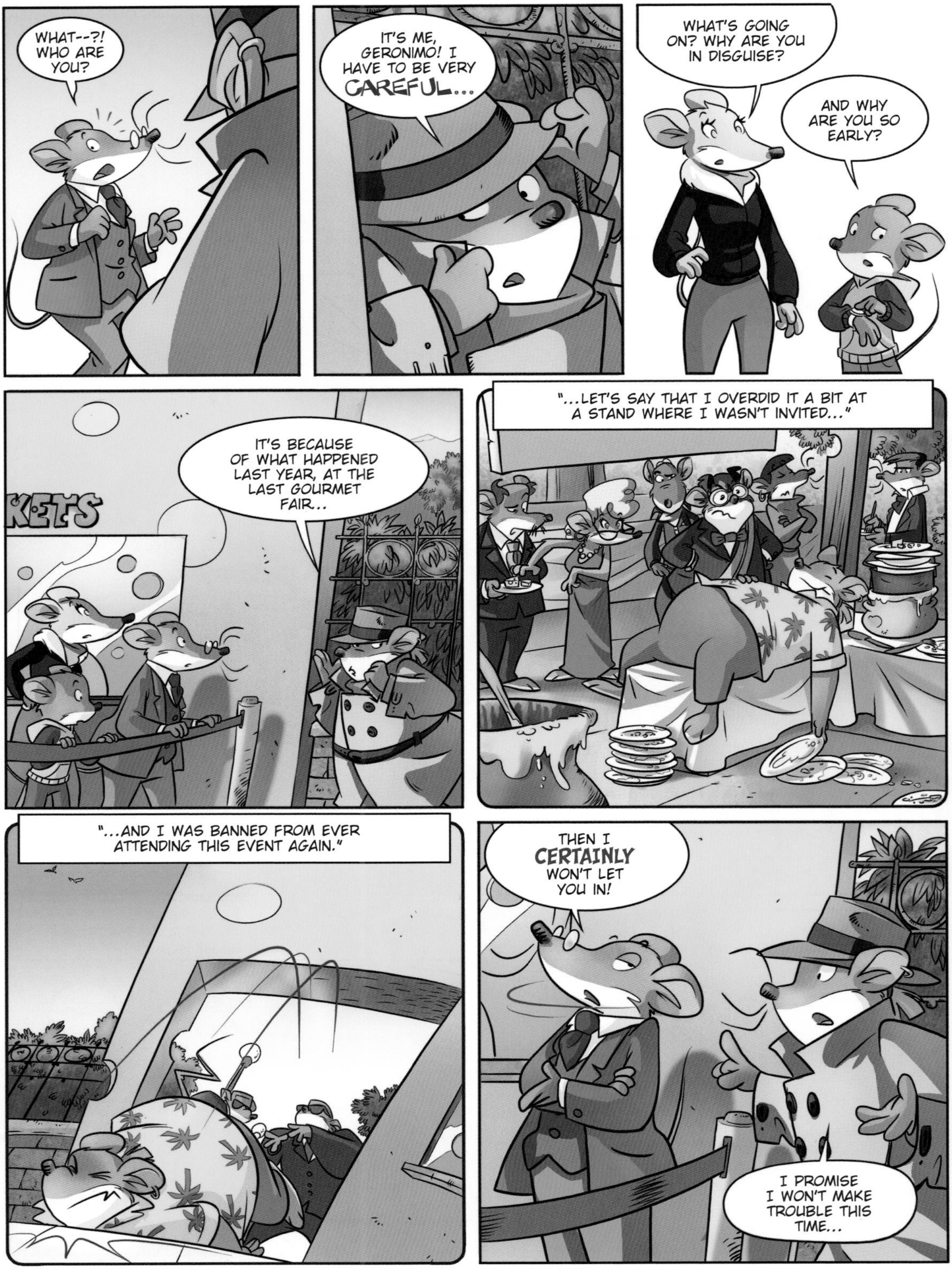
WHAT--?! WHO ARE YOU?
IT'S ME, GERONIMO! I HAVE TO BE VERY CAREFUL...
WHAT'S GOING ON? WHY ARE YOU IN DISGUISE?
AND WHY ARE YOU SO EARLY?
KETS
IT'S BECAUSE OF WHAT HAPPENED LAST YEAR, AT THE LAST GOURMET FAIR...
"...LET'S SAY THAT I OVERDID IT A BIT AT A STAND WHERE I WASN'T INVITED..."
"...AND I WAS BANNED FROM EVER ATTENDING THIS EVENT AGAIN."
THEN I CERTAINLY WON'T LET YOU IN!
I PROMISE I WON'T MAKE TROUBLE THIS TIME...

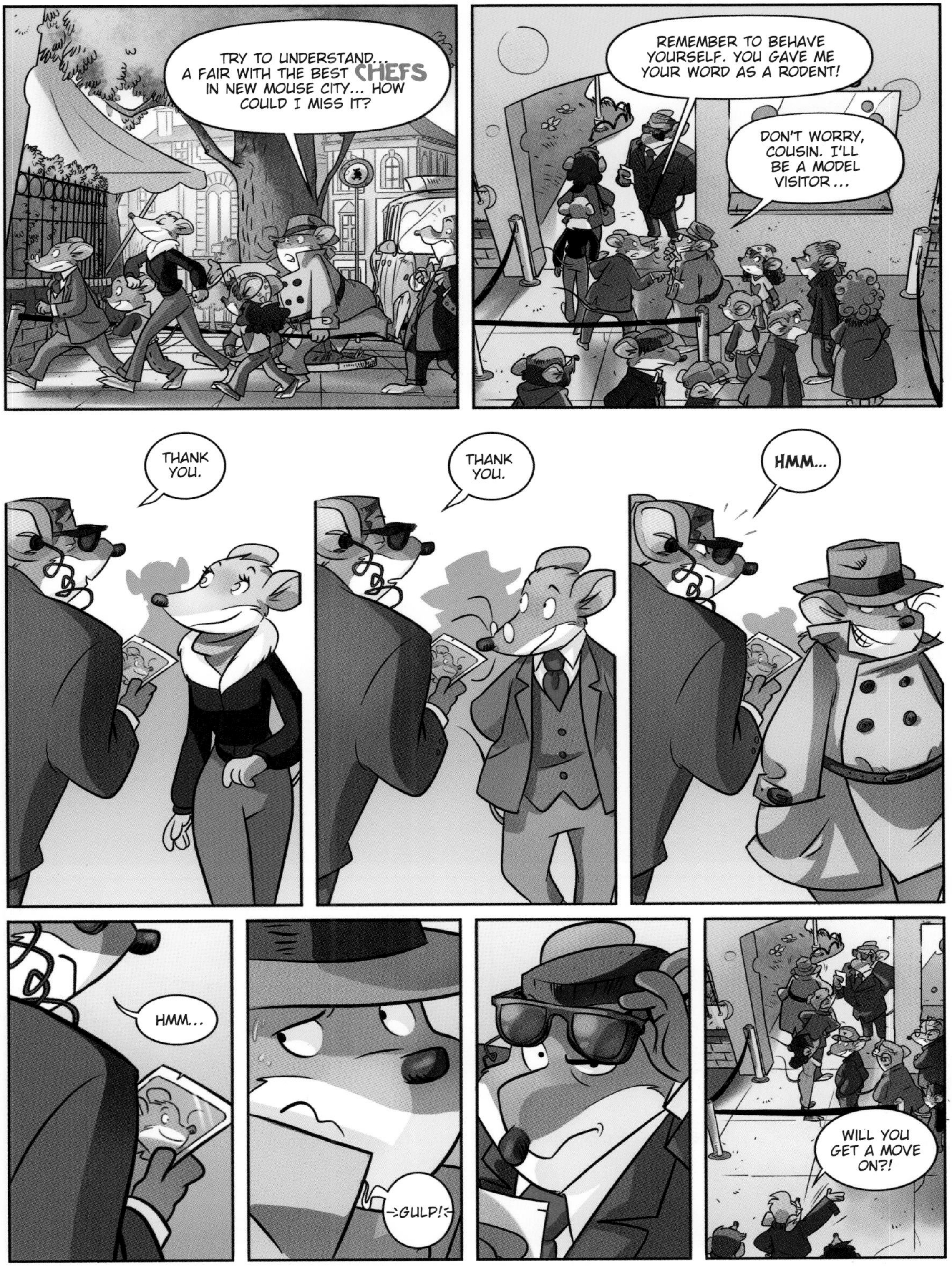
TRY TO UNDERSTAND... A FAIR WITH THE BEST CHEFS IN NEW MOUSE CITY... HOW COULD I MISS IT?
REMEMBER TO BEHAVE YOURSELF. YOU GAVE ME YOUR WORD AS A RODENT!
DON'T WORRY, COUSIN. I'LL BE A MODEL VISITOR...
THANK YOU.
THANK YOU.
HMM...
HMM...
GULP!
WILL YOU GET A MOVE ON?!

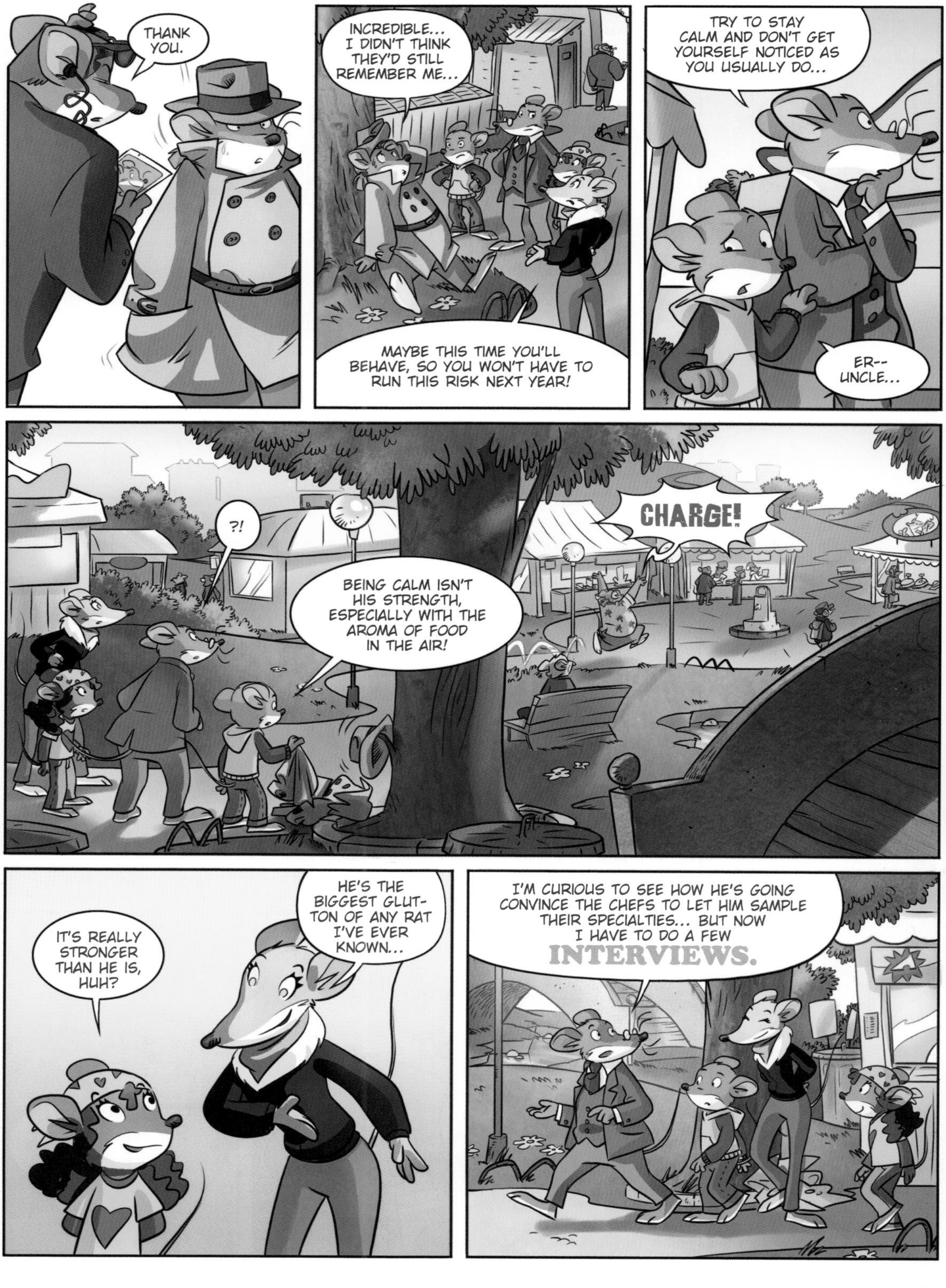
THANK YOU.
INCREDIBLE... I DIDN'T THINK THEY'D STILL REMEMBER ME...
MAYBE THIS TIME YOU'LL BEHAVE, SO YOU WON'T HAVE TO RUN THIS RISK NEXT YEAR!
TRY TO STAY CALM AND DON'T GET YOURSELF NOTICED AS YOU USUALLY DO...
ER-- UNCLE...
?!
CHARGE!
BEING CALM ISN'T HIS STRENGTH, ESPECIALLY WITH THE AROMA OF FOOD IN THE AIR!
IT'S REALLY STRONGER THAN HE IS, HUH?
HE'S THE BIGGEST GLUT-TON OF ANY RAT I'VE EVER KNOWN...
I'M CURIOUS TO SEE HOW HE'S GOING CONVINCE THE CHEFS TO LET HIM SAMPLE THEIR SPECIALTIES... BUT NOW I HAVE TO DO A FEW INTERVIEWS.

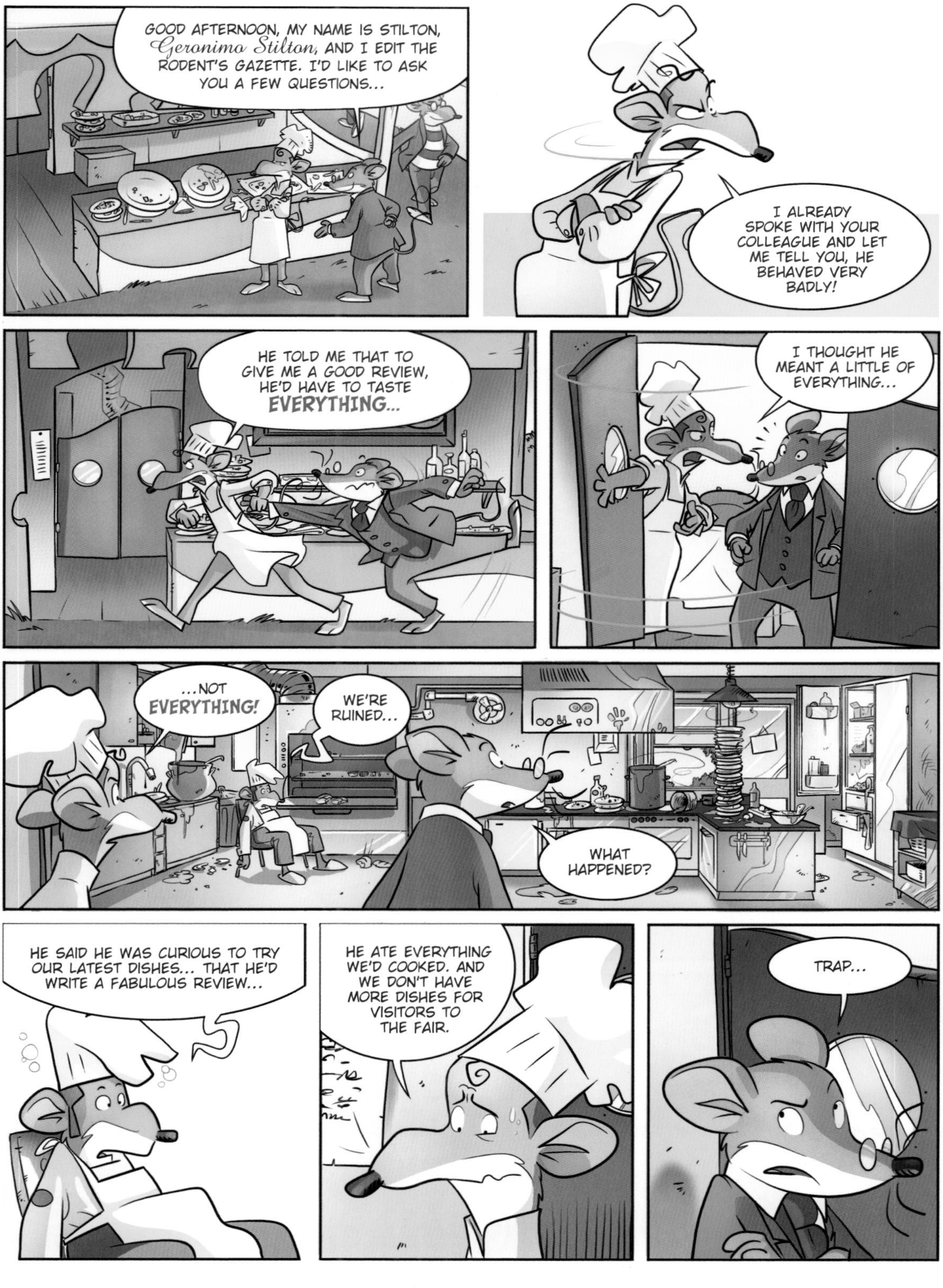
GOOD AFTERNOON, MY NAME IS STILTON, Geronimo Stilton, AND I EDIT THE RODENT'S GAZETTE. I'D LIKE TO ASK YOU A FEW QUESTIONS...
I ALREADY SPOKE WITH YOUR COLLEAGUE AND LET ME TELL YOU, HE BEHAVED VERY BADLY!
HE TOLD ME THAT TO GIVE ME A GOOD REVIEW, HE'D HAVE TO TASTE EVERYTHING...
I THOUGHT HE MEANT A LITTLE OF EVERYTHING...
...NOT EVERYTHING!
WE'RE RUINED...
WHAT HAPPENED?
HE SAID HE WAS CURIOUS TO TRY OUR LATEST DISHES... THAT HE'D WRITE A FABULOUS REVIEW...
HE ATE EVERYTHING WE'D COOKED. AND WE DON'T HAVE MORE DISHES FOR VISITORS TO THE FAIR.
TRAP...

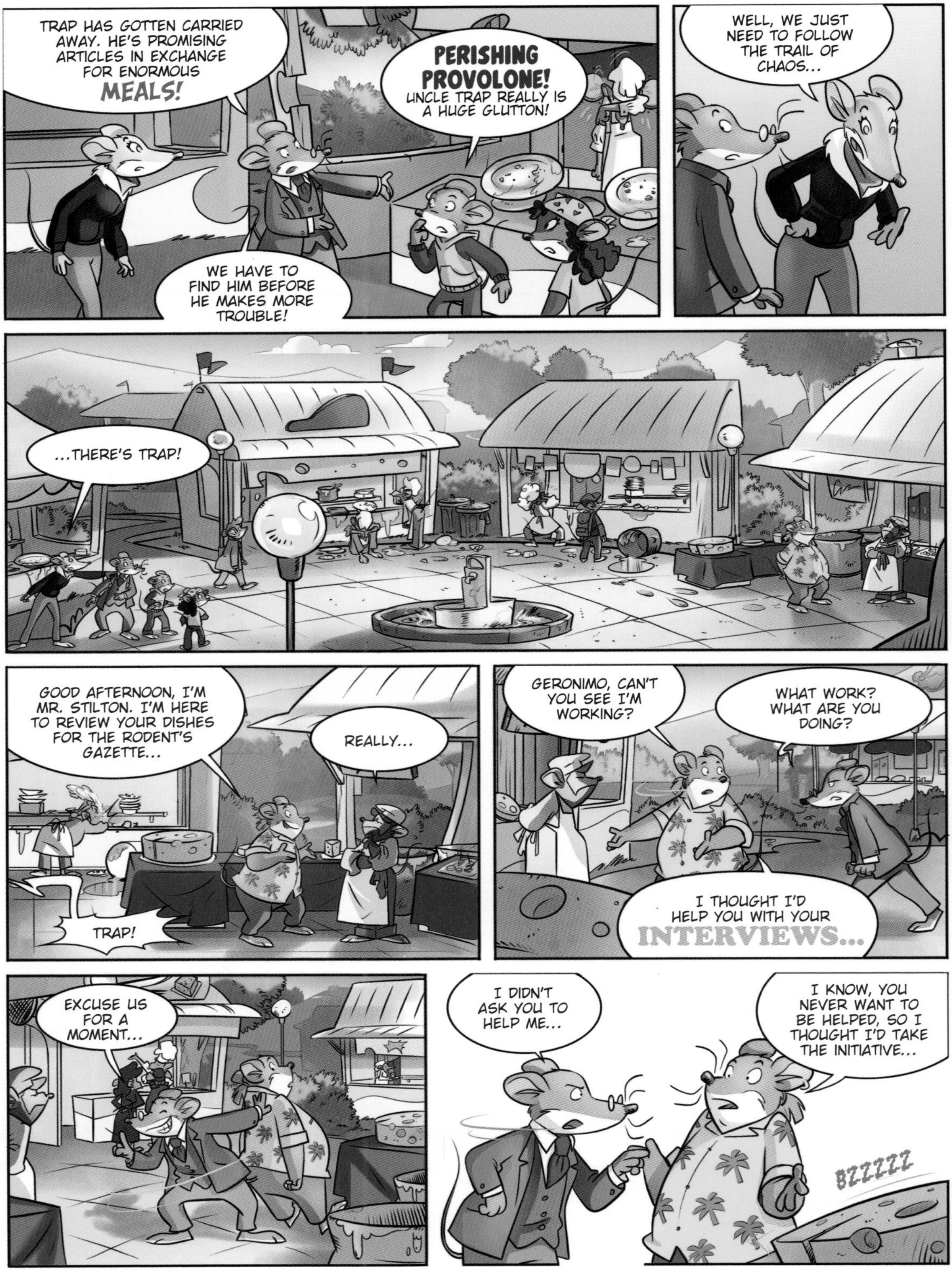

TRAP HAS GOTTEN CARRIED AWAY. HE'S PROMISING ARTICLES IN EXCHANGE FOR ENORMOUS MEALS!
PERISHING PROVOLONE! UNCLE TRAP REALLY IS A HUGE GLUTTON!
WE HAVE TO FIND HIM BEFORE HE MAKES MORE TROUBLE!
WELL, WE JUST NEED TO FOLLOW THE TRAIL OF CHAOS...
...THERE'S TRAP!
GOOD AFTERNOON, I'M MR. STILTON. I'M HERE TO REVIEW YOUR DISHES FOR THE RODENT'S GAZETTE...
REALLY...
TRAP!
GERONIMO, CAN'T YOU SEE I'M WORKING?
WHAT WORK? WHAT ARE YOU DOING?
I THOUGHT I'D HELP YOU WITH YOUR INTERVIEWS...
EXCUSE US FOR A MOMENT...
I DIDN'T ASK YOU TO HELP ME...
I KNOW, YOU NEVER WANT TO BE HELPED, SO I THOUGHT I'D TAKE THE INITIATIVE...
BZZZZZ

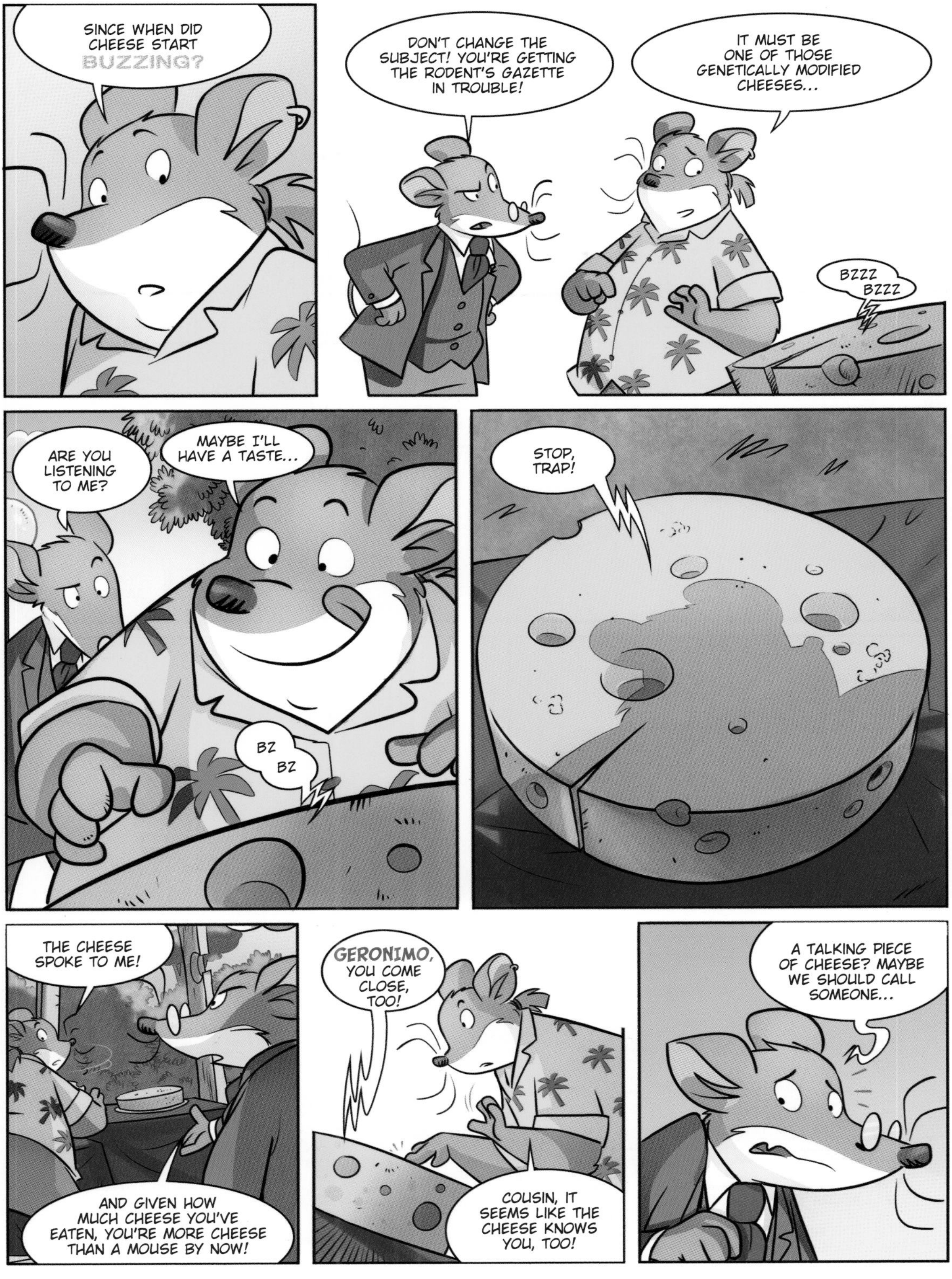
SINCE WHEN DID CHEESE START BUZZING?
DON'T CHANGE THE SUBJECT! YOU'RE GETTING THE RODENT'S GAZETTE IN TROUBLE!
IT MUST BE ONE OF THOSE GENETICALLY MODIFIED CHEESES...
BZZZ BZZZ
ARE YOU LISTENING TO ME?
MAYBE I'LL HAVE A TASTE...
BZ BZ
STOP, TRAP!
THE CHEESE SPOKE TO ME!
AND GIVEN HOW MUCH CHEESE YOU'VE EATEN, YOU'RE MORE CHEESE THAN A MOUSE BY NOW!
GERONIMO, YOU COME CLOSE, TOO!
COUSIN, IT SEEMS LIKE THE CHEESE KNOWS YOU, TOO!
A TALKING PIECE OF CHEESE? MAYBE WE SHOULD CALL SOMEONE...

WHAT CHEESE? IT IS I, PROFESSOR VON VOLT!

PROFESSOR, WHAT ARE YOU DOING HIDING IN A PIECE OF CHEESE?

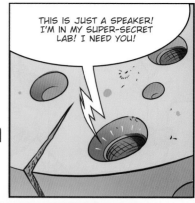

THIS IS JUST A SPEAKER! I'M IN MY SUPER-SECRET LAB! I NEED YOU!

UNCLE, I DON'T THINK IT'S....

I'M NOT *INSIDE* THE CHEESE!

WHAT HAPPENED? IS THERE A PROBLEM?

YES, THE TEMPOGRAPH, WHICH I USE TO MAKE SURE HISTORY IS NOT GETTING CHANGED, BEGAN **VIBRATING!**

THE PIRATE CATS?

I BELIEVE SO! THAT'S WHY I NEED TO YOU TO JOIN ME ASAP!

OKAY, BUT HOW CAN WE DO THAT?

YOU REALLY DON'T LIKE TO MAKE THINGS EASY, PROFESSOR!

SCIENCE WOULDN'T BE ANYTHING WITHOUT A TOUCH OF FANTASY... UH, TRAP?

YES?

THERE'S NO POINT INSPECTING IT. THE CHEESE IS *PLASTIC.*

OH.

I'VE PLACED AN ENTRANCE TO MY LABORATORY IN THE POT ON THE LEFT. YOU JUST HAVE TO GET INTO IT AND A PNEUMATIC TUBE WILL BRING YOU TO ME.

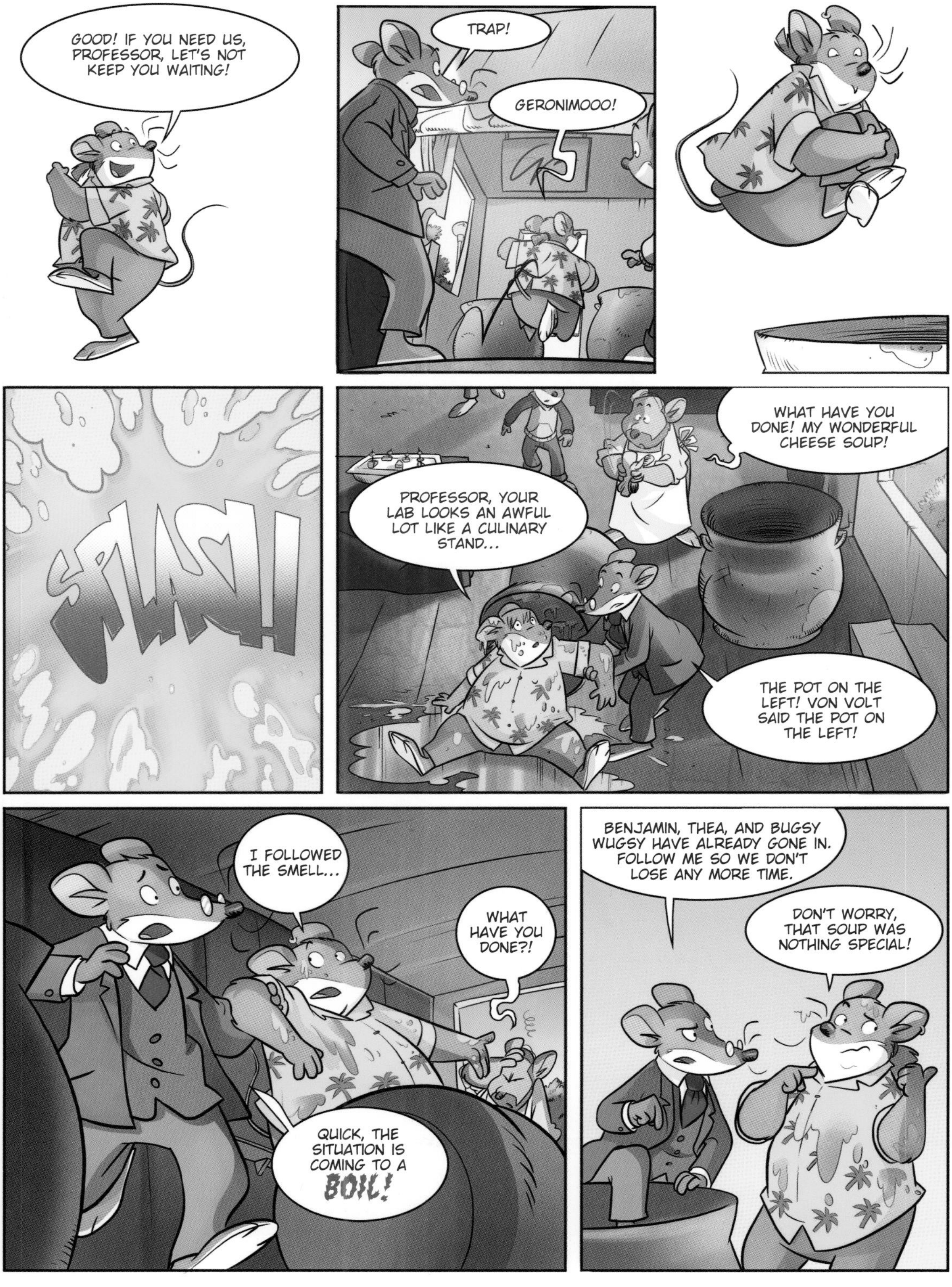
GOOD! IF YOU NEED US, PROFESSOR, LET'S NOT KEEP YOU WAITING!
TRAP!
GERONIMOOO!
SPLASH!
WHAT HAVE YOU DONE! MY WONDERFUL CHEESE SOUP!
PROFESSOR, YOUR LAB LOOKS AN AWFUL LOT LIKE A CULINARY STAND...
THE POT ON THE LEFT! VON VOLT SAID THE POT ON THE LEFT!
I FOLLOWED THE SMELL...
WHAT HAVE YOU DONE?!
QUICK, THE SITUATION IS COMING TO A BOIL!
BENJAMIN, THEA, AND BUGSY WUGSY HAVE ALREADY GONE IN. FOLLOW ME SO WE DON'T LOSE ANY MORE TIME.
DON'T WORRY, THAT SOUP WAS NOTHING SPECIAL!

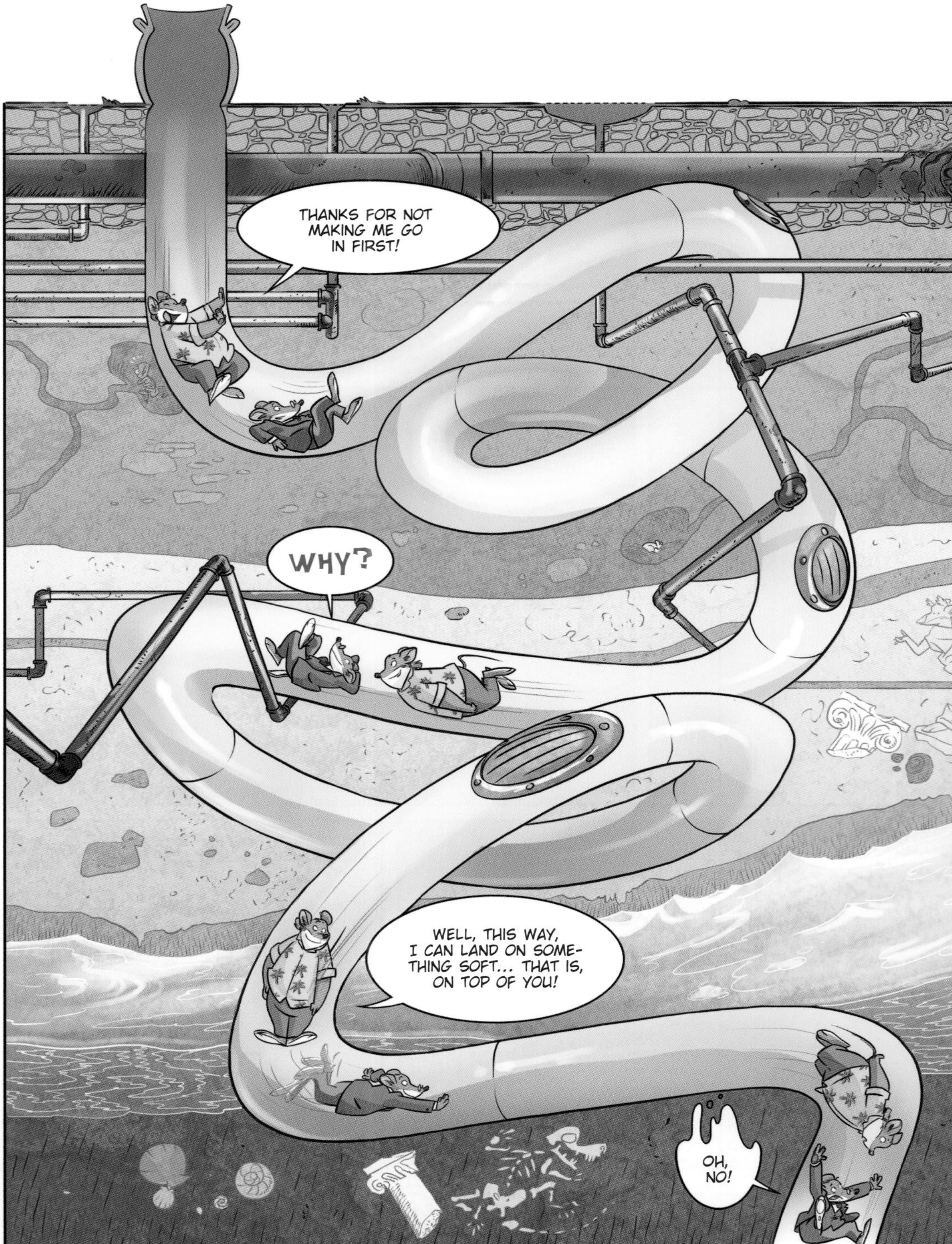
THANKS FOR NOT MAKING ME GO IN FIRST!
WHY?
WELL, THIS WAY, I CAN LAND ON SOME-THING SOFT... THAT IS, ON TOP OF YOU!
OH, NO!

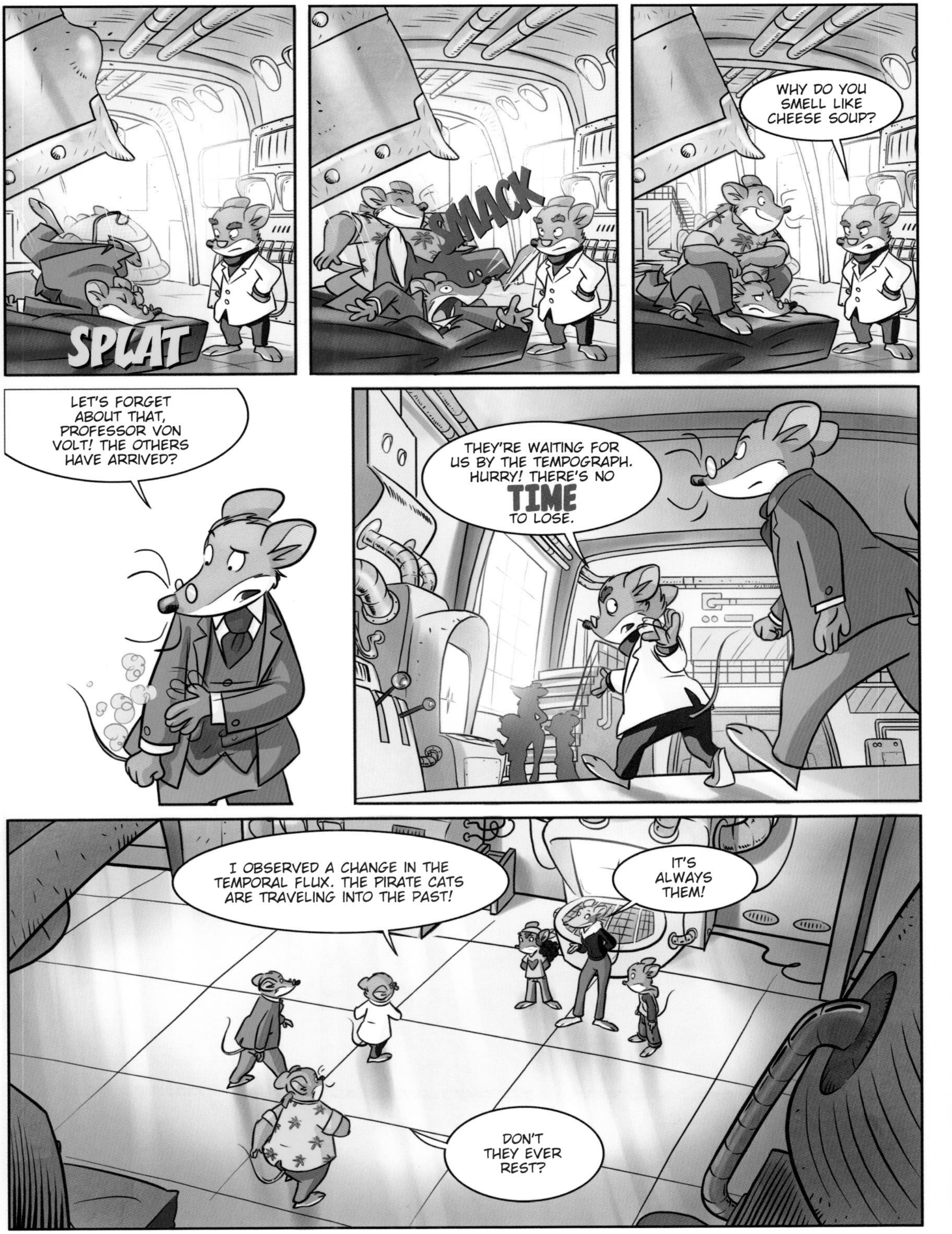
SPLAT
SMACK
WHY DO YOU SMELL LIKE CHEESE SOUP?
LET'S FORGET ABOUT THAT, PROFESSOR VON VOLT! THE OTHERS HAVE ARRIVED?
THEY'RE WAITING FOR US BY THE TEMPOGRAPH. HURRY! THERE'S NO TIME TO LOSE.
I OBSERVED A CHANGE IN THE TEMPORAL FLUX. THE PIRATE CATS ARE TRAVELING INTO THE PAST!
IT'S ALWAYS THEM!
DON'T THEY EVER REST?

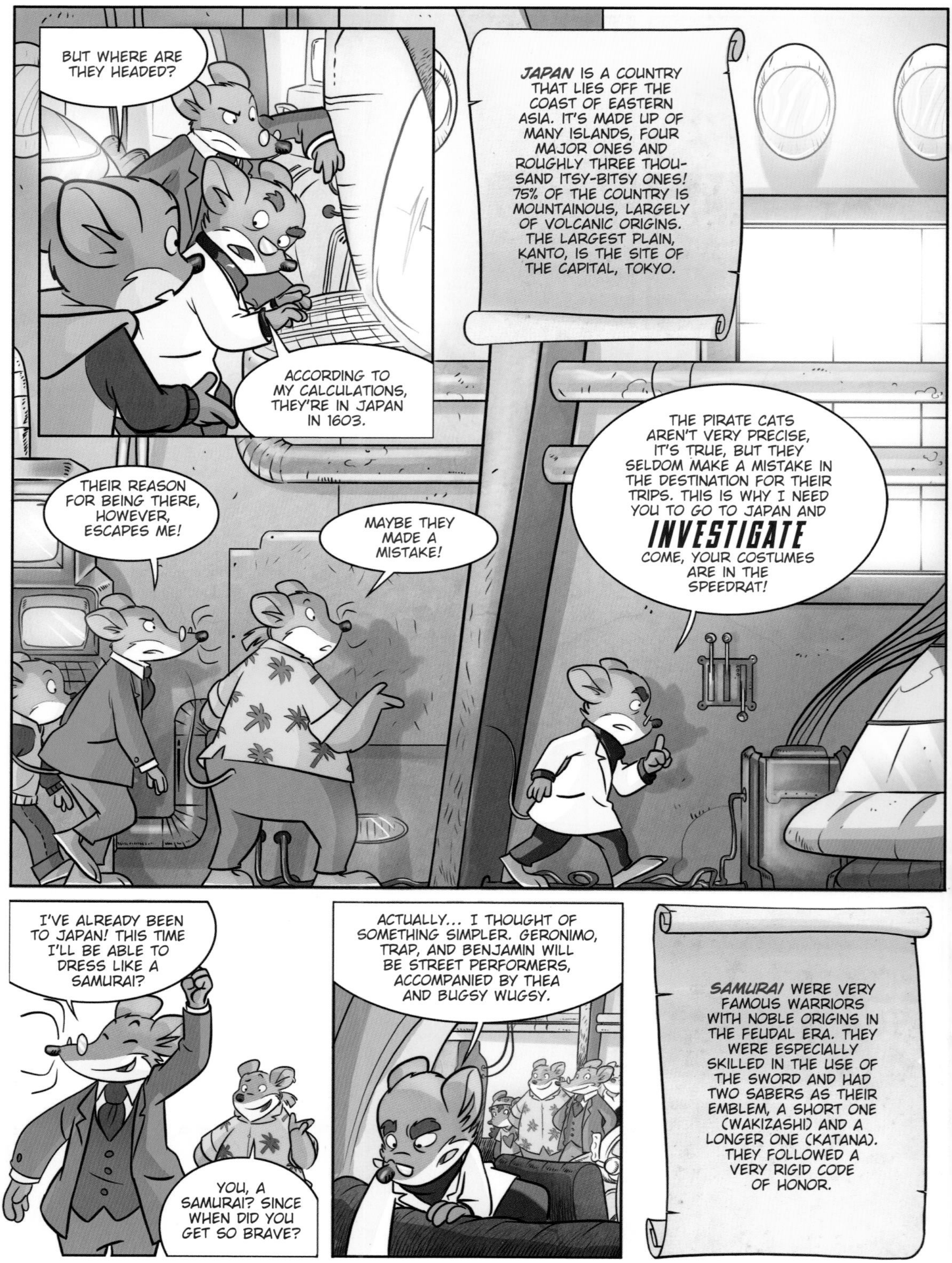
BUT WHERE ARE THEY HEADED?
JAPAN IS A COUNTRY THAT LIES OFF THE COAST OF EASTERN ASIA. IT'S MADE UP OF MANY ISLANDS, FOUR MAJOR ONES AND ROUGHLY THREE THOUSAND ITSY-BITSY ONES! 75% OF THE COUNTRY IS MOUNTAINOUS, LARGELY OF VOLCANIC ORIGINS. THE LARGEST PLAIN, KANTO, IS THE SITE OF THE CAPITAL, TOKYO.
ACCORDING TO MY CALCULATIONS, THEY'RE IN JAPAN IN 1603.
THEIR REASON FOR BEING THERE, HOWEVER, ESCAPES ME!
MAYBE THEY MADE A MISTAKE!
THE PIRATE CATS AREN'T VERY PRECISE, IT'S TRUE, BUT THEY SELDOM MAKE A MISTAKE IN THE DESTINATION FOR THEIR TRIPS. THIS IS WHY I NEED YOU TO GO TO JAPAN AND INVESTIGATE
COME, YOUR COSTUMES ARE IN THE SPEEDRAT!
I'VE ALREADY BEEN TO JAPAN! THIS TIME I'LL BE ABLE TO DRESS LIKE A SAMURAI?
YOU, A SAMURAI? SINCE WHEN DID YOU GET SO BRAVE?
ACTUALLY... I THOUGHT OF SOMETHING SIMPLER. GERONIMO, TRAP, AND BENJAMIN WILL BE STREET PERFORMERS, ACCOMPANIED BY THEA AND BUGSY WUGSY.
SAMURAI WERE VERY FAMOUS WARRIORS WITH NOBLE ORIGINS IN THE FEUDAL ERA. THEY WERE ESPECIALLY SKILLED IN THE USE OF THE SWORD AND HAD TWO SABERS AS THEIR EMBLEM, A SHORT ONE (WAKIZASHI) AND A LONGER ONE (KATANA). THEY FOLLOWED A VERY RIGID CODE OF HONOR.

VERY GOOD. THE COSTUMES ARE ALL HERE AND ALSO THE EQUIPMENT THAT WILL LET YOU UNDERSTAND THE LANGUAGE OF THE TIME. NOW, HURRY UP! YOU HAVE TO PREVENT THE CATS FROM CHANGING THE PAST!

DON'T WORRY, PROFESSOR, WE'LL SEE TO IT!

WHERE EXACTLY ARE WE HEADED?

YOU'LL ARRIVE A LITTLE BIT AWAY FROM EDO, THE ANCIENT NAME FOR TOKYO. HIDE THE SPEEDRAT AND DISGUISE YOURSELVES WITHOUT ANYONE DISCOVERING YOU!

TOKYO HAS BEEN THE CAPITAL OF JAPAN SINCE 1868, WHEN THE EMPEROR DECIDED TO MOVE THE SEAT OF THE GOVERNMENT AND HIS OWN RESIDENCE THERE. UNTIL THEN, IT HAD BEEN CALLED EDO, FROM THE NAME OF THE CASTLE (NAMED EDO-JO, BUILT IN 1457) THAT DOMINATED THE AREA.

THE PREPARATIONS WERE ALL MADE. ALL THAT WAS LEFT WAS TO BEGIN THE MISSION...

VRRRRRRR

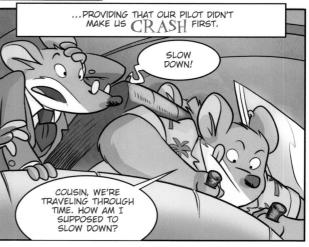

...PROVIDING THAT OUR PILOT DIDN'T MAKE US **CRASH** FIRST.

SLOW DOWN!

COUSIN, WE'RE TRAVELING THROUGH TIME. HOW AM I SUPPOSED TO SLOW DOWN?

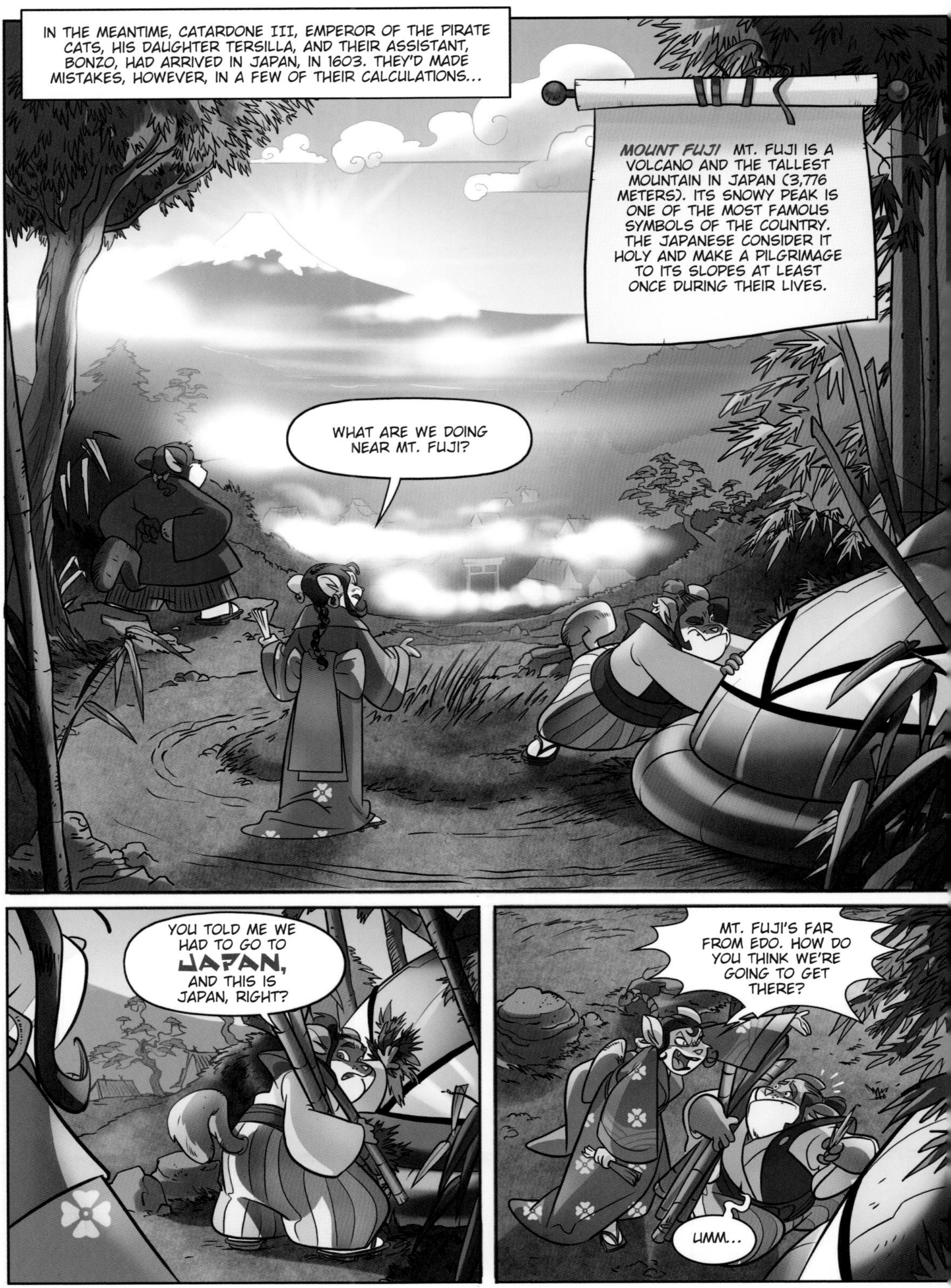
IN THE MEANTIME, CATARDONE III, EMPEROR OF THE PIRATE CATS, HIS DAUGHTER TERSILLA, AND THEIR ASSISTANT, BONZO, HAD ARRIVED IN JAPAN, IN 1603. THEY'D MADE MISTAKES, HOWEVER, IN A FEW OF THEIR CALCULATIONS...
MOUNT FUJI MT. FUJI IS A VOLCANO AND THE TALLEST MOUNTAIN IN JAPAN (3,776 METERS). ITS SNOWY PEAK IS ONE OF THE MOST FAMOUS SYMBOLS OF THE COUNTRY. THE JAPANESE CONSIDER IT HOLY AND MAKE A PILGRIMAGE TO ITS SLOPES AT LEAST ONCE DURING THEIR LIVES.
WHAT ARE WE DOING NEAR MT. FUJI?
YOU TOLD ME WE HAD TO GO TO JAPAN, AND THIS IS JAPAN, RIGHT?
MT. FUJI'S FAR FROM EDO. HOW DO YOU THINK WE'RE GOING TO GET THERE?
UMM...

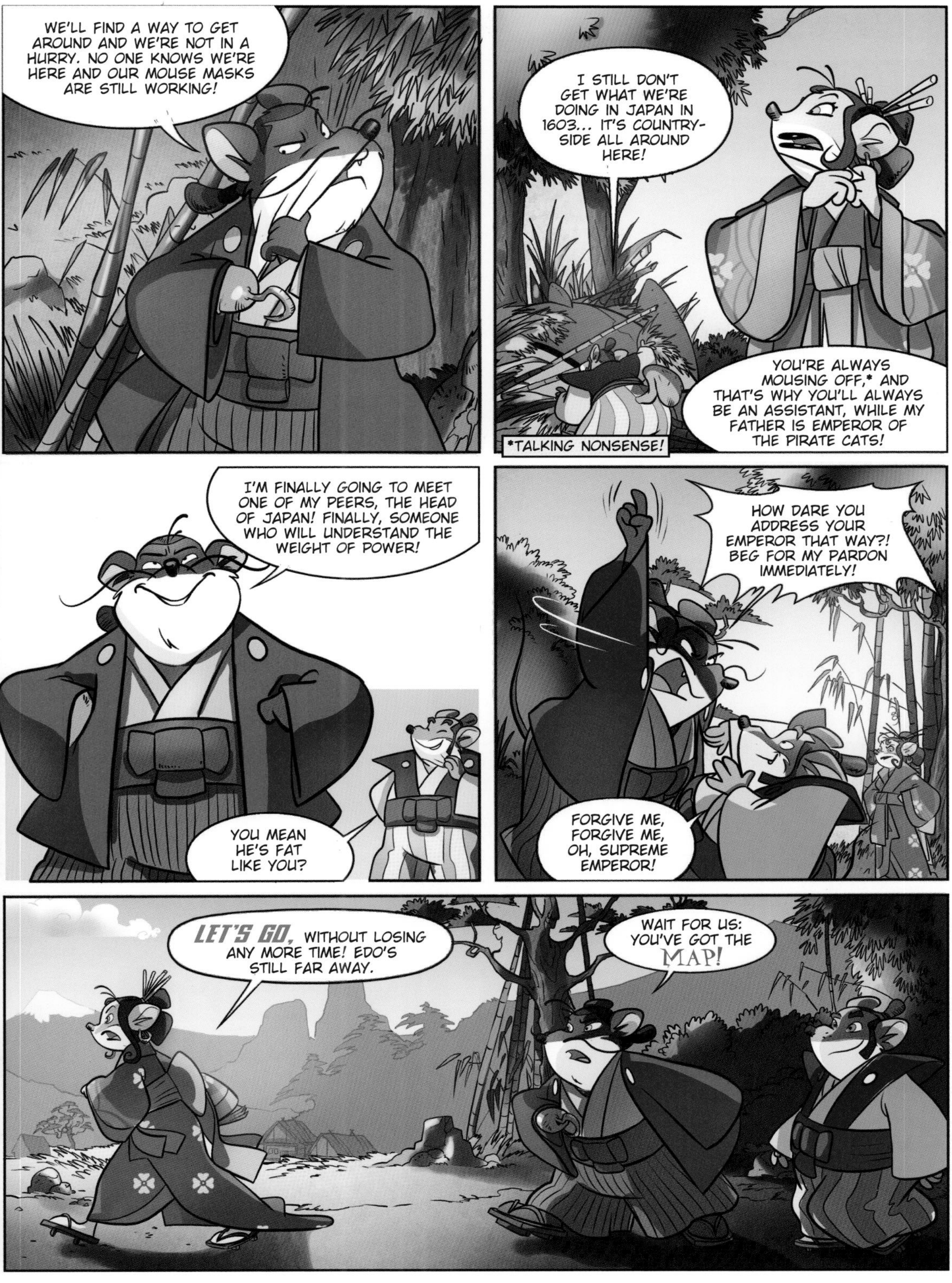
WE'LL FIND A WAY TO GET AROUND AND WE'RE NOT IN A HURRY. NO ONE KNOWS WE'RE HERE AND OUR MOUSE MASKS ARE STILL WORKING!
I STILL DON'T GET WHAT WE'RE DOING IN JAPAN IN 1603... IT'S COUNTRYSIDE ALL AROUND HERE!
YOU'RE ALWAYS MOUSING OFF,* AND THAT'S WHY YOU'LL ALWAYS BE AN ASSISTANT, WHILE MY FATHER IS EMPEROR OF THE PIRATE CATS!
*TALKING NONSENSE!
I'M FINALLY GOING TO MEET ONE OF MY PEERS, THE HEAD OF JAPAN! FINALLY, SOMEONE WHO WILL UNDERSTAND THE WEIGHT OF POWER!
YOU MEAN HE'S FAT LIKE YOU?
HOW DARE YOU ADDRESS YOUR EMPEROR THAT WAY?! BEG FOR MY PARDON IMMEDIATELY!
FORGIVE ME, FORGIVE ME, OH, SUPREME EMPEROR!
LET'S GO, WITHOUT LOSING ANY MORE TIME! EDO'S STILL FAR AWAY.
WAIT FOR US: YOU'VE GOT THE MAP!

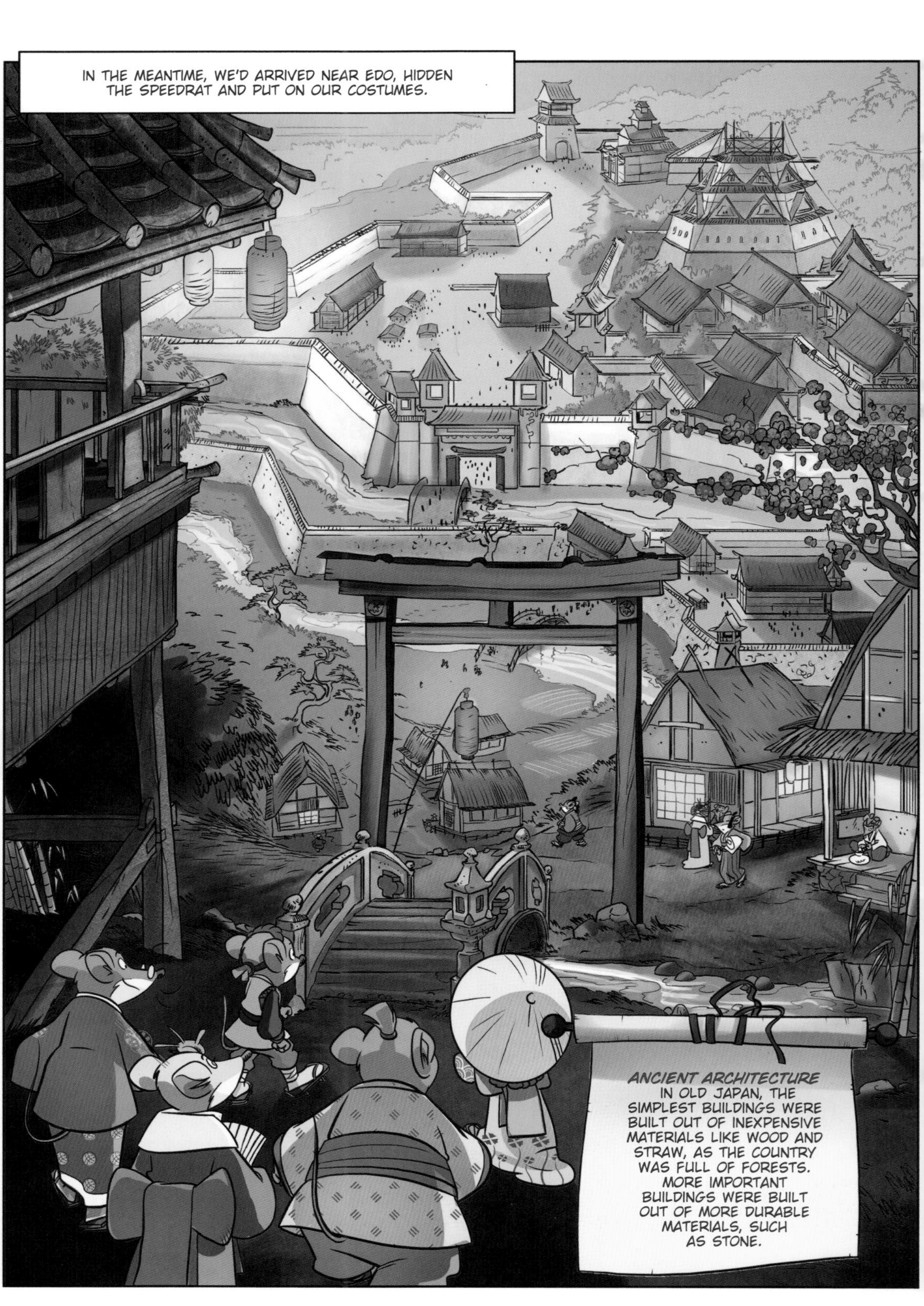
IN THE MEANTIME, WE'D ARRIVED NEAR EDO, HIDDEN THE SPEEDRAT AND PUT ON OUR COSTUMES.
ANCIENT ARCHITECTURE
IN OLD JAPAN, THE SIMPLEST BUILDINGS WERE BUILT OUT OF INEXPENSIVE MATERIALS LIKE WOOD AND STRAW, AS THE COUNTRY WAS FULL OF FORESTS. MORE IMPORTANT BUILDINGS WERE BUILT OUT OF MORE DURABLE MATERIALS, SUCH AS STONE.

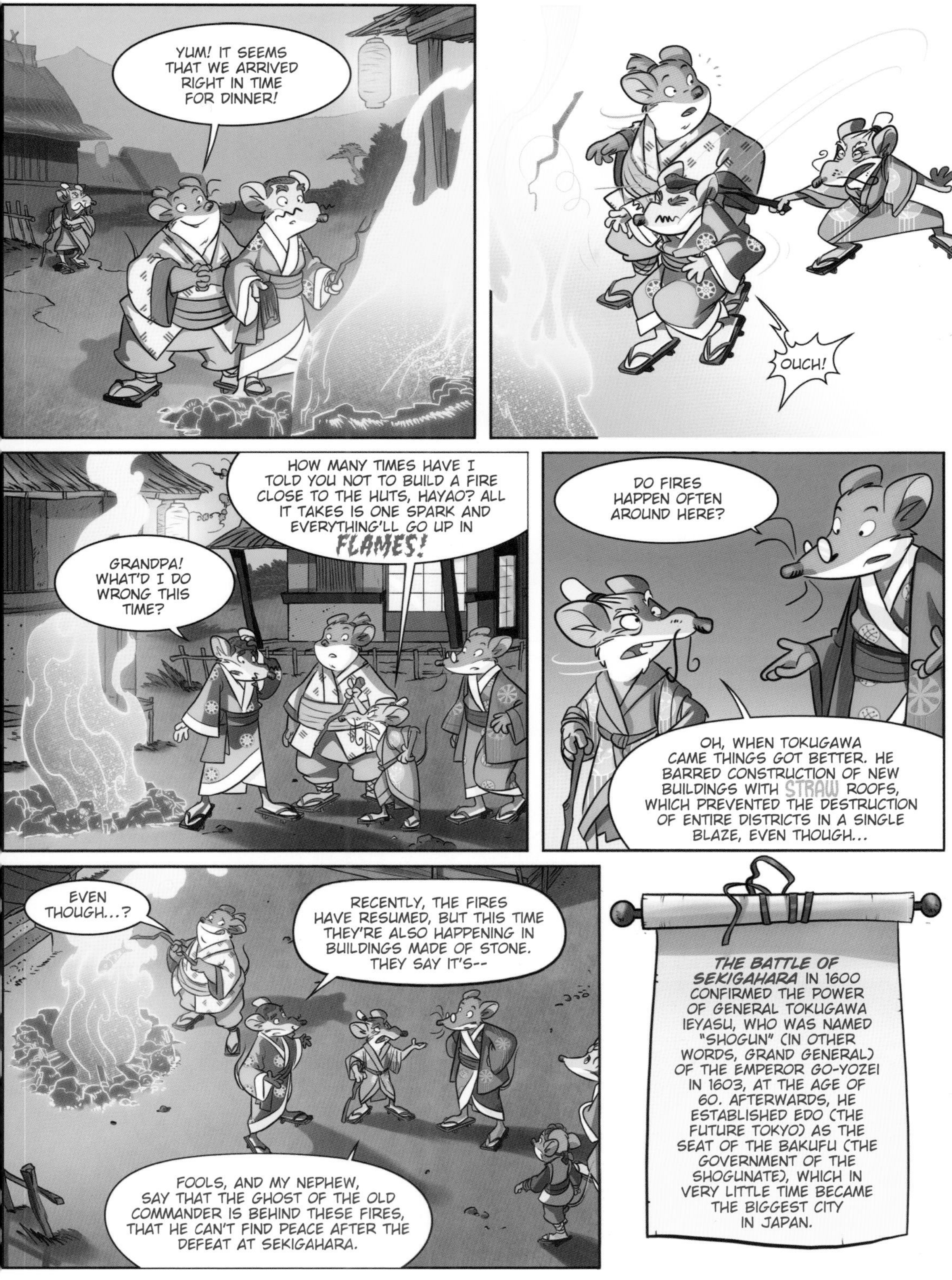

YUM! IT SEEMS THAT WE ARRIVED RIGHT IN TIME FOR DINNER!
OUCH!
HOW MANY TIMES HAVE I TOLD YOU NOT TO BUILD A FIRE CLOSE TO THE HUTS, HAYAO? ALL IT TAKES IS ONE SPARK AND EVERYTHING'LL GO UP IN FLAMES!
GRANDPA! WHAT'D I DO WRONG THIS TIME?
DO FIRES HAPPEN OFTEN AROUND HERE?
OH, WHEN TOKUGAWA CAME THINGS GOT BETTER. HE BARRED CONSTRUCTION OF NEW BUILDINGS WITH STRAW ROOFS, WHICH PREVENTED THE DESTRUCTION OF ENTIRE DISTRICTS IN A SINGLE BLAZE, EVEN THOUGH...
EVEN THOUGH...?
RECENTLY, THE FIRES HAVE RESUMED, BUT THIS TIME THEY'RE ALSO HAPPENING IN BUILDINGS MADE OF STONE. THEY SAY IT'S--
FOOLS, AND MY NEPHEW, SAY THAT THE GHOST OF THE OLD COMMANDER IS BEHIND THESE FIRES, THAT HE CAN'T FIND PEACE AFTER THE DEFEAT AT SEKIGAHARA.
THE BATTLE OF SEKIGAHARA IN 1600 CONFIRMED THE POWER OF GENERAL TOKUGAWA IEYASU, WHO WAS NAMED "SHOGUN" (IN OTHER WORDS, GRAND GENERAL) OF THE EMPEROR GO-YOZEI IN 1603, AT THE AGE OF 60. AFTERWARDS, HE ESTABLISHED EDO (THE FUTURE TOKYO) AS THE SEAT OF THE BAKUFU (THE GOVERNMENT OF THE SHOGUNATE), WHICH IN VERY LITTLE TIME BECAME THE BIGGEST CITY IN JAPAN.

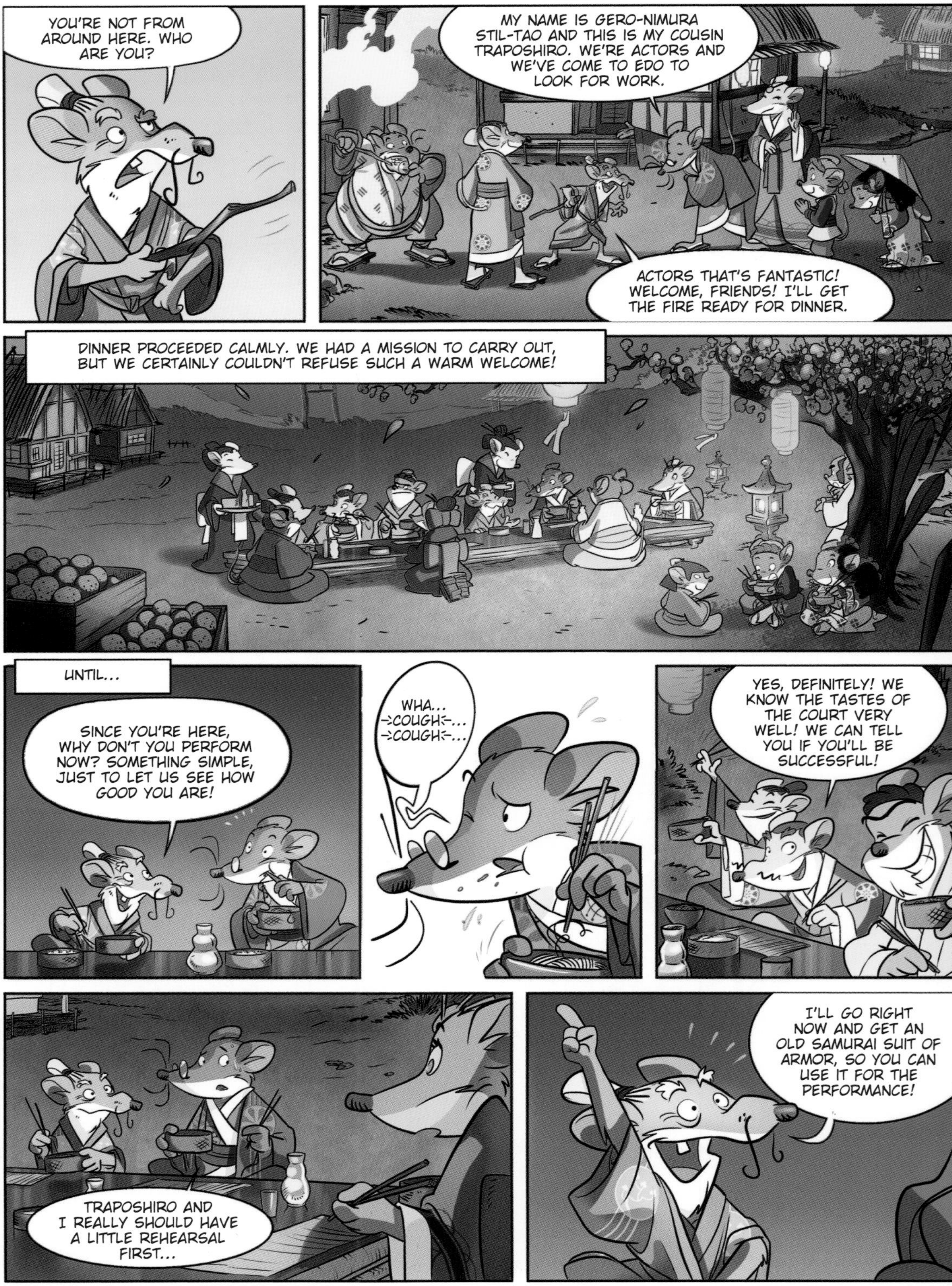
YOU'RE NOT FROM AROUND HERE. WHO ARE YOU?
MY NAME IS GERO-NIMURA STIL-TAO AND THIS IS MY COUSIN TRAPOSHIRO. WE'RE ACTORS AND WE'VE COME TO EDO TO LOOK FOR WORK.
ACTORS THAT'S FANTASTIC! WELCOME, FRIENDS! I'LL GET THE FIRE READY FOR DINNER.
DINNER PROCEEDED CALMLY. WE HAD A MISSION TO CARRY OUT, BUT WE CERTAINLY COULDN'T REFUSE SUCH A WARM WELCOME!
UNTIL...
SINCE YOU'RE HERE, WHY DON'T YOU PERFORM NOW? SOMETHING SIMPLE, JUST TO LET US SEE HOW GOOD YOU ARE!
WHA... COUGH... COUGH...
YES, DEFINITELY! WE KNOW THE TASTES OF THE COURT VERY WELL! WE CAN TELL YOU IF YOU'LL BE SUCCESSFUL!
TRAPOSHIRO AND I REALLY SHOULD HAVE A LITTLE REHEARSAL FIRST...
I'LL GO RIGHT NOW AND GET AN OLD SAMURAI SUIT OF ARMOR, SO YOU CAN USE IT FOR THE PERFORMANCE!

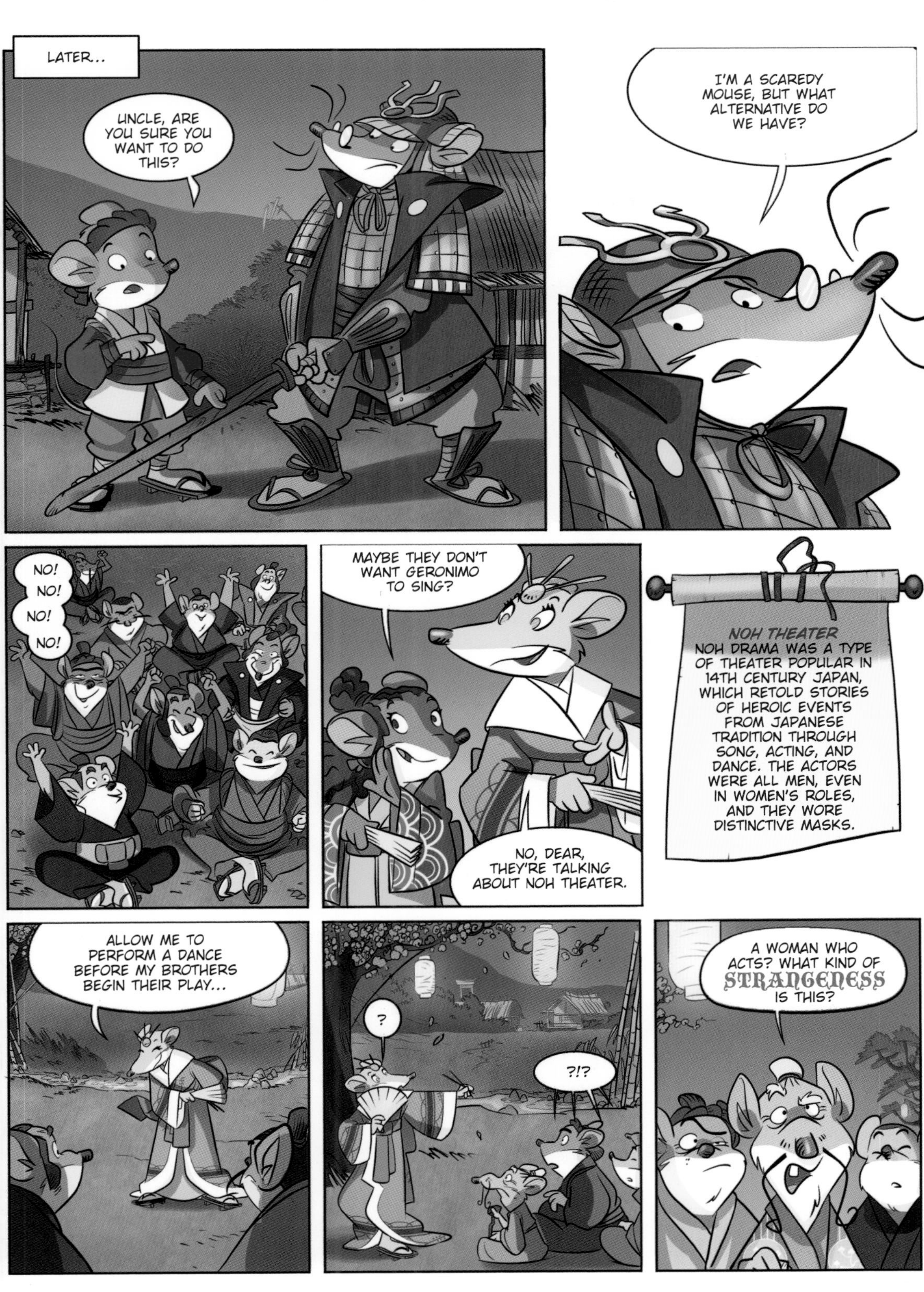
LATER...
UNCLE, ARE YOU SURE YOU WANT TO DO THIS?
I'M A SCAREDY MOUSE, BUT WHAT ALTERNATIVE DO WE HAVE?
NO! NO! NO! NO!
MAYBE THEY DON'T WANT GERONIMO TO SING?
NO, DEAR, THEY'RE TALKING ABOUT NOH THEATER.
NOH THEATER
NOH DRAMA WAS A TYPE OF THEATER POPULAR IN 14TH CENTURY JAPAN, WHICH RETOLD STORIES OF HEROIC EVENTS FROM JAPANESE TRADITION THROUGH SONG, ACTING, AND DANCE. THE ACTORS WERE ALL MEN, EVEN IN WOMEN'S ROLES, AND THEY WORE DISTINCTIVE MASKS.
ALLOW ME TO PERFORM A DANCE BEFORE MY BROTHERS BEGIN THEIR PLAY...
?
?!?
A WOMAN WHO ACTS? WHAT KIND OF STRANGENESS IS THIS?

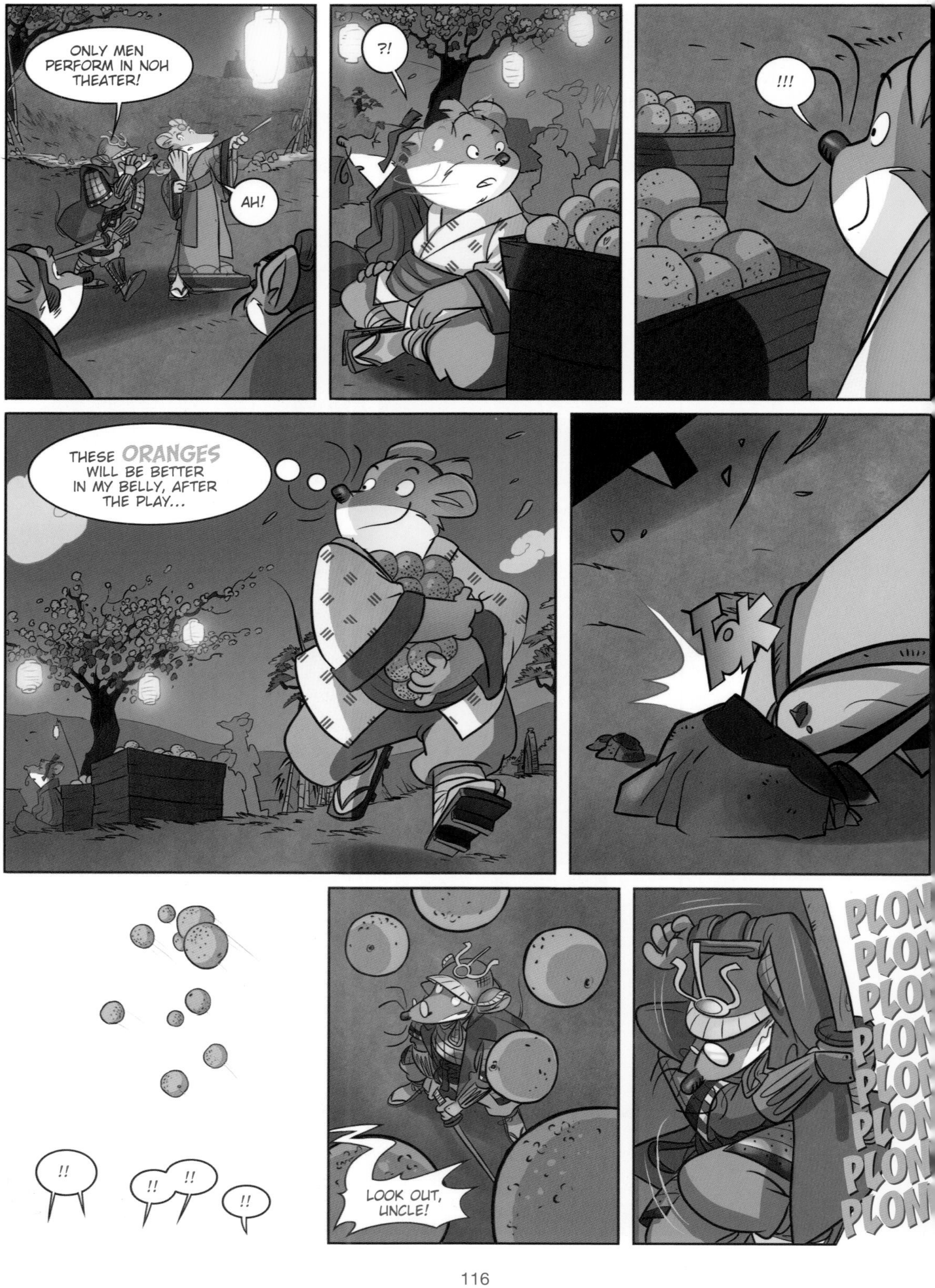

ONLY MEN PERFORM IN NOH THEATER!
AH!
?!
!!!
THESE ORANGES WILL BE BETTER IN MY BELLY, AFTER THE PLAY...
TOK
!!
!!
!!
!!
LOOK OUT, UNCLE!
PLON PLON PLON PLON PLON PLON PLON PLON

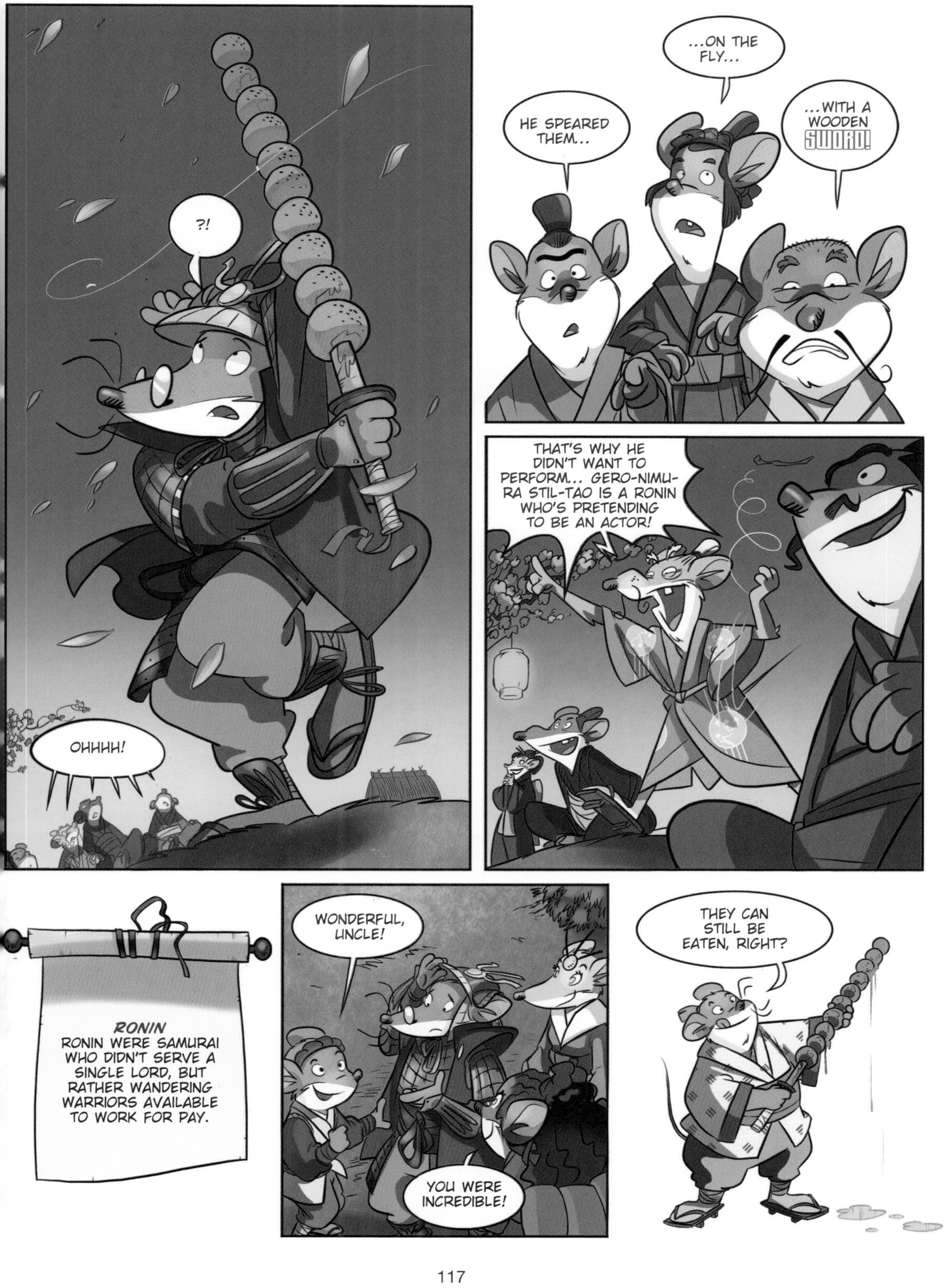
?!
OHHHH!
HE SPEARED THEM...
...ON THE FLY...
...WITH A WOODEN SWORD!
THAT'S WHY HE DIDN'T WANT TO PERFORM... GERO-NIMURA STIL-TAO IS A RONIN WHO'S PRETENDING TO BE AN ACTOR!
RONIN
RONIN WERE SAMURAI WHO DIDN'T SERVE A SINGLE LORD, BUT RATHER WANDERING WARRIORS AVAILABLE TO WORK FOR PAY.
WONDERFUL, UNCLE!
YOU WERE INCREDIBLE!
THEY CAN STILL BE EATEN, RIGHT?

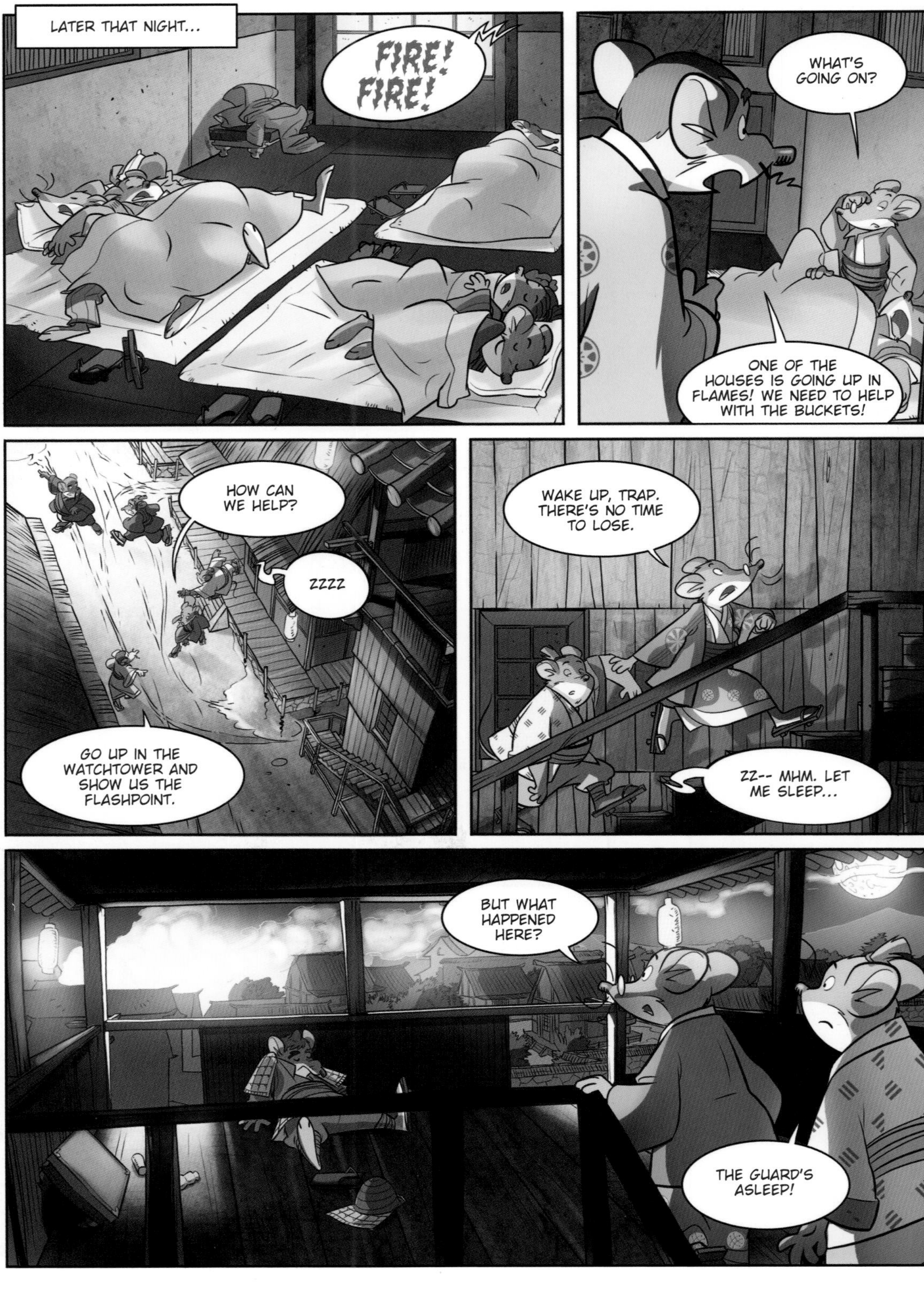

LATER THAT NIGHT...
FIRE! FIRE!
WHAT'S GOING ON?
ONE OF THE HOUSES IS GOING UP IN FLAMES! WE NEED TO HELP WITH THE BUCKETS!
HOW CAN WE HELP?
ZZZZ
GO UP IN THE WATCHTOWER AND SHOW US THE FLASHPOINT.
WAKE UP, TRAP. THERE'S NO TIME TO LOSE.
ZZ-- MHM. LET ME SLEEP...
BUT WHAT HAPPENED HERE?
THE GUARD'S ASLEEP!

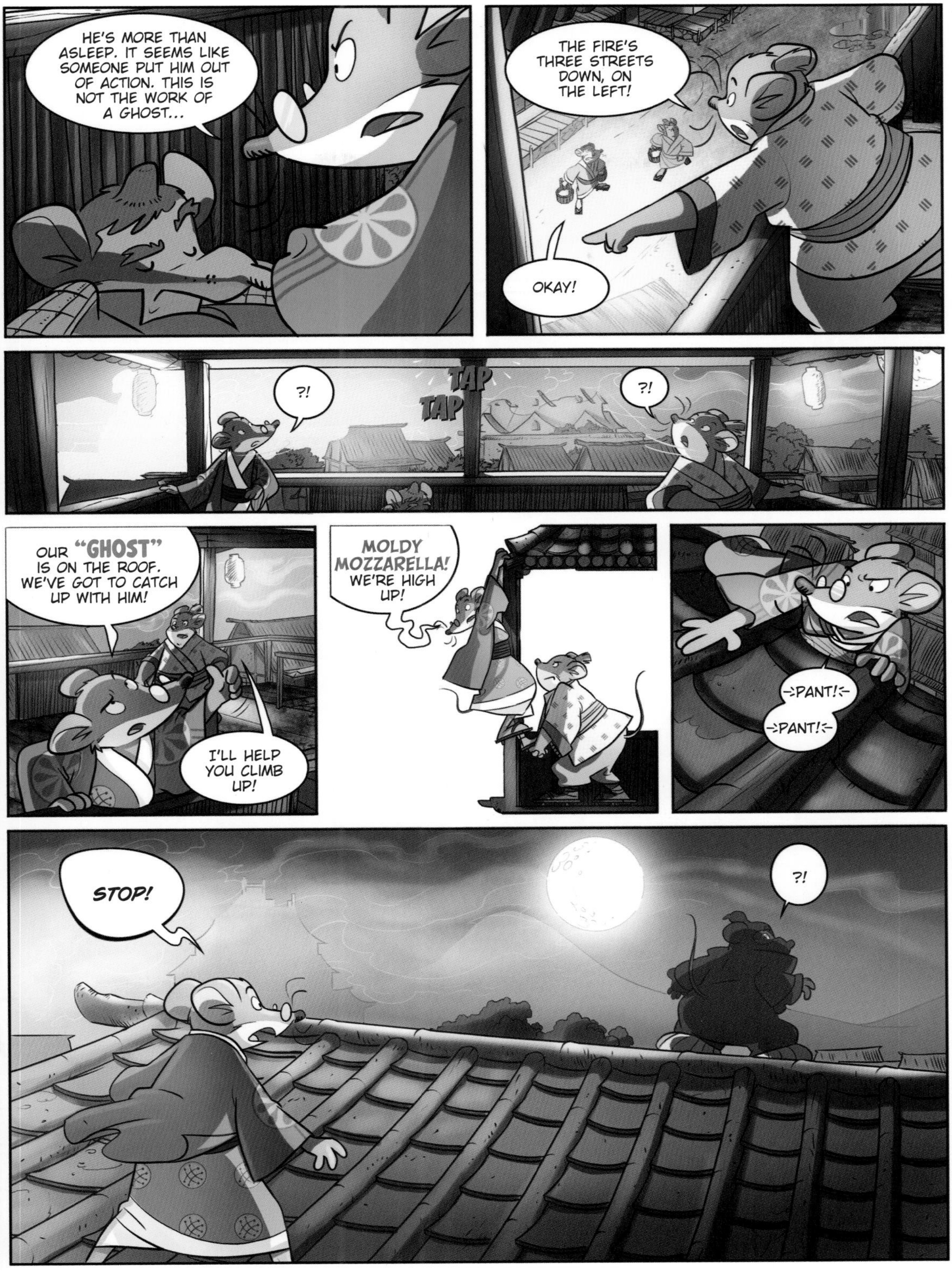
HE'S MORE THAN ASLEEP. IT SEEMS LIKE SOMEONE PUT HIM OUT OF ACTION. THIS IS NOT THE WORK OF A GHOST...
THE FIRE'S THREE STREETS DOWN, ON THE LEFT!
OKAY!
TAP
TAP
?!
?!
OUR "GHOST" IS ON THE ROOF. WE'VE GOT TO CATCH UP WITH HIM!
I'LL HELP YOU CLIMB UP!
MOLDY MOZZARELLA! WE'RE HIGH UP!
PANT!
PANT!
STOP!
?!

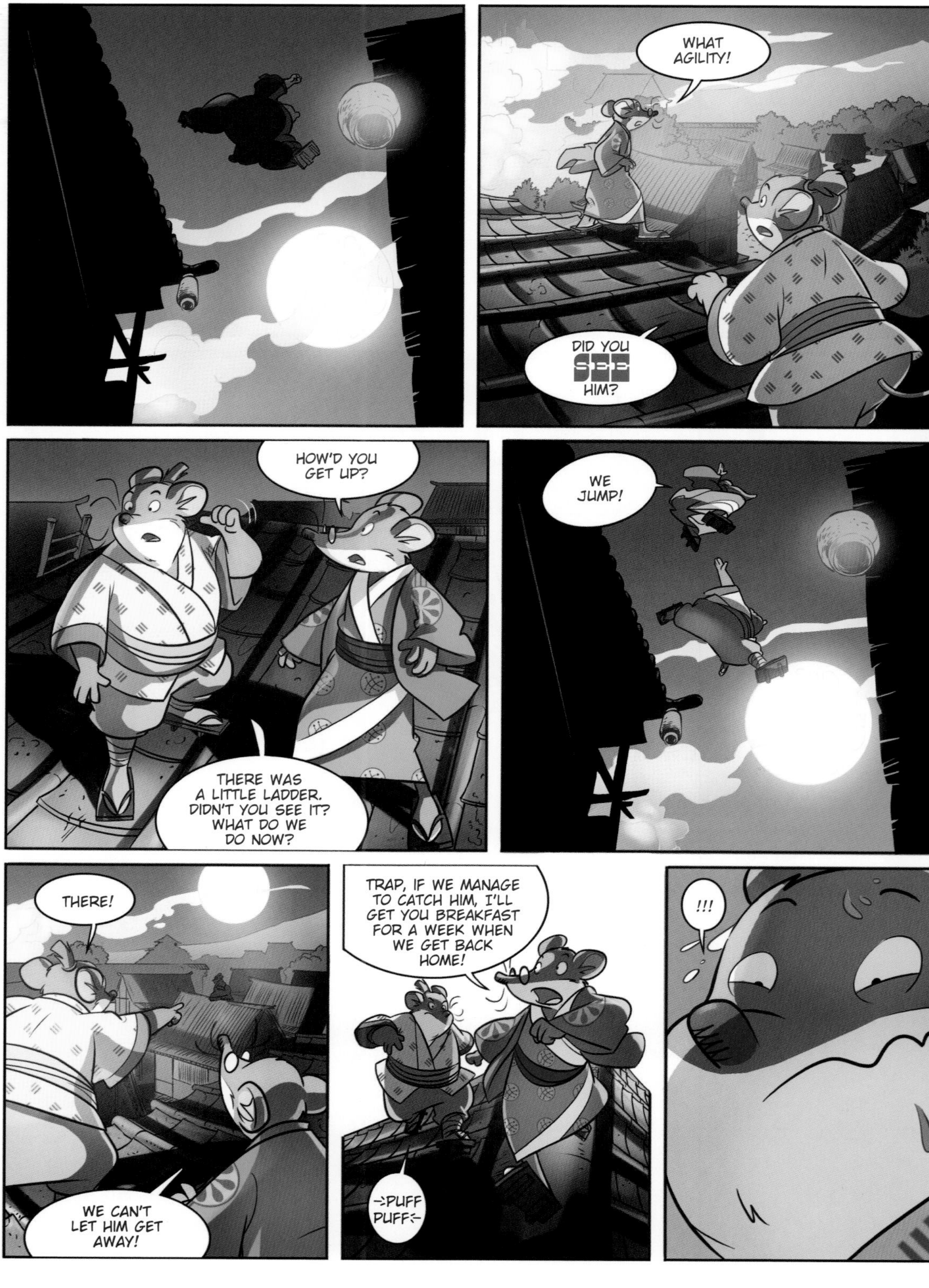
WHAT AGILITY!
DID YOU SEE HIM?
HOW'D YOU GET UP?
THERE WAS A LITTLE LADDER. DIDN'T YOU SEE IT? WHAT DO WE DO NOW?
WE JUMP!
THERE!
WE CAN'T LET HIM GET AWAY!
TRAP, IF WE MANAGE TO CATCH HIM, I'LL GET YOU BREAKFAST FOR A WEEK WHEN WE GET BACK HOME!
PUFF PUFF
!!!

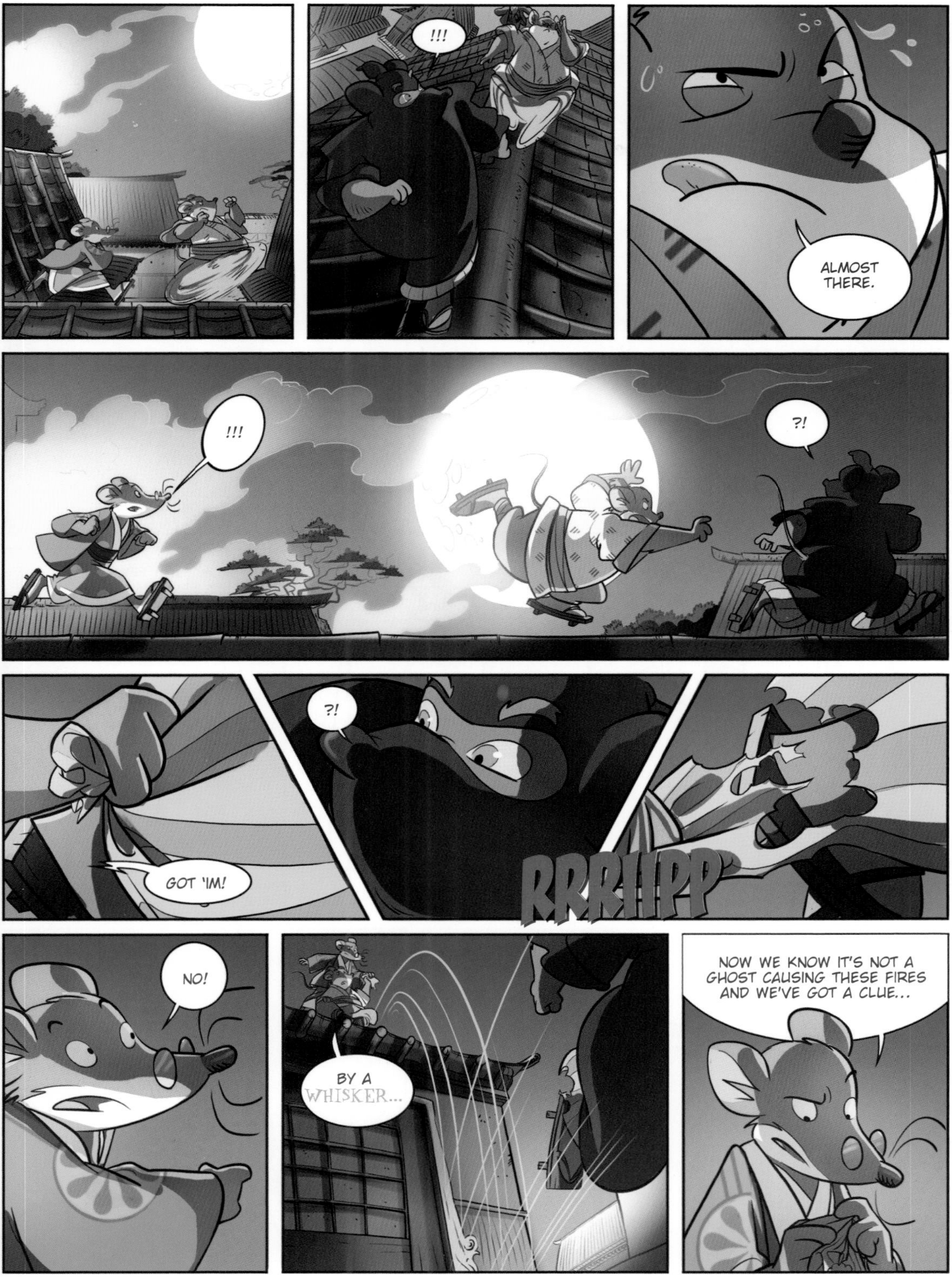
!!!
ALMOST THERE.
!!!
?!
?!
GOT 'IM!
RRRIIPP
NO!
BY A WHISKER...
NOW WE KNOW IT'S NOT A GHOST CAUSING THESE FIRES AND WE'VE GOT A CLUE...

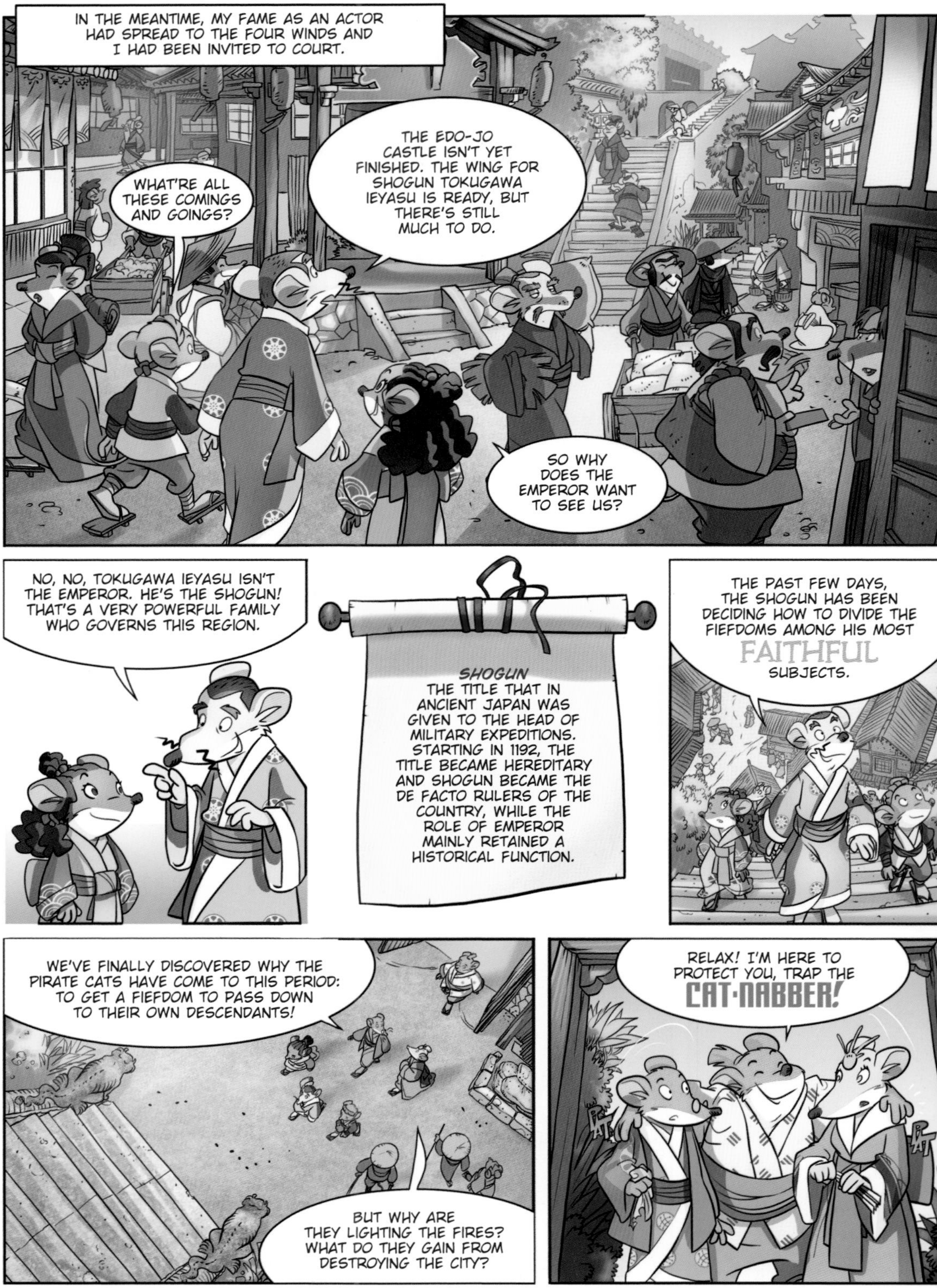
IN THE MEANTIME, MY FAME AS AN ACTOR HAD SPREAD TO THE FOUR WINDS AND I HAD BEEN INVITED TO COURT.
WHAT'RE ALL THESE COMINGS AND GOINGS?
THE EDO-JO CASTLE ISN'T YET FINISHED. THE WING FOR SHOGUN TOKUGAWA IEYASU IS READY, BUT THERE'S STILL MUCH TO DO.
SO WHY DOES THE EMPEROR WANT TO SEE US?
NO, NO, TOKUGAWA IEYASU ISN'T THE EMPEROR. HE'S THE SHOGUN! THAT'S A VERY POWERFUL FAMILY WHO GOVERNS THIS REGION.
SHOGUN
THE TITLE THAT IN ANCIENT JAPAN WAS GIVEN TO THE HEAD OF MILITARY EXPEDITIONS. STARTING IN 1192, THE TITLE BECAME HEREDITARY AND SHOGUN BECAME THE DE FACTO RULERS OF THE COUNTRY, WHILE THE ROLE OF EMPEROR MAINLY RETAINED A HISTORICAL FUNCTION.
THE PAST FEW DAYS, THE SHOGUN HAS BEEN DECIDING HOW TO DIVIDE THE FIEFDOMS AMONG HIS MOST FAITHFUL SUBJECTS.
WE'VE FINALLY DISCOVERED WHY THE PIRATE CATS HAVE COME TO THIS PERIOD: TO GET A FIEFDOM TO PASS DOWN TO THEIR OWN DESCENDANTS!
BUT WHY ARE THEY LIGHTING THE FIRES? WHAT DO THEY GAIN FROM DESTROYING THE CITY?
RELAX! I'M HERE TO PROTECT YOU, TRAP THE CAT-NABBER!

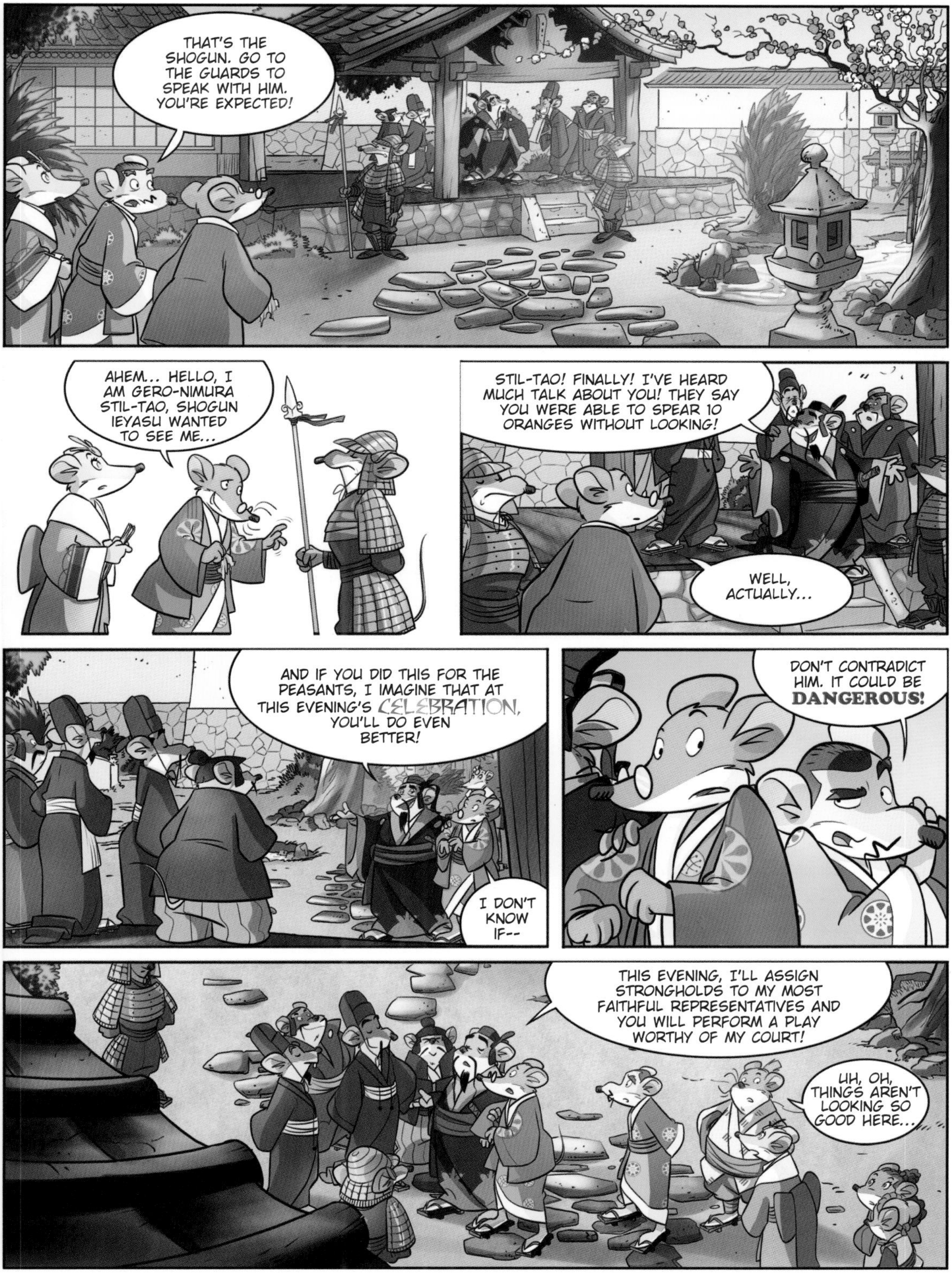
THAT'S THE SHOGUN. GO TO THE GUARDS TO SPEAK WITH HIM. YOU'RE EXPECTED!
AHEM... HELLO, I AM GERO-NIMURA STIL-TAO, SHOGUN IEYASU WANTED TO SEE ME...
STIL-TAO! FINALLY! I'VE HEARD MUCH TALK ABOUT YOU! THEY SAY YOU WERE ABLE TO SPEAR 10 ORANGES WITHOUT LOOKING!
WELL, ACTUALLY...
AND IF YOU DID THIS FOR THE PEASANTS, I IMAGINE THAT AT THIS EVENING'S CELEBRATION, YOU'LL DO EVEN BETTER!
I DON'T KNOW IF--
DON'T CONTRADICT HIM. IT COULD BE DANGEROUS!
THIS EVENING, I'LL ASSIGN STRONGHOLDS TO MY MOST FAITHFUL REPRESENTATIVES AND YOU WILL PERFORM A PLAY WORTHY OF MY COURT!
UH, OH, THINGS AREN'T LOOKING SO GOOD HERE...

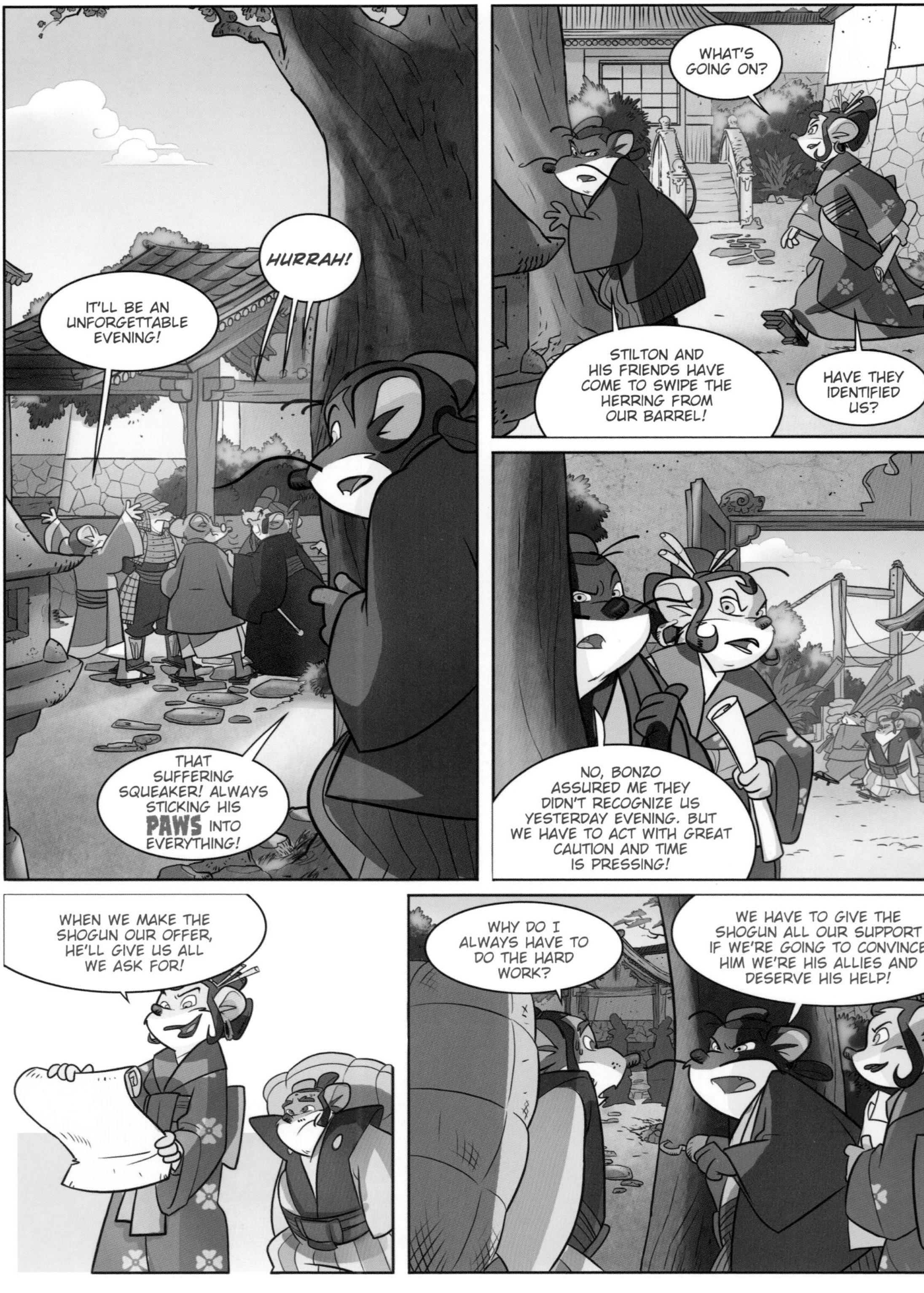
IT'LL BE AN UNFORGETTABLE EVENING!
HURRAH!
THAT SUFFERING SQUEAKER! ALWAYS STICKING HIS PAWS INTO EVERYTHING!
WHAT'S GOING ON?
STILTON AND HIS FRIENDS HAVE COME TO SWIPE THE HERRING FROM OUR BARREL!
HAVE THEY IDENTIFIED US?
NO, BONZO ASSURED ME THEY DIDN'T RECOGNIZE US YESTERDAY EVENING. BUT WE HAVE TO ACT WITH GREAT CAUTION AND TIME IS PRESSING!
WHEN WE MAKE THE SHOGUN OUR OFFER, HE'LL GIVE US ALL WE ASK FOR!
WHY DO I ALWAYS HAVE TO DO THE HARD WORK?
WE HAVE TO GIVE THE SHOGUN ALL OUR SUPPORT IF WE'RE GOING TO CONVINCE HIM WE'RE HIS ALLIES AND DESERVE HIS HELP!

EVEN THOUGH WE'VE ARRIVED AFTER THE BATTLE OF SEKIGAHARA, WE STILL HAVE A GOOD CHANCE OF GETTING THE FIEFDOM WE WANT AND BECOMING TOZAMA DAIMYO!

AND WHAT'S THAT!

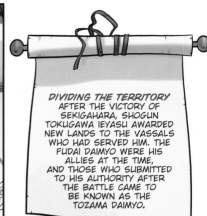

DIVIDING THE TERRITORY
AFTER THE VICTORY OF SEKIGAHARA, SHOGUN TOKUGAWA IEYASU AWARDED NEW LANDS TO THE VASSALS WHO HAD SERVED HIM. THE FUDAI DAIMYO WERE HIS ALLIES AT THE TIME, AND THOSE WHO SUBMITTED TO HIS AUTHORITY AFTER THE BATTLE CAME TO BE KNOWN AS THE TOZAMA DAIMYO.

BON-ZAI, DON'T SLACK OFF! BE QUICK WITH THAT SACK!

YES, OKAY!

THIS TIME GERONIMO AND HIS FAMILY CAN TRY EVERY WAY THEY WISH BUT THEY WON'T BE ABLE TO STOP US!

HEE HEE HEE!

HMM...

MAYBE THAT'S THE WAY TO THE **KITCHEN**...

TRAP, WE'RE IN TROUBLE!

GERONIMO HAS TO PERFORM TONIGHT AND WE DON'T EVEN KNOW WHERE THE PIRATE CATS ARE!

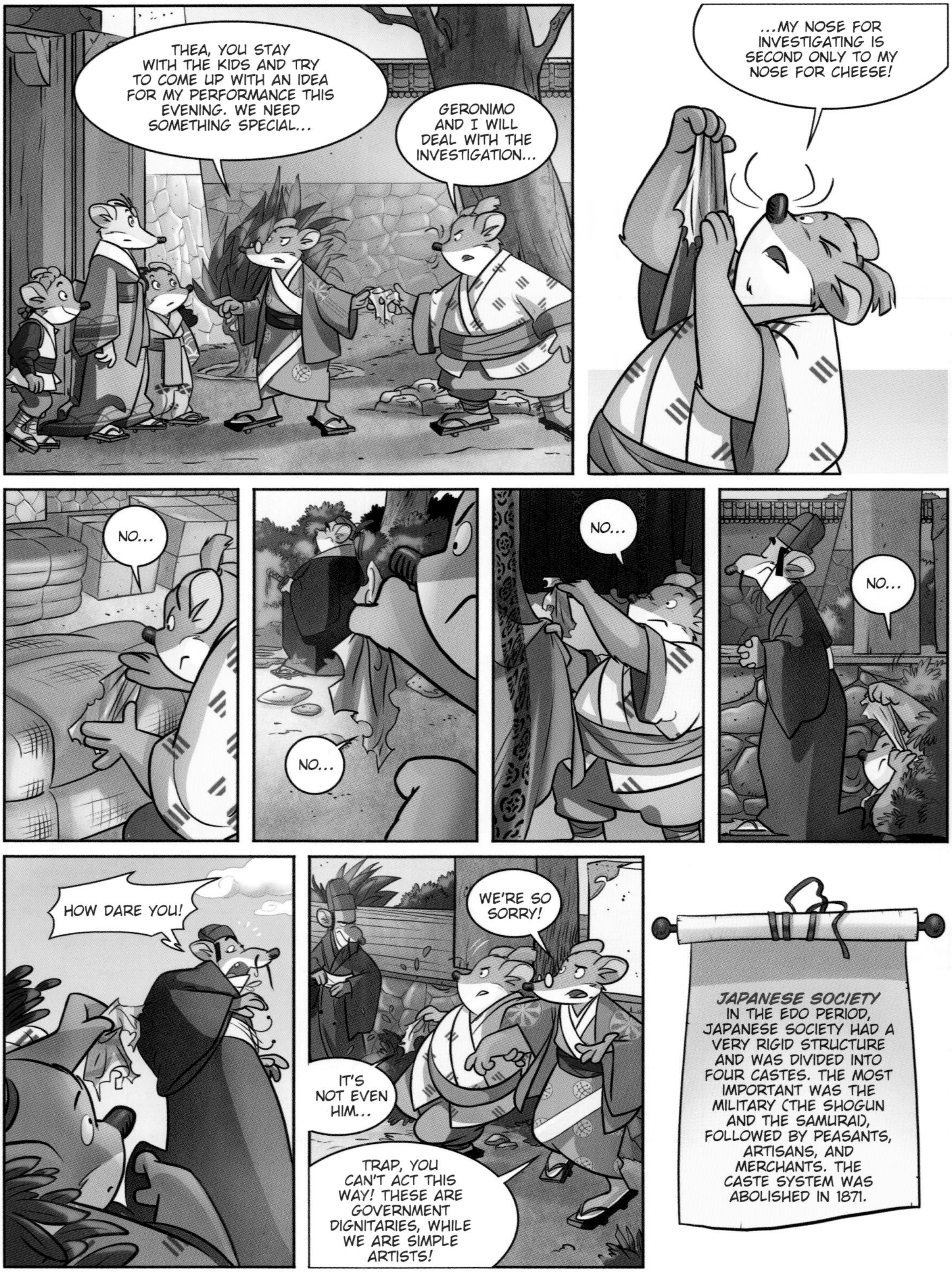
THEA, YOU STAY WITH THE KIDS AND TRY TO COME UP WITH AN IDEA FOR MY PERFORMANCE THIS EVENING. WE NEED SOMETHING SPECIAL...
GERONIMO AND I WILL DEAL WITH THE INVESTIGATION...
...MY NOSE FOR INVESTIGATING IS SECOND ONLY TO MY NOSE FOR CHEESE!
NO...
NO...
NO...
NO...
HOW DARE YOU!
WE'RE SO SORRY!
IT'S NOT EVEN HIM...
TRAP, YOU CAN'T ACT THIS WAY! THESE ARE GOVERNMENT DIGNITARIES, WHILE WE ARE SIMPLE ARTISTS!
JAPANESE SOCIETY
IN THE EDO PERIOD, JAPANESE SOCIETY HAD A VERY RIGID STRUCTURE AND WAS DIVIDED INTO FOUR CASTES. THE MOST IMPORTANT WAS THE MILITARY (THE SHOGUN AND THE SAMURAI), FOLLOWED BY PEASANTS, ARTISANS, AND MERCHANTS. THE CASTE SYSTEM WAS ABOLISHED IN 1871.

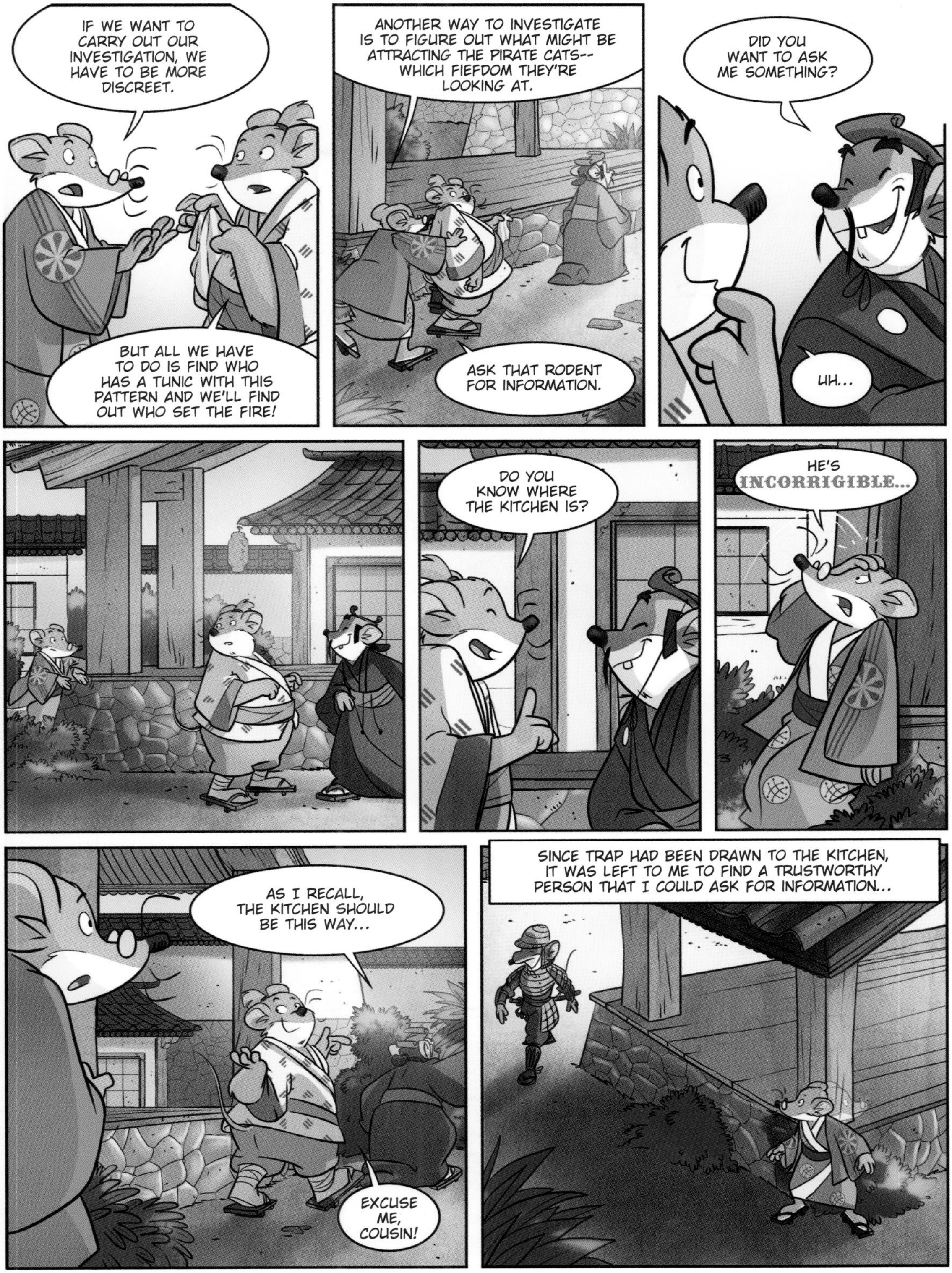
IF WE WANT TO CARRY OUT OUR INVESTIGATION, WE HAVE TO BE MORE DISCREET.
BUT ALL WE HAVE TO DO IS FIND WHO HAS A TUNIC WITH THIS PATTERN AND WE'LL FIND OUT WHO SET THE FIRE!
ANOTHER WAY TO INVESTIGATE IS TO FIGURE OUT WHAT MIGHT BE ATTRACTING THE PIRATE CATS-- WHICH FIEFDOM THEY'RE LOOKING AT.
ASK THAT RODENT FOR INFORMATION.
DID YOU WANT TO ASK ME SOMETHING?
UH...
DO YOU KNOW WHERE THE KITCHEN IS?
HE'S INCORRIGIBLE...
AS I RECALL, THE KITCHEN SHOULD BE THIS WAY...
EXCUSE ME, COUSIN!
SINCE TRAP HAD BEEN DRAWN TO THE KITCHEN, IT WAS LEFT TO ME TO FIND A TRUSTWORTHY PERSON THAT I COULD ASK FOR INFORMATION...

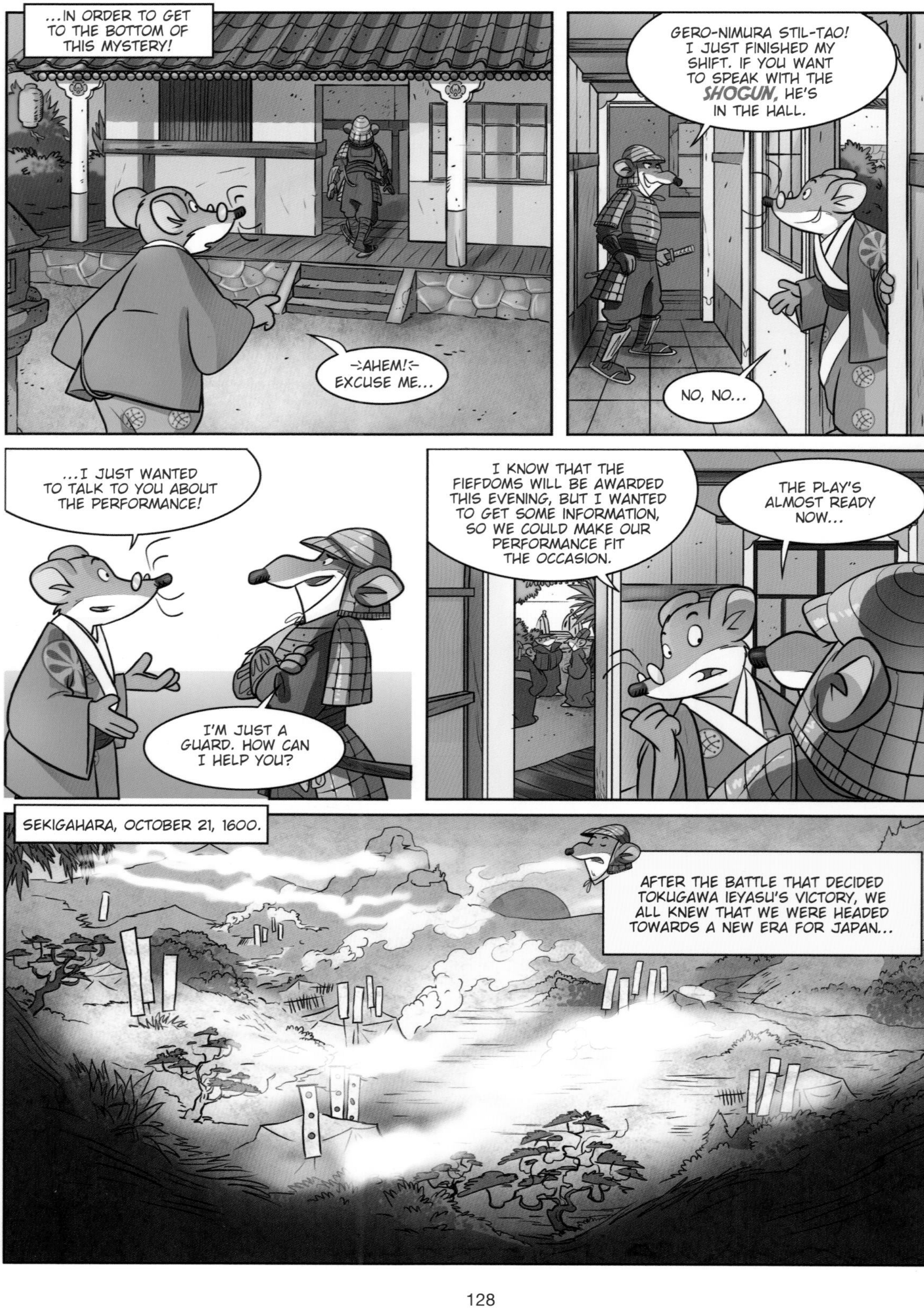
...IN ORDER TO GET TO THE BOTTOM OF THIS MYSTERY!
-AHEM!- EXCUSE ME...
GERO-NIMURA STIL-TAO! I JUST FINISHED MY SHIFT. IF YOU WANT TO SPEAK WITH THE SHOGUN, HE'S IN THE HALL.
NO, NO...
...I JUST WANTED TO TALK TO YOU ABOUT THE PERFORMANCE!
I'M JUST A GUARD. HOW CAN I HELP YOU?
I KNOW THAT THE FIEFDOMS WILL BE AWARDED THIS EVENING, BUT I WANTED TO GET SOME INFORMATION, SO WE COULD MAKE OUR PERFORMANCE FIT THE OCCASION.
THE PLAY'S ALMOST READY NOW...
SEKIGAHARA, OCTOBER 21, 1600.
AFTER THE BATTLE THAT DECIDED TOKUGAWA IEYASU'S VICTORY, WE ALL KNEW THAT WE WERE HEADED TOWARDS A NEW ERA FOR JAPAN...

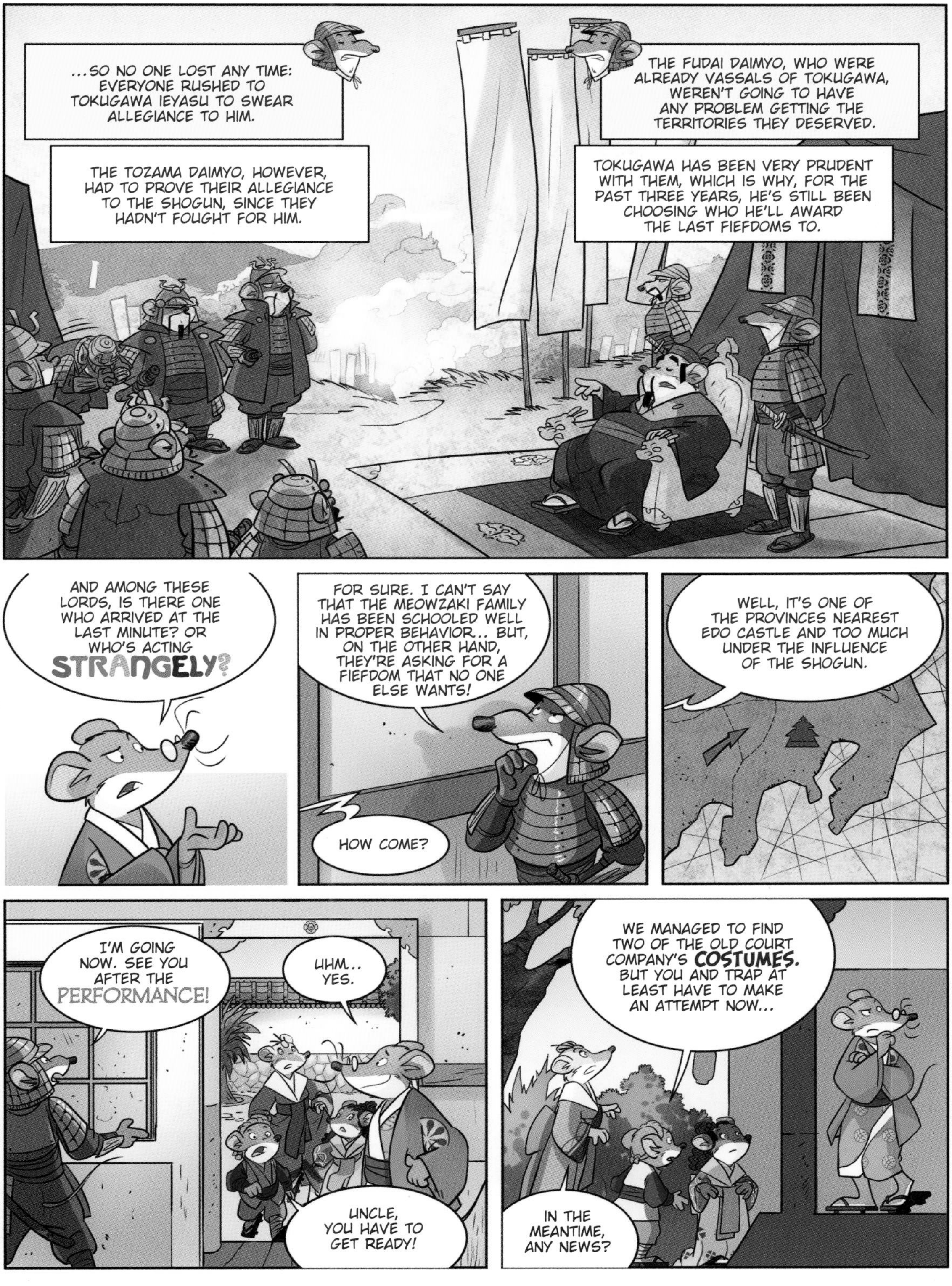
...SO NO ONE LOST ANY TIME: EVERYONE RUSHED TO TOKUGAWA IEYASU TO SWEAR ALLEGIANCE TO HIM.
THE TOZAMA DAIMYO, HOWEVER, HAD TO PROVE THEIR ALLEGIANCE TO THE SHOGUN, SINCE THEY HADN'T FOUGHT FOR HIM.
THE FUDAI DAIMYO, WHO WERE ALREADY VASSALS OF TOKUGAWA, WEREN'T GOING TO HAVE ANY PROBLEM GETTING THE TERRITORIES THEY DESERVED.
TOKUGAWA HAS BEEN VERY PRUDENT WITH THEM, WHICH IS WHY, FOR THE PAST THREE YEARS, HE'S STILL BEEN CHOOSING WHO HE'LL AWARD THE LAST FIEFDOMS TO.
AND AMONG THESE LORDS, IS THERE ONE WHO ARRIVED AT THE LAST MINUTE? OR WHO'S ACTING STRANGELY?
FOR SURE. I CAN'T SAY THAT THE MEOWZAKI FAMILY HAS BEEN SCHOOLED WELL IN PROPER BEHAVIOR... BUT, ON THE OTHER HAND, THEY'RE ASKING FOR A FIEFDOM THAT NO ONE ELSE WANTS!
HOW COME?
WELL, IT'S ONE OF THE PROVINCES NEAREST EDO CASTLE AND TOO MUCH UNDER THE INFLUENCE OF THE SHOGUN.
I'M GOING NOW. SEE YOU AFTER THE PERFORMANCE!
UHM... YES.
UNCLE, YOU HAVE TO GET READY!
WE MANAGED TO FIND TWO OF THE OLD COURT COMPANY'S COSTUMES. BUT YOU AND TRAP AT LEAST HAVE TO MAKE AN ATTEMPT NOW...
IN THE MEANTIME, ANY NEWS?

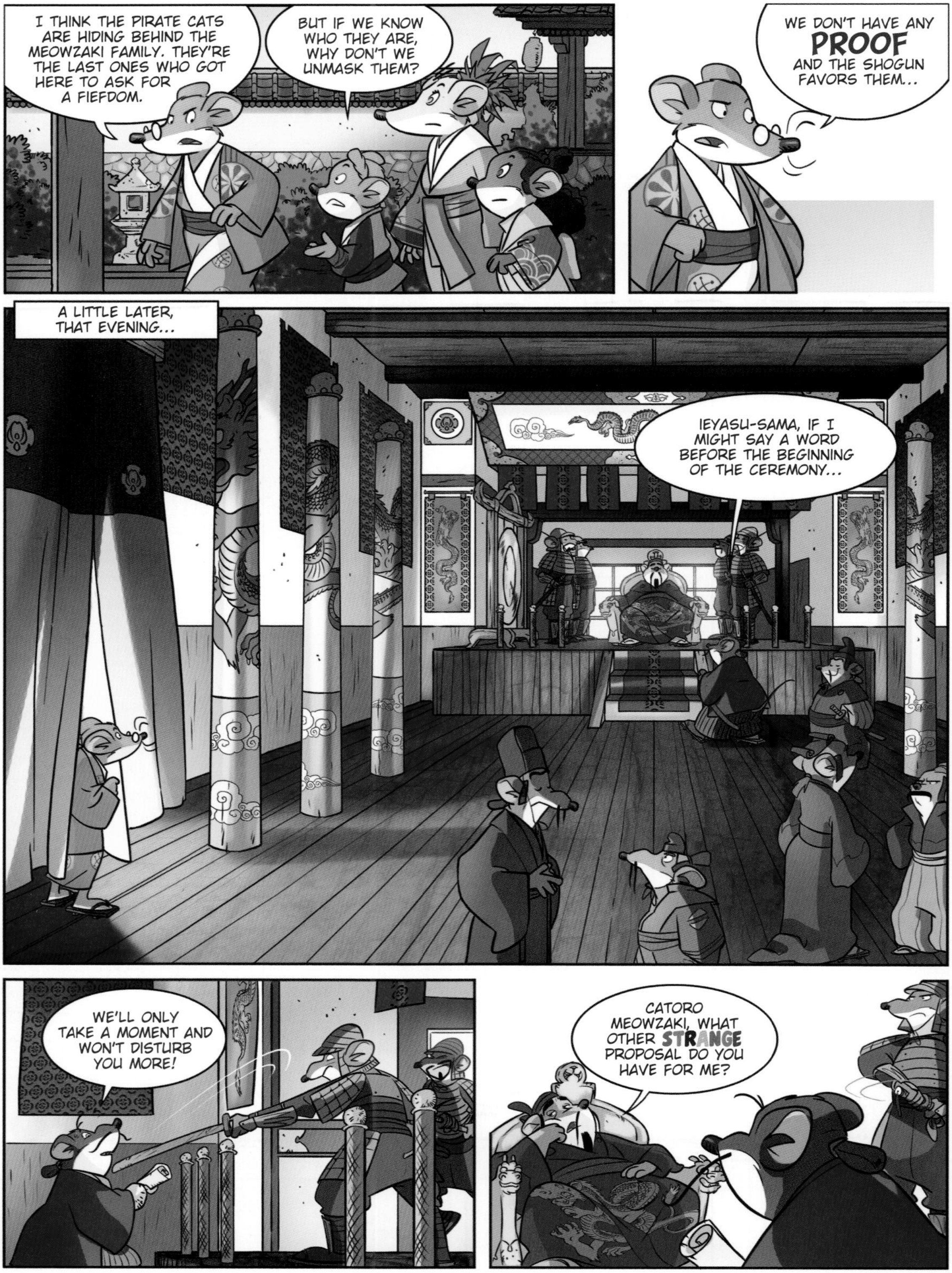
I THINK THE PIRATE CATS ARE HIDING BEHIND THE MEOWZAKI FAMILY. THEY'RE THE LAST ONES WHO GOT HERE TO ASK FOR A FIEFDOM.
BUT IF WE KNOW WHO THEY ARE, WHY DON'T WE UNMASK THEM?
WE DON'T HAVE ANY PROOF AND THE SHOGUN FAVORS THEM...
A LITTLE LATER, THAT EVENING...
IEYASU-SAMA, IF I MIGHT SAY A WORD BEFORE THE BEGINNING OF THE CEREMONY...
WE'LL ONLY TAKE A MOMENT AND WON'T DISTURB YOU MORE!
CATORO MEOWZAKI, WHAT OTHER STRANGE PROPOSAL DO YOU HAVE FOR ME?

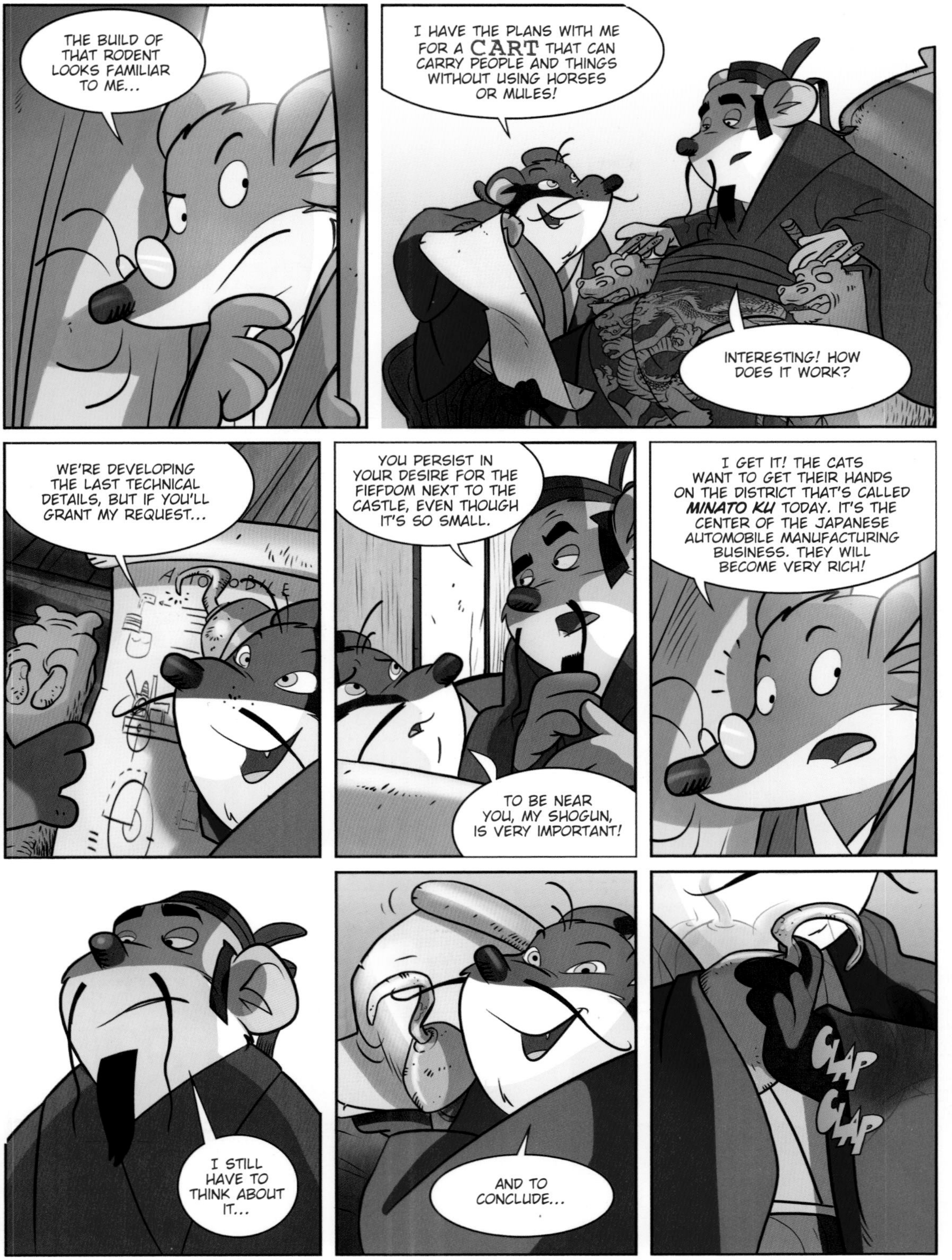
THE BUILD OF THAT RODENT LOOKS FAMILIAR TO ME...
I HAVE THE PLANS WITH ME FOR A CART THAT CAN CARRY PEOPLE AND THINGS WITHOUT USING HORSES OR MULES!
INTERESTING! HOW DOES IT WORK?
WE'RE DEVELOPING THE LAST TECHNICAL DETAILS, BUT IF YOU'LL GRANT MY REQUEST...
AUTOMOBILE
YOU PERSIST IN YOUR DESIRE FOR THE FIEFDOM NEXT TO THE CASTLE, EVEN THOUGH IT'S SO SMALL.
TO BE NEAR YOU, MY SHOGUN, IS VERY IMPORTANT!
I GET IT! THE CATS WANT TO GET THEIR HANDS ON THE DISTRICT THAT'S CALLED MINATO KU TODAY. IT'S THE CENTER OF THE JAPANESE AUTOMOBILE MANUFACTURING BUSINESS. THEY WILL BECOME VERY RICH!
I STILL HAVE TO THINK ABOUT IT...
AND TO CONCLUDE...
CLAP
CLAP

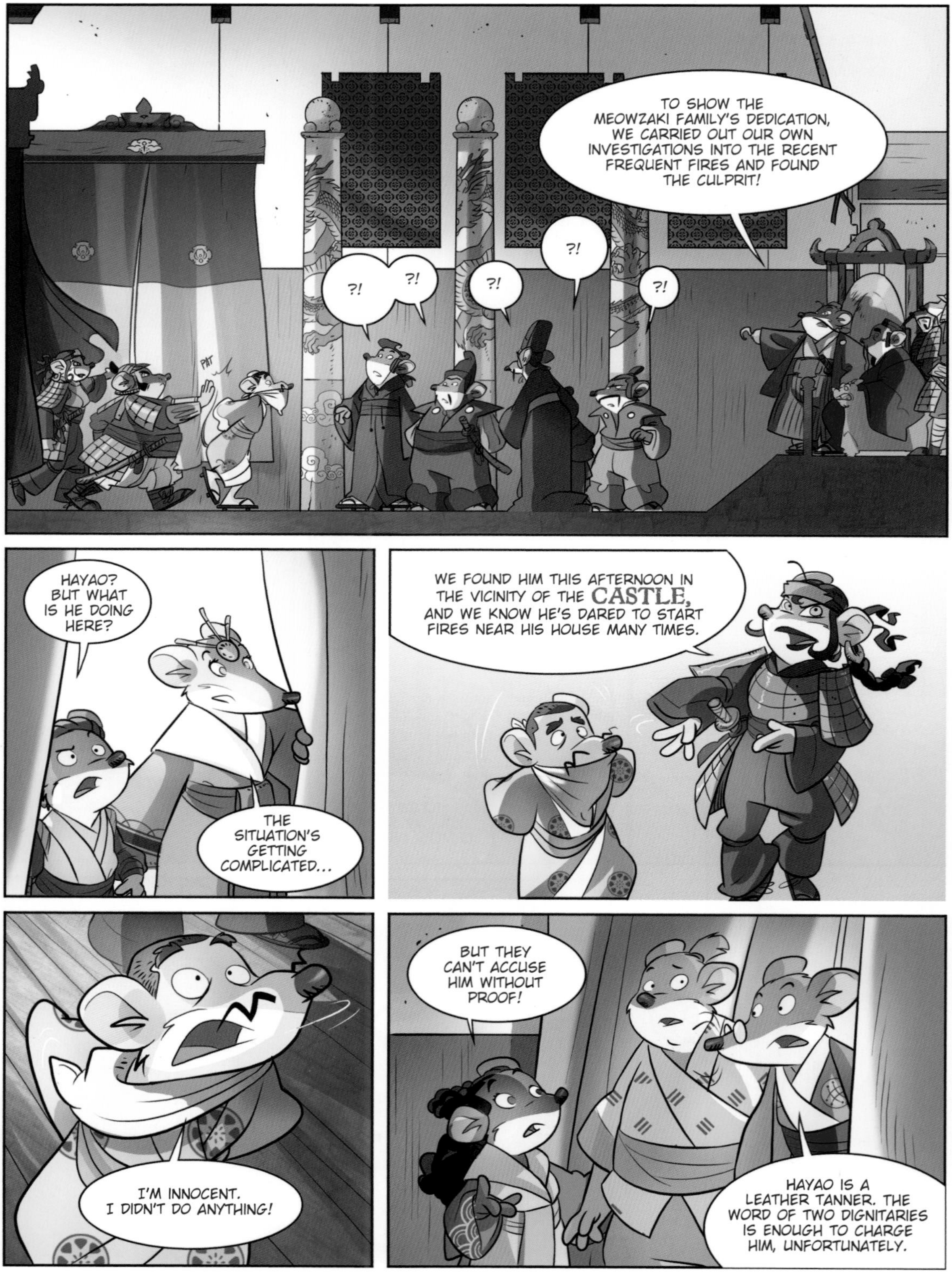
TO SHOW THE MEOWZAKI FAMILY'S DEDICATION, WE CARRIED OUT OUR OWN INVESTIGATIONS INTO THE RECENT FREQUENT FIRES AND FOUND THE CULPRIT!
?!
?!
?!
?!
?!
PAT
HAYAO? BUT WHAT IS HE DOING HERE?
THE SITUATION'S GETTING COMPLICATED...
WE FOUND HIM THIS AFTERNOON IN THE VICINITY OF THE CASTLE, AND WE KNOW HE'S DARED TO START FIRES NEAR HIS HOUSE MANY TIMES.
I'M INNOCENT. I DIDN'T DO ANYTHING!
BUT THEY CAN'T ACCUSE HIM WITHOUT PROOF!
HAYAO IS A LEATHER TANNER. THE WORD OF TWO DIGNITARIES IS ENOUGH TO CHARGE HIM, UNFORTUNATELY.

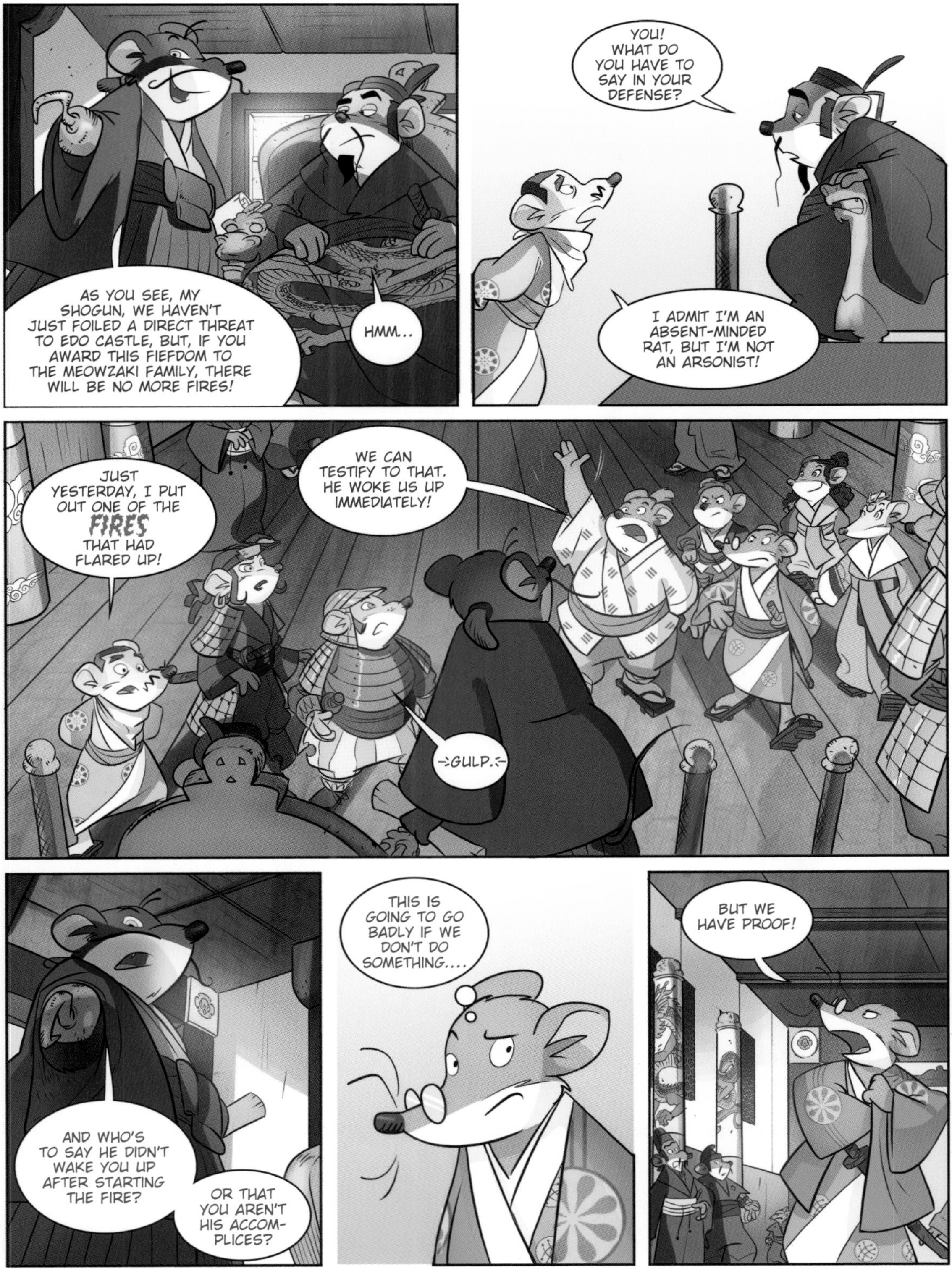
AS YOU SEE, MY SHOGUN, WE HAVEN'T JUST FOILED A DIRECT THREAT TO EDO CASTLE, BUT, IF YOU AWARD THIS FIEFDOM TO THE MEOWZAKI FAMILY, THERE WILL BE NO MORE FIRES!
HMM...
YOU! WHAT DO YOU HAVE TO SAY IN YOUR DEFENSE?
I ADMIT I'M AN ABSENT-MINDED RAT, BUT I'M NOT AN ARSONIST!
JUST YESTERDAY, I PUT OUT ONE OF THE FIRES THAT HAD FLARED UP!
WE CAN TESTIFY TO THAT. HE WOKE US UP IMMEDIATELY!
GULP.
AND WHO'S TO SAY HE DIDN'T WAKE YOU UP AFTER STARTING THE FIRE?
OR THAT YOU AREN'T HIS ACCOMPLICES?
THIS IS GOING TO GO BADLY IF WE DON'T DO SOMETHING....
BUT WE HAVE PROOF!

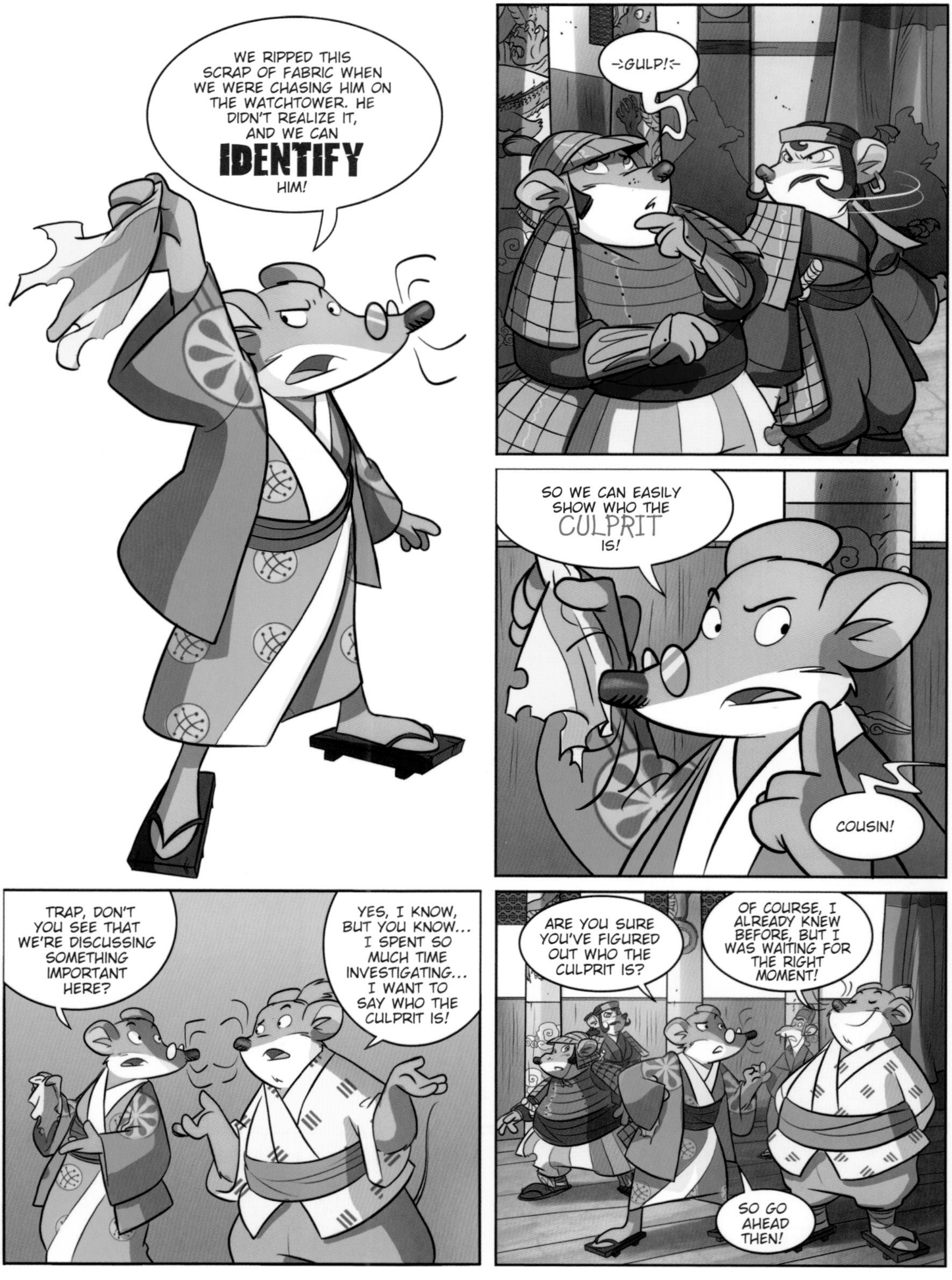
WE RIPPED THIS SCRAP OF FABRIC WHEN WE WERE CHASING HIM ON THE WATCHTOWER. HE DIDN'T REALIZE IT, AND WE CAN IDENTIFY HIM!
-GULP!-
SO WE CAN EASILY SHOW WHO THE CULPRIT IS!
COUSIN!
TRAP, DON'T YOU SEE THAT WE'RE DISCUSSING SOMETHING IMPORTANT HERE?
YES, I KNOW, BUT YOU KNOW... I SPENT SO MUCH TIME INVESTIGATING... I WANT TO SAY WHO THE CULPRIT IS!
ARE YOU SURE YOU'VE FIGURED OUT WHO THE CULPRIT IS?
OF COURSE, I ALREADY KNEW BEFORE, BUT I WAS WAITING FOR THE RIGHT MOMENT!
SO GO AHEAD THEN!

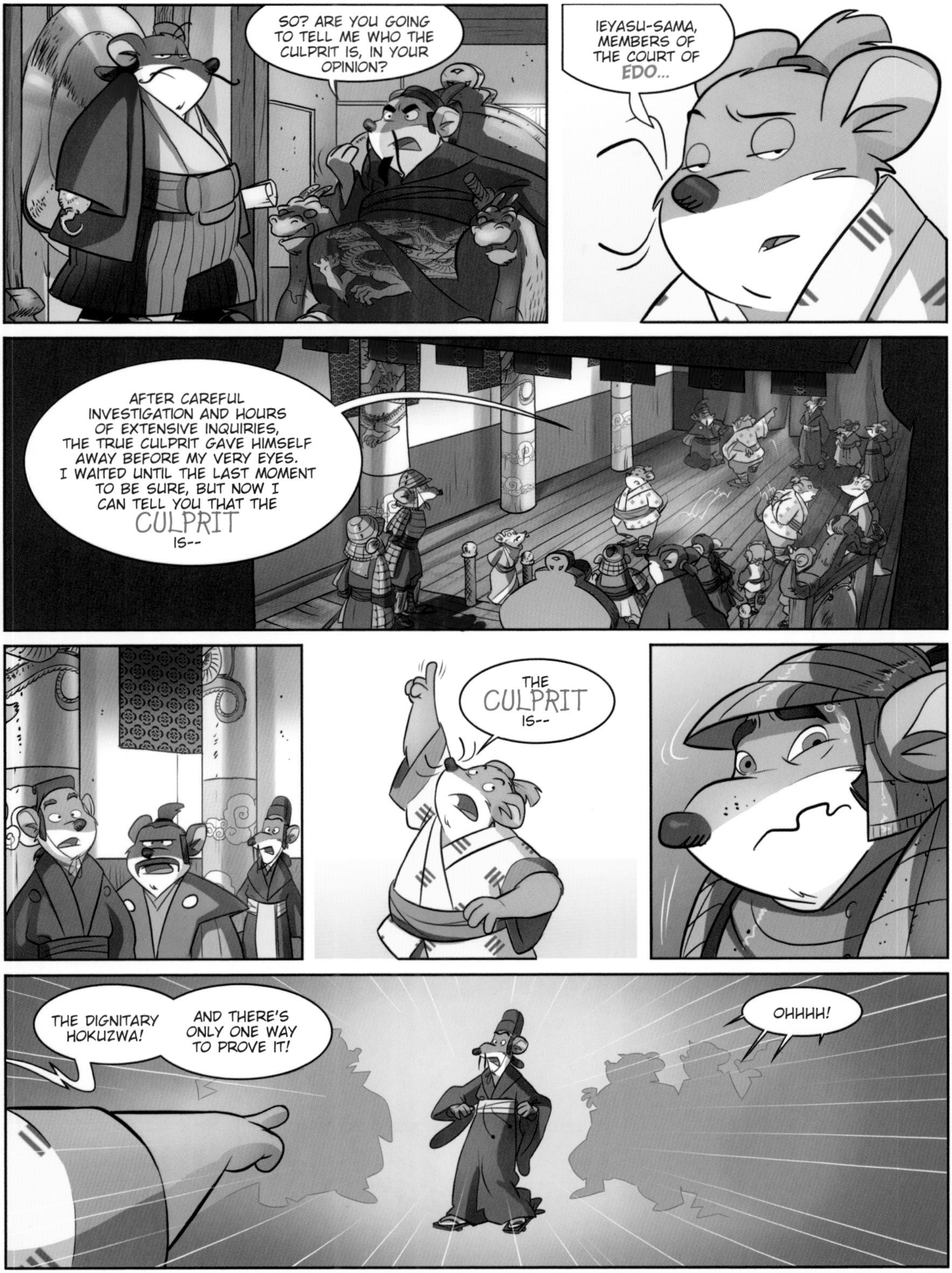
SO? ARE YOU GOING TO TELL ME WHO THE CULPRIT IS, IN YOUR OPINION?
IEYASU-SAMA, MEMBERS OF THE COURT OF EDO...
AFTER CAREFUL INVESTIGATION AND HOURS OF EXTENSIVE INQUIRIES, THE TRUE CULPRIT GAVE HIMSELF AWAY BEFORE MY VERY EYES. I WAITED UNTIL THE LAST MOMENT TO BE SURE, BUT NOW I CAN TELL YOU THAT THE CULPRIT IS--
THE CULPRIT IS--
THE DIGNITARY HOKUZWA!
AND THERE'S ONLY ONE WAY TO PROVE IT!
OHHHH!

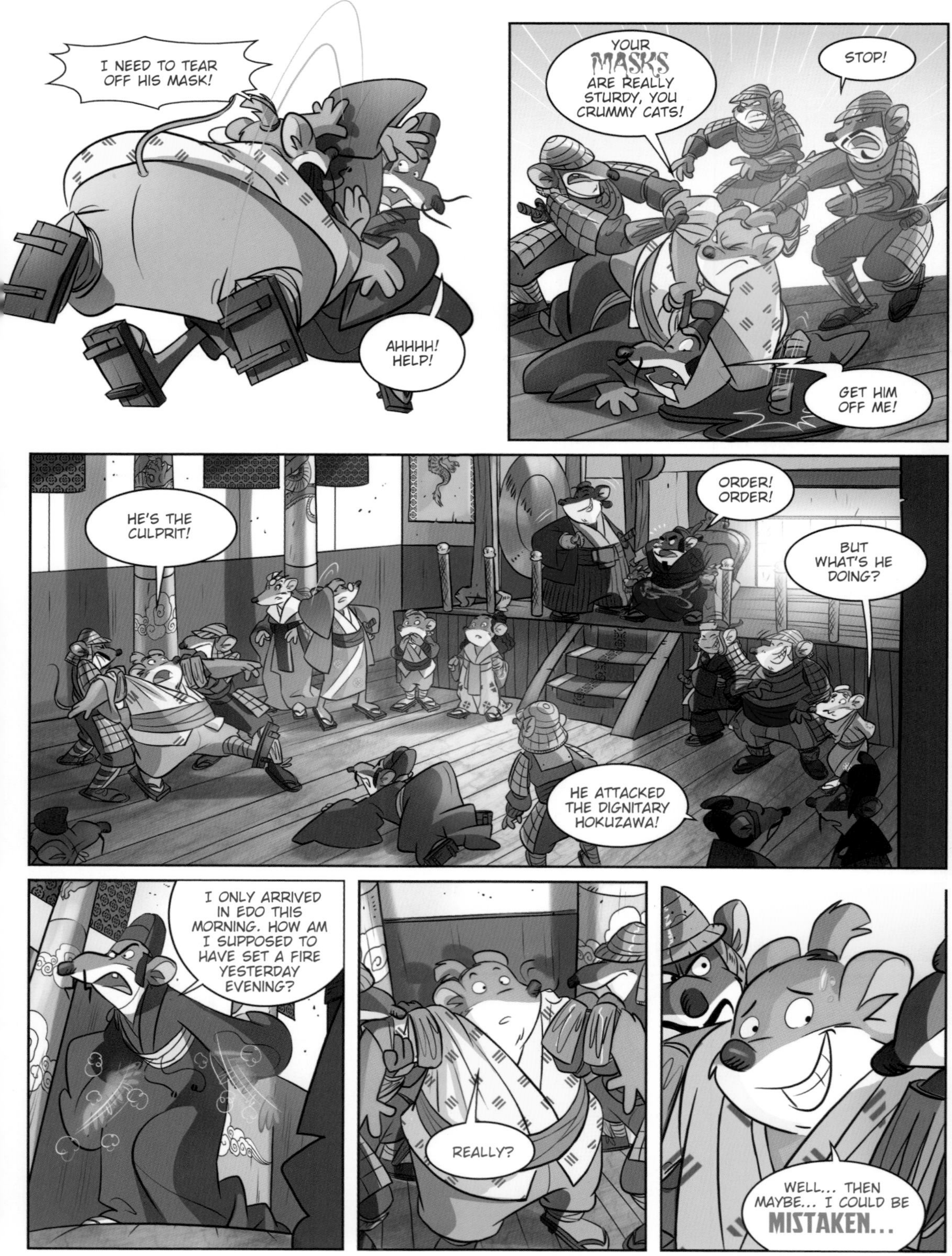
I NEED TO TEAR OFF HIS MASK!
AHHHH! HELP!
YOUR MASKS ARE REALLY STURDY, YOU CRUMMY CATS!
STOP!
GET HIM OFF ME!
HE'S THE CULPRIT!
ORDER! ORDER!
BUT WHAT'S HE DOING?
HE ATTACKED THE DIGNITARY HOKUZAWA!
I ONLY ARRIVED IN EDO THIS MORNING. HOW AM I SUPPOSED TO HAVE SET A FIRE YESTERDAY EVENING?
REALLY?
WELL... THEN MAYBE... I COULD BE MISTAKEN...

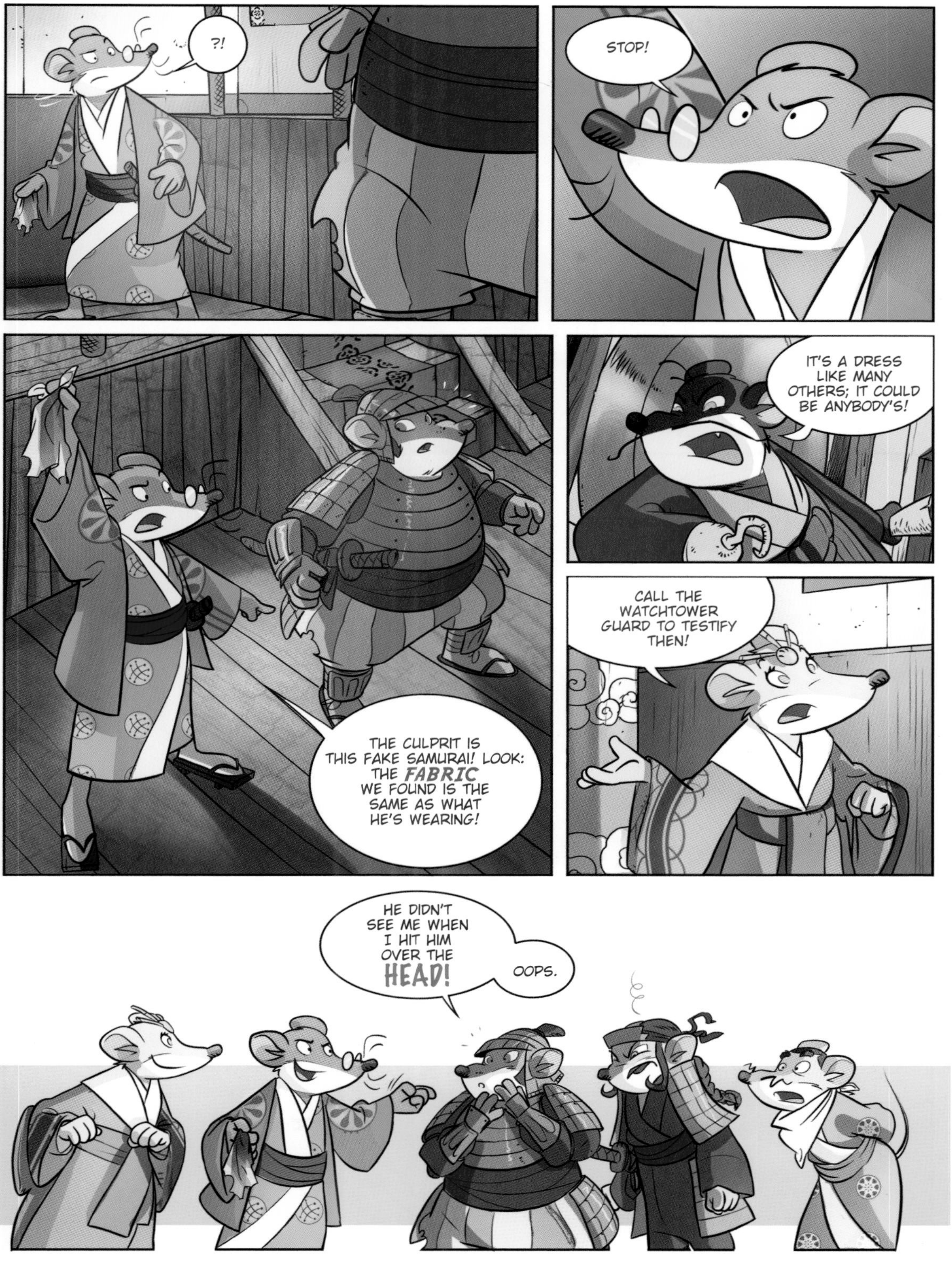
?!
STOP!
THE CULPRIT IS THIS FAKE SAMURAI! LOOK: THE FABRIC WE FOUND IS THE SAME AS WHAT HE'S WEARING!
IT'S A DRESS LIKE MANY OTHERS; IT COULD BE ANYBODY'S!
CALL THE WATCHTOWER GUARD TO TESTIFY THEN!
HE DIDN'T SEE ME WHEN I HIT HIM OVER THE HEAD!
OOPS.

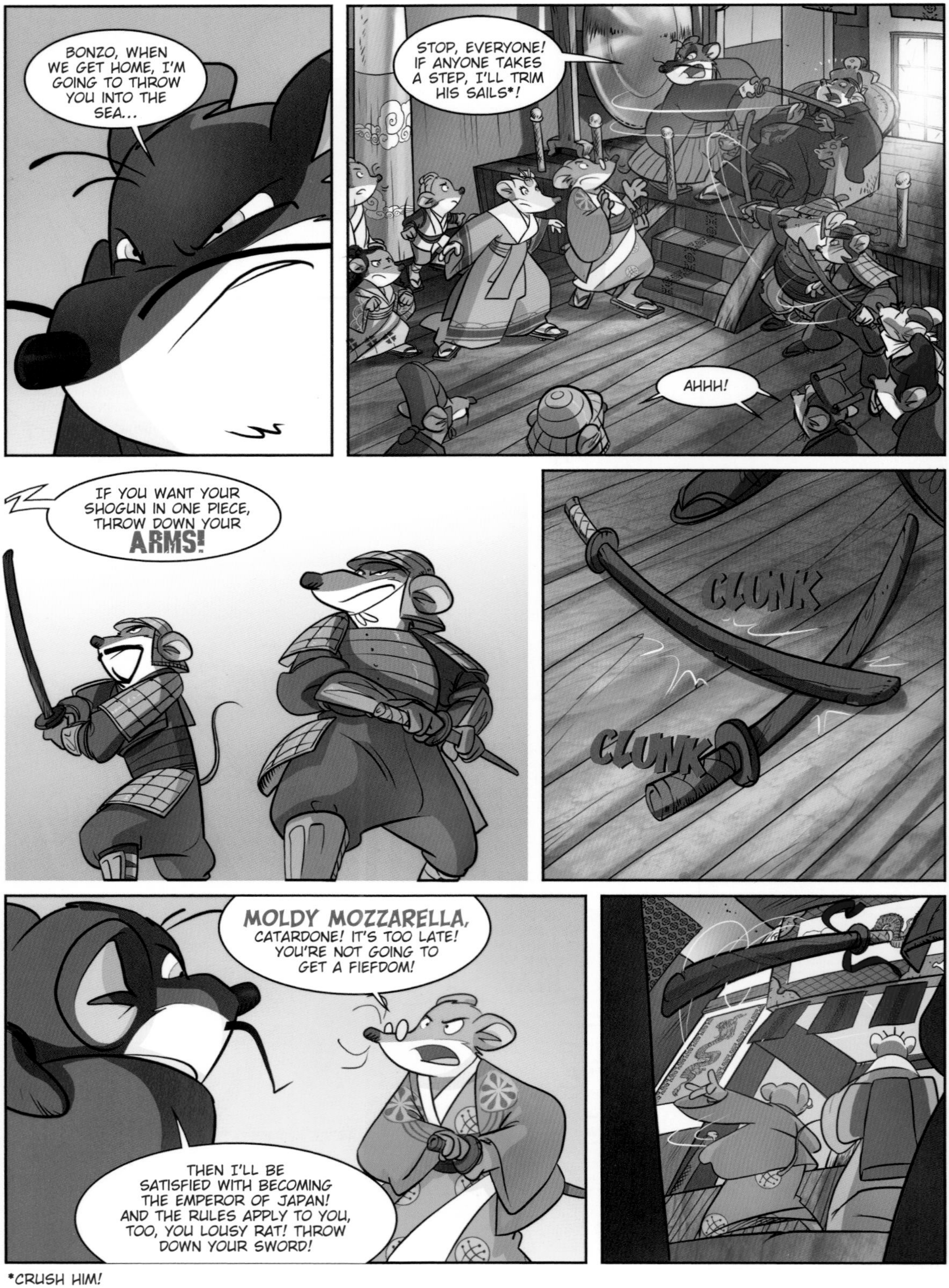
BONZO, WHEN WE GET HOME, I'M GOING TO THROW YOU INTO THE SEA...
STOP, EVERYONE! IF ANYONE TAKES A STEP, I'LL TRIM HIS SAILS*!
AHHH!
IF YOU WANT YOUR SHOGUN IN ONE PIECE, THROW DOWN YOUR ARMS!
CLUNK
CLUNK
MOLDY MOZZARELLA, CATARDONE! IT'S TOO LATE! YOU'RE NOT GOING TO GET A FIEFDOM!
THEN I'LL BE SATISFIED WITH BECOMING THE EMPEROR OF JAPAN! AND THE RULES APPLY TO YOU, TOO, YOU LOUSY RAT! THROW DOWN YOUR SWORD!

*CRUSH HIM!

CLUNK

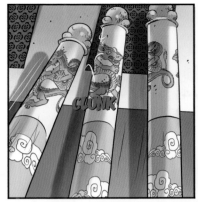

CLUNK
CLUNK

?!

CLUNK
CLUNK

SO I WILL BE THE **EMPEROR** OF THE CATS AND OF JAPAN AT LAST!

CLUNK
CLUNK
CLUNK

CLUNK!

GMMONG

BUT WHAT--?!

GMMONG

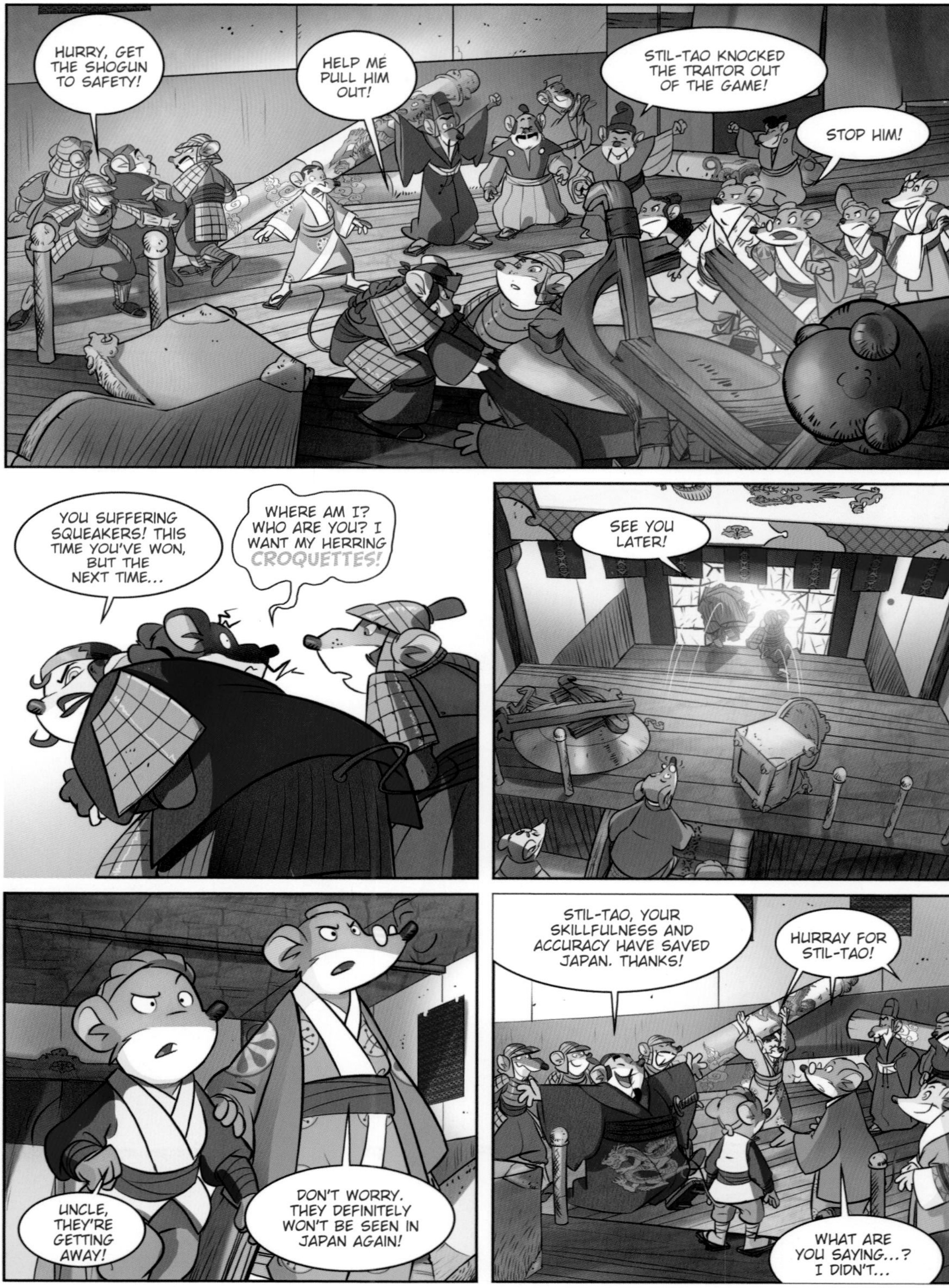
HURRY, GET THE SHOGUN TO SAFETY!
HELP ME PULL HIM OUT!
STIL-TAO KNOCKED THE TRAITOR OUT OF THE GAME!
STOP HIM!
YOU SUFFERING SQUEAKERS! THIS TIME YOU'VE WON, BUT THE NEXT TIME...
WHERE AM I? WHO ARE YOU? I WANT MY HERRING CROQUETTES!
SEE YOU LATER!
UNCLE, THEY'RE GETTING AWAY!
DON'T WORRY. THEY DEFINITELY WON'T BE SEEN IN JAPAN AGAIN!
STIL-TAO, YOUR SKILLFULNESS AND ACCURACY HAVE SAVED JAPAN. THANKS!
HURRAY FOR STIL-TAO!
WHAT ARE YOU SAYING...? I DIDN'T...

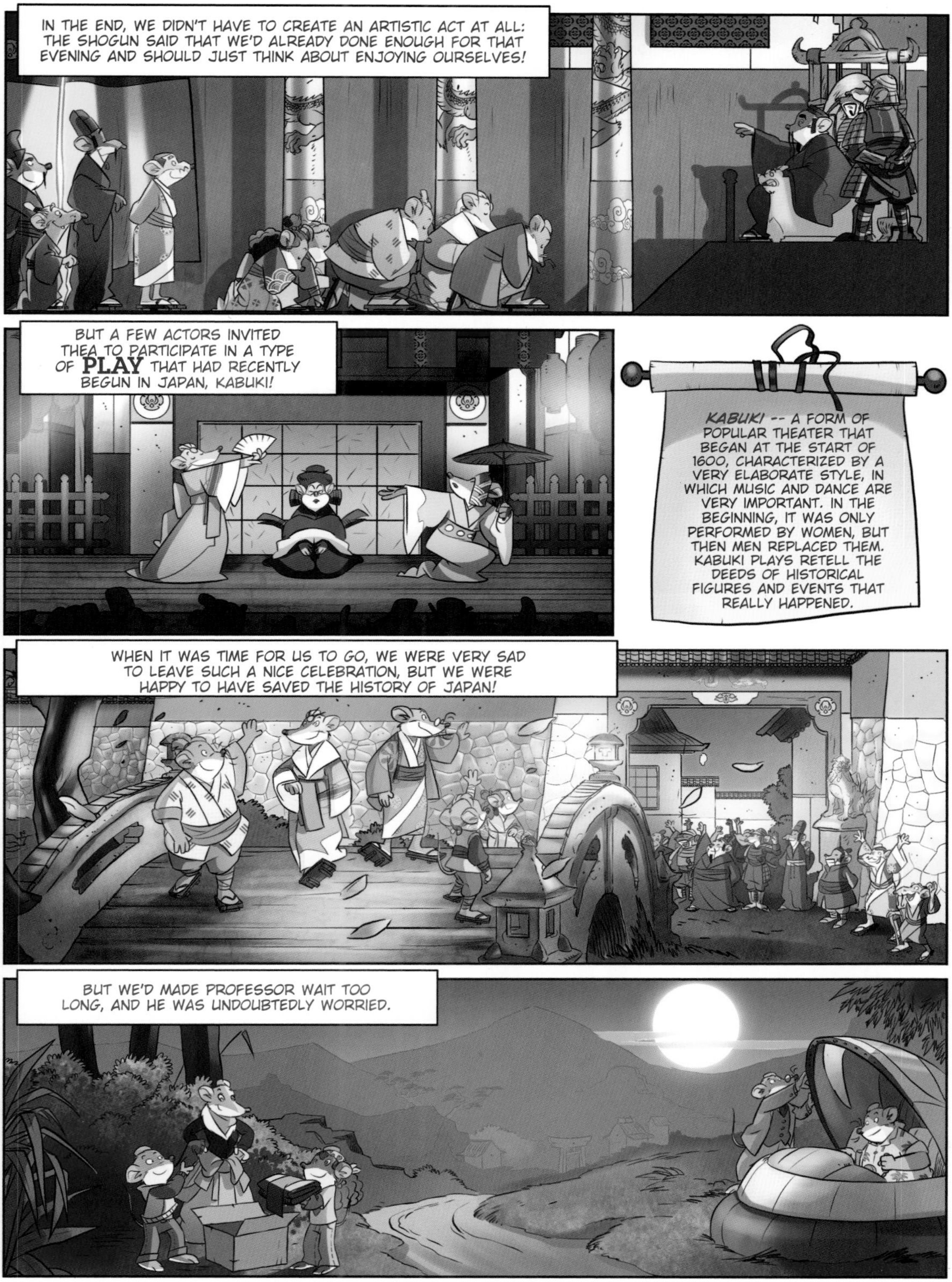
IN THE END, WE DIDN'T HAVE TO CREATE AN ARTISTIC ACT AT ALL: THE SHOGUN SAID THAT WE'D ALREADY DONE ENOUGH FOR THAT EVENING AND SHOULD JUST THINK ABOUT ENJOYING OURSELVES!
BUT A FEW ACTORS INVITED THEA TO PARTICIPATE IN A TYPE OF PLAY THAT HAD RECENTLY BEGUN IN JAPAN, KABUKI!
KABUKI -- A FORM OF POPULAR THEATER THAT BEGAN AT THE START OF 1600, CHARACTERIZED BY A VERY ELABORATE STYLE, IN WHICH MUSIC AND DANCE ARE VERY IMPORTANT. IN THE BEGINNING, IT WAS ONLY PERFORMED BY WOMEN, BUT THEN MEN REPLACED THEM. KABUKI PLAYS RETELL THE DEEDS OF HISTORICAL FIGURES AND EVENTS THAT REALLY HAPPENED.
WHEN IT WAS TIME FOR US TO GO, WE WERE VERY SAD TO LEAVE SUCH A NICE CELEBRATION, BUT WE WERE HAPPY TO HAVE SAVED THE HISTORY OF JAPAN!
BUT WE'D MADE PROFESSOR WAIT TOO LONG, AND HE WAS UNDOUBTEDLY WORRIED.

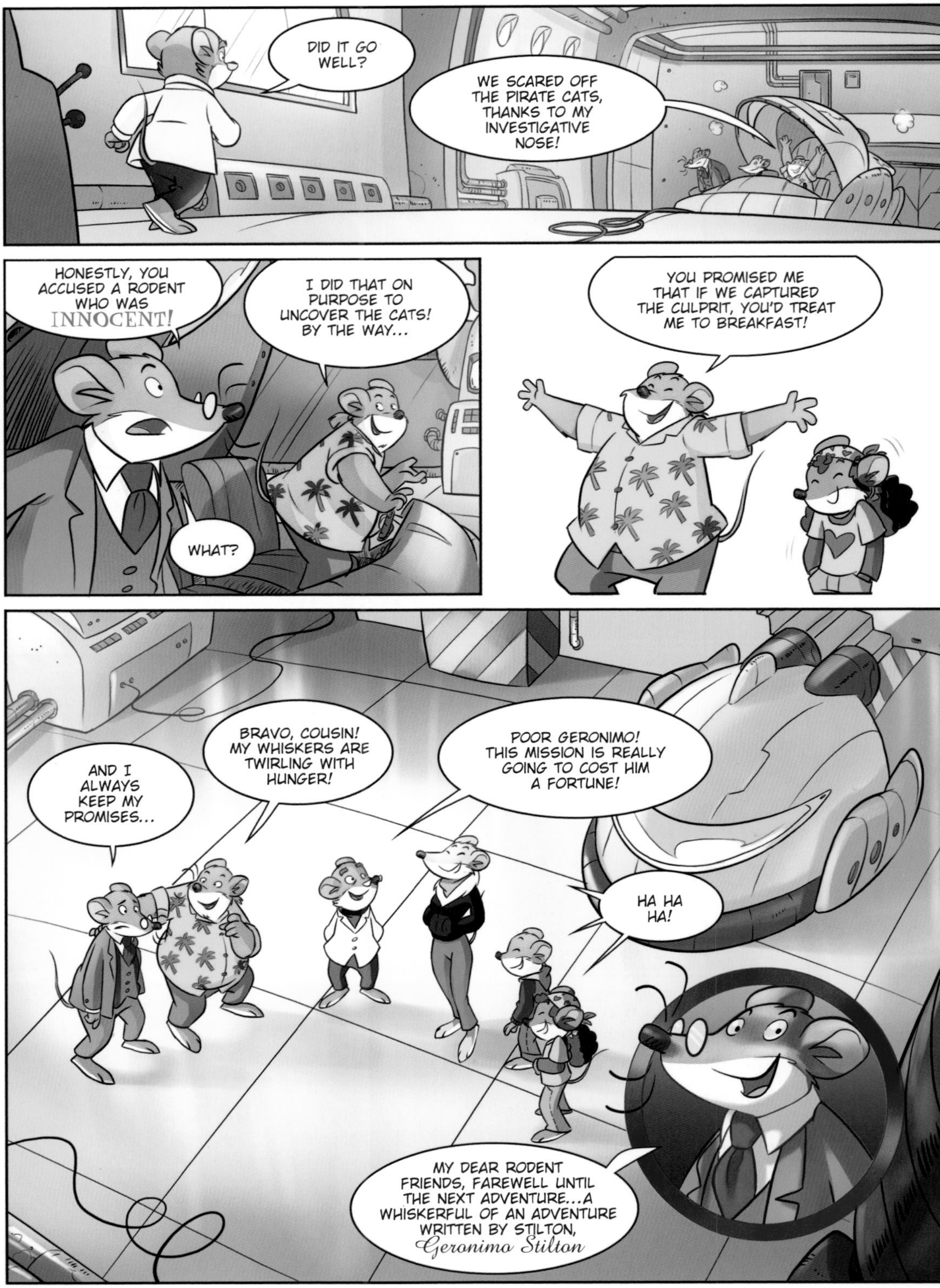
DID IT GO WELL?
WE SCARED OFF THE PIRATE CATS, THANKS TO MY INVESTIGATIVE NOSE!
HONESTLY, YOU ACCUSED A RODENT WHO WAS INNOCENT!
I DID THAT ON PURPOSE TO UNCOVER THE CATS! BY THE WAY...
WHAT?
YOU PROMISED ME THAT IF WE CAPTURED THE CULPRIT, YOU'D TREAT ME TO BREAKFAST!
AND I ALWAYS KEEP MY PROMISES...
BRAVO, COUSIN! MY WHISKERS ARE TWIRLING WITH HUNGER!
POOR GERONIMO! THIS MISSION IS REALLY GOING TO COST HIM A FORTUNE!
HA HA HA!
MY DEAR RODENT FRIENDS, FAREWELL UNTIL THE NEXT ADVENTURE...A WHISKERFUL OF AN ADVENTURE WRITTEN BY STILTON,
Geronimo Stilton

Watch Out For PAPERCUTZ

Welcome to the fourth future-friendly GERONIMO STILTON 3 IN 1 graphic novel, collecting three great GERONIMO STILTON graphic novels: "Geronimo Stilton Saves the Olympics," "We'll Always Have Paris" and "The First Samurai," from Papercutz—those cheesy wizards dedicated to conjuring up and publishing great graphic novels for all ages. Oh, and I'm Salicrup, *Jim Salicrup*, the Editor-in-Chief and Charter Subscriber to *The Rodent's Gazette,* here to chat with you a little about these timeless tales collected in this volume and to mention some of the other great graphic novels from Papercutz that you may find fascinating and fun...

I'm very thankful to Geronimo Stilton for saving the Olympics, otherwise I would've never met gold-medal-winning Olympic gymnast and bestselling author Laurie Hernandez a few years ago, when she gave an inspiring talk at a meeting of the Children's Book Council (visit their website at cbcbooks.org for lots of information about children's books), of which Papercutz is a member. She was there to talk about her new children's book, "She's Got This," not to be confused with her autobiographical bestseller "I Got This." If being an Olympian and an author wasn't impressive enough, she also competed on TV's hit show *Dancing with the Stars*. How cool is that?

Speaking of competing and dancing, have you checked out the latest DANCE CLASS graphic novel from Papercutz? This long-running Papercutz series by Béka and Crip features the adventures of dance students Julie, Lucie, Alia, and their friends, families, fellow students, and teachers, as they travel around the world to perform and participate in dance competitions. If you haven't been following their graphic novel series, don't worry—like GERONIMO STILTON their early graphic novels are being collected in a 3 in 1 format. DANCE CLASS 3 IN 1 is the perfect way to catch up and get to know the whole cast of characters.

Béka and Crip
3 Graphic Novels in 1
Dance Class
3 in 1
PAPERCUTZ

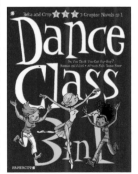

And speaking of Olympics, which we were before we started talking about DANCE CLASS, another Papercutz title has also presented a unique point of view regarding this real-life global event. In THE SMURFS #11, recently collected in THE SMURFS 3 IN 1 #4, we present "The Smurf Olympics" by Peyo. See the stars of the new Nickelodeon animated series compete against each other in their version of the Olympic games. Does Hefty Smurf win it all? You'll be surprised at who actually wins! (And it wasn't Laurie Hernandez, she's not super-tall, but she's not a Smurf either!)

But back to Geronimo Stilton... Here's a trivia question for you: What do the GERONIMO STILTON titles "We'll Always Have Paris" (from #11) and "Play it Again, Mozart" (from #8) have in common? Answer: Both titles are based on famous quotes from the classic movie *Casablanca*, yet while "We'll Always Have Paris," is a direct quote from the film, "Play it Again, Mozart" is a take-off on a line that's not in the movie, "Play it Again, Sam." The actual line is just "Play it." Now, some folks may think Papercutz readers might be far more familiar with THE LOUD HOUSE spin-off series THE CASAGRANDES than an old movie such as *Casablanca*, and that may very well be true, but that won't stop me from mentioning it. When I was young, there were references to all sorts of things that I didn't understand, especially in old Warner Bros. cartoons, until I was much older. And the thought of a young GERONIMO STILTON fan one day watching *Casablanca*, and after hearing those lines and thinking "Hey, I remember that from GERONIMO STILTON," greatly amuses me.

FABRICE ERRE • SYLVAIN SAVOIA
Magical History Tour
The Great Pyramid
PAPERCUTZ

By the way, the song in *Casablanca* that's requested to be played again is "As Time Goes By" which brings us back to our time-travelling mouse, Geronimo. In the premiere volume of Papercutz graphic novel series LOLA'S SUPER CLUB, by Christine Beigel and Pierre Fouillet, Lola also travels through time (or does she?) and at one point lands in Paris in 1900 and sees the Eiffel Tower. Guess Lola will always have Paris too.

And speaking of time travel, there's MAGICAL HISTORY TOUR, by Fabrice Erre and Sylvain Savoia, another Paperecutz graphic novel series that takes you back to important times in the past. Modern-day kids Annie and Nico explore the past together and discover all about the Great Pyramid, the Great Wall of China, hidden oil, the Crusades, the Plague, Albert Einstein, and Gandhi—and that's just the first seven volumes!

Which again brings us back to GERONIMO STILTON. I don't have much to say about "The First Samurai," other than if this was a Trap Stilton graphic novel, it would probably be called "The Last Ham on Rye." Instead, I'll just mention that you can follow the latest and greatest adventures of Geronimo Stilton and his friends and family in the all-new GERONIMO STILTON REPORTER graphic novel series from Papercutz (of course!). And of course, coming soon in GERONIMO STILTON 3 IN 1 #5 will be "The Fastest Train in the West," "The First Mouse on the Moon," and "All for Stilton, Stilton for All!" When it comes to great time-travelling graphic novels, Papercutz has got you covered!

See you in the future, Jim

STAY IN TOUCH!

EMAIL:	salicrup@papercutz.com
WEB:	papercutz.com
TWITTER:	@papercutzgn
INSTAGRAM:	@papercutzgn
FACEBOOK:	PAPERCUTZGRAPHICNOVELS
FAN MAIL:	Papercutz, 160 Broadway, Suite 700, East Wing, New York, NY 10038

Go to papercutz.com and sign up for the free Papercutz e-newsletter!

CATCH UP WITH THE NEW ADVENTURES OF Geronimo Stilton FROM PAPERCUTZ

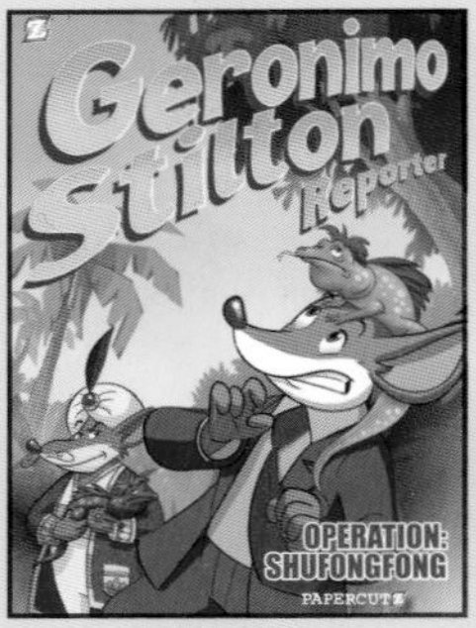
Geronimo Stilton
Reporter
OPERATION: SHUFONGFONG
PAPERCUTZ

GERONIMO
STILTON REPORTER #1
"Operation ShuFongfong"

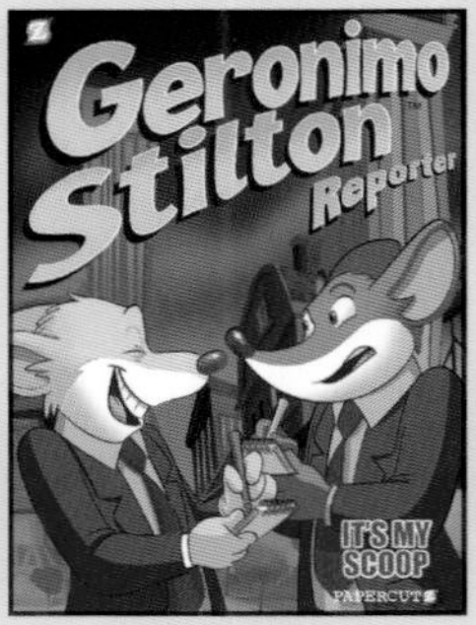
Geronimo Stilton
Reporter
IT'S MY SCOOP
PAPERCUTZ

GERONIMO
STILTON REPORTER #2
"It's My Scoop"

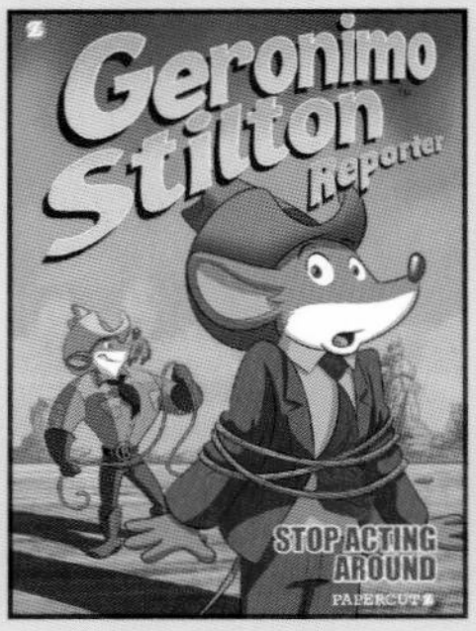
Geronimo Stilton
Reporter
STOP ACTING AROUND
PAPERCUTZ

GERONIMO
STILTON REPORTER #3
"Stop Acting Around"

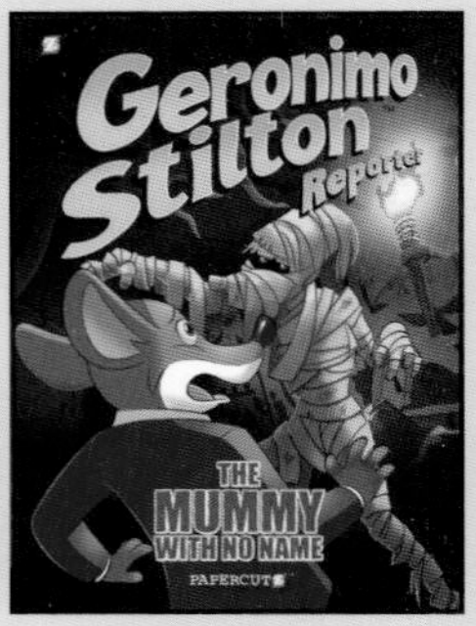
Geronimo Stilton
Reporter
THE MUMMY WITH NO NAME
PAPERCUTZ

GERONIMO
STILTON REPORTER #4
"The Mummy with No Name"

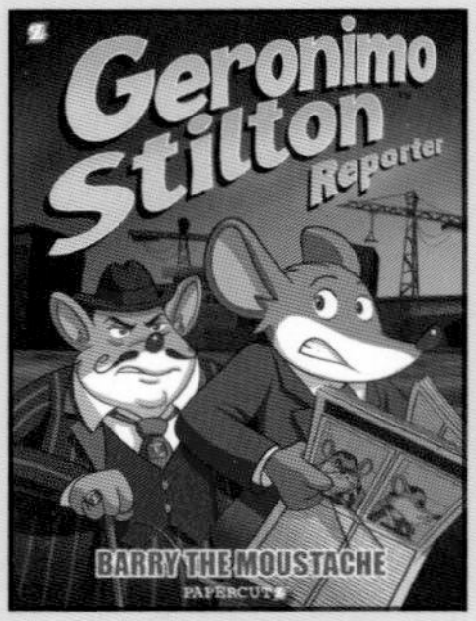
Geronimo Stilton
Reporter
BARRY THE MOUSTACHE
PAPERCUTZ

GERONIMO
STILTON REPORTER #5
"Barry the Moustache"

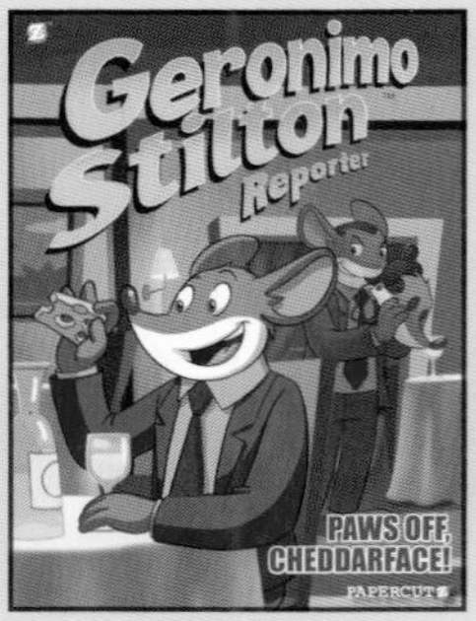
Geronimo Stilton
Reporter
PAWS OFF, CHEDDARFACE!
PAPERCUTZ

GERONIMO
STILTON REPORTER #6
"Paws Off, Cheddarface!"

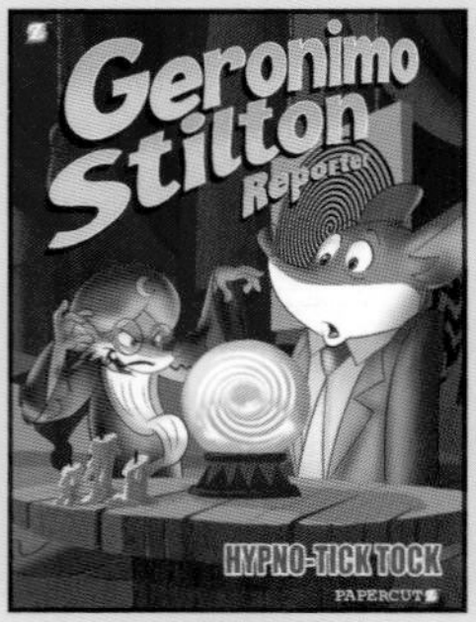
Geronimo Stilton
Reporter
HYPNO-TICK TOCK
PAPERCUTZ

GERONIMO
STILTON REPORTER #8
"Hypno-Tick Tock"

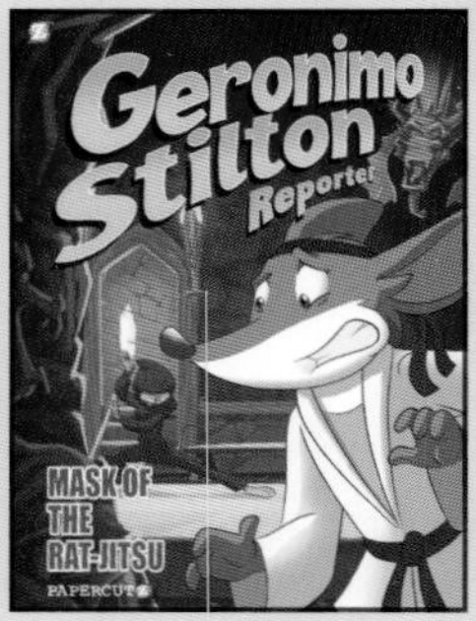
Geronimo Stilton
Reporter
MASK OF THE RAT-JITSU
PAPERCUTZ

GERONIMO
STILTON REPORTER #9
"Mask of the Rat-Jitsu"

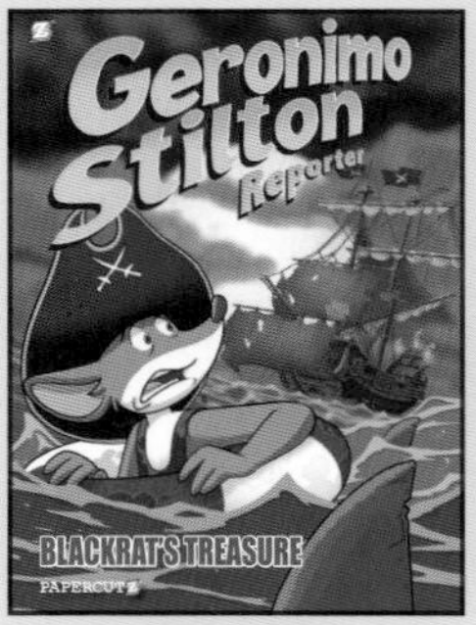
Geronimo Stilton
Reporter
BLACKRAT'S TREASURE
PAPERCUTZ

GERONIMO
STILTON REPORTER #10
"Blackrat's Treasure"

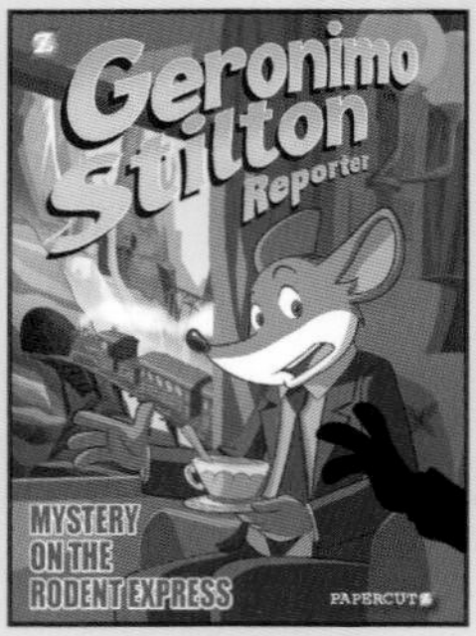
Geronimo Stilton
Reporter
MYSTERY ON THE RODENT EXPRESS
PAPERCUTZ

GERONIMO
STILTON REPORTER #11
"Mystery on the Rodent Express"

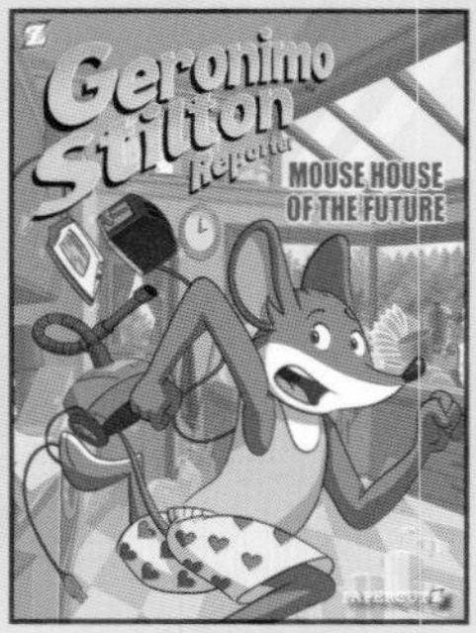
Geronimo Stilton
Reporter
MOUSE HOUSE OF THE FUTURE
PAPERCUTZ

GERONIMO
STILTON REPORTER #12
"Mouse House of the Future"

...ALSO AVAILABLE WHEREVER E-BOOKS ARE SOLD!

GERONIMO STILTON REPORTER Graphic Novels are availbale for $9.99 each in hardcover only. Order online at papercutz.com. Or call 1-800-886-1223, Monday through Friday, 9 – 5 EST. MC, Visa, and AmEx accepted. To order by mail, please add $5.00 for postage and handling for first book ordered, $1.00 for each additional book and make check payable to NBM Publishing. Send to: Papercutz, 160 Broadway, Suite 700, East Wing, New York, NY 10038.

See more at papercutz.com